East Of Egypt

Scott Grant

On The Road To Mandalay

Take me east of Egypt, where the best is like the worst. Where there ain't no missionaries and a man can raise a thirst. On the road to Mandalay where the flyin' fishes play and the dawn comes up like thunder, outa' China, cross the bay.

Rudyard Kipling

Chapter One: Mekong Heat

Bill Murphy whispered orders to his boat men as they passed by in column, with large sacks of raw opium thrown across their backs. He knew each sweaty face and marked his memory of them according to how they had behaved under pressure in fire fights, or ambushes, as thieves had often attempted to ambush them for their precious cargo. The day's heat had taken its toll and Bill Murphy allowed his thoughts to stray across the forceful currents of the muddy Mekong that sprawled along the horizon more like an endless sea than a river.

Bill Murphy had lived and breathed the vapor of this mighty river for more than half of his life and he knew every sand bar and tributary from its mouth at the delta, along the Vietnamese southern coast, up through Cambodia, Thailand Laos and Myanmar as it carved its way home to Mother China. Bill had been recruited straight out of the University Of Michigan where he took honors with a Bachelor Of Science in horticulture. The recruiter was not very impressed with his 4-H awards with dairy cattle but his eyebrows nearly left his forehead when he saw what Bill had done with hybrid crop exponentials.

That had been in the mid-sixties and America was growing fearful and weary of Marxist expansion around the globe. The mission of the CIA had always been the provision of accurate and up to date information to the President about America's enemies in foreign countries leaving domestic counter-intelligence activities to the FBI but some how the mission got blurry. Bill was offered a job as a Special Field Agent in Laos so he bade farewell to his older sister. She ran the farm after both parents were killed in a car accident when Bill was only twelve.

His sister had just gotten married to a young farmer Bill had known since early childhood so it wasn't as though he was abandoning her. The young man inherited his parents farm next door which expanded the land from one hundred fifty acres to three hundred fifty so as Bill saw it, it was time to strike out on his own and let Margie have the place.

He had a ton of questions but was always told he would learn everything when he had a "need to know." He respected authority and considered anything less to be tantamount to treason, so when the company finally came around to explain that he was wanted for his skill in increasing crop production and that his crop would be poppy plants used to process opium, he figured the government knew better than he of how to win a war.

Things may have turned out differently had he been exposed to the peace movement, but what philosophical reservations he may have once had he lost the first time he saw the bloated infant children, impaled by the North Vietnamese Army on bamboo spears. Their crime? Coming from a village suspected of cooperating with Americans.

Bill was perfect. He loved anything related to plant life was already accustomed to the humidity in Michigan and he didn't ask a lot of questions. Bill was trained by CIA old hands. Men who spoke several languages, mostly Asian tribal dialects such as the Hmong of Laos and the Han of Burma. Bill was a fast learner and soon could fend for himself in Thai, Cambodian, Vietnamese and the Hill Tribe dialects. The CIA became quite impressed with Bill's progress and before long, a team of Chemists from Hong Kong and Taiwan were flown in to teach Bill how to harvest and process the Papaver Somniferum plant, or Poppy. They taught him how to cull the ripe plant, just how to carve the grooves and after three, or four carvings, how to scrape the dried greyish brown secretions into collecting pots.

Then, they taught him how to convert raw opium into morphine and how to tweak the bleaches and chemicals to arrive at #4 grade, 99% pure, "China White" heroin. Bill worked constantly with the Burmese and Laotian generals to ensure security of the poppy plants and the labs where the heroin was processed. Bill became an old man in a young man's body. He had sex only twice before leaving college but in the Hills of Laos he was offered a different woman every day. He tried at first to politely refuse but was quickly told by an old hand that it would be an unforgivable insult to reject a gift. His other near mistake was openly gagging when the village Chief offered him the first bowl of soup on a sacred day festival.

He watched various men and women throw grubs and spiders in the soup, but the clincher was when he saw them drop in three live chickens, entrails, feet, feathers and all. He was about to ask the old hand if it were some sort of joke when the old hand cornered him and warned him that if he didn't eat the soup, they would lose the entire village to the NVA. Within weeks Bill was sucking on chicken feet with the best of them and he had even stopped losing all of his body fluids due to the ensuing diarrhea.

Bill never really considered himself a soldier but he learned how to be just enough of one to stay alive. Ambushes occurred often. He learned how to run straight toward the firing line as the shortest avenue of escape. He learned the various types of ambushes, from an "L" shaped one to a horse shoe ambush and even cantilevered ambushes that zigged and zagged according to the terrain and natural kill zones shaped by logical escape routes. Most importantly he learned to read the terrain well enough to trigger the ambush before he, or his Hmong tribesmen, were even in the kill zone. He fell in love with a Hmong woman who had the most beautifully shaped breasts he had ever seen.

No one even thought of using a condom and over a period of four years she bore him a daughter and a son. He was afraid to even ponder whether he had left behind any children with the many other jungle encounters he had.

Bill took on ever greater responsibility and was promoted ahead of others in his agent class. He organized the transportation of the drugs and equipment by initiating a charter with Air America, a CIA shadow company that was meant to keep Bill's operations at arms length from the political and legal entanglement that would have resulted from using military personnel and equipment in the secret war. He also arranged the regular remuneration of the tribes.

They were excellent fighters and were being paid handsomely to thwart their natural enemy the NVA along the Ho Chi Minh trail and to provide defensive forces for Bill's fifty heroin labs, but they carried bad joss. Bill spent half of his time in Laos and the other half in Burma building a relationship with the Han army generals and ferrying raw opium to his labs in Thailand and Laos but during the latter half of the war he drifted further and further away from reality and out of touch.

When Nixon and Kissinger declared "Vietnamization" of the war Bill was caught as much by surprise as anyone. When the NVA came pouring down from the north Bill was in Burma. A Burmese general let Bill take a small aircraft to go rescue his woman and kids but when he arrived he saw all three of them impaled on bamboo poles with the sharp end of each pole sticking out through their mouth and neck. He got back in the light aircraft with an M-60 machine gun and flew in circles shooting wildly at the countryside until he was himself shot down. An NVA patrol was hot on his heels and Bill knew his own death was imminent.

Suddenly a hand emerged from the swamp and pulled him down into the thick green bog. A camouflaged face came within inches of his own and a reed was shoved in his mouth as he was dragged under. He lost all track of time. He didn't know how long he had been beneath the water because each time he tried to open his eyes the green algae burned too much to bear. Finally, the same hand that dragged him down pulled him back up. "Who the hell are you?" Bill asked. "No. Who in the Hell are you?" The man replied. "I'm Bill Murphy CIA. Regional Operations Chief." "Not much region left to be Chief of Pal." The man grunted.

"My name is David Anderson. Special Ops team 22 . I'll explain everything later. Let's move! The Dinks are going to be really pissed when they get to the end of the trail I created for them earlier. Was that you shooting from the window of that Cessna? I watched you go down, that's how I was able to cut you away from the NVA before they could reach you." David said. Bill and David were running at full tilt when suddenly David tackled Bill and brought him down just before a spiked booby trap dead fall came whishing past. As they were getting to their feet an all black Huey Slick chopper came from out of nowhere dangling a rope with a foot stand.

David grabbed the rope and held Bill around his chest as they were scooped up and out of the thick jungle. The men were hoisted into the chopper as the M-60 guns opened up on the jungle below. The snap of ground fire tore bullet holes in the skin of the chopper as it spiraled ever higher. As Bill looked back, he saw the entire hill top where his family was go up in fireballs and plumes of smoke. "What the Hell is that?" Bill yelled as the chopper shuddered from the blast."B-52 strike. We learned that a whole village of Hmong were slaughtered by a regiment of Dinks so they cranked me up for some pay back. I called in the B-52's while we were running." David yelled.

Bill buried his face in his sleeve so David wouldn't see his sadness. Within an hour the chopper was setting down in a large hard spot, or base camp and David led Bill to a sand bagged bunker. To his amazement the bunker was a full sized saloon with a very long bar and mirrors every where. Other Operators, some bleeding from fresh wounds were sitting along the bar as though it were Friday Night Football. Appetizers and mugs of beer were abundant as well as bottles of Jack Daniels whiskey.

A large picture of Ho Chi Minh was plastered along the wall next to an official English Pub dart board. The bartender was re-loading a 9mm pistol with a silencer and reaching it to a couple of operators who were shooting a tight shot group on both of Ho's eyes. Suddenly, the man shooting cursed as a stray bullet made a hole in Ho's neck. "You lose Mother F---er!" The bartender said as the man pulled out his wallet and paid the bet. "Why doesn't he just buy a round?" Bill asked. "Because the booze is already free." David replied.

"OK, Super Spook, what in the Hell were you doing in Ho's kitchen? David asked. Bill gazed at Ho Chi Minh without eyes when suddenly six nude Viet girls dressed only in thigh high stockings walked in from a room behind the bar. Dancing on the bar to Steppenwolf's Born To Be Wild they let the men caress their pubis while stuffing dollars in their garters. It was all too surreal for Bill. He began to see his children and wife's faces and he felt about to lose his mind. "Hey! What's up Man?" David asked. "That certainly wasn't your first run was it?" "No. My family, I had a woman and two kids in that place!" Bill screamed as he collapsed on the floor. When he awakened he was in David's air conditioned room lying in his wet clothes. His entire body was shaking.

David returned with a large mug of coffee and Bill stopped shaking. Bill stayed in David's bunk for a few days. David came back at three am from a mission and they sat at the bar and talked for hours. "Hey! When can I sleep on my own freaking crate again dude?" David joked. "Tonight. Or today, since tonight is over. I'm going back to Burma. The war isn't over there, or in Laos and Cambodia. This one's on its last legs I'm afraid. You want a job Captain Anderson?" Bill asked with sincerity. "Whew! CIA. That all sounds scary, know what I mean?" David joked.

Within thirty six hours Captain Anderson received a Distinguished Service Cross and a set of orders from the Pentagon, releasing him to other official government capacities, or so the orders read. David had heard bits and pieces about the CIA's heroin ops and at first he made it clear that he wasn't a goddamned Pusher and that his responsibilities were 100% concentrated on defending Bill's operations. Thereafter he stayed completely outside the labs.

After serving Bill for two years David was called aside and let in on a scheme Bill had been hatching for a very long time. "David, I studied your jacket before I asked Langley to shake you loose from the army. You have an undergrad degree, Summa Cum Laude from Yale in Finance, with a minor in Business administration. How did you get to be such a Wild and Crazy guy?" Bill grinned "Long story. Runs in the family." David said matter of factly.

" I have a proposition if you're interested. I have been squirreling away a nest egg for when the Company realizes it isn't cool to stay in the drug business. I'd like to invest in you David. I have about three hundred thousand that I won't need right away.

I'd like you to consider an opening at Wharton for a Masters in International Banking operations." "Whoaah! Slow down. How do you know Wharton will consider a used up special operator with bonafide crazy assed P.T.S.D. ?"

Bill pulled an envelope out of his pocket. It was wrinkled and worn. "This is your acceptance letter. I took the liberty of sending your docs pretending I was you. I really laid on the nice guy shit and how all you want to do is get this part of your life behind you, the sooner the better and yadda yadda." Inside the envelope was Wharton's acceptance letter and a check for two hundred and ninety eight thousand dollars. Every penny Bill had been saving in his CIA account since he joined the company. David choked up.

At first David feigned anger but then he turned and bear hugged Bill and for the first time in his life he was rendered completely speechless. "Aren't you afraid I'll just go have one hell of a month in Las Vegas?" David asked. David I stay alive reading people. I know you like a book. You'll come back and by then I will have my post war shit together.

I want you to major in money laundering, not the kind that sends you to jail, but the kind that keeps us out." David delivered. He graduated with honors from Wharton but by the time he was ready to return to Asia to join Bill, Bill had just been tasked by the CIA to set up a duplicate of the Golden Triangle in Central Asia. Iran, Turkey, Afghanistan and Pakistan became known later as the Golden Crescent. To wait for Bill David became a banking consultant with Swiss A.G. in Zurich carefully biding his time.

Bill's mission was to thwart the Soviet invasion of Afghanistan by supplying arms paid for by CIA heroin in support of the new fundamentalist kids on the block, the Mujahideen. Bill looked at his convoy of boats along the Mekong loaded to the brim with raw opium. A few boats were still loading, so he let his mind go back again to the past. He remembered Pop Bailey one of the old OSS guys. Bailey was having an attack of conscience one night and decided to make it his singular mission in life to educate Bill on the sinister history of the CIA. Pop Bailey had traveled as an OSS liaisson officer with Mao Tse Tung during his hit and run war with the Japanese, all the way from Nanning to Yunnan.

He tried furiously to convince Bill that the U.S. had squandered a once in a lifetime opportunity to become staunch allies with China against the Soviet Union owing to Christian nonsense and fear of Marxism as espoused by John Foster Dulles. Pop Bailey went on to describe how every foreign policy failure and hot war since WWII had been a result of CIA involvement in American foreign policy. CIA suspicion of Mao led to Korea, suspicion of Ho Chi Minh led to Vietnam. "Just consider that the Brits took one look at the place, remembered Dien Bien Phu and said; Hey! You bloody Yanks wanna 'ave a go at the place ? Who ran the colonial system for the French? Bao Dai.

Who ran WWII political oppression in Vietnam for the Japanese occupation ? Bao Dai. Who ran it briefly for the British? Bao Dai. Who was standing in the doorway waiting for the Yanks? Bao Dai. Then when Kennedy looks like he's going to switch to the corrupt Diems, in comes the CIA and nails the Diems, with an assassination. I rest my case, about Vietnam." Pop Bailey had said. " We didn't found the agency to turn it over to such megalomania! But there's much more to come Bill. You'll see probably even more shit than I have before you get old and fade away as I'm fading away now."

"Pop was right." Bill thought. The problems in the Middle East started when the company decided Mossadegh was a Socialist. A Socialist! for Christ sake, not even a Commie bastard. The CIA does a number on Mossadegh and in comes Shah Reza Pahlavi. Who trains his Gestapo the dreaded S.A.V.A.K.? The CIA. When the Iranians stormed the U.S. Embassy at the behest of Khoumeini, who had been imprisoned and exiled by the Shah, it wasn't American people they detested, it was the CIA, who they correctly blamed for a generation of terror. "But the CIA was just attempting to stabilize the oil regions." Bill had countered. "Well they're far from stable now with the current repeat of the crusades anyone would have to agree." Pop Bailey replied.

"An infidel army is occupying a Muslim Iraq and no one there seems capable of getting past the fact that the country was forged by drawing a line around Mesopotamia which lumped three disparate groups, the Sunni, Shiites and the Kurds together all under one roof and why? To make it easier for the British map makers I suppose? Usama Bin Laden has been protected in Waziristan since the U.S. invaded Afghanistan to destroy the Taliban, while we slap the midget in Iraq.

Guess who funded and supported Saddam Hussein in his bloodless coup? Yep. The company. We liked the idea of a strongman to keep the buggers in line, just as we liked the Shah for the same reason. The CIA was tasked to keep the Commies out of our hemisphere. Starting with the sacking of Arbenz in Guatemala, the dubious suicide of Allende in Chile and CIA support of Pinochet's brutal use of off duty policemen and soldiers to form Death Squads. On to the Bay Of Pigs invasion in Cuba and continuing on with the use of CIA heroin to supply weapons to our side in Nicaragua and Santo Domingo. We have managed to really muck things up when you remain honest about it." Pop said. Pop Bailey was a smart man. Bill thought.

Bailey's eyes had actually filled with tears when he reminded Bill that in order to supply weapons to the Hill Tribesmen to fight the NVA along the Ho Chi Minh Trail, Bill had created the notorious narcotic agricultural region known as the "Golden Triangle." That Bill had hand designed an even larger and more effective region known as the "Golden Crescent" in Central Asia to provide weapons to the Mujahideen had made the phenomenon irreversible and had created a vast legion of drug addicts around the world even in his own country.

"Man, the CIA really bought and paid for you Bill." Pop had said. The old man's facts were difficult to dispute, but Bill was to be damned if he was going to shoulder responsibility for decisions made at far higher levels than himself. Where had it all really started? he asked himself. He knew the CIA had used him for their own nefarious reasons and as soon as the Soviet Union retreated from Kabul, he as well as the Mujahideen, had been left high and dry to fend for themselves in a hostile world. He felt far beyond a point where making a deep self examination would even be useful. It was far too grand to say this, or that person had created a global drug epidemic. It really started long before Bill came on the scene. It all really began when the Merchants of England decided they were willing to convert China into an unwilling trading partner, to acquire their rich silk, tea and spices, as well as jade diamonds, gold and emeralds.

The British government had created the East India Trading Company, that became so vast in its dealings it was said the sun never went down on its fleet of ships. They had already experimented with opium farms and laboratories in India and knew full well how addictive their raw opium product would be. Once released on an unsuspecting populace, the drug would buy China's precious goods and its government wouldn't be able to regulate it.

Bill had once read of how the unscrupulous British traders had bribed the Chinese Customs agents to let their product through the gates of Canton at such an alarming rate that it prompted a highly respected and reputable official named Lin Tse Hsu to close the port at Canton to all British merchants until the British government answered a letter he had sent to Queen Victoria appealing for her to intercede with her own subjects. Hadn't she in fact decreed opium to be an illegal substance, not fit for unregulated public consumption? "Why should it not be fit for Britain but be perfectly acceptable for China?" he had asked.

Queen Victoria had already forbade any British subject from kow towing, or even slightly bowing down to any foreign leader in China. She feared an uncontrollable legal repercussion from Chinese forms of justice upon British subjects. Without this formality of Asian symbolism however diplomatic relations had become impossible to transact officially. Lin's letter was never answered, or acted upon.

He closed Canton harbor to all British ships. The British opium merchants cried foul all the way to British parliament. By June of 1840, the British Navy was sent to teach the Chinese a lesson they would never forget. The Chinese were woefully unprepared for the technical violence of the Royal Navy and its contingents of Mariner Infantrymen.

The Chinese were forced to suit for an unequal peace at the treaty of Nanking. The opium merchants were not only allowed to re-introduce opium at the port of Canton but also at the ports of Ning Po, Amoy, Foo Chow and Shanghai. Lin Tse Hsu was humiliated and exiled to an insignificant post in Turkestan. Upon the demand of the Admiralty, British subjects were declared off limits to all Chinese courts.

The least noticeable degradation at the time, however hadn't been the unfettered release of dangerous narcotics on the country of China and the resulting epidemic of opium dens. The greatest degradation was in the declaration that henceforth China would open itself to Christian re-education and a renunciation of "Heathenism". This was a virus that was even more lethal than any disease the smelly Barbarians had brought to them before and continued on through history as the water mark of Sino-West relations. Who would win the war for the mind and spirit of China? Who would dare tamper with the inner soul of the Great Kingdom Of Heaven?

The East India Trading Company became the world's first international drug cartel, but the real battle lingered in history's shadows as China was carved into the partitions of raw power determined by its various War Lords. China's vast population absorbed and survived misery and death brought on by the onslaught of the quasi-government drug merchants, but the ultimate battle for her soul had to await two men who would struggle to claim her a century later. One, a peasant leader who dabbled in political philosophy the other a military oligarch whose American Christian, Wellesley educated Chinese wife represented a future of symbolic surgery to remove the Buddhist, Asian soul from the Chinese persona all in the name of a foreigner God.

America was so steeped in Christian traditions that it automatically sided with Generalissimo Chiang Kai Shek who promised, as so many dictators had before him, to establish a capitalist and democratic China under his leadership of the Kuo Min Tang, or "Nationalist Party". Mao promised a return to ethnic and nationalist legitimacy by way of his grass roots revolution which had defeated the Japanese invasion. Mao's victory in 1949 found his forces virtually chasing the Kuo Min Tang (KMT) forces out of China to the east and to the southwest.

The East KMT governed the Chinese island of Taiwan and the south western KMT escaped into the hills of Laos and Burma. The OSS metamorphosed into the CIA shortly after. The CIA hatched a scheme to use heroin, extracted from the poppy fields of Laos, Northern Thailand and Burma to trade for weapons that they believed would enable the ten thousand man KMT armies to attack and re-take China. They were soundly defeated by Mao's high spirited forces and chased back into Burma.

Disgusted with the outcome, the CIA essentially abandoned the KMT armies and left them to their own devices. Ten thousand man armies need to eat. Having learned how the poppy was used by the CIA to acquire weapons and supplies the soldiers became farmers and their generals became drug lords.

The Eastern KMT ran a very successful island country rivaling much larger countries economically and technologically, but a large segment of their society maintained the connection with the jungle dwelling drug producing KMT and a natural bridge was constructed by the KMT created triad societies who managed eventually to set up the worlds most efficient drug network ever known.

When the Vietnam war began it became once again an urgent CIA imperative to equip and train guerilla forces to stop the Viet Minh. No immediate funds were allotted by Congress for this purpose and thus began a mission that was to shape Bill's future life. He had been trained by the CIA to set up heroin regions and then had been discarded like an old pair of boots. What else was he to do? Return to farming in Michigan? Like a rusted weapon that remains deadly even when left lying on the battlefield Bill began his own drug cartel and brought David to his side to help him run it.

Bill found a comfortable niche in the Triangle as a "Producer". He didn't need a ten thousand man army as he was arms length from the actual growing and harvesting. He had no front line contact with the end user. He assumed some risk in transporting the raw opium from the Han and Meo mountains. His value added contribution was to transform the raw opium into 99% pure heroin and deliver it to the triad network in Hong Kong. What could be simpler? He kept the Meo happy with weapons and trinkets and the Han army in Myanmar satisfied with the latest army gear. He kept only twenty five percent of the street margin for the China White #4 he delivered to the triads. They seemed happy, yet Bill had always suffered from the instinct that told him that when everyone is happy things are probably about to explode.

Bill surveyed his boats as his thoughts continued to drift back and forth into his deep past. He lifted a Tiger beer from a cooler by his feet and took a long pull of its bitter sweet liquid, before setting the bottle down. The last two boats of his twenty boat convoy were covering their holds full of opium with heavy bags of rice. They would soon be ready for the voyage to Phnom Penh. Bill's thoughts took him to the Philippines. He thought about Manolo Alvarez of Manila.

The only other man besides David that Bill would entrust his life to. Manny was a mechanic. Not the kind who worked on cars, but the other kind. One of the most lethal assassins ever to emerge from the archipelago islands of the Philippine Republic. Manny was abandoned as a six year old boy on the mean streets of Quezon City. His mother, an aging prostitute, took Manny to a restaurant to celebrate his birthday. She bought him a cake with candles and while she lit them she told him to close his eyes and count to fifty. When he opened his eyes again the six candles burned brightly but his mother was gone.

He ran barefoot on the scorching pavement searching in every direction but he never saw her again. Manny begged for food from foreigners in Ermita and picked their pockets in Makati. He slept in alleys and abandoned warehouses until at the age of twelve he graduated to the big time by stealing a fish mongers gutting knife from an open air market. He stalked a very fat German man all afternoon. Following him from the shopping mall to his hotel where he waited for him like a predator cat in Africa.

The man walked to the whore house district in Ermita and was soon leading a young hooker to a cheap hotel where rooms were rented by the hour. It was getting dark so Manny crossed the street and waited in the shadows near the room. Finally, the girl left the room counting her pesos as she walked back out into the light. Manny sprang, pushing in the unlocked door to the room. The fat German man was just putting his legs in his trousers, when Manny exclaimed; "Give me your money!" Manny was tall for his age but his baby face caused the man to shake with laughter.

Manny grew angry and waved the knife, slamming the door behind him. "Go away shit man!" The German yelled. Manny wanted to frighten the man by lunging toward him with the knife but he tripped on a mound of used towels on the floor and plunged the knife straight between the rolls of fat, all the way through the man's heart. His eyes rolled back in his head as he came crashing down on a coffee table in the room. Manny tried to pull the knife out but it was stuck. He rifled through the man's trousers finding his wallet and a gold watch. He put the watch in his pocket and ran through the alley separating the money and throwing everything else away. He gasped when he saw a photo of the man with a skinny Filipina woman and three children.

He paused about to throw the money, picture and wallet to the street when suddenly he smelled the scent of chickens roasting on a spit. He stuffed the money in his shirt and threw the rest away. He bought a whole chicken and ate it while being chased by other hungry young boys until the chicken slipped from his hands and he escaped.

Bill first met Manny when he learned that some drug king pin in Burma had put a contract out for both David and himself. The Drug lord, a man named Kung Sa, had risen to the top of the heap. Four armies including his own ran the Han mountain region of Burma, or Myanmar, with a tight fist. Their operations still included some heroin trading but for the most part their business was almost entirely crystal methamphetamines. It seemed that Bill's triad associates had flooded the Northern Thailand drug district near Chiang Rai with China White that had only been stepped on twice. They were selling the junk at almost the same price as Kung Sa's methamphetamines. Who wanted Meth when China White was in town?

Kung Sa's profits began to plummet, so they declared the foreigner must go. Bill contacted his old CIA controller and got a list of heavy lifters in Asia. He liked Manny's profile and invited him to come to Phnom Penh. Manny spent the first week "investigating." He learned that Kung Sa had hired two Hitters from Bangkok. He stalked them to a run down hotel in Chiang Rai and the night before they were to fly to Phnom Penh to hit Bill and David Manny crashed through their door and put a round dead center in each of their foreheads. He then hacked off their heads and put them in a water tight carry on bag. He flew to Rangoon and left the bag on Kung Sa's door. He then flew back to Thailand and proceeded to take out two of Kung Sa's best men. Sakchai Suwanpheng was shot through his left eye from a distance of two hundred yards as he was riding in the lead vehicle of a convoy delivering chemicals to Kung Sa's labs in the Chiang Rai district.

Saengsanit Chaisri was strangled to death by garrote as he was eating his favorite Tom Yam Khun soup in his own kitchen. The message was clear. Although under house arrest by the Junta, Kung Sa could be reached at will. Kung Sa sent Bill a message that he wanted no further blood shed. Bill after all could not be expected to control what the triads did with his China White after delivery had been made. Bill paid Manny a cool two million U.S. and Manny returned home to his mountain fortress in Cebu.

Thus began a friendship that grew stronger each year. After the attack on the Twin Towers Manny began supplying Bill with critical HUMINT Human Intelligence that was both difficult and dangerous to obtain. Scores of Abu Sayef and Jemah Islamia terrorists were hunted down and killed. This solidified a vital contact Bill still had in Langley and it earned Manny priceless political capital at home in the Philippines. Not every cloud has a silver lining. It seems that seven families rule the Philippines at least all of its presidents have come from one, or another of the seven families. Manny's sudden notoreity created a jealousy between two of the families.

One dark moonless night a night assault was launched against Manny's stronghold in Cebu. Ex-NBI agents as well as ex-Philippine Army paratroopers used hang gliders to breach Manny's security. The teams sailed over the high stone walls of Manny's compound and took out his guards one by one. Manny narrowly escaped with his wife and mistress in tow to a safe house he kept in the mountains. Manny railed and pulled his hair when he learned that both of his wife's brothers had been killed in the assault. He called Bill in Phnom Penh. Within an hour a U.S. Marine chopper picked up Manny at his mountain hide out and ferreted Manny and the two women to a U.S. Navy ship that was sailing for San Diego. Bill's contact in the Company was at a very high level. Manny stayed in a CIA safe house in Rancho Bernardo, California for six months.

When his spies in the Philippines assured him he wouldn't be given the Nino Aquino reception, Manny made arrangements to fly to Malaysia and take a small fishing boat to Cebu. During the weeks that followed thirty seven men who had all partaken in the assault on Manny's stronghold were hunted down and executed. The conspirators, a Senator, a Congressman, and a Supreme Court Judge, were snatched from their homes in the middle of the night and taken to an empty warehouse in a remote location north of Manila. Manny's private physician was ordered to keep the men alive with adrenalin and Epinephrine injections to prolong the torture.

The three men were beaten to a raw pulp with baseball bats as they hung from the rafters on meat hooks. Manny's doctor finally fell to his knees and begged Manny to forgive him for letting the men die too soon. Manny kicked the dead bodies and held pictures of his wife's dead brothers near their faces as if the dead men could still see the reason for their own torture and death.

Bill lifted Manny and half dragged, half carried him away from the gruesome scene. Manny rented an entire hotel for the night not far from his home and had two dozen whores brought in as entertainment for just Bill and himself. They got drunk on Filipino rum and swore an allegiance until the end of time.

Manny's reputation spread and he began to receive lucrative contracts as far away as Dubai. He accumulated dozens of businesses and many square hectares of real estate but his prize possession was a resort hotel he had custom built in the center of the Bar district in Angeles City Philippines called The Emerald Of Asia.

Bill made a quick count of his boats. All were secure and awaiting his signal. Bill flashed a green beam of light and the convoy was launched. He had his boatman stay back to position himself to round up any stragglers. He watched fishermen weighing in their nets for the day, but the fish had all sounded to escape the surface heat. The convoy stretched out so as not to seem a convoy. Bill kept a wary eye on the shoreline while night descended on the Mekong river. Other small boats and sampans drifted past on their way north to Vientiane. The small boats appeared to be little pieces of wood on their way northward from the great Ton Le Sap lake that spread the shores of the river several miles across.

Chapter Two: A Twenty Kilo Bag

The sky was a symphony of fiery red with hues of yellow that brushed the shore line in a haze of burnt umber and gold. Another blistering hot day on the Mekong with searing heat and heart breaking humidity. Soon all boats on the river began to light their lanterns which swayed with the currents. This created the illusion that clouds of large fireflies were swarming in confusion and disarray as their soft, then brilliant reflections chased the rippling wavelets to the shore.

This was the heart of the Golden Triangle where the natural waterway confluence of the Mekong, Ruak and Mae Sai rivers performed a tripartite union with Thailand, Laos and Myanmar. Many children had been born on the floating bamboo villages of this mighty river and many men had died protecting their precious cargo of opium from pirates and thieves. Death existed here. If a bullet didn't claim you then Dengue fever, Malaria, Yellow Fever, or cerebral plague eventually would.

This load had been brought down from the Meo mountains first by a mule train and then by human mules who carried the raw opium in back packs hiding it in safe houses or even in freshly dug graves until bribes had been paid and soldiers had looked the other way.

Bill stayed low in his perch behind his dual mounted fifty caliber machine guns. This trip had been thus far pleasantly uneventful although the bribes had nearly doubled. He hoped the price surge was temporary. He understood that the spike in bribes had been a result of a massive drug intercept program the Narcs from the U.S. DEA and Interpol had been running for the past few days.

The pattern never seemed to change. Big Wigs would fly in from Washington, D.C. with shit loads of intercept aid money and expect to be chaperoned to the local danger spots by the host country police. They always pressed for immediate results to be able to account for their dollars at work. The predictable reflex would be heavy pressure from the top down until, as was the case in Bangkok, the police would round up pill popping addicts caught with methamphetamine pills, or a frying spoon. Then they simply lined them up in alleys and shot them at the base of their skulls. Why didn't they concentrate on the Crescent? That's where the serious quantity was coming from. The only thing Bill could figure was that the agents loved the sex action in Thailand and Cambodia more than they did the Middle East and West Asia. This load had already passed through the bribery zones along the river front of Laos. What now lay ahead was the politically instigated police intercept zones of Thailand and Cambodia.

Bill thought of his return from Afghanistan to Phnom Penh. He had lost touch with David while in Afghanistan owing both to his constantly busy schedule and the remote locations he was in. When his controller told him to pack up and leave his labs and fields in the Helmand province it reminded him of how the Americans left Saigon. No thanks for delivering Afghanistan back to Islam, no thanks for providing so many Stingers with your drug production that it caused the great Soviet Union to declare hand held surface to air missiles as the singular reason it lost the war, nothing. Bill thought often of his Hmong wife and children. They were only married by her Hmong tribal Chief, but Bill still thought of her as his wife. He began to hate the U.S. government for encouraging its Special Forces to convince the Hmong that they would always be supported and protected by Uncle Sam in gratitude for their valiant service to the U.S.A.

When it came time to bug out most of the Hmong were left to the wrath of the NVA. The ones who were shipped to the Central Valley of California near Fresno were dumped on what must have seemed to be a planet in outer space. Bill would never trust his government again for anything. There were good guys and there were bad guys, he knew that, but when politics and ideology were dropped in the mix it made everyone lie, cheat and kill to win at any cost. Survival driven betrayal. As simple as that.

The best and only real thing the CIA had ever taught him was how to produce pure heroin and get it to a buyer. It was the only skill set he needed to make so much money he could retire within eighteen months if he decided it was time. Bill thought of how he had used some of the drug money from the Crescent to buy a Land Rover in Karachi, Pakistan and how he packed five million dollars he had skimmed off the top of his last sale into compartments of the vehicle under carriage that he personally welded shut. He and the Land Rover rode on a Freighter to Thailand and Bill drove it to Phnom Penh to begin his new business. The CIA never knew that the money existed because he never added the heroin quantity he saved for his probable burn notice to his extensive monthly report to Langley. Vietnam taught him to plan for surprises and he learned the lesson well.

One day he was sitting at a side walk cafe along the river front in Phnom Penh when a shadow passed between himself and the glaring sun light. His heart skipped a beat. He almost reached for his ankle piece when he suddenly heard that unmistakable laugh. David was back and he had found Bill just as Bill always knew he would. The two exchanged bear hugs and Bill just kept shaking his head. Bill's body guard and driver had their hands inside their jackets until Bill explained that a long lost brother had finally made it home. "So when did you leave Afghanistan?" David asked. "About six months ago." Bill replied.

I tried to locate you using Wharton's data, but they only had a defunct address on Goethestrasse in Vienna. I figured you'd find me when you were ready." Bill said. David reached Bill a check for two hundred and ninety eight thousand dollars. Bill smiled and tore it in little pieces. "I told you before, it was an investment. Are you saying you don't want to join me?" Bill asked. "Hell no! I just want to work for you on a level playing field." "Money could never buy a life. You saved my life that day I met you David. So let's not worry about a little chump change and let's get busy making a lot more." Over the next weeks Bill was amazed at how David streamlined the operation. Bill had been living and working in an old warehouse not far from the Mekong just north of Phnom Penh.

David bought a large compound in the suburbs of Phnom Penh and established it as an NGO, or Non Government Organization. He named it S.H.A.R.I. or Sacred Heart Agricultural Research Institute. Working from the angle of Bill's education as a Horticulturist with hybrid grain research experience, David wrote the charter for an organization that was dedicated to finding a break through hybrid rice that would feed the hungry of the Third World. He easily acquired an affiliation with the W.H.O. World Health Organization and received a research grant from the U.N. F.A.O. or Food and Agricultural Organization. They received identification portfolios from F.A.O. that provided a pass that allowed them to travel throughout Asia without fulfilling typical visa requirements.

David hired a Cambodian staff and located them in an office in the center of Phnom Penh. They genuinely believed they were employees of an NGO. Then, David used three million of Bill's dollars to buy a bank charter in the Grand Cayman islands. He soon established a world wide banking network of affiliated banks that allowed him to transfer any sum of money anywhere in the world using the same status as a subordinate of a central bank.

The combined status of being a Christian not for profit organization that owned its own bank took S.H.A.R.I. completely off the radar. Gone were the days of brief cases stuffed with cash nervously brought to meetings with people who would just as easily kill you for what you carried as look at you. That had been many years ago. Since that time, together, Bill and David had amassed a billion U.S. dollars and prospects for the future looked quite good.

Bill ordered his boatman to tighten up his distance from the last boat. His boatman was a Khmer named Samnang which meant "Lucky" in Khmer. He chose him because he felt they could all use a little luck this night. Bill reflected about how surprised he had been to learn that both women and men share the same names in Khmer. He had once met a woman named Samnang in Martinis #1 disco, but she had given Bill the clap. He hoped his luck would change. "Hey Samnang! You also have sister named Samnang?" "No, just me name Samnang, Boss." "Good." Bill replied. "Me sister's names Kunthea and Chantrea.

Kunthea mean sweet smell and Chantrea mean moon light." Samnang volunteered. "I'm sure both very beautiful." Bill lied. "Yes, very beautiful." Samnang crooned. "Sweet smelling c--nt in the moon light." Bill thought to himself. Without warning a speed boat armed with a fifty calibre machine gun, turned on a huge flood light that had been originally mounted on an M-60 tank. Its million candle light powered beam was concentrated on one of Bill's boats.

"You want me attack Boss?" Samnang asked. "No, stay dark until we see how things go." Bill whispered. Bill could see a haze of droplets rising skyward from the river in the bright glare of the beam. The Thai Drug police quickly secured the boat with grappling hooks and were already leaping onto its deck with pistols drawn. The rapidity with which they found a twenty kilo bag of Bill's opium spoke volumes to Bill. He had a rat to find.

The Thai police appeared almost comical as they danced up and down while barking orders to their captives. Bill had trained his men well. They knew they had only thirty seconds to get beneath the water level. Suddenly the boat's crew including the two taken immediate prisoner dove beneath their boat. Bill saw the two white men, no doubt D.E.A. and INTERPOL, slap the shoulders of the Thai policemen to urge them to dive in after Bill's men but the Thai police weren't buying it. Instead they started shooting randomly into the black surly waters. Bill knew he had run out of time.

His men would have to come up for air soon and the Thai police would shoot them. Bill opened up on the Police boat with both fifty calibre's holding down both triggers as the boat exploded and disintegrated into a million shreds and pieces killing all aboard. Bill's men returned to their boat and re-joined the convoy. They were just fifteen minutes away from a safe haven. A small fishing village where Bill kept a team of laborers on standby. He called in his chopper support and within twenty minutes the opium had been cross loaded to pallets that would ride suspended beneath the choppers back to their compound in Phnom Penh.

Bill had a standard operating procedure for everything. He knew that the death of the two white policemen would make the Mekong impassable for at least three weeks. The response time of the Thai air force was one predictable hour. By then, there wouldn't be a trace of evidence to prove that any of his men had ever been there. Their boats had bags of rice with the S.H.A.R.I. logo, that included a picture of Christ on the cross. That's all anyone who inspected his boats would find. They dispersed after the cross load and headed for several villages along the way, where they would wait until they received a pre-loaded text message to inform them that it was safe to come home to Phnom Penh. Bill's S.O.P. or standard operating procedure also included the fact that the breach had to be found within a window of six hours.

Beyond that, the damage would not be containable. Bill hired all of his men personally. Someone he trusted had broken their sacred agreement. He had to be quarantined and outed before dawn. Bill's Chief of Security, a Khmer named Vibol hopped out of the lead chopper as soon as it landed at the LZ. He immediately replaced the crew of the arrested boat with a fresh crew and herded the original crew onto his chopper in hand cuffs. Vibol treated everyone as though they were guilty until proven innocent.

Bill released Samnang to take his chase boat to Samnang's Uncle's place, a fishing village just north of Phnom Penh. His fifties would be off loaded and hidden there and his chase boat would be moored along a covered floating dock. Bill ran to board Vibol's chopper and watched as the remaining evidence that his people had been there dissolved in the darkness.

Back at the compound the crew was isolated in five separate interrogation rooms. Bill went to his office and turned on the security monitors in each room. Vibol travelled swiftly between each room without any visible pattern, or method. He spoke so softly to each man that the interrogated had to lean forward to understand him. Forty five minutes into this round robin interrogation Vibol had just sat down again in room three with Amara, a man who had been with Bill's organization since the beginning. Suddenly Vibol shouted and slapped Amara across the face.

Then Vibol punched him and held a loaded .45 calibre pistol to Amara's temple. Bill ran swiftly to the room. Amara looked at Bill pleadingly. "Please Mistah Bill. I sorry. My sistah have brother in Cambodia Army. He Major. My wife say if he take only one bag opium he make Colonel rank. We have many bag opium. I no know Thai police coming want take whole boat. I sorry Mistah Bill. Please forgive!" "How did he make contact with you tonight Amara?" Bill asked. "He use cell phone." Amara sighed.

"I signal with blinking cell phone light. We text. No need talking." Bill was in a quandary. Although he believed Amara's story he didn't have a clue of what to do about it. Perhaps he could offer a huge bribe to Amara's wife and the Major to get them to keep their mouths shut about his organization. He was about to instruct Vibol to go get Amara's wife and the Major when an ear splitting explosion rang out in the room. Vibol had blown off the top of Amara's head. Bill was made temporarily deaf. He could feel his throat vibrate as he yelled to Vibol, but he only heard a vibrating hum as he yelled each word. Moments later his hearing returned. Vibol's men were removing the body from the room and cleaning up the blood, bone fragments and wiping the spray from the cement block painted wall.

"No worries Mistah Bill. We clean room good as new." "Vibol, f-ck the room! I am still trying to digest what just happened. Did you accidentally shoot Amara just now?" "No accident Mistah Bill. We must stop connection to drug police now, or they arrest and execute everyone. Wife Amara and Major must also die tonight. If drug police reach them first they take into protective custody. Learn everything about us. Conduct raid here before morning." Bill knew Vibol was right. Bill had killed before during fire fights but this was different. This was cold blooded execution.

"I know Vibol. You are right, but God Damn it! killing a woman is not something that comes easy for me." " Not only one woman, two!" Vibol corrected. "Two?" Bill gasped. "Yes. Major wife know every ting. Amara wife die, Major die she go drug police." "SHIT! Yes, I see what you mean Vibol." Bill said. "Amara have two small children. Major have two teen age son. All must die." "WHAT? No we're not f--cking baby killers. The two babies of Amara will be taken safely to an orphanage without leaving a trace of where they came from." " OK. Mistah Bill. You good man, but teen age sons must die. Khmer people talk in front of children. Teen age sons know every ting."

Bill bit his lip. He knew that each second he resisted Vibol's logic he lost irreplaceable face with Vibol and his men and worse the point of no return would soon be reached whereby the concept of survival would replace the concept of damage control. Vibol was right. "OK Vibol. Stop the leak. Tell me when it's finished." Vibol bowed slightly and left the room. Bill returned to his office and waiting by the door was his Chief Chemist Greg Hamilton an Englishman from Wales.

Bill rescued Greg from alcoholism. Greg was living with a Thai prostitute near Nana Plaza. She turned tricks to keep herself in Yabba Yabba and Greg well supplied with cheap Thai rum and brandy. When she became too ill to work Greg attempted to mug a foreigner to get money for their addictions, but he chose the wrong foreigner. Bill nearly broke Greg's arm until he realized how pathetically weak Greg was. Greg kept apologizing even during the robbery.Bill took him to a Thai restaurant nearby and bought him a meal. Greg began sobbing and recounting the miserable details of his life. When Bill learned Greg was a licensed British Chemist he made him an offer. As long as you remain drug and alcohol free you can work for me.

Greg cleaned himself up and quickly learned Bill's methods of converting opium into morphine and China White heroin. Greg now had a staff of seventy assistants and completely ran all of Bill's labs. "Cheers Bill!" "Hullo Greg! Are they finished off loading our opium yet?" "Yes. About twenty minutes ago. It's all tucked away in the supply bins absent one 20 kilo bag that the Thai police confiscated." "Good. You look worried Greg, what's on your mind?" "Oh nothin' really. Just heard two of the coppers was white cops from America and Europe like." "Yes. It couldn't be helped. They were on the verge of cracking us wide open so I had to take them out." "This means we're on the dole for a few weeks then?" "Looks that way." Bill replied.

"Why don't you process what we have for next months delivery and then give your fellows and yourself a two week paid holiday. Go live at the Chicken farm in Snooky." Bill said. Greg knew the S.O.P. procedure whenever white police were killed. He grinned and gave Bill a thumbs up as he always did when he was pleased about something. "Two White Coppers Bill? ya sure two weeks is long enough?" "Your Welsh arse had better be back on the pots in two weeks you Limey bastard!" Bill said with a smile. Greg laughed and walked out.

Bill poured himself a glass of fifty year old single malt scotch and leaned back in his large leather chair. He took a long pull of the delicate liquid and rolled it around his mouth letting it linger on his palate before gently and slowly swallowing it. The air conditioner blasted cool air across his sweaty brow as he felt the warmth of the single malt travel from his stomach to his neck and cheeks. He cursed beneath his breath as he thought about the two white breads. What else was he to do? Had they captured the crew they may have even captured Bill and David too. Bill loved the Khmer, but he knew them to be braggarts when you got them drunk. All the Thai police need to have done would be to treat their captives to a few cases of elephant beer and then let them brag about everything they knew.

Everything he and David had worked so hard for over the past decade would go up in smoke. The part Bill hated the most was the two teen age sons of the Major. When you're carving out a cancer in this business you can't go soft. It's kill, or be killed. It made Bill long for the day they could retire and just travel to anywhere. Bill was a tall man with rugged good looks. As strong as a bear and although his heart was good his involvement with drugs had made him strangely morose about their end effect. Bill could become as cold as a Cobra if his survival depended on it.

David was tall and very handsome. He was even stronger than Bill and was one of the best special operators ever to graduate from the Special Warfare Center at Ft. Bragg, N.C. He never told Bill about his real combat experience. Two years before he met Bill he had been on a Long Range Reconnaissance Patrol, (L.R.R.P.) deep inside North Vietnam looking for the American P.O.W. camps. He just missed finding them by a day. He found evidence all around showing that they had been kept there. Just as he was about to leave his eight man team ran into a group of North Vietnamese workers who had been sent to scour the camp and get rid of anything that may have been left behind.

A squad of NVA had come along as a protection detail and a fire fight broke out. David killed two men with his AK-47 and was engaged with two others hand to hand. Suddenly a third appeared from a hut and shot David in the groin with an AK-47. His team mates killed the remaining NVA and called in an extraction chopper. David felt a horrible burning where the bullet had ripped apart his leg muscle blasting a third of his femoral muscle out through the side of his hip. He pulled on the muscle to try to remove it and nearly passed out. He pulled down his trousers and discovered that the bullet had missed his penis by only a couple of centimeters.

"At least I'll go out with my dick in place." he thought. He watched the blood squirting in tandem with his heart beat and he knew he'd never make it back before he bled out. He started to recite the Lord's prayer and in the middle, he stopped praying and started laughing. He thought to himself "Lord you're gonna' do what you want with me either way so if you don't mind, I'll stop tryin' to lay a sales job on you." Suddenly the pain left him and he felt blissful and euphoric. He saw a white glowing light as he was hovering above his own body. Three of his team mates had been killed during the first thirty seconds of combat.

When the chopper landed his remaining team mates thought David to be dead and threw his dead team mates in on top of him. All the way back David was too weak to move an eye lash. He felt the horrible weight of his own dead and it stayed with him all of his life, both in his nightmares and manifested as claustrophobia.

"David leaned into Bill's office. "Doc says you nailed a couple of white bread cops tonight. What happened Bill?" Bill poured another glass of scotch for himself and one for David and gestured at the chair for him to sit down. "David, things were going along smooth as a baby's ass when suddenly a Thai Drug Police boat shows up and boards one of my boats. Faster than lightning they came up with a twenty kilo bag of raw opium so I knew we had a traitor. We are still on the verge of having our entire operation compromised. Really dirty things going down right now." Bill lamented.

"Tip off?" David asked. "Worse. Internal security leak." "Damn. That is bad. Any leads?" "Yeah. Vibol got Amara to roll. Seems his wife's brother is a Major in the Cambo Army and needed a sack of opium to get a promotion to Colonel." "D.E.A. Aid dollars at work?" "Most likely. The D.E.A. rolls in with deep pockets and suddenly all kinds of incentives to do drug busts start coming out of the wood work. Anyway I'm standing there in this nearly sound proof f--cking interrogation room and Vibol whacks Amara with a .45 calibre. My ears are still ringing." "Shit, you'd better get that checked out." "Aw the scotch is healing me already. At any rate, Vibol starts making out his hit list. He's gonna' whack Amara's wife, the Major, the Major's wife and all of the kids." "What? I'll freakin' whack Vibol first." "Wait David. I had the same reaction at first. But think about it. Amara's already dead. You know his wife is going to be standing at the police station tomorrow when he doesn't come home. So we whack her right?

Then, when the Major finds out both she and Amara will never answer the phone again he goes to the Cops, or worse, just continues the dialogue with them he's already having." "So we whack him then his two teen age sons who heard him bragging about making Colonel soon go to the cops. See how entangled this cancer can get?" "Did Amara have kids?" "Two toddlers, but that's where I put my foot down." Bill said indignantly.

"The kids are going to go to a good orphanage without any trace back to us." "Bill, are we best buddies?" "You know we are David." "Well whacking the grown ups is fine with me but taking out the two teen age sons is off the freakin map! Call Vibol and get this shit stopped about the teenagers Bill. I didn't sign on for shit like that." Bill screwed up his face and then nodded. You're right David. Sorry, I should have been more firm with Vibol." Bill hit speed dial to Vibol. "Yeah Vibol, it's me. Listen take out Amara's wife and the Major and his wife but don't hit the two boys. WHAT? SHIT! Really? Goddamn it. No I'm not angry Vibol. No don't go near the Thai Embassy. It's probably crawling with cops by now. No, no, not angry Vibol. Stay close to the Major. We will give your guys back up if they need it. We're on our way!" Bill looked shocked as he turned off his cell phone.

"David I'm sorry man, I tried. Vibol's assassins whacked Amara's wife and put the kids in an accomplices car who will get them safely to an orphanage. The Major's wife and sons were whacked simultaneous with the other hit. They're gone David. Sorry. The Major was intercepted on his way home. He doesn't even know that his family is gone. The Major confessed that he has an appointment in thirty minutes to meet with a Thai Drug Inspector at the Thai Embassy. The Thai cop called the Major while Vibol was standing there. Vibol got the Major to get the meet changed from the Thai Embassy to the Red Lion Inn. Quick thinking on his part. They're gonna take out the Thai copper in three zero minutes. Are you in, or out David?" Bill asked pensively.

"F--ck it, I'm in, but no more hits on kids OK?" "I promise David." Bill hit fast dial to his driver. "Mao I have a hot date get the SUV ready to roll in two minutes. Bring my new body guard, Veasna!"

The black SUV with windows so darkly tinted it was impossible to see anyone inside left the S.H.A.R.I. compound and drifted through the bicycles, motor cycles and cars like a star class yacht on a glass and metal sea. No one spoke but Bill's driver Mao sensed the urgency and cut in and out of the traffic with total disregard. Soon they were moving along the river front near the Buddhist wat. "Get us near the Red Lion Inn Mao, but stay in the shadows." Mao found a dark space beyond the street lights and squared the windshield with the front terrace of the Red Lion Inn and cut his lights.

Exactly five minutes had passed when they saw a Thai man dressed in black enter the restaurant. Close behind was a fat man with a very fat neck. His body was massive but he carried himself with the confidence of a weight lifter. The Thai man sat facing the front entrance, alone. The fat man who followed him in sat at a nearby table and ordered a large reistafle. It was delivered almost immediately and the fat man began to eat. Soon the Major flanked by Vibol and an assistant on each side neared the restaurant. The Major was shaking his head yes obediently while Vibol jabbed him on the neck several times with his forefinger.

Vibol disappeared in the shadows and the Major walked inside. After a brief exchange with the Thai, the Major took a seat at his table. The fat man continued eating without glancing at the man who was now with his superior. After a brief interval the Thai man pulled out a notebook and a pen but the Major shook his head no. The Thai man began to rise as though he were about to leave. Bill shifted uneasily in his seat.

The Thai man only stood to retrieve a thick envelope. He dropped it before the Major and sat back down. From out of nowhere Vibol's first assassin appeared and shot the Thai man in his left temple.

The Major lunged backward as the first assassin changed direction and placed a round in his left cheek and another in the center of his trachea. The fat man stood up so fast all of his rice dishes flew in every direction.

He pulled a Walther semi-automatic, but before he could get a proper aim a second assassin emerged from the kitchen and shot the fat man at the base of his neck. He went down thunderously, face first in the broken pile of dishes that had fallen earlier from his table.

The first assassin calmly walked to the table where the Thai man was sitting slumped forward with his left arm dangling beside the table and picked up the notebook and thick envelope. The second assassin in the meantime picked up each shell casing from both weapons. Customers were still screaming from beneath tables as the two men walked nonchalantly straight out the front door. One stopped to scoop up a large prawn which he took a bite of and threw the rest in a potted plant. Immediately, two Suzuki trail bikes pulled up and the assassins hopped on and disappeared down the dark streets toward Sharkey's Pub.

Vibol walked past the Inn and stared at the dark windows of Bill's SUV. Bill shook his head slowly yes." Damn. Damn. Damn. I don't like killing any more than the next man, but what we just saw was about as professional as it gets. Did you see the second guy stoop to police up the empty casings? F--ck!" Bill exclaimed. David didn't say anything. He was too busy trying to resist the downward pull of the whirlpool swirling around him.

He had sworn to start a new life with a Khmer woman he met one day strolling along the river front. Her name was Srey An and she was the most beautiful woman David had ever laid eyes on.

For the first time in his life the phrase "the face that launched a thousand ships" had true meaning for him. She had told him point blank that if he only wanted sex go to the Navy Annex, or the Walk About. If he was interested in a soul mate who would love him when all beauty had faded then read this book by Alan Watts about the Eight Fold Path Of Wisdom, or these beautiful little books by a Buddhist monk from Vietnam called Thich Nat Hahn. If you need classic, but general discussion read the Dhammapada by Eknath Easwaran. Study his little book called simply "Meditation."

"It should be called meditation for Dummies the way he holds your hand until you finally get it." She laughed. She was a Tigress in bed and thanks to a very brilliant Nun who taught her Oxford English and Western philosophy, she was able to carry on late night discussions of philosophy by Kant, Wittgenstein, Thomas Aquinas, Descartes, Nietzsche she knew them all by heart. The wonder of her was how she could take you on a magical mystery tour and explain everything perfectly within the concepts of Gautama Buddha.

She dressed plain during the day. She called the rags she wore her "Market Clothes." At night after you had grown accustomed to her daylight face, which she kept half hidden like a maiden of Islam, she would make you choke with surprise and desire when she wore dresses slit to the thigh. Then she'd finish you with her puffy, ruby red lips and her silky black hair. She became visible, or invisible, by caprice. Like the wind which shows itself to you in a field of grain when she wants to be seen, or blows clouds out to sea far beyond where you could ever find them again on your own, when she doesn't.

Bill sensed David's turmoil. He had suffered as much as David possibly could have about the deaths tonight. He didn't care about the greedy Major and his driven wife. He felt sorry that Amara was influenced by her and her husband. Now two more infants would grow up with hit, or miss parents. Bill silently made a vow to pay someone to find perfect parents for them and fund them all the way through university. The two teen age boys would be the hardest blood to wash from his hands. He knew that money could only compensate so much and beyond a certain point it was useless, or worse, it merely served to facilitate memories of pain. He knew David wasn't happy tonight.

What Bill worried most about was whether he blamed Bill, or whether he had simply reached the point where money had become poison. Bill was going to mention it to David. David's silence was unbearable at a time when Bill desperately needed his friendship. He was afraid to say the wrong thing so he said nothing.

"Mao, take us to Martini disco ." Bill finally said. "I need a beer, how about you David?" David remained silent nodding yes, without a word. When they arrived Mao and Veasna went inside first, even casing the women's bath room. When they were certain it was safe, they signaled Bill and David to come inside while they returned to the SUV. David stared at Bill for a few seconds. Bill was about to say something but David held up his hand and began to speak.

"Bill, I don't blame you for what has gone down in the past twelve, or so hours. It's the nature of the business we're in. If you blink you die. In fact, I am impressed with your ability to make life and death decisions so easily. I know your life has been just as rotten as mine. When you sent me out of the devils ass, I knew you were sacrificing everything you had saved in life to do it.

"I honestly think I would have eventually committed suicide if I had stayed in Laos any longer. Bill, we have a billion freaking dollars. You can take the lion's share, you earned it, but I'll be goddamned if I want to even be remotely associated with murdering freaking teenagers. I just can't do that mile with you, or anyone Bill. It consumes you.

You know, I had withdrawals from adrenalin shock at Wharton. I would lie in bed at night in a cold sweat at 3 am with my .357 Magnum at my temple, clicking off trigger snaps, never knowing the order. Death used to scare the shit out of me. Now it only fascinates me and sometimes mesmerizes me. My own death is something I have learned to deal with. Causing the death of others puts weight on my soul, so I have to somehow find a way to be more careful about how I give it than receive it. I find no meaning in needless murder and simple wealth accumulation. I guess what I'm saying is that I'll give it one more year and then I want to retire. Just no more kids, man."

"David, if you stand by me one more year I'll retire with you." "Really Bill? I plan to marry Srey An and leave the thrill and danger behind, but I can't imagine life with you further away than jogging distance." "So we have a year? Signed in blood?" "Signed in blood Bill." David vowed.

Bill and David were watching the big screen in the open air section. Suddenly three pretty Vietnamese hookers came in. They looked around and seeing Bill and David locked in conversation they started to walk back out. "Co di dau?" Bill yelled out. "Toi di choi!" The tall one yelled back. "We go Walk About bar" the other two answered. "You want ride? We go Walk About too." Bill answered. "Shuah!" The tall one replied.

The girls stood outside the SUV fickle as to who would sit where. Bill grabbed the tall one by the hand and led her to the back facing seat in the rear. She giggled as Bill whispered something in her ear. David sat in the forward facing back seat, flanked by the other two girls. As the SUV pulled away from Martini's Bill told Mao to head for the Walk About and to take the long way. Mao grinned at Veasna and rubbed his forefinger against his thumb. Bill always gave a good tip if he managed some vehicular sex.

Soon the tall girl's face disappeared into Bill's lap. The girl on David's right whispered in his ear. "You want two girl bare back blow job? Only five dollah each girl." "Shuah!" David said. The girls laughed and in moments they were both driving David wild. David was in ecstacy until the silence erupted in a half moan, half scream from Bill. "Have you finished yet good buddy?" Bill asked. "David felt the goddess of orgasm retreat back into her clam shell. He pulled both girls away and sat up straight. "Didn't make it this time Bill." "That's OK the night's still young."

They arrived at The Walk About Inn and bar and Mao parked in front of the Chaat Hour Hotel. After clearing the place Mao and Veasna returned to the SUV while Bill David and the girls went inside. Bill paid the girls, who proceeded to work the bar and pool table area for new customers. "David, grab a few shots of Stoly and meet me in the Men's room OK?" David bought two bottles of Stolichnaya vodka and grabbed a fist full of paper napkins near the sandwiches and followed Bill into the men's room. They took off their trousers and splashed their genitals with the entire content of both bottles. "Damn this shit is cold!" Bill exclaimed. David reached him a fist full of paper napkins. "Wait until you start to wipe the shit off!" David replied. "Ahhhh F--ck! You're right, man I'm on fire. My balls are roasting!" The Men's room was too small to get re-dressed so they walked out naked, pulling on their pants in the door way.

A drunk Kiwi laughed as he said; "Hey what av' we 'ere mates? a coupla' Poofs?" The bartender whispered in his ear and the Kiwi ran out through the open side doorway. "What did you say to him?" Bill asked. "Aw nuthin' mates just told im you were world champion Croc castrators." David and Bill laughed hard and deep. They had been through a great deal this day and both began to feel like getting the party started.

The bar girls who gave massages through the customers shirt for a dollar swarmed Bill and David as the bartender kept their glasses full to the brim. The girls were playing with their private parts through their trousers and with four women pawing at them at the same time they finally began to relax and enjoy themselves. "I was going to recommend going to Le Cyrcee, or Sophies for a team blow job David but I think the bastards shut them down." "Yeah, I heard Sophies is closed, but I'm not sure about Le Cyrcee." "F--ck it then let's go to Bo Ding."

"What's that a massage parlor?" "F--ck no. It's an apartment complex over by the Casino. A lot of the girls who worked the Viet massage parlors and even some of the girls who worked at KM-11 before the NGO, the International Ministry Of Justice, or IJM, got them closed down." Bill said. "Christians shaming the heathens?" David asked. "Yeah. But I think there really was some pedophilia going on there in the shacks behind the main fifteen houses." "Sick bastards, then they should have closed the place." David growled. "I agree, but the Christians don't want any prostitution in Asia, so if you Monger you get labeled a Pedo, or a sex trafficker." "Yeah. Like those holier than thou f--ckers such as Jim Bakker. They cry and beg for welfare check donations on TV and then spend it on Crack Hos." David said. "Too much big Brother nowadays."They don't have sex lives so they want to shit can the small amount of pleasure we have." Bill said.

"How about those hundreds of Catholic priests butt f--cking Altar boys?" Man I'd like to line all of those sick bastards up and empty a few clips." David added. "Now that's the David I knew." Bill said. "He's back!" "We have to get out of town for a couple of weeks David, so I made reservations to Clark in the Philippines. I've been promising Manny we'd visit him. You know he has that resort hotel in Angeles City. Let's go get our skulls f—cked out." "Hell Bill we can do that in Bangkok, or Pattaya." "Yeah, I know, but what the hell, let's visit an old friend and get f--ck stripped at the same time." "Powerful argument Bill." David agreed.

When Bill and David returned to the SUV Bill yelled to Mao; "Bo Ding and I don't want to hear any shit about it!" Mao shook his head no slowly but did as he was told. They drove past the Monument erected in 1956 to celebrate Cambodia's liberation from France. It was over run with prostitutes high on Yabba Yabba. Their pimps waved at the cars going by while a few of the girls hiked up their mini-skirts and pulled down their bikini panties to lure customers.

"David, Mao keeps warning me not to go to this place but what the f--ck, a little curiosity won't hurt. I was here once before and found a bed partner for the night. A twenty eight year old secretary who was moon lighting to support her Khmer husband's drinking problem. The place is under heavy police surveillance from time to time, so stay close in case we need to make an exit right." "Sounds like fun Bill." David said.

Mao pulled up to the curb and disgorged Bill and David about a block past the main entrance. Bill cursed a little about that. "Damned Mao is so paranoid he doesn't like to stop directly in front of the place." Bill grumbled. They ran between wrecked cars and a barbecue cart, passing two groups of prostitutes huddled together clad in bikini panties and bras and fish net stockings. Some had white painted faces that Asian girls believe is a way to look beautiful.

A large wooden door swung open and the men were welcomed inside a large ante chamber with a dilapidated sofa to sit on as the parade of females walked by. An older Khmer pimp who both Bill and David concurred looked like Pol Pot, came out grinning to get things started. He dialed a number on his cell that executed a string text message to all of the prostitutes in the building.

"David, here's how the set up works. The women we are about to preview are all freelancers who live within the complex. When customers come by they get a text message to come down in their sexiest garb. If selected they can boom boom in one of the short time rooms in the back. If you want take out they can be sent by moto to your hotel room. I never take Hos to my residence, you just can't get them to leave the next day. A short time goes for $5 bucks U.S. and includes both oral and traditional sex. Trouble is that the hygiene here is almost non existent. Most guys bring a bottle of rubbing alcohol to tide them over until they get back home to a hot shower."

In moments the girl parade began. The girls ranged from mediocre and over weight to drop dead gorgeous. Pol Pot #2 gestured toward the ladies. "Cost seven dollah short time here, ten dollah you take out all night." he said. The parade stopped and the girls shifted nervously, trying to prepare for rejection by pretending it didn't matter.

"Bill, I'm not finicky but except for the old hag on the end these girls all look to be in their low to mid teens." "Yeah, I saw that too David. OK let's get the f--ck out of here." Bill said. Suddenly a motor cycle came crashing through the large wooden door and came to a screeching halt in the middle of the cement floor. The man wore a helmet with a dark visor that he kept down to cover his face and a body length leather cover all. His bike bore license plates that said Embassy du Francaise. He nodded to Pol Pot#2 and went back toward the short time rooms.

It was obvious he was there on a regular appointment. "Great place Bill. Customers come dressed like astronauts to cover their identity." "Yeah, I wonder if he takes the helmet off when he's f--cking." Bill pondered. Seeing that neither David, or Bill were going to make a selection, Pol Pot#2 called David off to the side. "Come with me. I have special girl for you." he said. Pol Pot #2 took David down a narrow hallway and unlocked a door. Waiting inside were three semi nude pre-pubescent girls who couldn't have been a day over ten years old. They had obviously been warned to smile, because their forced smile was laced with fear of Pol Pot#2.

"Pol Pot #2 proudly explained; "All three "Originals" never have man before, you like, you take one, or all three one week. Five Hundred dollah U.S each." David's eyes misted over and he shook from the depth of his stomach with a primordial anger. He had lived and partied in Phnom Penh for six years and not once had he been propositioned so directly with children before, but there it was, raw and unmistakable. David grabbed Pol Pot #2 by the throat and shoved him hard against the wall. "You miserable f--cking pervert!" he yelled. From out of nowhere, two body guards ran toward the room. The first pulled a nine mm from his belt and aimed it at David's head.

Bill lunged past the second guard and delivered a crushing blow to the middle of the first body guards shoulder blades. He went crashing down across the floor. David turned Pol Pot #2 loose and scooped up the nine mm from the floor. The second body guard was just pulling the trigger to shoot Bill in the face when David squeezed off a round that blew away the side of the second body guard's head. Pol Pot #2 ran screaming from the room. The three girls ran along behind him. Suddenly, the man in the helmet with the dark visor ran from his room and crashed into Pol Pot #2. The man was still wearing his dark visored helmet but other than the helmet, he was completely nude.

He jumped on his motor cycle and crashed back through the wooden doors driving hell bent for leather out into the night time traffic of the Mekong river front. Outside the police had begun to take up firing positions from the buildings across the street. Prostitutes and pimps were describing wild debauchery in the building, the stories ranged widely, but upon one thing all were agreed, crazy foreigners had taken over the building and were shooting Asians indiscriminately.

Bill and David checked the entire lower building. The back door was being covered by a SWAT team with a flood light trained on the rear of the building. Police snipers lined the roof across the street and all of the windows along the sides of the building were welded shut with anti-crime bars. "We're freaking trapped David! Hey what made you come down hard on Captain Pimp?" "He tried to over charge me." David said with a stern look on his face. Bill started to laugh. Suddenly, a panel along the side of the hallway where the under aged girls had been kept popped open. Mao's head peeked out. His bushy hair was covered in dust and cob webs. "Come! Follow me Mistah Bill!"

The Khmer police outside were shouting profanities in Khmer on a megaphone as Mao, Bill and David moved along on their hands and knees pushing large rats aside along the way until they tumbled out through another panel onto a stairway landing. They raced up the stairs to a long hallway that led to a broken window without security bars. Outside on a ledge a twenty feet long four by twelve board connected Pol Pot #2's building with its adjacent building. They crawled across the board six stories off the ground gaining access to the adjacent building through another broken window. They scaled down another stair until they were able to crawl out through a side window on the ground floor. Waiting in the SUV with the engine revving was Veasna. As soon as they all dived in Veasna roared away knocking over trash cans to get back to the main street.

Mao, David and Bill were completely covered in dust and cob webs, but Bill demanded that Mao go off duty to receive his salutory beer at the Walk About. As they sat at an outside table Bill broke the silence; "How did you know about the secret escape Mao?" "My cousin, numbah one carpenter. He build. He say fat pimp worry police arrest him take cherry girls, so he build way to escape with girls, no get caught." Bill looked at his watch. It was three am. "David, it's been one hell of a night. We have an early flight to Bangkok and then on to Singapore where we can catch a connecting flight to Clark. What do you say we call it a night?" "Sounds good Bill." Both David and Bill each tipped Mao and Veasna fifty dollars each and then went home to take a long hot shower.

Across Phnom Penh whistles and sirens were blowing. Before he retired Bill called Vibol to assure him of Bill's complete satisfaction with the way Vibol had stopped the damage. You'll see a large bonus in this months pay check Vibol. "Just doing job." Vibol grinned. "Listen, one last thing before I don't see you for two weeks. You remember the fat pimp at Bo Ding? He gets sanctioned tomorrow, along with his ugly body guard. Use the same guys you used tonight. I really like their style. No Vibol body guard singular, one not two. Why? Because David already whacked the other one. Yeah Vibol, it sure as Hell has been one night for the books."

David called Bill seconds later. "Bill, I'm sorry about earlier in the evening. I know you didn't want those kids killed any more than I did. I'm OK now. As long as we are involved with China White it's a part of the territory. We must always make sure that we don't let conscience, or anything, slow down our reaction time, or we're as good as dead." "Thanks David. Thanks also for drilling that f--cker who had a bead on me. I thought I was a gonner for sure." "Hey! if you hadn't dropped that first son of a bitch I would have been deader than a door nail. We have to always cover each other's six Bill." David said.

"Yes David. That's what friends are for." "I'm really pumped about seeing Angeles City for the first time Bill." "You should be pumped. We're gonna have the time of our lives, just wait and see! David?" "Yes Bill." "The Pimp will be whacked tomorrow along with his remaining body guard. I put Vibol's boys on it already." "Hey that's just protocol Bill. Otherwise I'm sure he'd put one out on us." "He won't live long enough David. I'll see that he doesn't." "Good night Buddy." "Good night David my best friend!"

David thought about the fact that he had made his first kill in several years. What concerned him was how easy it had been. His instincts were just as fast and automatic as they had been along the Ho Chih Minh Trail. David hoped this night hadn't succeeded in dragging him back down into his old life, but if danger presented itself again, there was no doubt in his mind he would be ready. He would be anything but slow to respond. David felt no remorse for the man he had killed. He should have had higher standards than to be working for a pimp like Pol Pot#2 and perhaps he'd still be alive. Likewise the first body guard who would die tomorrow didn't deserve to live. He definitely had no remorse for Pol Pot#2. At least after tomorrow, he would never pimp a child again.

David was an amateur aficionado of Mac Arthur's campaigns in the Philippines and Asia in general and hoped he might get a chance to visit Bataan and Leyte once Bill settled in. He doubted Bill would be interested in any destination that didn't have bikini clad women on the menu. David loved women too, but he wasn't as addicted to them as Bill was. Mao was half asleep as he drove Bill and David to the airport. As they approached the drop off zone they were flagged to the side by a squad of police who carefully checked the under carriage of the SUV for weapons and explosives. Satisfied with their NGO and U.N. documents they were cleared for their flight to Bangkok. All across Southeast Asia security would only get even worse.

Platoons of Special Police spot checked passengers at every entry and exit. The news stands were filled with international headlines about a drug war on the Mekong. Even the airport at Singapore had double security and long lines of passengers waiting to be strip searched with their shoes in their hands. Finally, David looked out the window as Clark Field became visible through the puffy white clouds below. The humidity would be fierce, but endurable.

Chapter Three: Betrayal

Manny was standing in the small visitors corridor at the Clark airport beaming with excitement. He was very proud of his country. David noticed an occasional expression of sadness on Manny's face as he cast furtive glances at Bill which didn't seem to add up to the jubilation Bill openly expressed. Manny was a spitting image of Anthony Quinn, smile, gentle mannerisms, fiery eyes, the whole package. David always felt a bit strange making the comparison in his mind as he had actually met Mr. Quinn once in London.

He had been in a hurry to make a meeting with some bankers when his taxi became lodged in traffic. He paid the driver and hopped out to run the distance across Hyde park in his three piece suit to make his appointment on time. He was fated to be late that day for as he rounded a tall hedge he was sent sprawling by none other than Tony Quinn who was out jogging. Mr. Quinn was surprisingly tall and very dignified. David would never forget the humility of the man who was genuinely kind. Mr. Quinn was bubbling over with apologies.

He spent several minutes crawling on his knees in the wet grass to pick up David's documents which had gone spiraling in the breeze. David somehow couldn't imagine Manny being humble in any possible way. Then Manny surprised David by bending down to pick up David's heaviest suit case, the one filled with bank reports, financial manuals and books and legal records of the S.H.A.R.I. NGO. The second surprise for David was when they walked outside the airport lobby. Parked in the red zone with no policeman around willing to complain was a traditional Filipino jeepney. Parked in its multi-colored honor with windows open and engine running. A brand new shining jeepney and Manny was its driver.

Manny owned a stretch Limousine and had a small
army of drivers, but had chosen instead to meet his friends
in his favorite vehicle. David was totally disarmed and
began to feel an affection for a side of Manny he had never
seen before. Bill had described AC to David before, but
always ended up saying "Well it's just a place you have to
see for yourself." Manny drove past the manicured lawns of
Clark and David felt as though he were on the way to the
Officers Club at Ft. Bragg, North Carolina. They drove
toward AC and passed silently from one world into another.

As they drove the Perimeter road, known as Don
Juico blvd. the place began to resemble Bill's descriptions
more accurately. They drove past bars such as Roady's
Star Gate, Honey Ko's, Fire and Ice, Nasty Duck and
Foxy's where they began to see gorgeous women dressed
scantily beneath see through Victoria's Secret robes on
their way to work as dancers. Some of the women were
Maylay, of ethnic Filipino stock, but many looked
Portugese, Spanish, Japanese, Chinese and Korean. A few
were Eurasian and some were African-American.

"Damn Bill, these women are even prettier than you
described." Bill shrugged his shoulders as he grinned at
Manny with an "I told him so" look on his face. Dozens of
motor bikes with aluminum side cars that Manny called
trikes were weaving recklessly in and out of traffic as they
delivered the girls to their bars. Many SUV's with totally
darkened windows drove by, interspersed with European
looking men on Harley Davidson motor cycles. Buses and
many jeepneys completed the variety of vehicles. As trikes
stopped to unload bar girls David had to catch his breath.
The girls stretched their long smooth legs to the street
showing their panties as they climbed out. A few saw David
staring and winked, blowing kisses in his direction. "Damn! I
love this place already!" Bill and Manny chuckled as they
continued straight on to what had now become Fields
avenue.

Occasionally, jeepney's stopped in the middle of the street without warning to disgorge passengers. "Glad you're the one driving Manny. I'd already be in an accident otherwise." "Well, you get used to it David." Manny replied. Manny began to give David a two penny tour of Fields avenue. "David, there are roughly two hundred bars in AC give, or take. Each place has between a dozen and one hundred very pretty girls as dancers."

"At any given time, especially in what we call high Season between November and March, there are as many as five thousand women looking for business. Most are dancers who shuffle on a stage from about six PM until three AM unless some guy decides to take them back to his room. This is called a bar fine and was once a thousand Pesos. Over the last year a few bars broke ranks and kicked it up to one thousand three hundred Pesos." " Even three thousand in some places." Bill added. "It's still such a good deal to be able to take a stunner back to your room for just under forty bucks a night that it keeps AC competitive as a sex venue in Asia." Manny explained.

"A great many of the girls come here just for a few months to earn money for their families and somehow never cross the psychological bridge into whoredom. That's what makes them so special, I guess. They are more like girls you would expect to meet on college break in the West, in fact many are college girls who need to pay their tuition, or secretaries who moon light to pay the bills.

If you guys are up for it we can go bar hopping to a few of my favorite places later on after dinner." "I'd love it how about you Bill?" David asked. "Are you kidding? My dick is harder than a diamond engraver's tool!" Peals of laughter resounded over the noise of the traffic. Manny pointed down A. Santos street. "That's A. Santos street David. A genuine bit of history. It was a part of the first outcropping of bordellos when Clark Air Base first moved here." Manny explained.

"It deteriorated into what they now call "Blow Row". Most of the BJ bars have been driven out, or have been torn down to make way for pricey hotels, condominiums and restaurants but as we speak you can still get a very good bare back BJ down there for only six hundred Pesos. Downside is that the sanitation is unbearably bad. Speaking of which, I have a Dancer bar in my hotel and I'm the only one in town who compels my girls to get HIV tested on a regular basis. When we go out bar hopping tonight you can of course pick out any girl you like.

But if you permit me, I will send five each of my best girls to your suites. That's what I always do for Bill." "What's good enough for Bill is good enough for me." "Great! then it's done." Manny concluded. Manny's hotel, The Emerald Of Asia was exotically beautiful with a tropical motif. A blend of Indian and Malaysian art and an open atrium that brought a star filled sky straight down into Manny's expansive lobby. The open sky lobby had become the hotel's signature. Lush tropical plants brilliantly laid out throughout the property gave an aura of paradise to the place. Near the bar a jazz quartet, piano, tenor sax, drums and bass played flawless Australian and West Coast jazz. A drop dead gorgeous Filipina sang sultry blues songs as couples at nearby tables tapped along with the beat.

Children belonging to foreigners who married Filipinas long ago splashed and played in the shallow end of the gigantic pool complex. The lobby blended with the bar and the entire floor area was constructed of the richest marble money could buy. One could feel Feng Shui while stepping downward onto Terra Cotta Spanish tile that surrounded an olympic sized pool. Bamboo lanterns lined a perimeter stone wall with eighteen feet high water falls and Japanese bridges spanning across a creek full of Koi fish. The hotel was six stories high with three town-home style houses above on the Penthouse level.

These were never sold to the public, but kept for Manny's private use or open to such friends as Bill anytime they wanted to stay there. Manny pulled up to the front entrance and a small army of bell staff dressed in white tropical uniforms scurried to get the suitcases and drive Manny's Jeepney to his private garage where there was a Porsche Targa, a Mercedes 500-S and a long white stretch Mercedes Limousine. The Concierge, a tall and beautifully shaped Filipina who looked much wiser than her age of nineteen sprang from her desk joined by the older Bell Captain when they saw Manny enter the lobby. Manny smiled and addressed them both while pulling two magnetic cards from his shirt pocket.

"These two gentlemen have unlimited charge privileges at our bar, restaurant, gym and spa and don't have to register. Their passport can remain in their own room safe until they leave. Bill, still want your House Orientale ?" "That would be nice Manny." "Fine. David you may stay in the House Occidentale." Manny gave David's card to the Concierge and Bill's card to the Bell Captain.

"They will show you to your rooms gentlemen. It's ten until five now. Shall we meet for dinner at seven then, at my house? It's in the center. We call it the Temple House." Both men nodded with satisfaction and followed Manny's staff to the glass elevator that whisked them above the pool area to the Pent House level.

David watched the slender beauty bend slightly forward to insert the magnetic card in the sliding lock, while feeling himself breathing deeply. Her legs were so perfect and her bell shaped behind and waistline were sculpted by Michelangelo. Her shiny black hair fell to just above her buttocks and swayed when she walked. She could have been Helen of Troy, but David was determined not even for a micro-second to allow her to see his adoration for her. "This is Manny's house." David considered.

She may be a mistress of his. What a terrible thing it would be to f--ck up a brotherhood level friendship no matter how beautiful she happened to be." David thought. "Here is your living room and through the adjoining door is your library." She swung open a double door revealing a study with book shelves, packed with erudite collections of books and classics, reaching all the way to the eighteen foot ceiling. A sliding ladder to reach the higher shelves gave the library a nice finishing touch. A large, smooth green leather chair was centered on a real wood burning fire place and a cabinet stacked with top level stereo equipment. Up to date DVD's lined the large space by the window.

A flat screen Computer with broad band internet connection sat waiting on a leather and teak hutch. She led him out through a fully equipped kitchen with a gas grill and chopping block table centered beneath an iron ring of shiny copper skillets, utensils and pots and pans. Both the living room and Master bedroom suite had flat screen TV's that were beautiful Monet landscapes when the TV's were turned off. Large glass, French doors opened onto a wide terrace with four deck chairs for sun bathing. A Jacuzzi that was as large as a small swimming pool was lit up and its bubble jets were exploding in sparkling golden rays of light along the green tropical plants that lined the wooden deck and railing.

Tall shrubs kept each house private from the other but the view of the city lights below was breathtaking. David's suit cases had been delivered and set upon fold out tables in the Master bedroom suite. David reached the Concierge whose name was Julienne a fifty dollar bill. She smiled as she declined the gratuity, explaining that Manny's personal friends never tipped. It was almost as much as a week's salary, but she adamantly refused. "If you don't take it, I will tell Manny you made an indecent proposal to me." David said with a sly grin. She flushed and then began to laugh so hard they both sat down on the sofa.

She quickly corrected herself by springing to her feet, but this time with the fifty dollar bill shoved gracefully by David, into her jacket pocket. She resisted no further and left. Manny was sitting at Julienne's desk when she returned to the lobby. "Ok, I want the full report. Leave nothing out." he said with a stern look on his face . "Well, he was staring at my bottom all the way inside the House Occidentale." She said. "Of course. Go on." Manny said with an eager twinkle in his eye. " He gave me this." She held up the fifty dollar bill. "And you took it?" " I tried not to, but he made me laugh." "You mean he grabbed you?" "No not at all! He said that he would tell you that I tried to do something indecent to him if I didn't take the money." They both laughed out loud. Manny began to like David.

"That's something I would have done!" Manny said. "I know, that's why I took it." "Vile woman!" Manny said with a grin. "Ok. Get back to work you little Hussy!" Manny said with a smile. Julienne tried to pretend she was shocked at the name, but wound up giggling instead. Manny had known Julienne's father since they were boys in the same Manila barrio where Manny promised Eduardo that he would look after his family when Manny visited him on his death bed.

Eduardo had eight children and every single one of them had been sent to college by Manny after Eduardo passed on. Some had become nurses, others lawyers and one a doctor, with a successful plastic surgery practice. Julienne the youngest, said she wanted to run Manny's hotel so he sent her to Cornell for a degree in Hotel Management. She was now a Sophomore home for the summer and she followed her second father around like a lost puppy until he agreed to let her work as a Concierge. She was thrilled, both for the experience the job provided and for the opportunity however small, to pay Manny back for his kindness. Her mother made certain to mention to Manny that her daughter was still a virgin and that's how she wanted her to stay, until she found a decent husband.

Manny promised her that he would protect Julienne as though she was his own flesh and blood and as the Marquez family had learned, Manny always kept a promise. David was about to slide into the Jacuzzi, when he heard chimes. For a moment he was completely disassociated as to where in hell they were coming from until he realized that someone was at his front door. It was strange to be in a house and in a hotel room at the same time.

David couldn't find his robe so he wrapped a towel instead. He peered through the security aperture in the door and saw Bill's distorted eye peeking back at him. David swung open the door and Bill, dressed in a fluffy white robe holding two glasses of fifty year old single malt scotch stumbled in. "Careful David! This is the good stuff! I sent this scotch to Manny and he stocks the pent houses with it." He reached David one of the glasses. "Is she still here?" "Who?" "Julienne. The Concierge. Shit, I completely forgot to warn you. You can f--ck anyone in the hotel you please, but don't lay a finger on Julienne, in fact stay the f--ck away from her she's like the daughter that Manny never had." Bill said sternly.

"Thanks for one warning too late! I porked her in the Jacuzzi and now I can't get her to leave." Bill's eyes grew as large as billiard balls. "Please tell me you're shitting me David!" Bill said in shock and disbelief. "I'm shitting you." "Man don't ever do that to me again!" Bill cried out. "Really? when did she leave here David?" "Right after she gave me a very professional tour of the place." David replied indignantly. "I have to tell you though Bill, she had my heart pounding and had me taking deep breaths of air." "Tell me about it. Manny had her escort me the first time I stayed in the House Orientale and I ogled the piss out of her. I was just getting ready to hit on her, when she guessed that I was and rescued my ass just in time." Bill recalled.

"She began talking about how Manny had helped her entire family and paid every one's college tuition. How she was able to get into Cornell because of him. I came that close to stepping on my dick with a best friend." "I thought I was your best friend!" David grinned. "You are you miserable bastard. Can't a guy have two?" David smiled as he led Bill deeper into the penthouse. "Let me show you something David, that I don't believe even Julienne knows about." Bill said cryptically.

Bill went to the overhead oven in the kitchen and punched in a string of twenty numbers, ending with an "O-3" for Occidentale House # 3. Then, he led David into the Master bed room where a panel was sliding open slowly. The sliding panel concealed a hidden room. Once inside he punched in another string of numbers and a large wall safe opened. Inside was a large stack of one thousand peso bills, totaling five hundred thousand pesos, or about ten thousand dollars, U.S. Beside the stack of bills was a Glock-17 semi-automatic pistol and three clips of ammunition. Feel free to spend all of the money. Manny will replace the stack until we leave. Keep a running tally and leave dollars in the safe at the current exchange rate. "Will do!" David replied.

"Care to join me in the Jacuzzi?" David asked. "Sure!" Bill answered, as he opened the liquor cabinet and pulled out a bottle of the fifty year old single malt he had sent to Manny. At precisely seven PM David and Bill pressed the bell at Manny's door and were met by his doorman who ushered them to Manny's study. Manny's Temple House was exactly that, a Temple as well as a house. Nearly twice as large as either the House Oriental or the House Occidentale, it was filled with rare Mesopotamian, Egyptian and Arabian art. Dividing the living room from the dining room, was a floor to ceiling aquarium with a splendid collection of salt water fish. Crawling around on the bottom was a twenty pound Maine Lobster, who looked far too majestic to be sacrificed for a meal.

"Is he on the menu?" David joked. "No, King Louis the Fat is our resident sage and has received a presidential pardon from the last two Presidents of my country who were both here upon separate occasions. Besides, I'd feel like a cannibal if I ever cracked his shell." David applauded Manny's riposte with light clapping.

Manny's study had a rhinoceros head mounted above and behind his desk and an adjacent wall was filled with a twelve foot Marlin. Beneath the Marlin was a row of photographs taken of Manny on the fishing boat at the Cabo San Lucas harbor with his huge fish strung up by a small derrick crane. "My friends, please join me." Manny gestured toward the cream leather sofa before the real wood burning fire place. Manny sat in a large backed leather chair facing both his guests and the fire place obliquely. A young woman from the bar staff wheeled in a cart with Dom Perignon and chilled glasses, expertly opening the bottle with a pop while pouring the correct level of the bubbly liquid in each glass.

When finished she left the room, but kept a steady gaze on the glasses ready to return and pour as needed. "So tell me about your recent excitement fellows. I understand David hasn't lost the edge on his old profession. Perhaps he will put me out of business along the Mekong." Manny said, with a forced smile. David knew the sentence was loaded with a very complex layer of sarcasm, but he couldn't fit the pieces together. Was Manny jealous that he David had been re- established? or was it something else? "Not a chance." David said with a serious expression. "We could have used you Manny. But as I have always known since our days in Nam, David is a natural born killer and accounted well for himself." Bill replied sternly. "What of this other business? The shoot out near Laos and Thailand?" "Our TV news has been running that story a few dozen times a day. Was that you too David?"

"No. That was me. F--cking Interpol decided to go on a weekend river cruise with Thai counter drug police. They intercepted one of our boats using a tip off from a traitor. I had to do something. I love the Khmer, but if I had let them take the boat crew to Chiang Rai for interrogation our entire organization would have been compromised.

I simply couldn't risk it, so I popped everyone on the Thai police boat with my fifties." "Tip off?" Manny asked in a monotone. "Yes. One of the crewmen gave in to his wife's request to help her brother, who was a Major in the Cambodian army, to get a promotion to Colonel. The Major's Thai controller asked for a 20 kilo bag of raw opium and our crewman naively delivered it." "Already dead? All of them? Any kids?" Manny asked as his eyebrows furrowed. "Yeah. We had to put all but a couple of infant children in the ground before the Thai police and Interpol got to them." Manny rubbed his face with his large hands and massaged his eyes, as his past raced before him.

"Nasty business eh?" Manny said with a fake smile. "What are you saying Manny?" Bill asked, as his face began to flush red. "Nothing Bill. I know you're not a baby killer. You have to break a few eggs to make an omelet, eh David?" David didn't like the direction of the conversation and just stared blankly at the fire. "So you took out the people who were threatening you and now everything is back to normal?" Manny tried to bring the conversation back from the edge. "Yes, basically it was limited to the Thai policeman, the Major and his immediate family and of course our traitor and his wife. As you know Manny, better than anyone, a hit is never simple. Sometimes it spreads like gasoline on a dry field." "Yes. I know. No hit is ever simple. When you take a persons life you create a Tsunami in the future, by ceasing everything a person would have touched had he lived." " It's karma in its fiercest role I'm afraid." Manny said with a tunnel in his sad eyes. "Don't go getting soft on me Manny. You know you're one of my role models." Bill said with levity.

"If only that were true Bill." Manny replied. "Just never bring any of that shit to the Philippines Bill, not to my Tierra Madre." "For this, I have already given my solemn promise Manny." Bill said firmly, with a tinge of annoyance. "Well stay as long as you wish fellas, Mi casa Su casa, you know that don't you Bill?" "Yes. That's the main reason we came here Manny, to visit you and let things back home smooth out a little." "You know that hospitality is a two way street, don't you Manny? We'll always be there for you too." David enjoined. "David, get Bill to tell you about the time he saved my Pinoy ass by letting me stay in his house for six months. I was almost ready to take away his place by claiming squatters rights." "He already told me, Manny. You're a brother beyond a doubt." "Yes. Brothers. What would life be if we weren't ready to make sacrifices for each other, right?" Manny said with a far off look in his eyes.

"Hey David. You like lobster? I get it flown in. My hotel customers get the one and two pound lobsters. I over charge the shit out of them, but for my friends I always keep a fresh supply of five pounders. Come take a look at what we'll be having along with Argentinean filet mignon for dinner tonight." Manny led them to the kitchen, where his staff was busy preparing the evening meal. Swimming in a holding tank were three five pound lobster, as large as any Bill, or David had seen this side of Maine. No one spoke during the meal and when it was clear that all had finished Manny asked if anyone was ready to go Bar Hopping. David was unable to conceal his excitement about seeing the night life of AC for the first time.

They took a hotel SUV with two of Manny's best body guards Vasquez and Moreno. Each carried Glock 17's with a leather pouch full of loaded clips beneath their Filipino Barong shirts. The Barong shirts were loose and comfortable in the tropics and, like the Mexican Guayaberra were considered formal wear, that was even appropriately worn at high level affairs of state.

Vasquez parked the black SUV on Fields avenue and remained in the driver seat, with the engine running. He remained in communication with Moreno with a closed band radio and ear plug as Moreno entered the bar ahead of Manny, emerging with a thumbs up to Vasquez that signaled no threats inside. "This first bar is one of my favorites." Manny explained. "It's called the Lancelot and has about seventy to one hundred dancers at any given time all between the ages of eighteen and twenty eight." "On a scale of one to ten, with ten being a Stunner, I would estimate that fifty percent of the women here are sevens, twenty five percent are eights and fifteen percent are nines. The remaining ten percent are stunners." Manny said.

The three sauntered inside followed closely by Moreno who sat alone at the bar. They were led to a high cocktail table that provided an unobstructed view of the dancers. As soon as a short stocky mamasan saw Manny she rushed to his table. "Manny my love, why didn't you tell us you were coming? We would have closed the place to give you a private party." Manny embraced her. "Conchita my love. You are always so kind. In reality, I don't like a fuss made when I'm here, you know that." "Well at the very least Manny, you and your friends will not be able to pay for any drinks, or appetizers, they are all on the house!" "Thank you, so kindly Conchita. Give my regards to Helmut." "If I'm not mistaken he is right now enjoying free drinks at your bar." Conchita giggled.

Everyone chuckled and Conchita left Manny and his friends in private, but not before depositing a laser pen in his hand. He laid it on the table and began to peruse the dance line. "What is that for?" David asked. "Oh this. If we see a girl, or girls, we like, we put the laser beam on them and one of the hostesses will escort the girls to our table. Or you can merely call a waitress over and give her the girls dance card number. You see the round disk with a number?" "Yes, what are the cards for dangling on their bikini?" "Those are her license and ID cards." Manny said.

"The cards are color coded. Each bar has its own color profile. In this one, pink stands for Virgin and green stands for non-virgin. Red, means they are on their period. Many of the women who seek work here come from strict Filipino families and are still physically chaste. In order to make bar fine money they agree to perform oral sex only. Some are so gorgeous that they only agree to go bar hopping with a customer, who likes to walk into places with a beauty under his arm. You know, a date, or paid escort to be more precise." Manny concluded.

The place was full of middle aged and elderly gentlemen, but occasionally a younger man would walk in and the girls would scream as though a rock star had just walked in. It spoke volumes. It was all about the money for these lovely young women, that's why they were there but they were, none the less, very much in tune with what they would have preferred, if poverty hadn't been the spoiler. "Old guys pay the bills and young guys get to be the heartbreakers, Manny? Bill and I have had many late night discussions about this, for years, eh Bill?" Manny said.

"Yes, Manny came up with a paradigm he picked up from one of those self actualization books he used to read. What did you call it Manny?" "The Four Essentials Of Hedonism. The first is Money. Without money, nothing happens with the ladies.

Even if they marry you, if you stay broke, they eventually leave you, so like it, or not, wives are not much different than prostitutes who let you pay over time. The second part of the paradigm is Health. You can want all the way up into outer space but you need a vehicle to get there. If you can't get an erection because you are suffering from an illness, or pain, you are no longer a player. Next is time.

"You can be Arnie Schwarzenegger and have Bill Gates money, but if you busy yourself too much with your career you don't use your pleasure time very well." "And the fourth?" "The fourth has to do with geography or location. But it's more complex than simple geography. Local morality, social, or religious dissonence and such have a huge role to play. For example, you can be rich and healthy and have a long life, but if the lake is empty you won't enjoy the fishing very much." "In the West, structural feminism has forced a severe climate change on the psycho-social opportunities for sexual fulfillment." Bill enjoined.

"Political correctness has defined an almost impossible playing field that is anything but level. I equate PC with Fluorocarbons. Instead of the Green House, I call it the Shit House effect. Thanks to PC, A man has to prostate himself before a woman and doubly prove his sensitivity to female concerns, before he gets the slightest whiff of vaginal perfume. I believe you American men even wash dishes for pussy, at least the rumors abound." Manny smiled. "If you are over the age of forty five, you begin to experience the PC caste system." Bill agreed.

"Just peruse the personals on the internet. The oft repeated mantra in the female's list of requirements is that the male can be younger than she, not older. The West has developed a hatred for older people. If you are standing in line at the grocery store and get caught ogling the beautiful twenties girls who walk by, or even women in their thirties, they may just call the police on your ass. We are trained by society to covet and cherish beauty. When your own body is in disconnect with your concept of beauty, you're expected to close your eyes when a young woman walks by. How absurd! Instead of her, you're expected to focus on some old fat wrinkled assed woman who is in menopause and has become terminally frigid. What society giveth society taketh away. That's why you see a lot of older guys in Asia where they don't play by the same rules as at home."

"They get tired of getting kicked around and ignored so they vote with their feet and usually have much more of the great equalizer, money, to bring life back into balance." Manny said. "It's obvious you guys have put a great deal of thought into this." David said. "What Manny says is true David. It's a bit unfair and completely disingenuous to expect our preferences to change to fit someone else's concept of beauty, or of a perfect society." Bill concluded.

"It's like being raised on classical music, yet expected to stop listening to it as we turn fifty. A beautiful woman is a beautiful woman. That most of them are eighteen years old doesn't suddenly make them ugly does it? Here in Asia, age is equated with wisdom. People may stare a little in Asia when a salt and pepper guy walks by with a College freshman girl, but it's more in admiration and happiness for the girl who has found a solid pay check." Manny observed.

"As Asian women grow older they get more interested in some one to take care of them. In the West the stares would be stares of deep disdain and disgust. Many older guys who try to take an Asian woman back to the West to live, find a slew of younger guys obsessed with trying to take her away. His young wife is also deluged with fellow Asian women who have lived in the West for a long time.
They take the new girl under their wing to advise them on divorce as a way of wealth accumulation." Bill said. David digested the information and concluded that he and Srey An would always live in Asia, never in the Victorian west.

He scanned the rows of beautiful women dressed in bikinis. He had visited many clubs and sex venues in Asia but nowhere had he seen such a cornucopia of attractive and vivacious Hotties in one place and in such ethnic variety. As the ladies twirled past, like the gracefully sliding pages of a fashion model magazine twitching their hind quarters and shaking their breasts, their lovely faces changed from Malay to Japanese, Chinese to Spanish and Portugese.

Any one of these lovely creatures could be taken for the night for under forty dollars, with unlimited sexual service circumscribed only per prior negotiation and agreement. If the customer wanted some service that wasn't on the menu he would be guided to another girl, who was known to have similar tastes.

There were so many women to choose from the women were the aggressors. This was exciting to David while at the same time, strangely sad, as it removed them from the pedestal David had always put women on for most of his adult life.

They were here fighting for the attention of men twice their age because of poverty and a lack of alternative economic opportunity. One either passed on the possibility to experience carnal pleasure with them, or allowed himself to partake of their delicious flesh, while drifting into denial about the underlying circumstances. Of those who sampled these beauties only the strongest defended themselves from the illusion that an eighteen year old beauty, could actually fall in love with an old goat who had mostly used up his time on earth. If anything, the relationships were at best platonic and at worst, abusive and manipulative. "It's all about the money." David said out loud. "Hear Hear!" Bill repeated. David couldn't help but notice how peaceful all the men were. The place was absent the competitive aura of the West. Abundant women. Peace on earth, good will to men.

One simply thanked heaven that, at least once, before they died they were able to experience lovely women they could have never dared dream of in Bumf--ck Idaho. As younger men, in the inflexible places they came from, sex was so repressed that it was considered nasty and evil. Asians were not fettered by such damaging delusion unless of course they had been reached by a missionary.

Drink of this beauty and savor the memory, or gamble as the fundamental religionists be they Christian, or Muslim do that all pleasure worth enjoying awaited on the other side of death, not this one. The safe bet was to enjoy what was available, in the here and now. David thought of how he could easily walk through these bars and collect the seventy virgins, the Muslims were ready to die to claim and have them all, NOW. Yes, given time and health constraints have them now while he was still alive and breathing. Geography. Had the Muslims ever considered that the seventy virgins would be ghosts? David wondered. The man, also a spirit? What would it be like to sex seventy ghosts as a ghost? he mused.

David learned by speaking with a sweet dancer nearby that the going rate for a night with a virgin, in the Philippines would be fifty thousand pesos, or about a thousand dollars U.S. With his four hundred million U.S in the bank he calculated that he could defrock more than half of the available virgins in Asia if China were left out. He fought hard not to break out into a maniacal laugh, from which he may never return. David felt a great battle about to begin within himself. If life was measured by its most precious resource, which many would argue would be the best ever memory of sex, then the common denominator which allowed the possession of this most precious resource, had to be money.

If anyone needed further proof, there it was delivered beneath beautiful faces, carried on deliciously smooth legs, all available if one had the money to pay for it. You just had to sacrifice a f--cked up religiously influenced upbringing to be enabled. The well worn phrase he picked up in Thailand "It's all about the f--cking money!" implied a neutralizing sacrifice. " Without money sacrifice was assured. Throughout human history from Cleopatra, to Helen of Troy, men had been prepared to sacrifice their lives for a piece of ass. Money allowed cutting to the chase while sacrificing only one's boyhood ego.

In Asia, it was available for chump change. Many more things in life than women required sacrifice. Following some demented politician's concept of a perfect world involved wasted lives, the worst sort of sacrifice. Self awareness was the only escape and it came gradually at a great price. Some never escaped, they just suffered. "I had a higher purpose back then." became the mantra. David's journey toward the truth began when he tested the resolve of his North Vietnamese enemy and found him to be noble courageous and just as willing to die for his country as David had been ready to die for his. When it finally hit him that he was the invader and not the liberator he stopped believing in the propaganda. His government had created addicts in order to kill an ideological enemy and contain the spread of Marxism.

"Try to wrap your Christian glory around that fact for a while." he thought. His last great denial had been the one that allowed him to sell his services to Bill for an insane amount of money. He had become every bit as addicted to the money as the end user junkies had become addicted to the white powder his efforts had helped to provide them with. Now where had it led him? He and Bill were hiding out to stay one day ahead of the other great equalizer human justice. His thoughts made his mind reel as though he were about to explode. He had an uncontrollable urge to do something completely unacceptable socially such as throw his heavy glass at the mirror behind the bar. He felt the cold sweat break out on his forehead.

He could only think of how insane it was that he would be so very happy just to be holding Julienne right now instead of gazing at dozens of beautiful women who would be nothing more to him tomorrow than a fleeting illusion. "Are you alright David?" Manny asked. "Yes, I'm fine Manny. Just not used to the smoking and loud noise I guess." David lied.

"Let's head out to the next bar then and get some fresh air along the way. All of the bars we will visit tonight are within walking distance." Manny said, comfortingly.
Bill sensed that Manny wanted to speak with David so he dropped back with Moreno who scanned both sides of the street as Vasquez followed behind slowly in the SUV. "She doesn't belong to us, you know." Manny said softly. "I know. If she did she would already be yours." David answered without looking at Manny. "Yes. Mine. But fate never meant for that to be, so I let her think I love her as a daughter when it kills me deep down inside to keep my love for her a secret. Only you know this." "Your secret will die with me. If I knew her half as well as you I wouldn't have the courage to deny myself her sweet love." David said with a candor that surprised even himself.

"Yes you would. We are the same you and I my dear David. We suffer the same. I suppose we will both die painful deaths, simply because we deserve them." "Let us at least hope they are quick." David answered sincerely. Manny grinned and said "I am sure they will be so rapid we will have hardly had a chance to believe they were real."

"I must confess that I already love a Khmer woman but I have always known it possible that I could truly love two women at the same time. I suppose you find this strange Manny?" "Not at all. I love my wife and my mistress who we all pretend is a visiting relative and I also love Julienne. You are more Asian than Barang David. Far more." Manny had more respect now for David than he would have ever believed possible. He had passed Manny's first test of being able to recognize, with respect, the value of the love of just one woman and only just now David had passed his final test. The test of being unable to resist suffering for her in the midst of many other women. Manny understood the concept of loyalty, he simply never allowed himself to get loyalty mixed up with the profundity of beauty and its meaning within a steadily disappearing life.

Julienne was a special orchid, a captive in a ray of light consumed within a dark universe. Manny had seen that and now unbelievably he knew David had as well. Brothers of a single rose who would never stop bleeding from the thorn prick of being forever unable to touch, feel, or keep their life's dream. "David, we are tainted. That's why we will never deserve to be happy. You and Bill with your drug business and me with my miles of haunting faces of people I have dispatched. Most deserved to die and perhaps some didn't, but it was my hand that killed every single one of them. Your heroin starts out pure, but by the time it reaches the end user some very horrible chemicals get mixed in just to squeeze more money from the wretched. Have you heard about what the Mexican Cartels have started in the U.S.A.?" Manny asked.

"Cheese heroin derived from stepping on Black Tar heroin with Tylenol. Every bit as addictive as your #4 injectable stuff the Cheese heroin can be sold at two dollars a hit. Do you know who can afford two dollars a hit? School children. The rotten bastards of the Mexican Trafficante Cartels target school lunch money without flinching about the fact that they are killing an entire generation of children to make their profits." Before David could reply Bill caught up with them and the conversation was changed to where they were going next? Manny took them to ten other bars and David had begun to feel the power of this place. Angeles City was like no other place he had ever seen before. Bountiful with available women, but fraught with a delicate and dangerous infra-structure.

It only cost three thousand pesos, about sixty bucks to get someone whacked. Jealous Filipina girlfriends, or worse, greedy ones who were set to inherit more from a dead husband than a live one, often had their boyfriends, or husbands dispatched. A shadowy figure would emerge from a dark alley and whap! Two .22 Calibre slugs at the base of the skull and all options were closed. Bill had once described a gruesome execution.

It seemed a Black American who had a silver tongue finessed his way into an elite power circle of rich Filipinos. Doctors, Lawyers, Congressmen, Bankers, all were movers and shakers in Filipino society. No one would think of throwing a party without inviting Andre'. Unfortunately, Andre' had never taken the time to notice that he was a long way from Kansas. He would get drunk in his favorite, mostly Black customer frequented bar and start bragging loudly of how he had just f--cked a Congressman's daughter, or a Banker's wife and that he couldn't wait to see so and so's face when in six more months he would discover that his newborn child was a lot darker than he, or his wife.

The husbands waited for Andre' at the motel. He believed he would be meeting a lawyer's wife for another tryst. Her husband had cut off one of her nipples earlier to wrest a confession and the details of where and when Andre' would show up. Andre' was found three days later bloated and lying face down in a rice paddy. His skin had been battered over his entire body and his genitals had been ripped from his groin and stuffed in his mouth.

After leaving the Blue Nile and Bed Rock complex Manny took them to a small English pub named "Roy's Pub" down a side street from Fields Avenue. Darts, Billiards and friendly, quiet atmosphere welcomed them. Manny chatted with the English owner, an old friend and then joined Bill and David at a side table out of ear shot of the bar. "Well David, what do you think of AC?" "It's incredible Manny, beyond what I could have ever imagined." In his private thoughts David saw Angeles as well as probably the rest of the Philippines as just another place where too many children's dreams go unfulfilled and where too many bellies remain empty no matter who the self-made politician is who makes promises to the contrary. "Well, it isn't perfect." Manny admitted, as though he read David's thoughts.

"The bars are run as a cartel. The local politicos and police are constantly at the door to get their Tea Money and corruption is rampant. There's a small element of Rogue police who set up scams with naive visitors whereby they use under age decoys to entice them to a short time room and then follow with a raid where they scare the hell out of the tourist threatening him with a ten year prison sentence unless he coughs up as much as twenty thousand U.S. Dollars to buy a stay out of jail pass. I believe the dirty cop's days may be numbered though. They give AC a bad name. Never take a Freelancer here. Nine times out of ten she's a police decoy. Well shall we go back home?" Manny asked."Suits us", Bill said enthusiastically.

He hadn't been able to take his mind off the five women each Manny had promised. True to Manny's word as David and Bill opened their front doors they looked in to see five beautiful women. The women were dressed only in Victoria's Secret lingerie. Bill wasted no time. He had his five women strip away the lingerie and situated them in a line across the king sized bed and made love with each of them. He then fell asleep in the middle of his small harem as they stroked and caressed him. David's experience was completely different. He invited them all to join him in the Jacuzzi with two magnums of Dom Perignon and taught them how to hold their breath under water.

David's thoughts drifted to earlier in the evening when he saw the fire in Manny's eyes as he hatefully described the Mexican Trafficante's and what they were doing to children. "He blames Bill and me. What was that other thing he said to Bill? Don't bring that shit to my Tierra Madre." He suddenly turned pale as though he were bleeding out. "Goddamnit! Manny's going to either kill us or put us in jail". He mumbled to himself. David asked the girls to please take a shower and wait for him in bed, that he had forgotten to conclude some business with his friend. "Watch TV until I get back." David encouraged.

"Filipinas watch TV for hours ruining any romantic atmosphere known to man." Bill had said. David dried off put on his robe and went to the microwave where he plugged in the numbers Bill had given to him. The girls were all in the huge shower giggling and playing. David opened the safe and pulled out the Glock 17 and slid back the chamber. The firing pin had been removed. "Without it I may as well be waving my dick!" David mumbled to himself. David kept hitting Bill's door bell button until a dazed and somewhat perturbed Bill swung open the door. "What in the f--ck is up dude?" Bill said with a severe case of dry mouth.

"Manny said we are all tainted!" "David what in the f--ck? Are you drunk man?" "Hell no! Just go to your safe and check your Glock!" Bill started to wake up and ran to the microwave. He was soon inside his safe. A couple of girls wandered up to ask if everything was OK. Bill told them to go back to bed and that he would soon join them with a bottle of champagne. Bill snatched the Glock from the safe and snapped the firing mechanism back. "Look for your firing pin Bill." "Shit! There isn't one." "Manny had them removed. He kept the Glocks in the safe to ensure our false sense of security, but he is going to either do us himself, or roll on us to the Coppers." "Goddamnit David! You're talking about a brother here." Bill protested.

"I'm sure there is a perfectly credible explanation for this. What were you saying about being tainted?" "He told me earlier that we and he are all tainted. Too many sins to deserve to be happy. Shit like that. I started thinking about the look on his face when he said it, so I checked my Glock. Pin's been removed just like yours." "F--ck! I'm going to go ask him to his face!" Bill exclaimed. David had moved to the terrace where he could view the city streets below. Moving slowly into position was a black S.W.A.T. Police vehicle taking up a rear blocking position.It's team members slowly stepped out of the van and the leader pointed up toward the house Orientale.

Bill joined David and saw the S.W.A.T. vehicle for himself. Bill felt as if he had been stabbed in the heart by his own brother. "How could he f--cking do this to me after all I have done for him? Why? Was Manny insane? Had his conscience eaten his brain? Was he doing it because it would double his own power at home in the Philippines? "Manny captures notorious Golden Triangle Drug Lords would be the headlines." he thought. "Look. Let me think. OK? Go back to your place and get your clothes and shoes on. Then meet me at Manny's house. Stay in the back ground. He'll know we are on to him if he sees us both together." Bill cautioned.

David tip toed past Manny's Temple House and was soon back inside the House Occidentale. He removed the Filipino money from the safe stuffing his jacket and trouser pockets with it and took the most important records he had and placed them in the fire place. He turned on the gas jets and ignited the fire place. He then tip toed outside and crouched in a dark shadow near Manny's house waiting to pounce. David watched Bill ring Manny's door bell and listened as Bill made an excuse to come inside.

"Manny, sorry buddy but I have this Migraine headache probably from too much champagne. I couldn't find any aspirin, or Tylenol in the medicine cabinet, do you have something?" "Sure Bill, come inside." As soon as Manny turned to lead Bill inside Bill grabbed Manny from behind in a choke hold and dropped with him to the floor. Manny pulled a .32 Calibre Beretta pistol not much larger than a cigarette lighter from his pocket, but before he could unlock the safety David kicked it out of his hand and picked it up. "Why the f--ck are you doing this Bill?" Manny growled.

"No, Why the f--ck are you doing this to me? You son of a bitch! We discovered the missing firing pins and we know the Coppers are downstairs, awaiting your order to come inside." "How did you find out?" "Something you said to David flipped on his radar switch. Tainted. That's what you said." "We are tainted Bill. Me as well as you." "Poison to mankind. Your drugs kill hundreds of thousands of people everyday and you don't care. You just wiped out a whole family of Cambodians and it means nothing to you. Do one last thing that's good in your life and turn yourself in." Bill turned beet red and bit off a large section of Manny's left ear. The sound of his scream awakened the girls in the bed room. One of them tried to call the front desk and David shot the Telephone with Manny's .32 Calibre Beretta.

"Stop screaming! The rest of you girls crawl under the bed! Stop screaming, or I'll shoot all of you Godammnit!" David ripped out the phone wire and collected all five cell phones from the girls purses and stomped on each one. David found a second clip of ammo for the Beretta in Manny's pocket. "OK, Manny. Here's what we're going to do. Open your safe, or we drill you right now. "

They led Manny to the microwave while watching to make sure none of the five women escaped. Soon the safe was open and Bill pulled Manny's Glock 17 along with his ammo clips out. "Looky here David. Here's our firing pins." Bill scooped out one million Pesos and stuffed the money in a satchel David found in the closet. "Go get the other Glocks David. I'll keep everyone on ice here." David returned with the extra Glocks and ammo and placed them in another satchel.

"Manny keeps his King Air 350 Beechcraft at Clark. Manny you are going to get dressed I'll put a bandage on your ear and we will all head for your plane. Give instructions that we are taking you to the emergency room because you slipped in the jacuzzi. Tell your driver that I will take over. Speak only in English with everyone. If you say one f--cking word in Tagalog we will kill you and everyone in sight. Clear Kaibigan?" Bill spit out the word which means "friend" in Tagalog as if it were poison from a Cobra bite.

"You'll never make it out of here alive Bill. Give it up." "David, go shoot all of his whores." David was stunned. "Why can't I tie them up with bed sheets?" "It would take too long." "OK. I'll cooperate. Just don't kill anymore innocent people." Manny pleaded. "Everyone who dies tonight will have been killed by your betrayal, you bastard! " Bill shouted. "Just tell me one thing Manny, did you have this planned all along?" "No." "Well when did you decide to do this?" Bill screamed. "It came to me after speaking with David. He's a good man Bill and you're turning him into a rotten murderer, just like you and just like I used to be. You have to be stopped." "You'd never stop on your own and you'll drag David down with you!" Manny growled.

Suddenly a cell phone rang. Bill traced its ring to a drawer in Manny's study. Bill reached the phone to Manny. "Tell them ONLY IN ENGLISH to keep all their forces in positions in the rear of the hotel. Tell them your people have the front covered. Tell them to be prepared to raid the penthouse in one hour, that will give you time to move guests to safety before any shooting starts." Manny repeated Bill's instructions, word, for word. David moved an enormous desk in front of the bed room door to keep the women inside. Manny was quickly dressed and a make shift bandage had stopped the bleeding from his ear. The trio moved toward the elevator slowly.

The elevator opened and Bill placed Manny toward the glass side, to catch any possible bullets. In the lobby Moreno stepped forward concerned about Manny's ear. Manny continued to follow Bill's instructions by ordering Moreno to give Bill his SUV keys. Manny explained he had injured his ear in the Jacuzzi and that Bill would drive him to the hospital. As Manny and Bill passed by, Moreno caught a quick glimpse of the gun Bill held at Manny's back. He went for his Glock beneath his shirt. David cut him down with a short burst.

The three men leaped into the waiting SUV and were soon careening around the corner onto Fields avenue. A fast approaching flashing blue light with siren blasting began a hot pursuit. It was three thirty AM and all of the bars were closing. Women who hadn't been bar fined were walking toward jeepneys, waving at cars passing by. As the SUV flew past the Cherry Club bar and the ABC hotel, a trike driver tried to pull in front of the SUV to help the police. The trike driver was knocked fifty feet in the air, landing in a pile of smashed flesh and bones on top of some parked cars.

David held a gun at Manny's head. He saw a large white Hotel to the left front that looked like a church. There was a small clump of hedges nearby. "Let me out here Bill." "Turn around at the Petron station to come back and get me!" "What about Manny? I can't watch him and drive." "I'll take him with me." David said. David yanked Manny out of the SUV and pushed him sprawling down behind the shrubs. David crouched down behind Manny as the flashing light drew closer. When the police were almost upon them David stood up and emptied a clip into the windshield of the police car. Manny tried to jump up to run but David landed a karate kick to the back of Manny's knee which caused him to land on his face on the pavement. The police car slammed into a tree and exploded in flames. Trikes slowed down to watch the police car burn.

David lifted Manny and shoved him back into the SUV. "Bug out ambush!" Bill yelled. "Good shit David! Just like the old days along the Ho Chi Minh Trail." Bill said. "Some things you never forget." David said. "Those cops had families." Manny said in a low tone. "Shut the f--ck up or I'll drill you right here and now!" Bill growled. In minutes they were at Clark, pulling up to Manny's sleek Beechcraft King Air 350. This was Manny's most precious toy.

The King Air is a very elegant business twin turbo prop high performance aircraft. Its pressurized cabin allows it to cruise at twenty five thousand feet at an air speed of three hundred fifteen knots. Its range of seventeen hundred and sixty five nautical miles makes it a very popular aircraft for archipelago island hopping. It seats eleven passengers comfortably. Manny had the seats removed to make way for a large bed and a bar.

Chapter Four: Escape To Islam

"You won't believe this David but I forgot the keys." Manny said with a straight face. "You won't believe this either you bastard, but I'm about to cut off your dick and use it to hot wire this bitch." Bill replied. David reached inside Manny's pockets retrieving only his wallet which he shoved back inside Manny's trousers. "He isn't lying Bill." David reported. "Yes he is. He probably thought I didn't pay attention to details. He used to pick me up in Manila and fly me back to his place in Cebu. Manny keeps a set of plane keys on each of his vehicle keys." Bill tossed the SUV keys to David. "The green key unlocks the airplane and the red key starts the engines, right Manolo?" "Take the plane, but let me go for old times sake Bill." Bill shoved Manny in the back keeping his Glock aimed at Manny's head at all times. Both Bill and David were accomplished bush pilots. David would fly tonight while Bill kept Manny on a very tight leash.

Bill shoved Manny to the floor near the open door of the cock pit keeping his pistol trained on Manny's head all the while. David radioed the tower and explained that a small family emergency required an earlier than expected flight plan back to Mactan airport in Cebu. The sleepy tower controller assigned the runway and in seconds the prop wash was blowing debris behind the plane as they taxied for take off. Flashing blue lights were seen about a mile away headed for Clark. The expensive plane was routinely topped off with fuel and ready for departure. David opened the throttle and soon the aircraft was ascending into the still black night. The blue flashing lights were following in close pursuit, but no shots were fired for fear of hitting Manny. David leveled off at five thousand feet until Bill could give him a heading. "We have enough fuel for about seventeen hundred and fifty miles David. That should get us to Malaysia." Manny looked the other way pretending not to have heard about their destination.

"Plug 23 longitude and 15 latitude into the GPS for now. That will get us past Manila airspace and we can make corrections later. Drop down to tree top canopy to stay off radar. Head out over the Philippine sea to reduce line of sight detection." Bill said. Bill kept a safe house near the Malacca strait not far from the south Thailand border. They could fly there and remain hidden until they sorted things out with Manny, Bill thought. David looked up at the dark and forbidding sky while the luxurious plane descended as silently and as sleek as a panther, downward to tree top level. The ride became bumpier as they hit pockets of cold then warm air on their way to the sea coast. The stars were disappearing and the lights of the villages below took their place along the broad expanse and beyond.

David wondered if he would ever feel safe enough to come back to AC someday. "Probably not a good idea for at least the next one hundred years." He thought. He wondered if Julienne were asleep, or if she had been contacted soon after Manny had been taken. Mostly he thought of how much she would hate him once she learned that he, David played a part in Manny's abduction. "Wasn't meant to be. Manny was at least right about that." David thought. "I hope you both realize you're as good as dead!" Manny said coldly. "You're in my back yard now. By now, the Philippine air force will be scrambling with shoot down orders." David felt uneasy. They had been in the air for nearly twenty minutes but still no coast line. "I'm taking her up to ten thousand feet for a quick terrain check Bill." David warned.

"Give up man and land in Cebu. You won't like what happens next if you don't." Manny threatened. "Won't like what happens next?" Bill shouted. "I don't f--cking like what happened already! Who gives a shit about next?" Bill screamed. "Someone had to stop you Bill. I knew you wouldn't have ever listened to me about quitting the drug business!" "What about you Manny? You ready to give up being an assassin?" Bill asked?

"Yes, I am. I already have." Manny yelled. "But you were willing to turn David and me over to the f--cking cops. Do you have any idea what they would have done to us? They would have ass f--cked us with batons and then left us half dead to be raped in your medieval rat infested Manila prison by HIV infected zombies." Bill shouted. "I wouldn't have allowed that." Manny said. " In fact I can personally guarantee that you will be turned directly over to the U.S. Embassy if you land now. I know you won't believe this Bill but I've been made a better person by confessing my sins and embracing a life of dedication to our lord Jesus Christ. He will forgive you and David too, Bill." Manny said with sincerity. "F--ck you Manny! I can't believe this is you. Next you'll be trying to get me hooked up with the f--cking tooth fairy. Manny Alvarez, a f--cking born again Christian. This is just insane!" Bill shouted.

Manny began to consider his fate at Bill's evil hands. "OK Bill, you win. You keep the plane and land me in Samar or if it makes you feel safer, I know an obscure landing strip in Masbate. I'll make it home by boat to Cebu. That will give you a day's head start." "Aha. What happened to Christian forgiveness Manny? You two faced prick. One minute you're a born again f--cking Christian and the next minute you're giving me a day's head start. What kind of an asshole do you take me for? I'm supposed to let one of the most dangerous Hitters in Asia go free because he promises me a head start of a day? Give me the final respect of not insulting my intelligence!" Bill growled.

The plane cabin grew deathly silent. Suddenly, Manny landed a fist in Bill's rib cage that made him gasp for air. He then lunged forward through the cockpit door wresting the controls from David. The plane surged upward, stalled and then headed down toward the Philippine sea.

Bill struggled to recover, searching for the Glock on the cockpit wall which had now become the floor. The Glock had flown from his hand when Manny hit him. He found it, but lifting it during the downward G force was like weight lifting three hundred pounds with one hand. Bill finally got the barrel high enough. He aimed the barrel at the back of Manny's head and squeezed the trigger blowing off the back of Manny's skull. Manny slumped over onto the passenger seat beside David.

David was now using every pilot skill he knew from his training in an A1E Sky Raider in Vietnam, to pull out of the death spiral. Just before the plane plunged into the ocean at three hundred knots David pulled the King Air out of the dive. In the nick of time the powerful plane with over a thousand horses of power in its Pratt & Whitney engines caused the main frame to shudder as it went skimming along the surface at fifty feet above sea level. Bill looked down at the body of a man that just hours before he would have taken a bullet for.

Now, he had been the one who killed him. Bill became choked with emotion and came closer than at any time since his childhood to crying. David saw Bill's eyes water over and knew he had better do something to pull him out of it. "Hey, what was that shit Manny was going on about the Filipino Air force and what was going to happen next?" "You didn't see the tracking transponder near the GPS antenna? Manny had to install it for his insurance company because of the size of his theft policy. If we don't de-activate it we really will be saying Good Morning to the Philippine air force. Keep it steady at this altitude." Bill crawled forward, reaching over Manny's lifeless hulk to open the passenger door. He opened the door and shoved Manny's body out and sat for a moment in the blood drenched seat. Then he climbed out onto the wing. Holding on to a lip above the cabin he edged his way to the transponder.

He used a pocket knife to cut through a rubber coated cable. He unscrewed some mounting screws and twisted the transponder out of its housing. Bill shoved the trans- ponder inside his shirt and climbed back inside the cockpit. "Brrrr. It's colder than shit out there David!" "Did you get it?" "Yeah." Bill pulled the transponder out of his shirt. "It has an internal battery that has a life of seventy two hours. Fly back inland low over the jungle canopy. We'll drop it there and make them look for us with a land, instead of a sea search.

Depending on how long it takes a ground party to find the transponder it should buy us a little more time to put some daylight between our asses and the Philippine Air force." "Roger that!" Soon they were flying just a few feet above the tall Banyan trees below. Bill waited until the vegetation was as thick as could be and then he tossed the transponder. "OK David. Head south again over the water and stay as low as this baby can fly without taking a swim." David flew so low above the ocean that the spray from the waves beaded up across the windshield.

"Bill, I have a feeling we don't have to worry about being followed. Asian cops seldom react quickly without getting tied up in layers of authority and bureaucracy." "Doesn't apply in the Philippines David." "They copied American systems pretty well during America's era here. They have corruption at every level, to be sure, but if they feel cheated, or that their sovereignty has been breached they cooperate remarkably well with each other. Manny had a contingency for everything. That's why he was such a good Hitter. He always had a fall back plan." "What happened to his fall back plan with us? "David asked. "He went a little nuts I guess. His decision to stop our drug operations was obviously a spontaneous decision that was triggered when he had that conversation with you. He probably figured the SWAT team he called in, would catch us riding whores and completely vulnerable. You're only allowed one major mistake in life and I guess that was his. Thanks to your instincts we're both still alive and kicking."

"I just hope we make it out of Philippine air space Bill." "We will. Now that we're on to what Manny's contingencies may have been, I am beginning to visualize what he may have done. First, Manny would have calculated that if someone stole his plane the regular police would have probably been helpless to do anything about it. He would have written standard operating procedures for his second in command to contact the Air force directly and give them the frequency of his transponder. He would have explained his actions to the president of the Philippines the next day to cover the ass of the Air force Commander who scrambled jets for him. I played golf with Manny not long ago and we partnered with a guy named Colonel Mike Fernandez who commands the Seventh Tactical Fighter Squadron over at the Basa Air force base.

Basa air base is fairly close to Pampanga and AC. All Mike could do is bitch all afternoon about how the Filipino government f--cked him out of a bunch of F-16's. Seems the Americans were so keen on getting Filipino air power up to the task of fighting the Moro Independence Liberation Front, down in Mindanao and keep them in check, as well as the Abu Sayef and even the Filipino pirates, that they diverted an order of F-16's from Saudi Arabia to Manila instead. Even found financing for the Filipinos." Bill said.

"The Filipinos got together and figured out for themselves that if they ever needed F-16's the Americans would wind up flying them for free so why pay for the cow when you have the milk for free?" "I thought you said the Filipinos are thin skinned about their independence from America?" "They are, but when it comes to huge chunks of money all of that shit goes out the window. The Filipinos took the money and spent about a tenth of it on seventeen AerMachi S-211A mini-jets." Bill explained.

" The fat cats pocketed the rest. There's no such thing as the "trickle down effect" in the Philippines. It's more like the dried shit effect that doesn't even roll down." "So instead of F-16's the Filipino people got stuck with toy jets to defend their country?" "Hey David who said anything about the S-211A being a toy? It's a bad assed little jet. It does all the aero acrobatics for dog fighting, has a range of Fifteen hundred plus miles, it has IFF Friend, or Foe ID transponders, air to air missiles and the whole nine yards. It's main drawback is that its airspeed is only four hundred fourteen miles per hour. But that's faster than what we're flying now so if they pick up our scent we are still f--cked big time. Our best hope is to hug the ocean and hope we make it out of Filipino air space south of Mindanao.

All of their S-211A's are stationed up here on Luzon because the government continues to have coup de etat jitters based on their history. They want their most powerful weapons close enough to Manila to keep their eye on them. Once we reach Masbate and Palawan they just have OV-10's and Choppers. We may have a chance with them." "What if they pick up our tail with the S-211A's?" "Then we don't make it to Palawan, or Masbati, or Malaysia. It would go down like this. They have our radio frequency. They would use it to speak with Manny. After a few seconds if they didn't start hearing a bunch of Tagalog, they would end us with their air to air missiles." Bill said.

Bill stared back at the coastline near the place where they dropped the transponder. Three S-211A's dropped down out of the sky to canopy level dropping flares to mark the spot. "Mike Fernandez' boys just found the transponder David. Let's hope it takes the ground party another hour to discover that a transponder is all they have. If the search party is already nearby we could find ourselves under hot pursuit." Bill said. David increased his air speed to a level three hundred knots and prayed they wouldn't hit a rogue wave.

They flew low across the water until Bill spotted Palawan island. Both men sat stiffly, intensely realizing that at any moment the Philippine jets could swoop down behind them and blow them to pieces before they could realize they were dying. They began to breathe a little easier when they passed beyond the twelve mile distance between Philippine territory and international waters. To avoid Malaysian interceptors they continued to fly low beneath radar. " We should be skirting the south east coastline of the Sprattly islands in about an hour. The Filipinos patrol the shit out of that airspace because they are in contention with Malaysia and a host of other countries about who owns what there." Bill expained.

"We have plenty of fuel, so do a box around the place or we may just pick up some Malaysian, Filipino, Viet, or even Chinese fly boys around there." Bill said matter of factly. "Yeah, don't worry, I'll give them a wide berth. Hey I knew you bought a rice farm in Malaysia to use as a safe house. Is it near Kuala Lumpur?" David asked. "No. It's actually up the coast of the Malacca Strait, about one hundred miles south of Georgetown. About an hour by air south of Phuket, Thailand. "I'll need some headings when we approach the Malaysian coastline." David said.

"No problem. Weather's clear, so we should be able to fly Line Of Sight by then." Bill replied. "The area got pretty hammered with the Tsunami. Not as hard where we will be and certainly not as hard as Phuket, but many thousands of people lost their lives with that one, along the entire coastline." Bill reflected. A band of light yellow sky was forming along the eastern horizon behind them as they flew southwest toward Malaysia. Bill's safe house included a small airstrip that he had used when he flew in supplies for the U.N. Tsunami relief effort a few years back. That is when he got the brilliant idea to buy a rice plantation in the name of S.H.A.R.I. as a perfect N.G.O. cover for a safe house.

The huge rice barns were perfect for emergency storage of drugs when needed. He let the Muslim family go on running the place keeping the profits of their crops. He asked only that the Great house remain available when ever he needed it. The family lived in a large farm house on the property, reserving the main residence for Bill. Along they flew on a cushion of air. An occasional wind current provided some breath taking turbulence, but David held the craft steady on course riding just above the tips of the low cresting waves.

Once, Bill saw a small formation of jets as they were completing the last leg of their box around the Spratly Islands but Bill couldn't tell which country they belonged to and soon they had flown away in the opposite direction. At last they saw the coastline of Malaysia in the distance. Bill punched his data into the GPS. "Damn David! We only need a three degree course correction and we'll be dead on." David adjusted to the new heading and kept the King Air level and steady as they flew the jungle canopy. "Take her up two hundred feet and flip on the auto pilot switch and I'll take over." Bill said.

David ascended two hundred feet and put the plane on auto pilot. Bill slid in behind him then switched off the auto pilot and descended back down to canopy level. In an hour they had reached the west coast
of the Malaysian peninsula and Bill brought the King Air up to an altitude of five hundred feet. "See those large houses and hangar off to the right down there David?" "Yep! Is that the place?" "That's the place." "Well Bill, haven't you sort of over shot the runway by a few kilometers?" Bill chuckled. "Go back to the bed in the cabin. There's a button on the right side." "Push it and the mattress unit lifts up hydraulically. You'll find two Paraglide Commando chutes Manny keeps packed and on board." "Chutes? What do we need chutes for? We're riding in a perfectly designed luxury aircraft. I'm a paratrooper, but why in the f--ck would I want to jump and leave this beautiful airplane behind?" David joked.

"What? You thought we were going to steal Manny's plane and take it back to Cambodia?" " I must confess Bill the thought did cross my mind." "This plane is so hot David it's a f--cking wonder it didn't melt before we got it here. Within two weeks every King Air on earth will be visited by the friendly Beechcraft safety and security teams and using a design blue print that encodes a serial number in the most obscure of places every legal unit will be cleared. Any King Air thereafter that flies with tail numbers that are not on Beech Craft's list will be immediately seized by local customs and held for the legal owner. In our case murder charges would be tacked on to theft charges." "OK. I get the picture. We're ditching over water, I assume?" David asked.

"Let's take it up to an altitude of about ten thousand feet you jump first and track toward the shore. With the light landward wind we have you should be able to crab to the beach without even getting wet. I'll be right behind you." David collected the money bag and the weapons. "Bring the money, leave the weapons. We'll be among friends here. Not all Muslims are bad guys." "That's very true, but not even one little Glock?" " OK. Bring two Glocks and several clips of ammo." Bill said as they began the ascent to ten thousand feet. Bill found a deep gorge along the coastal shelf and put the plane on auto pilot until they were both in their chutes. He strapped the satchel with the money and the weapons to David's front webbing. He took the plane off auto pilot and yelled "Stand in The Door Motherf---er!"

David held up his middle finger grinning broadly as he stepped out onto the small ladder step and pushed away. Bill then aimed the plane vertically down, crawled to the larger cabin door and leaped from the aircraft. He watched David below tracking with a full Delta body position toward the shoreline as he did the same. Within seconds they both watched the white foamy implosion of the King Air as it disappeared in a wide pattern of bubbles and waves.

Chapter Five: Jihad In Siam

They both popped at three thousand feet and toggled their chutes all the way to the beach. They hid their chutes beneath some ferns and palm leaves and started walking through the deep sand, toward the coastal road. "Bill, I hate to tell you this, but you have Manny's blood all down your back side." "Oh shit!" Bill groaned. He ran to the waters edge and flipped over on his back, into the low surf. As he stood knee deep in the water, David filled his hands with gobs of wet sand and scrubbed the blood away. On the coastal road, a flat bed truck stopped to give them a ride.

A rice farmer who was a neighbor from just beyond Bill's place recognized Bill and grinned as they shook hands. After the flat bed left the coastal road to turn on to a road full of chuck holes David thought of how smooth the King Air had been in comparison. "Bill, just how much did Manny pay for that King Air?" "He bought it last year for just over six million bucks." "Really?" "Yes, really." "Bill, I don't like the way you amortize capital goods." They laughed at the remark, but both knew it would have been suicide to keep Manny's plane.

Bill waited respectfully for Omar to send all of the women to the back of his house before knocking on the door. Omar was a thin man with most of his front teeth missing. His face was weather worn and wrinkled, but he had a wonderful twinkle in his eyes and smiled broadly at his benefactor. Omar spoke English haltingly, but with surprisingly good pronunciation. "How long stay Mistah Bill?" "Only a day, or two Omar. We came for the birds." "Ah, the birds! Bill want see birds?" "That would be nice Omar! "

"David was completely perplexed. "Birds? What birds?" he wondered as he followed Omar and Bill to the large buildings near the air strip. Omar slid open the huge doorway and standing there, in a majestic half light, were two Caribou cargo aircraft painted ghost grey on the bottom and jungle camouflage on the upper half of the entire fuselage. "Remember these babies David?" Bill asked, with no small amount of pride. "Remember them, hell I see them when I close my eyes especially during orgasm!" David had been inserted in Laos and Vietnam for a great many of his top secret missions by this sort of aircraft. Designed and manufactured by De Havilland of Canada the Caribou became the perfect jungle hopping plane. With a useful payload of three tons and a range of fifteen hundred plus miles it graced the jungle canopy with excellence and solid reliability. It's air speed was just over two hundred miles an hour, but considering its missions speed was not as important as durability and performance.

It could land and take off on a dime. It didn't really need an air strip. A water buffalo trail worked just fine. "Where did you find these Bill?" "The Australian Air Force was upgrading and they held a fire sale. I only bought two, I should have bought four, but I didn't want a bunch of questions about them being thrown around at the Phnom Penh airport. Anyway I think two will serve our needs." Omar excused himself to go tell his wife to prepare lunch for his guests.

"We can always find two more if we need them David, but after last week I only know we are no longer an Opium Navy. Instead, with these Caribou, we will become an Opium Air Force." "How much did we spend?" David asked" I thought you'd never ask. I bought them for two hundred fifty each." "That is a good price! For the six mil Manny spent for one King Air 350 we could have had twenty four of these." David marveled.

"They are both topped off with fuel and are ready to fly us to Phnom Penh. Both even have flight plans that just need the dates filled in. We will fly them both home as soon as I speak with Vibol and Dr. Hamilton to be sure there will be no unwanted welcoming parties waiting for us." "These planes will allow us to cut our processing time and transportation staff considerably, but aren't you worried that the Khmer will get pissed off if we can't keep them as employees?"

"David, it's precisely because we had an internal leak that I decided to use this option. I will employ everyone somewhere, just not within our lab Ops anymore. Hamilton will keep his people, we'll keep the most trusted guys we have to load and unload cargo from our planes and that's it." "Are you going to land the "Boos"on the street outside the NGO?" "Wouldn't that be cute? Hell no. We will establish a rice farm like this one and land our opium from Burma and Laos, outside Phnom Penh and truck it buried beneath bags of research rice to our lab in the city. Body guards, truck drivers and laborers shouldn't total more than two dozen people." Bill calculated.

"I see you've put some thought into this Bill." "Except for pilots David. For now I guess that's you and me." Bill said. "I will fly for you until you get one, or two more pilots but I don't want to get back into the Ops again Bill." "I know. Besides, I need you to keep doing what you do so well." Bill replied. Omar had his wife and two teen aged daughters bring the late afternoon dinner to the great house where Bill and David were settling in. The men made small talk about Omar's farming chores and it became clear through the course of the meal and the after dinner tea that Omar was interested in becoming more involved in Bill's NGO operations. Omar excused himself at dusk to say his prayers and Bill asked David to join him in a room upstairs that he had turned into an office and study. "Omar would probably croak if he ever found out what we really do." David said. "There are a lot of things about Omar that may make you croak David." Bill replied.

"What, for example?" "Well, for example that he belongs to the same Muslim terrorist group that bombed Bali. He's an Imam and bomb maker and is respected and feared by the regional police. That he conducts raids into southern Thailand and has harbored Jemah Islamiah groups right here on this very rice plantation from time to time." "Jesus! You're right, I'm croaking." Bill chuckled to hear David confess his total surprise. "Aren't you worried that his Ops could compromise us Bill?" "To the contrary. I may need him down the road. As you know David, the Golden Crescent now produces about ninety three percent of the world's opium. After Al Qaeda and the Taliban moved into Pakistan and Afghanistan and that stupid bastard Mullah Omar, no relation to our Omar, destroyed my labs and most of the Poppy fields it also burnt all of my usable contacts there. The opium we're pulling out of Laos isn't enough to keep a cat alive." Bill lamented.

"Burma is our main source now and we are only able to operate with the Shan, thanks to General Jon Kern who is one of a handful of top commanders in the Shan State Army. As separatists, they keep the Myanmar army out of the Shan region of North Burma. The Junta has gained in strength, however and may move on the Shan Army someday soon. If that happens I wouldn't trust the Junta well enough to continue doing business in Myanmar.

If anything happens to Jon Kern we're properly f--ked." Bill said. "What if we expand our cooperation with Omar, here in Malaysia? Could he help get our asses in the door with the Taliban Mujahideen back in Afghanistan and Pakistan?" "David I wouldn't want to be back in that Hell hole for all the tea in China. What I would consider doing with Omar is let him front the opium collection in Afghanistan." "We could ship the raw opium in rice bags like we do in Cambodia only from Pakistan, across the north Indian Ocean over to some place like Somalia. We'd have to hire a big assed army in Somalia though to maintain security. The soldiers we'd find there would want to use our product themselves.

We are talking extreme circumstances here. I have no final contingencies yet." Bill frowned. "I'm sure it must have been pretty hairy at times in Afghanistan." David said almost apologetically. "Hairy? Every goddamned minute of the day. I was the CIA controller of a guy named Gulbuddin Hekmatyar. What a guy! He was as hard as nails. He founded a Mujahideen army called Hezb-i-Islami. Our combined mission was to protect and expand Poppy production in the Helmand Valley, as well as run a few dozen heroin labs near Koh-i- Soltan, just across the border into Pakistan. That son of a bitch hated Russians so bad it was only rare that he ever took even a single prisoner.
Instead, he beheaded them with a sword. If there was a bunch of them he just mowed them down with a machine gun. He always kept his word with me though and that's all I gave a shit about." Bill said.

"What happened when the Red Army pulled out?" David asked. "Hekmatyar eventually became Prime Minister, as well as a whole bunch of other important positions in the post Mujahideen government, but then the Pakistanis got involved with their ISI, Inter Service Intelligence and helped create the Taliban and eventually helped welcome in Al Qaeda. David, by the time the party was over and the CIA retired my ass, in the late eighties, we were producing a thousand tons of raw Opium a year. Pakistan alone was pulling in about ten billion dollars a year net, on heroin sales." "That's a lot of product Bill." David said.

"Today I hear they're producing nine thousand tons a year. Now David, that's a lot of product." "Shit! Is Hekmatyar still the head Drug Lord over there ?" "Nah. He fell into trouble with a war lord named Mullah Nasim Akhundzada. Hekmatyar's Hezb-i-Islami army got their asses kicked by Nasim's boys and things just sort of went down hill, power wise, for Hekmatyar after that. He did manage to get some revenge though when he had Nasim assassinated."

"The war between Nasim's people and Hekmatyar kept him from becoming a bigger player with the Taliban and Al Qaeda even though it was Hekmatyar and his Hezb-i-Islami that rescued Usama Bin Ladin and Al Zawahiri's asses at Tora Bora. Hekmatyar took them up into the mountains of Waziristan and as far as I know, not many more than him know where Usama is today. Al Qaeda replaced the Mujahideen as the new radical terrorist Islamic fundamentalists. Hekmatyar just wanted Afghanistan to be free of all foreigners, including Al Qaeda, so he fell out of grace. He still attacks the Coalition and NATO forces from time to time, but as far as I know he lost his Golden Goose in the heroin trade as I hear he depends on money filtered in to him from the West through illicit Islamic charitable organizations." Bill said.

"So there wouldn't be much we could do to get Ops started in that place?" "They would behead us on sight David! We could do all the sales jobs on them you'd like and it wouldn't amount to a sack of dried shit. The arable land is already being tilled for Poppy to the last hectare and they aren't short on buyers. Usually they just trade raw opium for weapons and spending money. The various war lords with their armies protect their buyers who ultimately process the raw opium in Pakistan.

Everybody is already running a couple hundred labs to cut down on the bulk from raw opium into 99% pure heroin at a factor of ten to one in reduced weight and size. They wouldn't want us two white breads within a thousand miles of their Ops. Besides once they found out that I am ex-CIA and worked with Hekmatyar they would roast our balls and make us eat them before separating us from our heads. If they only knew the magic that you have with laundering huge sums of money they would let you live, but me? No way Jose'." "How are they laundering nowadays?" David asked. "As far as I know they are really hurting. Billions of drug dollars that they can't get to their soldiers because the world financial institutions have put their systems in serious shut down."

"They have to resort to small amounts of e-money and Digital cash such as M-money and other cellular type money transfers that use money changers, who move from town to town to avoid having to register with the Feds. They have had to cancel terror strikes because of funding problems." Bill said.

"M-money. That's how even the Mexican Cartels launder their drug money. They would all have an orgasm if they had a system like the one you set up for me." "Yeah, but they would probably f--ck it up with some weird trans-action like sending a few tons of C-4 to some European country on their Master Charge card." Both men had a deep laugh with David's last remark.

"Just out of curiosity David, what sort of system would you set up for those Neanderthals?" Bill asked. "Well, first of all, I would rather die than help them kill innocent people, but to answer you in a theoretical sense I would probably set up a Brazilian swap meet. A bazaar that dealt strictly in cash with no paper trail. That would allow an easy slide out of dollars into euros. Since it has already been done in Brazil inadvertently, I would probably pick another Latin American country.

Perhaps a country like Paraguay." David mused. "Back to us Bill, what about Pakistan? Could we make it there somehow?" "Oh David! Even worse than Afghanistan I"m afraid. Until he was assassinated, back in 1988, a General named Zia Ul Haq, ran Pakistan with an iron fist. He was killed in a plane crash, made to look like an accident. Even took out the American Ambassador and most of Zia's military staff. Zia's brother was commander of the NWFP the Northwest Frontier Project, where most of the processing of Afghan Opium into 99% pure heroin had been going on.

After Zia's death, his brother and several members of his staff were arrested and jailed. They jailed Zia's personal Account Manager for smuggling a huge stash of pure heroin into Norway, but a few years even before all that. Anyway, not long after Zia was out of the picture Benazir Bhutto became Prime Minister. Immersed in the misery and shame of how her father had been murdered, as a result of an earlier coup de etat, her first course of action was to go after the Inter Service Intelligence folks. She didn't make a lot of friends by attacking the government's infra structure. Imagine if the FBI and CIA were under the same hat with unlimited powers of summary execution and martial law then you would achieve an approximation of ISI.

The ISI was given the task of keeping Afghanistan from becoming stable, to ensure Pakistan's own security and were considered indispensable so Benazir was only partially successful in paring them down. Afghanistan was much more manageable as a client state so ISI helped the CIA engineer a rise to power of the Mujahideen. That was because the CIA created the Islamic Brigades and needed the Mujahideen to cause the Soviet occupation to fail.

The recent assassination of Benazir by Al Qaeda was an obvious counter thrust, to thwart an attempt by the USA to seat a broad coalition of secular and liberal representatives to replace Musharraf, after his party lost the elections. The U.S. Strategy was to continue the clean up of ISI that Benazir began years before by steering her back into power. Her national zeal and political ambitions combined with America's narrow interests got her whacked. Furthermore David, there's an Egyptian cleric named Sheikh Essa who is a fierce rabble rouser and mouth piece for Al Qaeda. He took up residence in the NWFP of Waziristan in a small town called Mir Ali. His particular firebrand theme of Islamic fundamentalism preaches that even non-practicing Muslims should be considered to be Infidels and beheaded.

He has many followers both in Pakistan and Afghanistan called Takfiri. He has called for all political institutions in both countries to be dismissed and replaced by a universal Emirate that will rule by Sharia law in pretty much a return to the old Taliban. He cried out constantly for Benazir's death and a day after she was killed the Americans sent a Predator over to his place and blasted his house with a Hell Fire missile. He was seriously wounded but somehow escaped and is being seen as omnipotent as a result. A few weeks ago the Americans dropped in for a visit with another Predator in the NWFP and took out about thirteen Al Qaeda. One of them was Abu Laith al Libi. A week earlier they took out a Top Taliban South Waziristan Commander named Mullah Nazir who was meeting with none other than Zawahiri, himself. Somehow Zawahiri left before the drone launched its missile. Not the first time that his fat ass has narrowly escaped. Can you imagine the f--cking intrigue and betrayal involved in that?" Bill asked.

"The point I'm trying to make here is that if the Taliban and Al Qaeda didn't kill us the Americans would. Not my preferred sort of work environment." "Mine either." David said. "Bill, if we get greedy we'll kill our f--cking selves. As you know, the global street price of China White is about fifty eight U.K. pounds per gram, or roughly one hundred twenty five dollars U.S. per gram. We pay five dollars of that one hundred twenty five, to the Shan and Meo for processed raw opium.

We keep a clear profit after expenses of about nineteen dollars a gram, or nineteen thousand U.S. per kilo. The rest goes to the Chinese triads. In spite of that, we make nineteen million a ton and we don't even have the risk of dealing with distribution. We should be planning our retirement instead of worrying about opening new sources of supply in the Golden Crescent." Bill grinned widely at David's comment.

" You're right of course David, but there's just one little thing we need to do to hedge our bets. We need these nice little safe houses to retreat to when things get bad everywhere else." "What's that?" David asked. "Go look out the window and tell me what you see." David moved to the curtain and looked out beyond the rice paddies to the airport hangar. "I see three deuce and a half trucks being unloaded." David answered.

"Could be weapons and ammo from what I can see. Who are they Bill?" "Omar's guys, about forty troops. They're loading our Caribous with re-supplies mostly small arms, RPGs and C-4 for their Ops in Southern Thailand. " "What the fuck! You had this shit planned all along!" David yelled out. "Yes. but not for another two weeks. This shit with Manny threw me off schedule." "When did you intend to tell me about it?" "Now?" Bill answered flippantly. "Thanks a lot Bill!" David said sharply. Bill chuckled at the exchange.

"Let's take a nap. I'll brief you on the mission at twenty one hundred hours. We'll be back before breakfast tomorrow morning." "Shit Bill! I'm having trouble keeping up with you." Bill smiled and said "Let's walk over to the hangar and meet the troops. There's something else over there I'd like to show you anyway. "When David and Bill appeared from behind the olive drab trucks, one of Omar's soldiers raised his AK-47 aiming at Bill's face. "Don't want to shoot your pilot, do you son?" Bill quipped. The soldier lowered his weapon, as the other soldiers ridiculed him and began to laugh. Bill led David inside the hangar to a small office with shades drawn. Once inside, Bill pushed a button inside a desk drawer and a secret panel slid open. Inside was a large computer desk with state of the art computer equipment and accessories. It had a satellite broad band internet connection and some other equipment for encoding both voice and Mpeg video feed.

"Get a load of this David." Bill said as he sat down and began pecking at the key board and clicking the mouse. To David's astonishment, a clear view of Bill's secret office interior at the S.H.A.R.I. compound in Phnom Penh came into focus. The office was quiet and still except for the pendulum of a clock on the wall behind the desk. On a shelf clearly visible was a digital calendar clock which gave the twenty four hour military time display as well as the current date in real time. "Damn Bill! What is this?" "It's my sure fire way of knowing whether we have been compromised. This digital imaging is kept on a month long video recording that is activated by motion sensors.
What you are looking at now is live, but the recorder only comes on when someone, or something enters the room." "Your a bloomin' genius Bill!" David quipped.

"Not really. I actually got the idea when I saw it being used in a home security advertisement. Modern technology my friend. It's there so why not take advantage of it?" "Yes why not? Bill, I am still having trouble getting my mind wrapped around your association with terrorists. Quite honestly it's bothering the hell out of me." "Never think downstream David. Number Four China White is our product. It will always bring us into business with people who are unsavory downstream. That doesn't enter into the picture upstream that's where we are, upstream. When we sell our China White, it leaves upstream and goes downstream. If I allowed myself to worry about what they do with the shit, or with the money they get for it I would already be a dead man many times over." Bill observed.

"Stay upstream with me David and we will be wealthier than our imaginations could ever make us. Omar has a right to protect Islam, David. If his Ops involved attacks on Americans of course I would refuse to help him. I know a lot of Westerners were killed in Bali and although he was a member of that Jihadist group, he fought like Hell to prevent the attacks from happening from the inside.

His beef is with Thailand. From what I understand he has good reasons to lead a resistance against the Thai Junta." "F--ck the nap Bill, I need to know more about the mission tonight before I feel comfortable flying against the Thai." "Fair enough, but let's at least go back to the Great House. The air con works better there." Bill and David had perspired through their shirts from the heavy humidity.

"Does Omar really stay in his Bungalow when you're not here?" David asked. "F--cked if I know. I doubt it I sure as hell wouldn't would you?" Bill exclaimed. "F--ck no man, this humidity from the coast is a dog." When they were settled in the Great House Bill pulled a couple of Tiger beers from the refrigerator.

He drew down a map of the Thai and Malaysian border from a heavily used map roll away attached to the ceiling. "As you know David, the Thai and Malaysians have been waging a cultural and religious give and take, in the southeastern three provinces of Thailand known as the Pattani region for a long time. Most of the people who live there are ethnically Malay, speak Malay and are Muslim. They have been trying their damnedest over the last century to separate themselves from Thailand, but the stubborn Thai are hearing nothing of it." Bill said.

"Most wars have been fought for one of four reasons. Race, Religion, Language and economic ideology. This conflict has it all. Economically, the only investments the Thai have sent to the Pattani have been mainly bars and whores. That has deeply insulted the Muslim culture. The Thai border juts down into Malaysia like a large claw claiming people and land that the Malays feel belong to mother Malaysia." Bill continued. "Religious adversity, cultural adversity, linguistic and even racial adversity. It's all there. Add stubborn ignorance from the Thai leaders and you have a volatile cocktail indeed." Bill observed.

"As I said, the tussle has been going on for decades but there was a major resurgence of the separatist movement in 2001. Can't say whether it had anything to do with the Twin Towers in New York. I doubt it was more than coincidence but I can tell you that since then, our pal Omar has been hip deep in the training camps of Al Qaeda and the Taliban in Pakistan and Afghanistan. Anyway, where the f--ck was I? Oh yeah, there's four major separatist groups at work in the Pattani region." "PULO, BRN, GMIP and the BRN Coordinate. The BRN Coordinate are the baddest asses in the valley and have conducted most of the bombings and assaults on Thai Police facilities. They are also the ones who beheaded a bus load of Buddhist monks and have even beheaded Thai students.

Have you guessed by now? The BRN Coordinate are Omar's boys." "The ones who beheaded the Thai are the extreme right faction who Omar despises. The ones you just met are new recruits and are a small element of the BRN group. Let's see. Thaksin really stirred the shit up in 2005 when he used heavy handed tactics and gave an asshole General Sonthi Boonyaratkalin pretty much the power to hold summary executions and was otherwise pretty rough on the peasants in the region.

Then Thailand had its coup de etat in September 2006 and the Junta came on with a lot of empty promises and things got even worse than when Thaksin Shinawatra was Prime Minister. To give you an idea of how things have gotten out of control there were 1,400 casualties from the violence when the Junta replaced our boy Thaksin in 2006. As of January 2008 that figure has now reached 3,700 and is still climbing." Bill added. "We will be flying in fresh weapons and troops to an airstrip in Yala Province just here." Bill used a small pointer to indicate the air strip.

"I will have a checklist ready when we go to the planes to inspect cargo and passengers, let's say at about twenty one hundred hours. We will fly canopy to avoid radar and should have a nice clean in and out. The air strip will be lit for ten minutes only with upwardly visible # 10 cans filled with sand and kerosene." "They will be lit when we cross the IP. We should be unloaded within ten minutes and we'll take off immediately after the stacks are removed from the Boos. Radio silence all the way through except to warn of imminent attack.

The Thai have a squadron of F-16A jets on call for the region armed to the teeth that fly Close Air Support for day time missions. They have a heavily armed variety of choppers with air to air, air to ground rockets, 40 mm cannon and fifties. Enough to chew our asses up if we get caught. If we get discovered fly west to the Malacca strait and then down the coast back to the hangar. Hot pursuits shouldn't cross the border back into Malaysian airspace, but given how things have heated up I wouldn't bet the farm on that. Questions?"

"Bill, I will not fly if these guys are going to behead any more Buddhists." David declared. "I happen to be in love with a Buddhist woman you met her, Srey An." "This is a re- supply mission David. No one is beheading anyone. Any other questions?" "Yeah, when can I get a change of clothes?" "They are waiting by the shower in your bathroom. I gave Omar's wife your clothes sizes months ago." "One other thing Bill. I know how important Omar is both as a safe house keeper and as a possible partner for Ops in Afghanistan, but I'm having trouble getting pumped up enough to fly a mission against Thailand. Can you give me something to piss me off a little, or at least get a feeling that I'm on the right side?" "Well f--ck David! You remember the time we got caught up in that raid in Nana Plaza and how the Thai cops started herding the girls we'd already paid for into their Paddy Wagon?

Remember how we tried to politely explain that to the little Thai Police Captain who got on top of the bar with his jack boots and used a mega horn to tell all the foreigners to stay back, or he would shoot us? The Thai are wonderful people man, but give them a gun and a badge and they go nuts with power. Well, that's sort of what happened in the Pattani region." Bill observed.

"Over the years, the Thai police have raped and pillaged until the Malay peasants said they weren't going to take this shit anymore. To add insult to injury, the Thai entrepreneurs tried to turn the place into a mini Pattaya by bringing bars and discos into the place. Muslims do not like whores and alcohol in their face, but the Thai just said f--ck em' and did what they wanted with the place.

OK, you want something to get pissed off about? How about the Tak Bai incident?" "What was that?" David asked. "Well in October of 2004, all hell broke loose with the insurgency when the Malay people got wind of a really stupid blunder by the Thai Police. It all went down just here in Narathiwat province." Bill points at the map. "Six Muslims were caught delivering weapons to the insurgents and the Thai Police of course arrested them.This caused a riot
and the Thai Army was called in to handle it. The crowd went wild demanding the men's release and the Army replied with water cannons and tear gas.

Seven men were shot dead. Hundreds of local Malay men were arrested and made to strip to the waist. The Thai soldiers tied their hands behind their backs with plastic restraints and then stacked them on trucks six layers deep to save petrol and transported them to a military prison in Pattani. It was a very hot day and the trip lasted five hours. When they arrived at Pattani seventy eight prisoners had suffocated to death.

"Thaksin tried to white wash the tragedy by saying that the men who died were dead because they had been fasting for Ramadan. Two years go by and the new Prime Minister, Surayud Chalanont offered a clumsy apology and violence erupted in the region and quintupled over night." "Damn! OK. This isn't about Thailand, or a fatwa against Buddhists, it's about a corrupt junta in Thailand, that doesn't really represent the peaceful will of the Thai people. I'm in! " David said firmly.

"I knew you'd agree once you had all the facts." Bill said with a smile. Bill and David spent nearly an hour with pre- flight inspections on each Caribou and its human and materiel cargo. Each man's AK-47 was inspected to ensure that no rounds had been chambered and that the safety's were on. Grenade pins were taped over to ensure that none would be snagged and detonated inside the aircraft. When both aircraft and all personnel were inspected and certified by Bill, or David, the men boarded the aircraft.

They found places to sit, or lie down for the two hour flight. Omar chose to ride with David. David was an unknown article and a good leader would always choose to remain near an uncertain factor, to protect his men from the unexpected. Bill had elected to fly lead aircraft and would be the first to cross the IP, or Initial Point. Once the IP was crossed technically speaking, there would be no turning back until the mission had been completed. Aborted missions were only aborted before the IP and both Bill and David held fast to those rules. The night was clear and painfully bright.

Bill had carefully planned this mission to occur when the moon would be a sliver and the darkness would offer a higher possibility of success. Two things had forced the mission during unfavorable circumstances. First Manny had gone Christian and second, Omar's people were fighting a valiant, but losing battle and their only hope was the men and weapons Bill would deliver to them with the moon at his back. It was to be a mission of mercy to the desperate.

"Joss." Bill thought as he surveyed the luminescent jungle canopy on the horizon. He circled the rice farm once before heading north east toward the IP. He could see David's Caribou lifting off the air strip as he throttled down for a descent back to a canopy level flight.

David thought of the young faces he had looked into when he inspected their weapons. Just boys, really. A seasoned combat veteran could always detect a cherry. You could smell the fear on them without having to see it in their eyes. These young boys would soon know what he knew and feel what he had felt, for the first time.

David compared the psychological impact of war on youth with an allegory he called the death of a rose. A loss of innocence would be the first petal to fall. The next would be the loss of beauty, especially if the carnage was in their faces. The remaining petals, such as love for mankind and the belief that mankind is inherently good, not evil, would fall slowly, or rapidly depending on whether the action was hand to hand. Their hearts would oscillate from cowardice when they cried out for their mothers, to bravery and unselfish heroism when they did impossible things to save their brothers in arms.

Their young minds would be sculpted by their specific experiences and scarred for life. After all the petals had been stripped bare by the stark reality of war the lonely thorn covered stem that remained would always be a symbol of their new reality. Their new character would use this day to measure limits of mental endurance for each day for the rest of their lives. The boundaries which had been stretched far beyond anything else human society could ever rain down upon itself, established. The only good thing they could draw from war would be the confidence they would have within the expanded dimensions of their new lives. "What doesn't kill you makes you stronger." David mused.

David had a heightened sense of alert, as he watched the skies, waiting for a Thai F-16, or a combat chopper which could take his own mind back to its own boundaries once more. As he scanned the horizon, he remembered a book by Paul Tillich, a German theologian who taught metaphysical studies at Harvard.

The book was titled "The Courage To Be." In it, Tillich defined the courage of a soldier as a form of fortitude, or "Tapferkeit". Not the highest level of courage because ultimately, saving a fellow soldier's life, would result in restoring that soldier's ability to continue delivering death to other human beings. A higher form of courage, "Herz Mutig," Tillich reserved for someone who died to save women and children. Both types of sacrifice would use up a life, which was all anyone had to give, but the sweetest sacrifice was the one which saved the innocent. David thought of Sun Tzu and "The Art Of War." How battles were won, or lost, first in the mind and heart of a soldier and an army, well before the battle lines were ever drawn. That's what had given the North Vietnamese an edge the Americans could never over come. The North Vietnamese were fighting foreign invaders in their own homeland.

The mistake America's leaders made, was placing far too much importance on ideology. The real battle was a battle for the defense of the Homeland. The very same reason America won its own war of independence. A search for meaning and purpose, or ideology, was never as important as the battle which had to first be fought and won in the hearts and the minds of the common folk. The Americans never quite developed a love for the South Vietnamese that was equivalent to the demanded sacrifice. America once suckled the philosophical breast of France for her own most treasured concepts of liberty during her own revolution. France stormed the Bastille to rip back their freedom from the hands of the corrupt Bourgoisie, yet both countries had tried to deny it from the people of Vietnam.

The Americans had to first fight a war with their own people in order to fight a hellacious war with a determined enemy in a foreign and unforgiving place. Technocracy had so alienated America that its leaders were completely out of touch with the most precious of its own principles. Out of touch with the real heart beat of the nation. The Vietnam war was lost in America's streets and college campuses well before the first bullet had been fired, just as it had been with the French at Dien Bien Phu. American military leadership finally realized they were losing the moral high ground and attempted to initiate programs to reclaim the villages from the NVA, but in the final scheme of things it had been too little too late. Too much, too wrong. History left to sort out the colossal mistakes. The little book of Sun Tzu read by America's generals, but never really understood by those who could have made a difference.

What enabled young men such as the ones on this plane, right now, to be willing to sacrifice their very lives? Some by strapping on explosives, to turn themselves into human bombs? To them it would be considered the highest form of Herz Mutig but David knew it would never rise above the level of Tapferkeit because innocent life had been the target. A Jihad where the victims were innocent women and children could never approach Herz Mutigkeit. In fact, it would never rise far above simple cowardice. The North Vietnamese had committed incredible horror because they believed the means was justified by the end. A liberation of their nation from post colonial oppression. They were right, about the end but not about the terror. David imagined that the Pattani Muslims would also someday win their war against the Thai in spite of the terror they had committed against peaceful Buddhists. Why? Because they owned the long term higher moral ground. Defending their homeland trumped the terror they committed to win it back or did it? David tried not to cloud his mind with any further thoughts of morality. He was still battling for his own mind.

He needed to dismiss Manny's call for redemption, from the vast moral wasteland, of being a link in the chain of the production of China White. How much longer could he stay upstream with Bill, keeping his life as a Drug King Pin separate from his concept of good and evil in humanity? David said his mantra and began to put distance between himself and the type of thoughts that would dull his instincts of survival in combat. Using instruments and visual references, Bill soon announced on the intercom that he was crossing the IP. He turned on the red interior lights. As soon as the lights turned green, it would signal time to exit down the lowered ramp of the aircraft.

As Bill approached the air strip, which was little more than a cow path he could see four pick up trucks, sitting dead center on the landing strip. He had no choice but to break radio silence. "Bird Leader Two, this is Bird Leader One, over." "Come in One." David replied. "Be advised nest is full. Four eggs sitting in the middle of the nest. Over." David thought for a second and then shook his head. "Omar are you in touch with your people on the ground?" "I thought we have radio silenced." Omar replied. "Omar, I think your people have four vehicles sitting on the trail Bill is supposed to be landing on."

"He can't land until they clear the runway." Omar turned on his cell, dialed a number and began issuing hateful noises into it. Immediately the pick up trucks moved off the runway. David looked down at the airstrip and noticed that the number 10 cans had not been lit and mentioned this to Omar. "Don't tell them to light them now Omar, it's bright enough already." Omar issued vitriolic sounds into the cell phone and then clamped it shut, making spitting noises to himself, long after the cell phone had been shut off.

Bill brought his plane down as light as a feather and lowered the ramp to enable the troops and cargo to be unloaded. Three of the troops had exited, when from behind a tree line, a Thai combat chopper lifted up vertically and fired two missiles that sailed past Bill's Caribou by mere inches.

He immediately throttled all the way, while lifting the ramp and strained to lift it airborne again. The Thai chopper flew in hot pursuit and was attempting to get a radar lock on the ascending aircraft. David watched from above. "Get an RPG ready to fire Omar! Hold the stick steady, right here." David instructed. He strapped his web belt to a D ring near the side cargo door and leaned out with the RPG. The wind caused him to wobble, but he forced the RPG point to be parallel with his own aircraft as the Thai chopper hovered to get a shot on Bill's aircraft. He fired. The RPG hit the Thai aircraft squarely in its engine.

The Thai chopper became a huge ball of white, hot gas as it exploded into a million shards and splinters. Omar was so excited he screamed "Allah Akbar!" as David resumed flying the Caribou. Omar pointed down at the three men left behind by Bill's sudden departure. They were fighting for their lives against a crack platoon of Thai Special Forces troops. Bill radioed David. "Leader Two, Leader One, over." "Leader Two, over." "Leader Two, fly to the alternate LZ, this one's hot, over." "Roger Leader One, Wilco!" Bill flew to the alternate LZ about five miles east of the hot LZ.

The trucks awaited there, per Omar's instructions to go there if the first LZ became hot. He landed and his cargo and the remainder of his troops were off loaded within minutes. Soon Bill was in the air, circling, but David's aircraft was nowhere to be seen. Seeing the three men pinned down David circled back and landed further down the trail.

He kept the engines idling as he grabbed an AK-47 and several clips of ammunition. He ran down the ramp grabbing two RPG's before bounding off the end of the ramp. Seeing this, Omar and all of his twenty troops ran behind David toward the heated fire fight. They approached the three men from the rear of the berm they had taken cover behind.

At first the three were afraid they had been encircled by Thai, but quickly judged from the tall silhouette that it was the American. Thinking they were fighting against a small force the Thai soldiers began to leap frog toward the berm intending to over run the position when suddenly twenty five AK-47's opened up on full automatic chewing ten of the Thai soldiers to pieces in the first five
seconds. David fired his two RPG's wounding several of the remaining Thai troops.

Omar began to ready his troops for a counter attack but David pointed at the Caribou and started running toward the plane. Omar started running behind David and soon all of Omar's men including the three who had been rescued were running along behind as well. The plane was quickly boarded and airborne again within seconds. Soon, David was landing at the alternate LZ. His plane was being unloaded when the three young boys he had rescued came to him at the cockpit, tears streaming down their faces mumbling "Allah Akbar, tank you mistah David! " David had an urge to give them a group hug, but suddenly put his feelings in check. Instead, he looked at them firmly and said "You are welcome." He then saluted them and said; "Go with your brothers and fight with courage for your country and its people!" Omar ran from the plane hiding his face so the foreigner wouldn't see his tears. David didn't know it, but the three young soldiers he had just rescued were Omar's younger brothers.

He promised his sister, who had raised them after Omar's parents died that he would protect them with his life. Instead, it was this foreigner who saved them and Omar would never forget this night. Omar sat quietly in the hold of David's empty Caribou all the way back to the rice farm. His heart overflowed with gratitude to David, but his shame for not having been the one who led the rescue to save his own brothers was unbearable. He didn't know why he had felt so helpless.

Perhaps, because those three young lives were more precious than his own life that he feared the consequence of failure enough to have momentarily doubted his own abilities. He didn't know and couldn't even ponder the reasons he froze. He just knew that he would never again support the killing of innocent foreigners. Against all he had been taught since childhood he now knew beyond a doubt that infidels couldn't help their ignorance and should be loved as a brother until they learned the ways of Allah, God willing.

Bill locked the hangar, then returned to the Great House and walked up to David's bed room door. He wanted to discuss the events of the evening, but as he slowly looked in he saw David asleep on the floor in a deep and fitful sleep. He was back in Vietnam, along the Ho Chi Minh Trail on the very same long range recon patrol he had been on in his nightmares for the past quarter of a century. At sunrise the intense Asian sun filled Bill's room like sparklers on the fourth of July. He stumbled for the bathroom and had finished his shower before he realized that the exotic aroma that filled his nostrils was from spice and food. He shaved and quickly put on fresh clothes to go downstairs to discover what was making such a racket with his olfactory nerves.

He walked down the stair and was so pleasantly surprised that he had to sit down and let his eyes have the first feast. Seated around a very long table, filled with a dozen varieties of Reistafel and tropical fruit were four lovely young women between the ages of eighteen and twenty six. Each had faces painted with white make up and ruby red lipstick. Asian women believe the whiteness enhances their beauty more than their own lovelier, darker skin. They sat backs straight looking forward with very serious expressions until a nude David tumbled over Bill rolling down the steps with his genitals waving in the breeze. He rolled to their feet by the table.

The girls screamed with laughter as David bowed and wrapped a dinner napkin half way around his hips covering the front like a fig leaf, but not the rear. He mumbled about "no privacy" and "Bill why didn't you warn me?" as he stumbled back up the stair with his butt cheeks moving in unison. Bill was gasping for air as he laughed along with the girls. "David, you're so f--cking funny!" was all Bill could repeat over and over. The girls began to leave but Bill asked them to "please stay" and they sat back down still giggling at what they had just seen. Bill got dressed excused himself and walked down the path toward Omar's bungalow.

Omar met him halfway on the path. "I hoping you didn't mind Omar ask women to be your guests Mistah Bill." "Not at all Omar, we are grateful for the companionship." " I know I can never repay Mistah David for what he do last night." Omar continued. "I want thank both of you for what you do for Malay people. Mistah David risk his life, save my three younger brothers. My sistah cry all night with happiness when I tell her what David do." "What did David do?" Bill asked. Omar gave Bill a detailed account including how David saved Bill's plane from certain disaster.

"I saw the chopper explode, but I thought one of your people shot it down from the ground." Bill stood for a moment taking it all in. Bill knew that if they had been back in Vietnam a Congressional Medal Of Honor would have been awarded David for his heroism last night. Now, even better he had earned the love and gratitude of a wonderful Malaysian family. Bill had never tried to bring a woman back to the Great House in order not to insult Omar's Islamic sensibilities and wham, in one stroke David had a houseful of beauties who were at their disposal. "Speaking for David, you are welcome Omar. God is great!" "Yes, mistah Bill! Allah Akbar!" Bill excused himself and returned to the Great House. David was already making the girls laugh with jokes and magic tricks when Bill walked in.

"David, can I speak with you alone?" David walked out on the veranda with Bill. "What's up Bill?" David asked. "About last night. I'm still digesting this myself. Omar tells me you led an assault on an entire platoon of Thai Special Operators to save his three brothers. Not just Islamic brothers, but honest to God flesh and blood brothers."

"So?" "So? That's all you can say? I mean that's some heroic shit David!" "There weren't many options Bill. The three kids were getting left behind by the change in LZ's. They could have tried to run Bill, but those brave assed teenagers were holding their ground against a platoon of Thailand's best soldiers. You want heroes? Those three kids were the f--cking heroes Bill. They were suckling little boys yesterday afternoon, but when I looked down in the night at them I saw three brave men sharing ammunition clips and throwing f--cking grenades.You can't just leave people like that to die without joining them. What ever they were before they're our brothers now Bill and you can't let brothers die without doing something." David said.

Bill stood in awe realizing that there were layers to David that he was only just beginning to discover. "Damn I'm glad you're my brother David." "Me too Bill. Let's go enjoy the spoils of war." Bill smiled broadly and went back inside arm in arm with David. The girls didn't speak a single word of English. Bill knew only a few words of the local Malay dialect. "I still can't understand why Omar sent these fine ladies to us Bill. I thought he was a devout Muslim." David said. "He is. These girls aren't whores David. Well, not by the standard Western definition we would use any way. Each of these girls no doubt had an unsanctioned love affair with a young Muslim man and lost her virginity in the process. Muslim Mothers are very strict. They perform random, unannounced inspections of their daughter's hymen, to ensure chastity." Bill explained.

"When it was discovered that these ladies had been disloyal to future husbands they had been betrothed to Muslim honor dictated that they could never marry a respectable Muslim man." "Had they been in Iran, Pakistan or Afghanistan, they would have probably been stoned to death in what they call an "honor killing" by their father, or brother. But here in Malaysia they are used on special occasions such as this one to serve as concubines and companions." "Our gain, someone else's loss." David said. "Exactly!" Bill replied. " I almost forgot, David. Thanks for saving my ass again last night!" "My pleasure Bill!"

Bill watched David, as he kept the girls laughing. He felt in awe of him now. Some men have great oratorical skills and move nations with words. David was a man who affected life through courageous action. "Give me one David for a million of the other kind, any day." Bill thought to himself.They all feasted on their Malaysian breakfast and when it was clear that Omar would keep them from being disturbed they went upstairs and made love like innocent children. They fell into an exhausted sleep until evening.

When they awakened David used sign language pretending to swim to ask if anyone would enjoy going to the beach. "I think they'd like to go, they just don't want to be seen frolicking with us." Bill said. "Who will see them? We can use one of Omar's jeeps and we can wait until after dark to go." When Bill explained this they all smiled and nodded their heads yes. Bill filled a canvas bag with two Mac-17's and several clips of ammo and a few grenades. He knew they wouldn't need them, but felt better having them near.

The girls described a special lagoon with their hands that had a private secluded beach with soft white sand. When they arrived the lagoon was just as the girls had described. It was fed on a constant basis with fresh sea water that circulated from tidewater that escaped back to the sea. After a blistering hot day the water felt cool and inviting to David who volunteered to plunge in first.

Bill parked the jeep beneath a spreading Banyan tree in the dark and stripped off his clothes as David had done before him. He watched as the girls undressed. By now both he and David knew each lovely young woman intimately, but he still felt a lump in his throat when he watched their lovely voluptuous full breasts wobble as they leaned over to peal away their panties. The moon caressed the lagoon with a glistening path of shimmering light. The silver reflection from the water danced along the creamy smooth surface of each woman's skin in a dazzling haze.

This in turn created an aura of playful light that sparkled in a base relief of their silhouettes against the water. When they waded chest deep into the dark lagoon their breasts heaved in rhythm with the cool surrounding water. Their hair became curly when wet until they resembled the women David admired in the Gaugin Tahiti paintings.

David swam with each woman, pausing to kiss them and feel their smooth bodies against his own. Bill joined the group huddled together like a great ball of tiny fish, ever circling and caressing each other in unison.

Bill and David became aroused which in turn aroused the women. While two women kissed and suckled the men above the water, the other two spread their legs and pushed themselves onto the men below the surface. They swam and rotated until both Bill and David reached a blissful climax. They floated almost in a dream state, a dream from which no one wanted to wake up until the ever so faint hum became a sputtering vibration from a million miles away beneath the star studded sky. David reacted first followed shortly by Bill. "I see it Bill. It's a sea Otter flying low, about a kilometer out at sea." "Yes. I see it too David." Suddenly men were exiting the aircraft in a low level insertion with full UBA underwater breathing apparatus. The divers were followed by the flat splash of a rubber inflatable. Bill put his forefinger over his lips to warn the women not to utter a sound.

In moments the women were shivering as they stood near the still warm hood of the jeep getting dressed. The girls pulled their clothing off the windshield and began trading articles of blouses, slacks and under garments, in an attempt to find their own. Bill waved his hand palm down urging the girls to put on what ever they already had in their hand. One girl attempted to light a small flash light to find an ear ring until David took it from her. When he drew his finger across his throat the girls finally understood that the men in the water meant danger. One of the women made a motion with an imaginary steering wheel that told the men that she knew how to drive.

The group pushed the jeep back onto the main road and the women drove toward home. Bill opened the canvas bag and divided the Mac 17's ammo and grenades with David. He then pulled the cell phone Omar had given him from the bag and hit speed dial. "Yes Mistah Bill. You OK?" "I'm OK Omar, but you have what appears to be a six man team of special operators on the way to your place NOW! They're in a rubber raft headed for the beach near the lagoon. Good! You know where I'm talking about? Yes Omar small weapons probably demolitions too. Just a guess at this point, but unless the Malaysian navy is having night training they're probably Thai Special Ops who followed our signature back to where we live. Two minutes? They will be here in two minutes! I will engage. Come as fast as you can! Out."

"David, on my signal let's take out the lead two. You take the left side and I'll take the right! Then walk your fire down to the last ones." "Roger Bill!" Bill and David took up firing positions on the high ground overlooking the beach trying their best to calculate where the tides and current would most likely deliver the raft. "If my guess is right, they'll land about center front of our positions. That will give David and me a clear initial shot. " Bill thought. "We'll have a good base of fusillade cross fire for the rest. At all costs they must be kept away from Omar's family and our Caribous." Bill thought.

Bill knew that they would bring enough demolition, probably C-4 to level the hangar and the houses and probably take only Omar as prisoner and kill the rest of his family. David was thinking just as intensely as Bill. "Why not just raze the place with their F-16's?" David wondered. "Because it would start an open war between Malaysia and Thailand, that's why! An in and out Special Ops hit could be blamed on rival terrorist groups, but an F-16 attack would have an unmistakable Thai finger print."

"This, based simply on the (BDA) Bomb Damage Assessment their weapons left behind." David concluded. David could see the dark mass moving faster than the current. "Those lazy bastards have a motor on that rig. Shit they are headed too far north of us. They'll probably put to land about a hundred meters north of Bill's position." David thought. David crawled on all fours as fast as he could until he reached Bill. "Bill! They have a f--cking outboard motor they'll miss us by a hundred meters further north!" "Yeah I see that now. F--ckers are too lazy to be SEALS that's for sure!" Bill and David crawled backward until they reached a tree line.

They stood up at the tree line and ran full tilt until they reached their new positions just as the raft was being lifted and carried toward them by six men with automatic weapons, three per side. Bill gave the signal and opened up with a short burst followed immediately by David. Both lead men were dead when they hit the ground. The two in the mid section of the raft returned fire lying low in the sand while the two in the rear dove back in the water and disappeared.

A brief fire fight took place when one of the two men firing from the raft pulled out a hand device and began shouting in Thai. Within seconds two F-16A's exploded their after burners as they headed back vertically from their strafing and low level bombing attitude.

"Incoming." David yelled as he and Bill dove for cover behind some clumps of beach grass. Suddenly the entire beach shook as the jets unloaded two, two hundred and fifty pound bombs on Bill and David's previous positions. Bill and David were thrown six feet in the air as their weapons popped out of their hands caused by the shock of the bomb blast. They were both made temporarily deaf by the concussion. A hand grabbed David by the arm. It was Omar.

"You OK Mistah David?" "I think so Omar. Yep, still have all my body parts." Omar ran to Bill who was slapping his ears to try to hear. "You OK Mistah Bill?" Bill turned his head so the ear that had been facing away from the blast could pick up Omar's words.

" What's that Omar? Yeah, I'm fine. How's David?" "He OK, Mistah Bill." "There are four enemy left alive. Two on the beach and two in the water." Bill said" "No, three on Beach dead. One on beach alive. Two escape in water get away for now. We find tomorrow." "Will this place be submerged in Malaysian reporters tomorrow?" Bill asked Omar. "No. Both country's governments want keep entire affair secret. If Thai Junta admits it violated our airspace they be forced to have reason why spread around the world that we are fighting Jihad to liberate the Pattani."

"Both countries maybe suffer from open war. Once again my deepest tanks to you and Mistah David. You nearly killed defending land of Malaysia. You never be forgotten for bravery." "Thank you Omar. I am afraid this means we must leave with the planes tonight. Intel satellites will have detected the explosions. Once they review their data they will also learn there was a fire fight and they will have tracked the signature of the Thai jets back to their base." Bill explained.

"This entire area will get dedicated bird time and my face and David's face will be put through an intense search. Our files were erased when we worked for the Company in Laos but we have lived profiles since then, as NGO businessmen in Cambodia. We have no choice but to leave as soon as we get cleaned up." "I'm sorry Mistah Bill. You both be missed very much." "Mistah Bill. I mean to tell you earlier, but this attack make me forget it. There was loud buzzing noise coming from your office in hangar."

"Get David and I to the hangar immediately Omar! please!" The night air in the open jeep to the hangar awakened both Bill and David. Once inside Bill pressed the button in the desk and the panel slid open. In live time they watched in shock as Vibol was being tortured at Bill's desk. Two men, one Thai and one Khmer, were removing Vibol's fingers one by one. His screaming was hard to bear. Both men spoke in Khmer, but Vibol who knew he was being videotaped courageously answered only in English.

"I told you! I don't know about heroin contacts. I just driver for NGO." Bill frantically typed and used the mouse and soon had captured both men's images. Bill then transferred them to a contact at the CIA's ultra secret database that he paid dearly to use. Yet another finger was removed by a heavy pliers sort of instrument as Vibol passed out. Then a pop up appeared on the computer screen. The pop up was divided into two frames. Both the Khmer's face and the Thai's face had a string of data beneath their photos . The Khmer was a corrupt Colonel in the Cambodian anti-Drug Task force stationed in Phnom Penh.

The Thai was a notorious Drug dealer from Bangkok who dealt almost exclusively in Amphetamines, but was according to the data, very interested in expanding into heroin production and distribution. "I have no choice David. I have no choice. Vibol was my very best soldier." As he said this to David, he held down the control button and typed in a string of numbers. Suddenly the three men's heads exploded outward like pumpkins as their bodies slumped to the floor. In Bill's office in Phnom Penh an implosion bomb had gone off. The vacuum it created in Bill's office caused the three men's brains to explode through their eye sockets and nasal passages. Their bodies slumped to the floor.

Nothing else in the office was destroyed, not a paper on Bill's desk had been disturbed other than the spattered brain matter and blood. "Damn! They must have really tortured Vibol to get him to take them to your office." David said. "No. He took them there voluntarily. He knew I would end his pain. He helped install the system I used to bring it to an end. I regret that he suffered while we were engaged at the beach, but at least we ended his misery and took out his killers at the same time. He was a good man." Bill said.

"After we get back, anyone who was connected with these two are already dead." Bill used the mouse and scanned both the interior and exterior of the compound. No one else was there. Bill doubted that either the Khmer Colonel, or the Thai Drug trafficker had time to tell anyone where they were going and why. They must have been driving around when they spotted Vibol and somehow got the drop on him. Bill thought. Bill saw an older model black Mercedes parked beside the compound on a side street. Using the computer he placed an internet call to Mao, his driver. "Mao, this is Bill."

"Hello mistah Bill!" "Mao, there is a black S-500 Mercedes parked on the side street beside our compound. I need for you to get rid of it. Search it. Retrieve anything you find and then have it driven out of town and destroyed. Leave nothing behind that could be identified. There are three dead bodies in my office. Put them in the Mercedes and pour acid on them. One of them is Vibol. He died heroically for us Mao. Light some candles and incense at the Wat Phnom for him. Leave a basket of rice, sweet cakes and fruit." "Yes, Mistah Bill. I do right away." "Thank you Mao. We will be home tonight. Call Dr. Hamilton and tell him to come back to work tomorrow with his entire team." Bill rang off.

"Things are sure getting heavy are you certain we should go back after this?" David asked. "Yes, David. Those two wouldn't have been working together for the Interpol, or even the Cambodian police, certainly not for the Thai police. They were just trying to exploit our organization for money and territory. If we had anything to fear from Interpol it would have already happened." Bill saved the data on the Khmer Colonel and the Thai drug trafficker to the hard disk and then removed the disk and put it in his satchel. He then asked Omar to come inside. "Omar here is a Bill Of Sale, I just printed out a few minutes ago and signed. It should be taken to your lawyer. It transfers this rice plantation and
all of the buildings back into your name in payment of services rendered, however, you are now on the Thai Air Force target list map here." Bill warned.

"Omar, sell the place and find a new house to live in far from here." Bill said. "How can I repay generosity? Of course I find new and safer place and you will always be my honorable guests anytime you come back." "Thanks Omar. In this envelope you will find enough money to run this place until you can sell it. All of the computer equipment is yours. In this attache' case is a little over a million Philippine pesos." Bill said.

"Please divide this money with the women. They made David and myself happier than I think we have ever been." "They were gift from me Mistah Bill. You no need pay them." "Yes and we are very grateful to you Omar. As you gave them to us as a gift, please give them money from us also as a gift." David had checked and topped off both aircraft. "We're good to go Bill!" "Great David. Let's fly line of sight up the coast until we're about two hundred fifty miles north of Phuket, Thailand. Here's the eastward heading that will take us home to Phnom Penh. I will guide you in to the new hangar I bought north of Phnom Penh about twenty five clicks. Radio silence unless you have an emergency. Hang close and hug the canopy my friend."

Omar's wife brought some pastries and fruit, as well as a large jug of tea for both aircraft. After hugs and small talk the two Caribous were lined up on the airstrip and within minutes, both were circling the rice farm. Bill headed out to sea and both flew the coast line due north. Several hours later Bill was flying low along the Mekong with David close behind. Shortly after Bill bought the Caribous he bought a few hectares of land not far from a river front village along the Mekong, about a thirty minute motor bike ride north of Phnom Penh. Bill had a large corrugated steel hangar built there that was large enough for both of his helicopters, as well as the two Caribous.

It was in fact large enough to house two C-130e aircraft which Bill someday considered buying to replace the Caribous. The two aircraft were flying low along the Mekong when Bill dipped his wings to signal they had arrived. Bill began a wide circular landing pattern and lined up with his airstrip. He broke radio silence to call his hangar to let them know to keep the runway clear. Bill landed first and David circled once more to give Bill a chance to taxi to the hangar before landing the second plane. After David also taxied inside the hangar Bill's workers set about re-fueling both aircraft and servicing its engines. Bill pulled two Tiger beers from the office refrigerator reaching one to David. They sat on Bill's desk and discussed their next moves.

"Get a couple days rest David. I will be occupied with changing our operations from Navy to Airforce." David chuckled at the vision. I will probably bring Vibol's brother in as his replacement for Head of Security. His name is Anchaly. He's every bit as good as Vibol. Maybe better when you consider his motivation to get some payback for his brothers death. I'll tell him Vibol pulled the pin on an implosion grenade to stop his torture. I'll erase the tape. I don't want him to know it was me that pulled the trigger. "

Chapter Six: Triads In The Wire

Khmer can be funny about death, they often blame the messenger. "Anchaly probably wouldn't understand that Vibol just couldn't be saved, that he was dead as soon as those two picked him up." Bill said. "Oh, as an experienced Hitter, I'm sure Anchaly would understand, but as a Khmer whose brother was tortured and then had his brain exploded things could definitely get a little hazy. I'd just do as you suggested. Tell Anchaly that Vibol was being tortured to death and that he committed suicide, with a grenade. " David concurred.

"That he kicked the pin out of the grenade under the desk, which also killed his torturers. Anchaly will like the revenge angle, I'm sure." David said. "Yeah, that's the cover story and I'm sticking to it. Listen, we should have one ton of China White ready for delivery to Hong Kong in a couple of weeks. Let's make this delivery together OK?" "Sure. Why not?" David replied. They finished their beers and jumped on their two Honda motor cycles and headed for the compound. Mao brought Veasna along to help lift the bodies. He first entered Bill's office to search the bodies for the keys to the Mercedes. He found them in the Colonel's pocket.

The bodies had been there for only an hour and a half, but without air conditioning the air tight room was getting some what gamey. The smell of death permeated Mao and Veasna's nostrils even though they held handkerchiefs over their faces. Death, in a humid environment smells like rotten garlic. Even the most cast iron stomachs empty at the slightest contact with the nauseating odor. Mao threw up on the Thai followed closely by Veasna, who vomited on Vibol. "F--cking idiot." Mao shouted. "Couldn't you have thrown up on the Colonel, instead of Vibol?"

"What f--cking difference does it make? Let's just get this shit job over with OK?" Veasna shot back. The faces of the dead were grotesque. Their heads had come apart along the cranial sutures. Their eyes dangled from their sockets still connected by the optical cords. They seemed to have bled surprisingly little, but Bill's Persian rug was saturated with foul smelling body fluids.

Mao and Veasna spread open three black rubber body bags, with zippers. They squirted a blue foam, on each body, with a very dense concentration of hydrochloric acid to dissolve the teeth, face and hands. Mao and Veasna struggled, until exhausted, to get the bodies up the stair and into the boot of the S-500 Mercedes. Dead bodies seemed to weigh more than live ones. Mao drove the Mercedes out of the S.H.A.R.I. compound followed closely by Veasna in the black SUV that trailed slowly at a distance. Mao then headed for an obscure stretch of untilled land out near the
Vietnamese emigre village, about ten kilometers out of town. Shortly after leaving the compound Veasna noticed a black Toyota Four Runner behind Mao some two car lengths away.

He rang Mao's cell. "You have a tail." Veasna said. "No shit? Which one?" "The black Toyota." "I see him! How long has he been there?" " He joined us a block after we left the compound!" "F--ck! OK. Listen carefully Veasna. Don't follow him too closely. I want him to believe he is safe. Remember where we took the girls we met at the Karaoke last week?" "Yes, out by the old Viet village." "Remember the narrow road with minefields on both sides?" "Yeah sure so what about it?" "Once on that road Veasna you can't turn around, you can only go forward, or back. I will lead him onto that road and start to burn the Mercedes. He will probably follow me onto that road. As soon as he does you race in behind and block his ass. Get your weapon locked and loaded in case he doesn't let us take him prisoner."

"OK Mao, as soon as I see the flames his ass is blocked!" Mao led the Toyota out of town and meandered, from one old road to another until at last he came to the "alley of death" appropriately named because of its location among the minefields. Veasna had taken a different route in order not to be seen by the driver of the Toyota. Mao glanced occasionally in the mirror and was alarmed to see the Toyota without Veasna anywhere in sight. He thought of calling him on the cell, but he didn't want to spook the man in the Toyota.

Mao drove onto the road and stopped near a clump of hedges. He stepped out of the Mercedes to relieve himself. Still no sign of Veasna. "Damn him." Mao mumbled. He reached inside the Mercedes and chambered a round in his Uzi and shoved it inside his shirt. He caught a glimpse of the Toyota. It hadn't entered the old road, but was instead hanging back to observe.

Mao busied himself with turning the gasoline cans upside down inside the car. He opened the boot and poured one of the cans over the dead bodies. He then rigged a thermite grenade with some fishing line and placed it in the back seat, stretching the line out through a slight crack in the driver side window. The driver of the Toyota came closer to see what was going on. Mao pulled the fishing line and the Mercedes exploded in a massive ball of flame and began sending thick black smoke in the air. The Toyota driver had driven a few feet onto the road when he decided it wasn't a good idea. He put the Toyota in reverse, but before he could exit in reverse Veasna came roaring out of nowhere and sealed him off. He opened up on Veasna's SUV shooting out the driver's side window and shattering the windshield. Veasna dived out of the passenger side and began firing at the Toyota shooting out its rear window.

Mao ran beyond the flaming Mercedes and took a squatting firing position waiting for the Toyota driver to make his next move. It came in a split second. The Toyota driver drove out onto the soggy field, to attempt a U turn, which would allow him to by pass Veasna's SUV. Whoomp! The Toyota was blown ten feet in the air straight up, its doors flapping like the wings of a black stork frightened by a crocodile. It seemed weightless at first, suspended in time, but then it came down hard on its rear end like an elephant that had been shot between the eyes. Veasna yelled at the Toyota driver, first in Khmer, then in English. "Come the f--ck out of there with your hands up, or you're dead Bitch!"

Mao ran past the fire with his Uzi aimed at the Toyota and joined Veasna, behind the S.H.A.R.I. SUV. Suddenly the Toyota erupted in flames and it's driver threw away his pistol and crawled out with his hands in the air. He made it half way to Veasna and Mao when Whoomp! his center torso was vaporized. His legs stood for a brief second from the waist down then slumped to the ground. His right arm went spinning in the air and landed on the Hood of Veasna's SUV. Mao stood staring at the arm frozen by the sudden implications of what lay before him.

He saw the unmistakable Red Dragon tattoo with the calligraphy of the Wo Sing Wo triad. He also saw the Red-Pole 426 insignia which meant that this man was an assassin for the 14 K triad out of Hong Kong. "Shit brother. This guy is Chinese. An enforcer for the triads in Hong Kong. Notorious original gangsta fools bro! " "You can tell all that shit just from a tattoo? Where did you learn to read Chinese?" "My Moms is Chinese. Where the f--ck you think I got my name fool?" That evening when Bill arrived at his office he expected to perhaps still smell either the bodies, or the chemicals, or both, but he didn't expect body parts. "What did Mao do David? Cut the bodies up and forget an arm?"

Lying in a clear plastic bag on Bill's desk was the arm of the triad enforcer. "That's some strange shit Bill. Wait a second, check out the tattoo! That's a triad tattoo man." "Can you read Chinese David?" "Sorry, I fell asleep in calligraphy class." "I can't read it either. I'm sure Mao will fill us in, but in the mean time take it out of the bag and let's finger print this guy." Bill said. David removed the arm from the bag and held it while Bill rolled each finger and the thumb across an ink pad. Bill then scanned the print card into a file and sent it to the CIA super data base.

In a few minutes a photo with data appeared on his computer screen. It read: "Li Chen Yi, thirty six year old Hong Kong Chinese male, Red Pole #426 Enforcer for the Wo Sing Wo 14K triad. Specializes in assassinations and extortion. Last seen in Hong Kong within last two weeks in a Kowloon restaurant with Huang Ho Hui, #489 Leader of Wo Sing Wo triad. Both men experts in martial arts in particular use of an eighteen inch pointed meat cleaver. Consider armed and dangerous. No further information available."

"Well he's no longer armed and I doubt he's still dangerous." Bill remarked and both men laughed. Just then came a tap on the door. Bill turned on his security screen to see Mao and Veasna standing outside his door. He quickly buzzed the electronic lock to let them in. "What's up with the Kung Fu arm?" Bill asked. Mao saw the face of the assassin on the screen and was surprised that Bill had found the man so fast. "He follow me from here when I take Mercedes to destroy near Vietnamese village." "I see first." Veasna said. "Then when he enter narrow road with mine fields, both sides, he try to turn around in mine field. Blow up." Mao finished. "He was no doubt tailing the two men who grabbed Vibol." Bill observed. "He watched the Mercedes to see where it was going next."

"He couldn't have seen you load it with bodies, so he must have assumed the men were slouched down in the seats. He's an assassin. You were driving away with his hits so he followed you. Good work fellows. You get credit for the kill even though you didn't shoot him. Anti personnel mines, even a beer bottle up his ass works for me." Bill said.

Mao and Veasna grinned widely. This meant an extra few thousand dollars with their paycheck this month. After they left, David spoke. "You aren't really going to dismiss this so easily are you?" What ever the exigent circumstances a triad assassin working right in our back yard is very serious." "I agree David. I just didn't want to pump up those two just yet. We can only assume from this that the 14K are not working within the good graces of the Ma family. Bill slipped his hard drive from the Malaysian safe house computer into a computer near his desk.

He brought up the split screen with the faces of Colonel Pao Thoeun and the Thai Meth dealer and heroin Pusher wannabe, whose name was Sanya Lumsiri. Bill stared at the Cambodian Colonel's face and started to remember. Bill hated Khmer Coppers. The definition of a corrupt Cambodian cop was dependent upon whether, or not he had gotten caught. They were all on the take. It was just a matter of who offered the highest bribe with the lowest threat of being exposed later. Bill never killed anyone who hadn't deserved it in one way, or another, except maybe the kids in the Amara incident. "Can't think about collateral damage now." Bill actually felt that his hands were clean. "Let's start with what we know. These two were trying to muscle in on our operation. Perhaps a disgruntled friend of the major Vibol killed, or even one of our own employees. Some one who knows our operation wants us gone." Bill said.

Chapter Seven: Permanent Sky

"We cannot assume just because Li Chen Yi was a talented assassin that he was here to assassinate anyone. Yet, he works for our major triad customers in Hong Kong. Was he here to kill us or the two bastards who grabbed Vibol? I trust my Hong Kong connection but lately my trust instincts suck. We have a delivery to make in three weeks. We should put a lot of thought into how we want to manage it, doing absolutely none of it according to routine, or business as usual. Whomever set this up may still have a lot more in store for us." "I completely agree." David said.

After a brief hesitation David said; "Bill, I'm going to get laid tomorrow night, Big Time." "Srey An? David you're a dog to lay that on me when I'm going to be so busy I can't even think of women." Bill moaned. David chuckled. "Man's gotta do what a man's gotta do." "You got that right partner!" Bill said with a look of envy. "Get out of here Dog without pity!" Bill growled. David laughed and left.

Srey An was probably the most beautiful Cambodian woman alive. She was an infant when Pol Pot's manic rage was a scourge of Kampuchea. At least a dozen people died hiding her from the butchers who took away life as it was served up to them. In fact, not even an infant was safer than anyone else. The Grim Reaper took every life in its path as the evil Pol Pot and his dreaded S-21 group executed men, women and children with hammers to save bullets.

She was found on the streets at the age of five by some missionaries who placed her in their Christian orphanage. They taught her English along with the urgency of loving a beautiful woman with a beard, named Jesus.

She would steal away nearby and sit for hours watching the strange bald men in saffron gowns, enter and leave their Pagoda. They seldom spoke and always begged for their food. Once she found the courage to enter their Pagoda and found it frightening. Candles were lit everywhere and fruit was strewn at the feet of an enormous golden statue of a fat man who stared off into space as though nothing, or no one else really mattered. As she turned to leave an elder monk stood shadowing above her. In an instant white doves flew inside and circled the Pagoda landing near the fruit and rice placed at Buddha's feet.

The monk picked up Srey An in his arms and took her to Buddha. "Do you see how the little birds who are full of life feed at the feet of our most sacred one?" he asked. "Yes." came the little voice. "Someday the little birds will leave this world we know and fly even higher in another world until they learn our master's secret, which will allow them to remain in a permanent sky. Look about you child. Do not think about sadness and death, for in between there is also youth, health, vigor and life, in its most beautiful circumstances. All are connected by change.

Until Buddha breathes his wisdom in our hearts we are all prisoners of change. You are a child of Buddha. It is your birth right. Never forget where you entered life, for your spirit will leave it in the same place. Go my child and know that Buddha is not outside of you, but that he awaits you in your heart of hearts. Take the memory of this moment with you child and in your darkest hours remember how the little birds were sustained at the feet of Buddha. Remember there will always be disappointments, but not hard to find in between there are simple pleasures of life, that are Maya. Nothing is as it appears. All things have secrets. Go find them and live each rich experience until change takes you to other places no more. When you hear the Pagoda bell let it remind you that you exist, here and now."

That a bell will always ring as the faithful remind you that you will exist forever, but think not so much of the future lest you lose the sweet present." She stared at the face of Buddha and watched the birds fly away through an open window. Although she was always polite and grateful to the missionaries for the kindness she received from them at last she had found her Buddha, who would take her back to her Asian heart where she belonged. Srey An grew into a breathtakingly beautiful woman and once after making tender, delicate love with David she told him the story. There after, he always called her his "Little Bird" whenever they were alone.

Because of her beauty many Khmer politicians and businessmen coveted her, each desiring to make her their concubine. She played with them and accumulated bank accounts and gifts, but she never made a promise that would end her opportunity to meet the right man someday. A night with Srey An had cost some, as much as ten thousand U.S. dollars and others, such as David, not a single cent.

David had always outsmarted women who tried to use the "sex for free" trap. Nothing is ever free. Even wives have subtle price lists for their treasures. Go cheap on a birthday present, or complain too loudly about a credit card invoice and watch the quality of your sex life disappear. "It's all about the money." David thought again. But it really was different with Srey An. He knew she had been a Courtesan to survive. All Asian woman without monetary resources traded sex for gifts. Some were indeed outright whores, but David felt completely different with Srey An and was beyond blaming her for surviving in the only way she really could have. He paid Srey An's monthly rent and food and bought her lovely dresses, and traveled with her to their favorite romantic get aways in Asia. He would marry her soon enough. No need to hurry. He knew she loved him too and would wait until he asked her to marry.

Asia had taught David not to become obsessed by extremes, or to be in a hurry. When a reason to be extremely happy arrives pinch yourself if need be until you bleed to bring your soul back into balance. When things become unbearably sad, for what ever reason indulge in laughter and frivolity to the very brink of insanity if necessary. Never let your balance get unbalanced. It all sounded good in theory, however, in the case of Srey An who fulfilled his life so perfectly David knew he would remain forever out of balance yet enjoy utter and complete happiness. He loved her and the love she gave him was enough to fill a vast and empty desert with a sparkling blue sea. He had not the slightest doubt that she would wait for him so why hurry?

When Bill started his career in heroin production in the Golden Triangle he was mentored by three old OSS men. He kept his mouth shut and his ears open and learned vital things from each of them, storing away only what he felt was worth keeping. He liked Bill Jeunesse right away not merely because they shared the same first name, but because Bill Jeunesse was serious and intelligent. A man who knew more about the Hill Tribes than any other English speaking man alive. The CIA considered Bill Jeunesse their Hill Tribes expert and relied heavily upon his advice.

Bill Jeunesse's father had been a missionary in the Shan region of Burma where Bill Jeunesse was born. Bill Jeunesse grew up speaking all five of his region's tribal languages. He proved invaluable to Bill Murphy not merely in being able to understand what the Shan were saying, but why they said it and the customs that shaped their ways. Bill Jeunesse had a Hill Tribesman's attitude about Opium. He understood that come what may someone would be growing and selling Opium, so why shouldn't his tribes get a fair share of the income?

Tony Rich was as different from Bill Jeunesse, as night and day. A CIA mercenary and a butcher who paid five hundred Kip, or one dollar to his mercenary drug army soldiers, for an ear of a Pathet Lao soldier and five thousand Kip for an entire head. Tony taught Bill how easy it was to be hated by paid mercenaries, but the one bit of wisdom David learned from Tony was that the threat of violence often works even better than the real thing. Especially if you are building a drug army, but the threat must be supported with actual violence that is swift, reliable and consistent, if it is to remain dependable as an instrument of power.

The last, Pop Bailey, was a religious man who felt that in order to bring Heathens to Jesus you had to first get them economically stable. Pop Bailey taught Bill opium's intricacies from planting to harvest and along with the chemists brought in by the CIA from Hong Kong Pop taught him how to convert the poppy into opium, the opium into morphine and the morphine into 99% pure grade #4, China White heroin.

At about the same time that Bill and David were risking their lives for their country in Laos and Burma a Hong Kong triad family of the Teo Chiu triad, which was a dedicated heroin dealing ring, came onto the scene. Their leadership was divided into three clans belonging to the family "Ma" of the Dragon Syndicates. The first was Ma Sik-Yu, or "White Powder Ma" then his two younger brothers Ma Sik-Chun, or "Golden Ma" and Ng Sik-Ho, or "Limpy-Ho." Ma Sik-Yu understood quite well that the best way to succeed in the heroin business was to control the product from production to distribution. So one day he decided to take a trip from Hong Kong to Burma. There, White Powder Ma met with a CIA agent named Bill Murphy. Bill later introduced Ma to General Li Wen-Huan who was on the CIA payroll, but was anxious to receive funds from the Poppy fields he controlled.

He needed the funds in order to pay his ten thousand man Kuomintang army. The General was keen on acquiring a steady relationship with Ma Sik-Yu to use Ma's developing international heroin network, a network the CIA had been unable, or unwilling to create on its own. Bill's main interest was Ma Sik-Yu's Hong Kong banking connections. He needed a bank that would support his drugs for arms deals without leaving a paper trail. A deal was struck and the arrangement allowed the Ma family to become the richest Chinese in Hong Kong.

Their big break came as the mules they sent regularly to New York got busted and did hard time. Establishing connections in prison that eventually enabled the Chinese to crack the American heroin market that had been previously the sole domain of the Mexican and Colombian Cartels. The Ma family went legitimate with their enormous wealth forming a media empire called the Oriental Press Group which still owns outright the Oriental Daily News, Hong Kong's most elite news organization. Their real estate empire includes all manner of businesses but their prize possession remains their Media empire which is the largest in Asia and is run by Ma Sik-Yu's son Ma Ching-Kwan.

Shortly after the end of the Vietnam war the Hong Kong police made a move on the three Ma brothers however, they were tipped off and made a dash for Taiwan where Ma Sik-Yu still had Kuomintang connections. Ironically since the Ma's could no longer remain directly involved with the Golden triangle Ma Sik-Yu eagerly embraced Bill with open arms when Bill came to him in Taiwan after leaving the CIA to propose a continuation of their business. With Ma Sik-Yu as his exclusive buyer of processed heroin Bill became the primary processor and supplier of China White in South East Asia which Ma simply redirected further on to his triad's global network.

This provided David with a secret banking initial point for his cash deposits. Ma Sik-Yu's bank used affiliate bank transfers which did not receive the same scrutiny of an individual, or a corporate deposit, shell, or otherwise. Furthermore, his deposits were reconciled and transferred immediately to his chartered bank in the Caymans, which denied any curious eyes a blip on the financial radar screen to follow. It was laundry as fresh and crisp as it could ever hope to be.

At worst, it had the potential to excite a federal bank inspector, but since the more stringent anti-laundering laws had been passed in Hong Kong in 1995, not a single case had ever been prosecuted. Hong Kong had been under such pressure to reform their anti-laundering laws that an arrangement such as Bill's was rare, in fact unavailable to other drug dealers. If Bill was being shadowed by one of Ma Sik-Yu's triads he would have to weigh his reaction carefully. He and David would meet with Ma Sik-Yu after their next delivery of a ton of heroin in Hong kong, and get to the bottom of it.

David called Srey An. Whenever he needed his soul cleansed this Khmer stunner was the doctor. Her glossy red lips and shiny black hair that descended over solid breasts that wouldn't wobble more than a centimeter on the toughest dirt bike trail set the man on fire. Her hour glass figure and long legs destroyed David by large increments. His most vile thought was her command and vice versa. "Oh David, you no love me. You have forgotten Srey An. Confess." "If I forgot lovely Srey An why are we speaking?" "David, it's because you had a cosmic accident and dialed my number by technological mistake, tell me so I can erase you from my life." David laughed out loud at this. "Srey An meet me at the French restaurant by the Ministry of Justice at eight O'clock for dinner and I swear I will prove that you are the only woman in my life."

"How shall I arrive there? Moto driver who wants to pimp me by Monument, David?" "No naughty girl. I will send a driver to fetch your glorious and sexy behind. He will arrive at your apartment and await you at seven thirty exactly." "Oh David, perhaps you do love Srey An. At the very least you are gifted at making Cambodian woman suffer with false hope." "Srey An, I do love you and it is my foreign heart that suffers under such cold and calculated mistreatment by an Asian woman who is blessed with beauty by Buddha, himself." "Shall we dance after dinner David? I need to bring correct shoes, yes?" "Bring all of your shoes but wear no panties." "Oh David! I was ready to give you my heart, but now you speak so commonly." "Seven thirty Srey An?" "Oh David, how can I refuse you?"

David arrived at seven, early enough to secure a table and allow himself the small indulgence of an order of Foie de Gras, with a bottle of very delicate Sauterne to sip while waiting. He would treat this as a sample and order more as an appetizer for Srey An after she arrived. Srey An arrived at half past eight. David was on the verge of desperation to see her and the hour and a half he waited had seemed like an eternity.

She glided in like a Goddess who had made a wrong turn in heaven. The look on David's face of excitement and delight told her no excuses would be needed for her tardiness. She wore a sheer brocade gown that David bought for her in Bali. At first glance it gave an illusion that her pubis was visible, but upon closer inspection one could see the sequins and feathers that created the effect. Her supple breasts filled the upper part of the gown comfortably. Her oval, pink nipples were nearly visible through the sheer material. David wanted to ravage her on the table, but constrained himself, ever the perfect gentleman.

Bill made a few phone calls and set in motion an entirely new organization. They were going air mobile. Bill hated the higher risk of interception on the water, especially after the recent close call on the Mekong. Things were even worse near Hong Kong and Macau. Guangdong on the mainland had replaced Hong Kong as a main heroin hub. Many of the triads were moving there. An inland drug route now stretched from Myanmar, just across the border from Riuli China, and Chiang Rai, Thailand, all the way to the South China sea just north of China's borders with Laos and Vietnam.

If Bill could convince Ma Sik Yu that a channel could be set up that used semi-tractor trailer trucks he could deliver more heroin than ever to the port at Guangdong. He could set up all of his production in Laotian Labs and pay the Laotian generals for protection. The Chinese could also be bribed. Dangerous, but still a viable option no matter how you looked at it. The bribes would have to be high though. given the execution without trial by the Chinese police of anyone caught trafficking. Still however, taking raw opium down the Mekong for processing had become something of a turkey shoot. You either adapted to change in this business or you got swallowed by it.

David felt Srey An's toe move along the inside of his leg beneath the table. He was impossibly aroused before she had even arrived just thinking of her smooth body next to him, but this was more than he could stand. "Still want to go dancing at the Heart Of Darkness, after dinner?" David asked. "No, I want you to take me on this table here and now." She purred. "Sorceress." He whispered. "Then take me to my place and take me on the floor." She said with a naughty smile. Both had barely touched their food but David called for the check. Soon, David and Srey An were twisting like Snow Leopards in the back seat of the SUV.

Veasna was craning his neck to steal a glance in the rear view mirror but finally stared straight ahead at the road. "No woman, even a beauty like this one was worth losing a good job over." He considered. Soon, they were at David's villa. David and Srey An were re-buttoning their garments. "I thought we were going to my place." Srey An remarked. "I'm sorry, I forgot to tell Veasna." "That's alright David, let's stay here. I like your view of the river better than mine anyway." She said.

Veasna was pleased to hear her say that. David's TV and stereo equipment were state of the art. At her apartment he would have to remain out in the SUV. Here, he could listen to his favorite rap stars and relax on a large leather sofa. Veasna made himself comfortable on the sofa while David and Srey An retired for the evening upstairs. David had a panoramic view of the Mekong from the Japanese bridge, to the river front Wat, but David was only interested in the view before him who was removing her panties as he ripped off his shirt in utter anticipation and desire.

David pulled her to him and they searched each others mouths with their tongues. Their finger tips delicately caressed and probed each others secret pleasure places. Srey An pushed David backward onto his king sized bed and moved with the agility of a jungle cat to his manhood taking him teasingly into her mouth holding still, while her darting tongue pleasured him. David became the aggressor and moved his tongue tip more lightly than a butterfly's wing. He took her to the heavens and back and just before the first light of dawn, he mounted her and they exploded as one into the distant cosmos of their dreams. They collapsed in each others arms and he watched her beautiful breasts rise and fall with each breath she took until he too fell into an enchanted dream where life stood still. He had his first non violent dream since he was wounded in Vietnam.

David decided he would ask her to marry him after their loving was finished then thought better of it slipping the large diamond ring he had bought for this night into her slipper beside the bed. He would propose to her in the morning on the terrace as they watched the sun rise over the Mekong river.

Veasna loved to listen to Gangsta hip hop. He didn't want to risk disturbing David so he plugged in the Doe skin large leather ear phones and cranked up the volume to several decibels. He slipped some Fifty Cent into the player and lay back on the soft sofa. Just as some people are able to fall asleep though they live near a freeway, or a train track, Veasna fell asleep listening to Ludicris and Dr. Dre. He awakened as the sharp meat cleaver sliced through his trachea.

The assassin lifted the steel blade to get more force with a second thrust to take the blade all the way through the neck bone. In his last moment Veasna flipped the switch in his hand which changed the loud music from ear phones to speakers. The noise was like a bomb going off. David leaped to his feet pulling a .357 magnum from beneath his mattress as he flew from the bed. He took Srey An by the hand pulling her to her feet as he pointed in silence to the bed. She was sobbing, but she obeyed and crawled beneath the bed. David assured her that he would be back soon. "Stay here, no matter what you hear!" He told her. David edged his way beyond the door and crept toward the head of the stair with his Magnum gripped in both hands ready to fire. From behind a large palm plant a man leaped through the air toward David. Before David had an opportunity to target the man he was upon David slashing with a sharp eighteen inch meat cleaver. David blocked his slashing move and hit the man across his forehead with the barrel of his pistol. The two rolled down the stair punching and jabbing as they tumbled to the bottom.

The man was dressed in black like a ninja with black skull cap and black face mask. He was an expert at Kung Fu landing on his feet as he somersaulted away from David's flying kick. He in turn threw a death kick toward David's throat. David parried the kick, extending his right hand beneath the man's leg as he fired ripping the mans groin apart. The bullet tumbled through the assassin's abdomen and exited through the top of his skull. A second assassin emerged from the direction of the dining room. It was Veasna's assassin. He threw his meat cleaver at David.

It sliced along David's neck lodging in the teak wood mantle behind David's head. David fired three shots. The shot group was so tight it literally decimated the top of the man's skull. David checked the front and rear doors quickly to ensure there were no others.

In the pale morning light David looked down at the floor and saw Veasna's head lying a foot away from its body. Veasna's big brown eyes were wide open. They stared toward the top of the stairs as if he was still protecting, still warning David from beyond death. David swallowed hard when the message reached his mind through the screaming noise of the stereo.

David leaped up the stair so fast it felt his heart would explode. He smashed through the doorway just as a third assassin began to empty a full clip into the mound of bed spread, sheets and pillows on the bed before him. He spun around and pulled the trigger of his Glock 17, but it made an empty clicking noise. David shoved his magnum in the man's chest and unloaded his remaining two rounds in rapid succession. The man flew backward, crashing through the French doors behind him and went sprawling in death across the terrace. David screamed "I'm sorry Srey An! You can come out now." The cd came to an end downstairs. The silence that now filled the room was a million times worse than the loud music that had filled it just moments before.

David wasn't afraid of a man on earth, but he was frozen and helpless now as he stared down at the last place he had seen her alive. He couldn't find the courage to look beneath the bed. He stood for what seemed an eternity begging her to please come out.

Then, he finally dropped to his knees and looked beneath the bed. Her beautiful brown eyes stared back at him in a painful silence. Through his blurry, tear filled eyes he saw her once lovely face now torn apart by the assassin's bullet below her upper lip. From her nose, to her chest her face and neck were gone.

David tugged gently and lifted her limp body up into his arms. He carried her out onto the terrace to the view she had loved so much just as the first sliver of sunlight flashed from the horizon to the shore of the river below. This was Srey An's favorite time of day, he thought. "Life begins every morning at this time." She used to say to David. "If you miss it each day you are only half alive." He trembled as he held her. He softly talked to her calling her his little bird. "Go now to Buddha my little bird. Fly away now to your permanent sky. Take my heart with you my sweet little bird and keep it with you until we are one again. He held her and covered her lower face with a silk pillow case he pulled from the very pillow she had laid her head on.

He was still standing there holding Srey An when Anchaly's men burst in with weapons at the ready. Anchaly kicked the third assassin's body as he yelled "All Clear!" Bill gave David space to grieve. "Take the men downstairs Anchaly." Bill silently closed the terrace door behind him and went back downstairs to help Anchaly collect intelligence. David stood with Srey An for an hour. Then he came back inside, got dressed and transported her body to the Wat, to prepare it for a Buddhist funeral.

When he was ready he gave Bill a call on their secure line. "I need for them to bleed Bill." "They will David. They hit my place too. Mao is dead. They beheaded him too."

White Powder Ma was tilling some plants near the perimeter hedge of his massive penthouse mansion at the top of his Oriental Press Group building. The building towered high enough above the city of Taipei to be able to look down at aircraft and helicopters that flew below. His private phone rang. His secretary answered. "Kind father your nephew Ma Fai-Zhi is in the lobby and wishes to pay you a visit." "Ma Fai-Zhi, the errant son of Golden Ma, Ma Sik-Chun, my dear younger brother has come to pay me a visit? Something must have gone wrong and now he wants more money, or worse, my personal intervention." Ma mumbled to himself. "Well, if he cannot follow simple instructions then he must learn the hard way as I had to do and his father before him." Ma thought. "Have him escorted to me and tell the escort to remain nearby until he leaves." "Yes, dear father."

When Ma Fai-Zhi had first come to White Powder Ma to beg for his intervention in Ma Fai-Zhi's quest to enter the heroin trade White Powder Ma had advised him to take over his connection with the American Bill Murphy. What could be simpler? Let the American, convert the opium into China White. He had proven more than reliable over many years. His heroin was as good as any the world over. Let him assume the production and risks. Things had gotten much worse since White Powder Ma had controlled nearly all of the output of the Golden Triangle. There had always been enough opium for everyone. But his greed filled nephew had insisted that he wanted to replace the American and control the product from the Golden Triangle to the streets of America. "Why should it not be so?" Fai-Zhi had argued.

His triad Wo Sing Wo now controlled all the networks from New York to Los Angeles and San Francisco and all points in between including Europe. Why should Bill Murphy be allowed to stand on the neck of distribution to take a share that rightfully belonged to those who moved the product at great risk from Asia? White Powder Ma had even tried to present his share of the heroin business to Ma Fai- Zhi as a gift, as he no longer needed the source of funds. His media empire had made him the richest man in Asia. If Ma Fai Zhi would only agree not to change what had been both a profitable and an air tight arrangement with the American he could have White Powder Ma's share. But no these youngsters must always re-invent the wheel.

Bill Murphy had always delivered exactly per arrangement. Their system had been fool proof because they had enjoyed a mutual trust. Bill would visit White Powder Ma pretending it was a social courtesy offering his person as collateral until Ma's bank would transfer the pre-agreed amount of money depending on the load. Bill's assistant David would call Bill to confirm receipt of the transfer as Ma's assistant would board the small freighter carrying the heroin beneath sacks of rice confirming the purity by random test and the quantity by weight. Neither party had ever cheated the other out of a single gram.

When both parties were satisfied, Ma would lift his tea cup in a toast to his old partner and the marksman positioned and ready to kill Bill Murphy from a nearby roof top would lower his rifle. No cash had ever changed hands as it was always handled electronically by Ma's own bank in Hong Kong. Others in the trade had always been tempted to kill each other for the large sums of cash and product, but the electronic transfer seemed to remove this temptation altogether. The American had even used Ma's bank to deposit cash from other transactions.

Ma had always known every move the American made and not once had it threatened Ma in any way. Ma Fai-Zhi believed that if White Powder Ma turned over his Shan contacts as well as his Meo tribal contacts, he could control the product without Bill Murphy and virtually own the Golden Triangle. Out of a reverse filial piety since White Powder Ma was a strict adherent to both Confucianism and Taoism, he had consented to allow Ma Fai-Zhi to make a virgin trip to Myanmar and Laos to see for himself.

If the contacts in both places agreed to supply Ma Fai- Zhi as well as Bill, what harm would there be? That would merely fall under the category of "Free Enterprise" an American concept that had served White Powder Ma quite well. "Well, let us see what Fai-Zhi has done with the contacts I gave him." Ma ventured. Ma Fai-Zhi walked out on the terrace waving his hand to dismiss the armed escort who ignored the gesture and waited for the signal from White Powder Ma, to retreat which never came. Ma Fai-Zhi bowed, but sat down before his uncle had taken a seat. The armed escort shifted uneasily at this obvious snub of protocol and good manners. The second snub came when Ma Fai-Zhi spoke first.

"Uncle, I attempted to pay a visit to the American before going to Myanmar and Laos believing it would make you happy that I tried to pay fair notice to Bill Murphy before I made contact with the suppliers, but he became very angry and began to shoot my body guards. I barely escaped with my life." "What have you done, you fool? Tell me the truth! I know when you are lying!" White Powder Ma growled. "Go back to your stupid plants and flowers old man! You think you are the only one who knows how to sell the white powder?" Ma Fai-Zhi raised his hand to slap his uncle, but the guard lunged between them with a thrust that nearly broke Ma Fai-Zhi's arm.

With his free hand Ma Fai-Zhi pulled a snub nosed .38 caliber and shot the body guard in the face killing him instantly. White Powder Ma's secretary ran for the phone and Ma Fai- Zhi shot her too. White Powder Ma ran for a desk where he kept a revolver but Ma Fai-Zhi beat him to it. Ma Fai-Zhi used his belt to tie the old man to a chair. He then placed a cell call to four triad members waiting in the lobby. "Come to the Penthouse. I'll let you in to the old f--ck's place. Hurry! "

White Powder Ma shook his white head slowly. "I was warned that someday I would be punished for my involvement with the White Powder. The I Ching even told me so. I drew an evil hexagram that told me I would be betrayed by my own blood and so it has come to pass. Tell me exactly what you did and maybe I can still fix it with money." "Shut up old man. Do you think you are the only one with contacts?" "Who are your contacts Fai-Zhi? Who would chase a young man's dream and leave a sure thing behind?" "I had a Thai who understands the heroin trade even better than you." "I also had a Khmer Police Colonel who would have protected my operation inside Cambodia." "Had?" White Powder Ma asked incredulously.

"Someone, perhaps you tipped off the American Bill Murphy that we were coming and both contacts were assassinated. So far I have lost six good men, including our Enforcer to the vicious mad dog Bill Murphy, but he will soon be eliminated. The Shan and Meo will do business with me at a lower price, as there will be no one else to sell to." Ma Fai-Zhi boasted. "This is far worse than I had feared. You have lost the American now, even for me." White Powder Ma said sadly. "Why for you? He doesn't know that I am connected with you." Ma Fai-Zhi retorted. "He is a man from the old CIA, your days are now numbered on this you can rely." Ma Sik Yu growled. "Foolish, cowardly, old man." Spat back Ma Fai-Zhi in return.

"Did you think that I don't know the routine you have established with his delivery of heroin to you? I even know the serial numbers on the filthy rice freighter he always uses to bring you the heroin. There is a delivery every month sometimes a Quarter ton, sometimes a half ton sometimes an entire ton, or more of product. If you wish to live you will give me the time and date of the next delivery. Our triad will use it to finance our operations in the Golden Triangle."

"Foolish boy. Even if I gave this information to you do you believe he would deal with you now after what you have done?" "Old ruinous dog. He will think he is still dealing with you. I will be present for your meeting with him and as soon as my men have boarded his boat it will be my man who is on the roof top, but this time the CIA Murphy will die." Ma Fai Zhi chuckled.

"If you do exactly as I say I may spare your life because you are my fathers brother." "If your father knew what you are doing he would kill you himself." Ma Sik Yu growled. The door bell rang. Ma Fai-Zhi let in his four triad men. "Get those two bodies bundled up and take them out and dispose of them. Uncle call your executive and tell him you are not feeling well and have decided to take the next few weeks off. That you may even decide to travel if you feel better. Tell them you absolutely do not wish to be disturbed by anyone."

The four triad men busied themselves with cleaning the blood away and removing the bodies while Ma Fai Zhi locked his uncle in his master bed room after removing the telephone from that room. He ransacked desk drawers searching for notes, or documents that might indicate when the next delivery was scheduled. Since the early days White Powder Ma had marveled his colleagues with the details he kept filed away in his head. Ma Fai-Zhi would find nothing.

Chapter Eight: Turf War

Li Jing-Xan was not alarmed that her sister, Li Wan-Xi had not come home in two days. Quite often Ma Sik-Yu would take her with him on a sudden business trip and Li Wan-Xi didn't always have an opportunity to notify her sister that she would be gone for a couple of days. However, when four days had gone by without a single phone call from Li Wan-Xi, Li Jing-Xan began to worry.

Then, when her sister's line was constantly busy, she could bear it no longer. Against strict orders never to call the main number, she dialed it anyway. The crude and impolite man who answered was a stranger. When asked if Li Wan- Xi could come to the phone the man answered that she had been sent on a business trip in behalf of Ma Sik-Yu. Li Jing- Xan knew that this would never be possible because in addition to being Ma SikYu's secretary her sister had been a nurse maid. Without her the old codger would probably over, or under dose his medications and croak. She commiserated for two hours before calling again and had been told abruptly to "F--ck Off!"

Li Wan-Xi had repeatedly admonished Jing that if she ever turned up missing she should use the key in the large teak wood cabinet hanging inside on a hook to open a small chest where she would find exact instructions. LI Jing- Xan trembled as she opened the small chest. The instructions began: "Do Not Call The Police. Over the years our dear father, has become friends and partners with an American man named Bill Murphy. I have been his contact person for our Dear Father. Here is his contact information. Call him and give him this cell phone number. It is a secret phone that allows only incoming calls to our Dear Father to prevent abuse should it ever fall into the wrong hands. The American will know what to do."

Li Jing-Xan wondered why her sister always referred to Ma Sik-Yu as "Dear Father." He had never done anything sweet, or tender for Li Wan-Xi, but that was just her sister. Li Jing-Xan dialled the number in Cambodia and was so nervous she nearly changed her mind. She was about to hang up the call on the third ring when an American man answered the phone. "Hello?" A moment of silence was followed by Li Jing-Xan's tiny voice. "You mistah Murphy?" "Yes, who is this?" "My name Jing. My sistah Li Wan-Xi tell me call you if she go missing. She give me numbah for cell phone Ma Sik-Yu." Bill quickly wrote down the number. "Thank you miss Jing." Bill said.

"Wait. Can I give you my numbah. You call me please when to find sistah?" "Yes, of course!" Bill then called Ma's cell. It was set on vibrate and was muffled beneath Ma's pillow, but after several rings Ma realized it was the cell and quickly answered. "Ma here!" Ma said excitedly. "Ma, this is Bill Murphy." "Mistah Bill. So glad you call." "Yes, I received a call from your secretary's sister Jing. Is Li Wan-Xi OK?" "She dead Mistah Bill. Long story. My evil nephew kill her and body guard and hold me hostage in my bedroom until time to meet for exchange of cargo and money transfer with you. He want kill you, keep product and money too. Probably kill me too. His name Ma Fai-Zhi, he belong 14K triad in Hong Kong." "Ma, here's how we should proceed. I will call back on your main line. I'll announce that I am Bill Murphy and that I wish to speak with you. They
will no doubt listen in. I will explain that our shipment of one thousand kilos is ready to arrive at the designated place on Saturday afternoon instead of next week. Instead of meeting you at your apartment in Hong Kong as usual, I will say that I would like to meet somewhere else. How about a Dim Sum restaurant I know in Tsim Shat Sui?" "Not good Mistah Bill." Ma said.

"You stand out like big thumb. Place for Locals. Not many foreigners come there. Wanchai, same same, too much Susie Wong. You come instead Lan Kwai Fong. Bigger place, more foreigner, connect also to Soho. I own restaurant name Blue Dragon. Set up meet for there. I have room upstair. Private, but have large terrace and window see inside. You arrive day before. Tell my manager password "Red Sky". He hear dat, he do whatever you say."

"Perfect. Don't worry Ma. I'll get you out of this." "Thank you Mistah Bill." Bill hung up the phone and his mind began to reel with the ramifications. Had the triads forced White Powder Ma to give up the contacts in Myanmar and Laos? He called Jon Kern on the secure line. Shan Army General Jon Kern answered in Shan dialect. "General, it's Bill Murphy!" "That's interesting, as I have been informed that you are dead." "I am not surprised. Ma Sik-Yu has a nephew who belongs to the 14K triad. He has kidnapped Ma and tried his best to eliminate me. That is one of the reasons I am calling, General Kern." "And the other?" "I have acquired two Caribou aircraft that can easily handle our product pick up when it's ready." "Bill, I hope you understand when this nephew Ma Fai-Zhi came calling he even had Ma's password. He also offered me something I couldn't refuse." General Kern explained.

"You know that I have added five thousand soldiers to my defense army. They need weapons. In addition, Ma Fai- Zhi agreed to throw in ground to air missiles we can use to shoot down the Junta insecticide planes that are trying to eradicate our Poppy Fields." "Did he establish a protocol for delivery of the weapons and pick up of the opium?" Bill asked. "Yes, in fact he did. His vessel, the Yunnan Rose, is a barge that can clear river bottom." The General said. "General, he will never make it past the river patrol north of Louang Prabhang and if he does the Thai will put a scope on his ass before he can get the cargo to you."

"I assume it is my opium that you were intending to trade for the weapons?' Bill asked. "That is correct. I believed you were dead Bill. "Yes. I understand. What if I fly in those same weapons and exchange them for the opium? I don't need an airport just a solid road without too many chug holes say about three, or four hundred meters long." "You just described the driveway to the compound at my camp near Tachilek." The General said. "I know it well. Any details on the barge?" Bill asked. "Yes the Yunnan Rose has a Hong Kong registry number, it is 374727. My spies inform me that it is moored about twenty clicks north of Houay Xay, Laos, along the Mekong."

"Perfect. I'll be contacting you soon to arrange the exchange." "Good to know that you are still alive Mister Bill." "Thanks General. See you soon!" Soon after setting up their NGO in Phnom Penh six years earlier, David and Bill met the bartender in the Walk About bar. A big, burly fellow who had been trained in the Australian Special Forces. He was a brother.

He never asked what business you were in he just asked what the mission was and within a few short days he could assemble a team of six ex-S.A.S. and Australian ex-Special Ops mercenaries. It offered a ready pool of talent and experience as long as the pay remained high. In fact they were adrenalin junkies who were ready for anything. Over the years David had stayed in contact with his favorite six. David contracted all six. After dividing them into three two man teams, he briefed them describing three missions. "The first, is to rescue Ma Sik-Yu, a trusted business associate being held hostage in Hong Kong possibly already murdered, the second, to eliminate enemy triad members by blowing up a freighter in the Hong Kong harbor and the third, to capture the Yunnan Rose, near Houay Xay Laos. We will transfer its weapons cargo by air to Tachilek.

He immediately put the men in pre-operations quarantine in his villa. Each was provided Mac-17 automatic pistols and AK47's with thousands of rounds as well as dozens of hand grenades, RPG's and various hand guns. They were provided uniforms. Phase Alpha, the hostage mission was civilian clothing low profile, tropical, tourist apparel. Phase Bravo, the seizing of the Yunnan Rose and transfer of weapons cargo to Burma was jungle fatigues. They were stripped of all identification and assigned code names, Raptor One through Raptor Six. Bill and David were simply Leaders One and Two.

Each of the men were in excellent physical condition and had seen action around the world, from the Falklands to Iraq and Afghanistan. Bill used his CIA database contact to acquire recent satellite photos of the Blue Dragon restaurant and its surrounding environment in Lan Kwai Fong. A special bird tasking was ordered for the Yunnan Rose, justified by Bill's contact from a highly reliable source that it was suspected of transportation of weapons and drugs. A satellite photo of the Kwai Chung container port was also obtained. The photos were pinned to the Mission board and studied in intimate detail by all team members. Soon David had written a complete Operations Order that broke down each man's assignment and the mission time line in hours, minutes and seconds, for each assignment.

Bill placed the call to Ma SikYu's main number. "Hello, my name is Bill, may I please speak with Ma Sik-Yu?" The man stuttered for a moment and an audible change in the tone indicated that Bill had been put on a speaker. "One moment please. I get him for you." Ma Fai-Zhi was alerted and White Powder Ma was hustled from his bedroom to the phone. "Remember! We must know exactly the time his freighter will be in Harbor and approximately where." Ma Fai-Zhi whispered in his uncle's ear. White Powder Ma Shook his head yes. "Hello Mistah Bill?"

"Hello Ma Sik-Yu. Thank you for taking my call. Ma Sik- Yu I am calling to ask if we may please deliver your product load on Saturday afternoon at two O'clock. We finished earlier than expected." "Saturday at two O'clock? Yes. That is OK. Same time to meet my place?" "Yes, same time, two in the afternoon, but may we please meet in Lan Kwai Fong? I have other business there later after we are finished. Do you know anyplace there where we can meet in private?" "Yes. We can meet at Blue Dragon restaurant."

"Can you find it?" "Yes. No problem. See you on Saturday at two in the afternoon at the Blue Dragon in Lan Kwai Fong." "Yes. Bye Mistah Bill." "Bye Ma Sik-Yu." Ma Fai-Zhi leaped in the air with excitement. "YES! Now I have you Mister F--ckhead Bill! I will show you some triad revenge. You did well uncle. Remember! If you do anything Saturday to tip him off you will die on the spot." White Powder Ma stared silently out the window at the ominous sky.

"I should have listened to the I Ching. Look what the White Powder has done to us. I am plotting to kill my brother's son. No matter how this turns out if I live beyond Saturday afternoon I will never deal the White Powder ever again." Ma Sik-Yu thought sadly to himself. Bill arrived at David's villa in the late afternoon. When he walked in the room jumped to attention. Clive Middlebury, an ex-SAS Sergeant Major known on the mission as "Raptor One" loudly announced "Leader One! Attenhut!" "Bill smiled, but out of respect for the team's military traditions he simply shouted back "Death Before Dishonor!" The room erupted with "Hurrah!" and everyone took a seat before the enlarged satellite maps which showed the Victoria harbor of Hong Kong with red flags pinned to the target areas. Map two was a high relief map of the Lan Kwai Fong district.

"The targets believe this freighter to contain certain items of value which they will attempt to take by force. This freighter has markings they will recognize. We believe they will tail this freighter all the way to the Kwai Chung Container Port sometime after it enters Hong Kong Harbor. It will not contain the cargo they expect. Instead, it will contain two hundred fifty pounds of C-4 plastic explosive, rigged for command detonation by cell phone. As soon as team Bravo, or Raptors Three and Four are clear and our targets have forcefully boarded the freighter Raptor Three will make the cell call from the escape craft which is a high speed twin engine boat. This escape craft is maintained on the freighter. Raptors Three and Four will leave for Hong Kong tonight aboard the demolition rigged freighter.Questions?"

"We should arrive at the harbor of Hong Kong at 1400 Zulu?" "Yes." David replied "What about bloody Customs? At fourteen hundred hours the Container Port is quite busy." Are you Raptor Three?" "Yes Sir!" "Kevin, You will abandon ship while the hostiles are boarding it. Exit the freighter on the north side and move quickly away prior to command detonation at your discretion. Trust me, Customs will not be a problem." "Collateral damage expected Sir?"

"Two Hundred fifty pounds of C-4 will blow the bottom out of the freighter and kill anyone within two hundred feet of epicenter. Try to stay away from other non-targeted vessels as best as possible. We believe our targets will be the only boat within two hundred feet of your freighter, as they will wish to board you." "Yes Sir, but two hundred fifty bloody pounds of C-4 should kill all the little fishes along the South China coast." Kevin remarked. "We want to leave a message." Bill said. "That you will Sir. Loud and clear." Kevin enjoined.

"After you pass Vietnamese customs and have reached the high seas remove all forensics. Nothing left on the freighter that can be traced back to us by the police." David said. "Understood Sir. I doubt there will be much left after the blast." Everyone laughed at Raptor Three's last remark. "After the freighter is destroyed you will leave Victoria Harbor in a Westward direction and ditch your speed boat just here at Discovery Bay an upscale little place on the northeast coast of Lantau Island, by this dock."

"You will then blend in with the crowd and take the public bus to the Hong Kong Airport. Bus number DB02R runs each half hour to the airport via Cathay City. The entire trip is just under thirty minutes. Team Alpha, Leader One and myself will arrive at the airport minutes after the Hostage rescue. The Hostage will have his Lear jet parked at the airport ready to return to Taipei. After we have freed him we will all then depart for Phnom Penh aboard our Caribou. Our hostage will go back home in his Lear."

"Simultaneously with, or shortly after our Hostage rescue mission Raptors Five and Six will conduct a raid on a flat bed barge with a team of nine Khmer headed up by our Chief of Security Anchaly. Raptor Five, John, is an experienced pilot with many hours flying a Caribou. He will be your ride. I will accompany you tomorrow Raptor Five to check list your Caribou and have you do a test flight. Bill don't forget to have the guards drain the airstrip long enough for the test flight and of course on the night of the mission." David said. "Our airstrip will remain dry until all missions are concluded." Bill replied. "This barge, the Yunnan Rose is moored north of Houay Xay, Laos. Just here on the map in a small estuary. A bird mission picked it up yesterday. It is loaded with weapons and explosives. All care must be taken to avoid destroying its cargo. The cargo may be booby trapped. Do not lose that cargo."

As David said this, he looked at both Anchaly and his team, as well as Raptors Five and Six. All nodded to the affirmative. "I expect you to use scuba and silent kill to capture that barge. I don't want a single frog to be awakened on the shoreline. You will conduct your raid at fifteen hundred hours on Saturday. This should provide you with the element of surprise. Once you have captured the Yunnan Rose take it to your LZ and off load the cargo to your Caribou. Raptors Five and Six you will then fly back to Phnom Penh using the empty second Caribou we bring. Anchaly and his men will float the Yunnan Rose empty back to Phnom Penh. We may need it for further missions." David said. Raptor Six, Roy Schipper spoke up. "Sir, this may be significantly after your Ops in Hong Kong. Is there a chance that someone in Hong Kong may tip off the targets on the barge?"

"Good question. You will read in the Ops Order that if you do not receive a call from me, fifteen minutes before launch time, you will scrub the mission, abort and return home." David answered. "Silence will mean our mission in Hong Kong was not a success and I will most likely be dead." A somber mood descended on the room, as each man understood the gravity of the mission they had already accepted. Raptor One spoke. "Prisoners Sir?" "None." "Yes Sir!"

"Now then, simultaneous with the harbor explosion Raptor One, who is our sniper expert, how many kills Sergeant Major?" "Hundred seven Sir!" "Yes, well Clive Raptor One, will take out their sharp shooters who will most likely have taken up residence in the hotel next door. Sergeant Major you will catch a plane to Hong Kong that leaves in two hours." "Recon the roof of the Blue Dragon and act as our Forward Observer. Send SITREPS by SAT phone.

You may pick up your sniper rifle suitcase at this address. It has already been arranged with an old contact of Bill's in Kowloon. You will find it to be state of the art. After you make your kill, throw it from the roof into the garbage bin, beside the restaurant in the alley. Either wear surgeons latex gloves, or wipe it clean. There will be a black, English style taxi waiting one block east of the restaurant. If we are not there within three minutes after you make your kills then leave without us and lay low at your favorite place until it's safe to book a commercial flight back to Cambodia." David instructed.

" Raptor Two will go with you and act as your spotter and rear guard." Raptor One broke in with a question. "I'm not certain yet, just how busy this restaurant is, but by sending me to recon its roof, this early, aren't you concerned that we may tip off the enemy?" "Excellent question. No. The Manager of the Blue Dragon will cooperate fully with you after he hears you repeat the password "Red Sky". Apparently his employer, who is also the hostage made this arrangement some time ago. Obviously, you should remain out of sight and do not stay in the same hotel as your targets." "Oh I shan't do that Sir. The mission is to kill them at fourteen hundred hours on Saturday, not a few days before." The room erupted in a chain of laughter.

"Raptors One and Two, you are Team Alpha. Raptors Three and Four, Team Bravo. Raptors Five and Six, with Anchaly's detachment, Team Charlie. Radio silence except to report mission failure. In case Bill, or I cannot speak freely our standard reply will be; "I'm in an important meeting and can't be disturbed." What we will really mean will be; "what the f--ck happened?" Call signs frequencies and other communication devices are listed in the Op Order." Raptor One asked David; "Sir, who are the bad Guys?" "Murderers, Kidnappers and Thieves." Bill broke in.

"They killed two of my drivers who were the best two body guards I have ever trained. They killed David's woman. Shot her in cold blood like the f--cking cowards they are. They have kidnapped one of their own who we will set free on Saturday. They are 14K Chinese Triads who want to steal our livelihood and bury us." "They have buried them f--cking selves!" Raptor One yelled. "Hurrah!" The room erupted. Bill waited for silence.

"Gentlemen, I said we would pay you twenty five thousand U.S., each up front and twenty five thousand after the job is done. I have just decided to pay you the full fifty thousand tonight. You will also receive a nice bonus when the job is finished!" "Hurrah!" Pandemonium broke out as David passed out cold Tiger beer and the men gathered to take their evening meal. The Sergeant Major and Raptor Two departed, as well as Raptors Three and Four. All had their detailed instructions and the equipment to carry out their mission. Raptors One and Two made the evening flight to Hong Kong without incident using the passports Bill and David had provided. They stashed their money keeping only the operation money passed out at the Ops briefing and then met at the Phnom Penh airport.

They took separate rooms in a seedy hotel in Kowloon and went straight to bed. In the morning they took the ferry to Hong Kong Island and pretended to sight see in So Ho. When they were certain they were not being followed they wandered into the Lan Kwai Fong district. By noon they passed by the Blue Dragon restaurant and were pleased to see that it was open for lunch and already filling with customers many of whom were White foreigners. The Sergeant Major fumbled with the menu and eventually ordered some fish with fried rice and hot and sour soup. Feigning the desire to learn more about how the soup was prepared, he asked to speak with the Manager.

The waiter didn't understand and brought out the Chef who believed the customer to be upset with his cooking. After several uncomfortable minutes that was attracting attention from other patrons the Sergeant Major threw up his hands and waved the waiter and Chef away. This angered the Chef who ranted all the way back to the kitchen throwing pots and pans. The noise caught the attention of the Manager who was doing paper work in his office on the second floor. He came down to ask what was the matter and was led to the Sergeant Major's table. "Are you the Manager?" The Manager spoke very broken English and quickly called on a Swiss customer who had been a customer for several years who spoke perfect Mandarin and Cantonese.

The Swiss man came with the Manager to the Sergeant Major's table. "May I be of assistance sir?" The Sergeant Major was embarrassed. He couldn't just blurt out the password to a perfect bloody stranger, now could he? He employed a clever ruse. "Yes, my good fellow, we seem to be having a language crisis." "I am thinking of becoming partners with a Chinese bloke in a restaurant we are opening in Liverpool. The name of the place will be "Red Sky" and I was just wondering what the calligraphy would look like on the sign above the place."

"Oh, that's easy" said the Swiss man who drew the Chinese characters for red and sky. "Thank You so much my good fellow!" "You're welcome." said the Swiss gentleman who returned to his table with a curious expression. The entire time the Swiss man and Sergeant Major were speaking the Manager of the Blue Dragon remained frozen stiff. The Sergeant Major took the calligraphy and reached it to the Manager who stared at it for several seconds before he bowed and said "please come with me." The Manager led the Sergeant Major and Sean Morris, Raptor Two, to his office. "Please take seat." He politely said. "Who to you this Red Sky please?" "You know very well who, Ma Sik-Yu." said the Sergeant Major.

"Him have trouble? With who?" "We are not aware of many details. Only that on Saturday, at two in the afternoon he will be brought here as a hostage. He wants no police to be involved. He will meet two Americans in your upstairs conference room with the terrace and large sliding glass doors. The people who will bring Ma Sik-Yu here, are now holding him prisoner. His kidnappers are from triad 14-K and their leader is Ma's own nephew." The manager looked both frightened and angry. "What can I do to help." He asked. "We will need access to the roof. Is there a room on your top floor where we may possibly be able to stay on Friday night?" Clive asked.

"Come, I show you." The manager replied. He led the two men to the top floor where he pulled down a folding ladder from the ceiling. He then unlatched a door to the flat roof. Clive and Sean crawled out onto the roof on all fours over to a three feet high perimeter wall. The Manager felt somewhat ridiculous to be crawling on the roof, but he didn't stand, or complain. As the three peered out over the empty lot beside the restaurant Clive asked, "Why is this lot empty?" Wu Ho Ya, the manager replied "New construction office building begin next month." "I see."

Clive removed a small laser device from his pocket and shot a beam to the adjacent hotel. "One hundred fifty meters." he mumbled to Sean, who recorded the figure in a small notebook. Clive spoke, as Sean wrote in the notebook. "Four floors, flat roof like this one. From the TV antenna it appears there's a wall around the edge of the roof, deep enough to assume a sitting, or a kneeling firing position. Ten windows per floor." Clive said. "Impossible to tell which window, until their shooters get here, or whether they will shoot from the room or the roof. Roof is too unstable as the shooter will have to lean on the perimeter wall exposing his weapon. Most likely a window position inside the room, but we must wait and see."

"Heavy drapes on each window will make it easier to eliminate rooms, as we look for the last minute open drapes. Well, quite right then! See here old fellow, what is this?" Clive pointed to a small tool shed in the middle of the Blue Dragon restaurant roof. "We keep broom, mop and cleaning supply there." "I see, do you suppose we could get it cleaned out and a couple of mattresses tossed in? I noticed on the way up your sleeping quarters have no windows. That won't do. We must have observation of the hotel constantly." "We do right away. You sleep on roof Friday?" "Yes. Can you make us some noodles and tea on Friday afternoon? Once we go upstairs we won't be coming down until our job is done." "Yes. Make excellent meal for you." "Cheers!" Clive and Sean said.

Clive and Sean took the ferry to Kowloon and then a taxi to the address David had given them at the Ops briefing. A wrought iron gate gave the old house an air of English aristocracy. Once inside, however, the decor was a blend of Ming and Han dynasty. Green dragons spewed water into a Koi fish pond near the brocaded ante chamber. Once inside, the abundance of ancient Chinese artifacts made the house seem more like a museum of art, than a dwelling with wood carved furniture and hand painted cranes on silk framed by mahogany teak wood.

Sean's eyes rolled around as he whispered; "This is quite a fokkin gun shop if I've ever seen one!" "Yeah mate. It's a bloody cover job and a good one at that." A matronly, dignified, elder Chinese woman dismissed the butler and invited them into her office where elegant high backed chairs were drawn to a long table with a metal top. She pushed a button under the table and a man carried a weapon case out, set it on the long table, opened the case and then stood back. "I believe you will find this weapon to your satisfaction." she said.

"Jesus fokkin Christ Sean, will ya av a fokkin look at this! "Sorry Madame, it's just.... The Chinese woman smiled and held up her hand to signal no offense. "Wot izzit?" Sean asked. "Mate, it's an L-115-A3. The most serious state of the art sniper rifle in the British arsenal. The British government commissioned Accuracy International Ltd. to produce five hundred of these, total, for British snipers to use in the Helmand province against the bloody Taliban of Afghanistan. It's even more powerful than the L-96 it replaced. Fires a heavier round. The L-96 could only fire with complete accuracy at a distance of one mile. This brute does the same job at about one point four miles. At that range it can still penetrate a soldiers steel helmet, or the door of an automobile.

It's scope can penetrate heat haze which has always been the primary limitation of long term accuracy. SAS used to employ a single sniper and a spotter for missions, now they deploy six snipers and spotters because this weapon is so accurate they can do silent kills of six targets all at bloody once, that. The spotters assign the targets and like punishment from the heavens six people go down at the same bloody time. Can you imagine what that does toTaliban morale?" "Jesus." Sean muttered. "I see you know your weapons sir." The lady cooed.

"Thanks Mum, but I regret to inform you I cannot accept this weapon. Not because of the expense. I'd gladly buy it from you for me-self, but shan't use it now because it is about ten times too powerful and unwieldy for the job. If my employer could have reconnoitered the target ahead of time he would have never chosen this weapon." "What about the other weapon he ordered for your partner?" She asked. Let's see. Yup. Perfect choice of weapon. XM-8 light weight assault rifle. Fires 5.56X45 mm NATO ammunition. Weighs two and a half kilos, is a gas operated weapon with a rotating bolt and has a rate of fire of seven hundred and fifty rounds per minute. Magazines hold thirty rounds." Clive added.

" Do you have the one hundred round double drums?" "Yes, I do." "Can you take this Infantry configuration XM-8 back and exchange it for three XM-8's? One in a "Sharpshooter" parasniper configuration with a 3.5X Scope?" "Most certainly and the other two?" "Make the other two both XM-8's in the compact mode, with the shorter barrel. Give us a couple thousand rounds of ammunition. Do you have flash grenades?" "How many do you want?' "Two each." "Do you happen to have K-Bar knives?" She nodded yes.

"How do you wish to reconcile the transaction changes, shall I call my employer? Mum." "No need. Bill has had an account with me since the old days. Add two K-Bars. Is that it?" "Yes, thanks much." Clive replied. "Out of curiosity, Mum, I know the U.K. pays about five thousand Pounds per rifle for the L-115-A3 and it's nearly impossible to get them if you aren't still in the military, how much would this one have cost, had we taken it?" "Ten thousand Sterling and change." She replied. Sean's eyebrows went to the top of his forehead. "How long will it take to change the order to the XM-8's?" "You're in luck. Both of my gun smiths are here. Can you come back in an hour, or would you care for some tea and wait here for the order?" "We'll wait Mum."

As the men sipped Green tea Clive explained why he changed the order. "I had to make the changes Sean. Can you bloody see us lugging that monster up the stairs, just to blow the head off a bugger only one hundred fifty meters away? I wouldn't be able to live that one down in a hundred fokkin years mate!" Clive said with disgust. "I'm glad you know your weapons so well." Sean replied. "You also bloody know that I don't need no fokkin spotter at that bloody range?" Clive said sharply. "Great! What am I doin' here then Clive?" "You're bloody covering me arse, that's what! Don't you bloody forget it either mate!" "Oh yeah right then! I almost bloody forgot!" Both men chuckled.

Within an hour the weapons and ammunition were divided between two canvas bags with carrying straps. The two men shouldered the bags and returned by taxi to their hotel in Kowloon. The nosy desk clerk in the cheap hotel where they had rooms stared at the two heavy bags as they waited for their room keys. "Been out shopping!" Clive said to the little man. "Chinese Toys." Sean explained. Both men chuckled as they disappeared in their rooms, to fine tune their toys.

The voyage of the S.H.A.R.I. freighter, had been a steady, but uneventful one until it left Cambodia and entered Vietnam, headed for the mouth of the Mekong delta and the South China Sea. Raptor Three, Kevin Steele, was an ex-Royal Navy frigate Commander. He was cross trained with the American Navy Seals and was as tough as nails. Ted Waverly, Raptor Four was an ex-Australian Special Forces Captain.

They were quite peaceful fellows except when they were drinking. They had once held off an entire company of Thai police in a beer bar in Pattaya. An ignorant bar manager had attempted to cheat Kevin out of three thousand Baht, which he claimed the two owed for lady drinks for every girl in the bar. Ted had already paid the bill to include a generous amount of lady drinks and had even left a decent tip.

When three Muay Thai martial arts experts suddenly appeared and lunged at Kevin both Kevin and Ted chewed them to pieces in ten seconds flat. The Thai police Captain ordered thirty of his best policemen to attack and secure the two men. The first five policemen were broken to pieces and disarmed. The remaining twenty five surrounded the place and were held at a stand still. Finally, both the British and Australian Consulates flew down from Bangkok to arrange a surrender of all weapons and an immediate deportation of both men to Melbourne, Australia.

That had ended their stay in Thailand, but not South East Asia. They returned to Phnom Penh and had since drifted occasionally to Laos and Vietnam on odd security jobs. This assignment with David, who they had grown to trust completely had been a God send for both men who had nearly come to the end of their finances. They were still not certain about Bill. He seemed more like a typical American, throwing his money about like it had no bloody end. They couldn't believe he was paying every bloody man on this mission the same fifty thousand American, each! "Even the bloody Khmer for Christ sake!" Ted had said to Kevin.

"It's his bloody money Ted, he can fokkin set it ablaze with a match if he wants to." Kevin had replied. "Yeah, mate that's true, but if he could've waited to fly our arses back from Hong Kong we would have done the whole fokkin job for the same fifty he paid us and dash the fokkin bonus we woulda done it all mate. Instead he hires a bloody army to do a two man job." "Maybe he has his reasons Ted. Maybe he wants someone to believe they're up against a whole fokkin army, know what I mean? Like why would he want to blow up a perfectly floatable tin can such as this with about twenty times more C-4 than he woulda needed to sink the old bitch?

Americans are the least understandable of her majesty's subjects throughout the Common Wealth. Right up there with the bone headed Roos in my books." "Get thee stoffed!" Came Ted's reply. Both men laughed. Ted sheepishly informed Kevin of a new discovery. "There's a fridgie in the galley mate. Full of Filipino beer and Tiger beers too." Ted observed. "If you take a single drop, I'll fokkin shoot you. No drinkin on a mission." Kevin said sternly. "I know. I was just testin ya mate!" Ted retorted. There was a crescent moon this night. It slipped mischievously between dark wispy clouds. It's silver reflection scattered across the wake of the freighter like small fragments of glass.

Muddy water seemed blacker at night and took on a crisp mirror like quality. Kevin had on running lights to avoid hitting other boats, but he had no protection against hitting sand bars, other than to hug the middle of the river and hope. The flood lights of the small Vietnamese speed boat suddenly changed the soothing darkness into a hostile assault on Kevin's eyes. The loud speaker added to the insult. The voice began in Vietnamese then changed to Khmer and finally English. "Hold fast and prepare to be boarded. This is the Vietnam River Police and Customs. Please have your ship's log, cargo manifest and immigration documents, ready for inspection." Within minutes three Vietnamese policemen and two customs inspectors had boarded the freighter. "How many persons are on this freighter?" "Myself and my engineer Sir." Kevin answered.

"Your manifest says you are carrying five hundred kilos of hybrid rice. What is that?" "We are a U.N. affiliated religious NGO that performs research on rice, to multiply crops for impoverished countries. This load is headed for a laboratory in Taipei, Sir." Kevin said solemnly. The lead policeman pointed at the stair and the two inspectors went below.

The rice was packed in fifty kilo bags and stacked on top of the bag which contained the two hundred fifty pounds of C-4. Detonation cord was wrapped tightly around that bag and concealed by loose rice. An electric detonator rigged to a cell phone with a spare battery switch was laying beneath the rice with a wire antenna extending vertically to the outside of the freighter through a maintenance hatch. The police commander perused the documents and waited for his customs inspectors. They returned soon and shook their heads no. "It seems they are satisfied with your cargo Captain, but I am not satisfied with documents." "Oh? What is wrong?" Kevin asked.

"You have no document showing permission from our Department of Agriculture to transport foreign grown rice through our territories. I am afraid I must ask you to follow us to our port. Your ship will be seized along with all valuables on board until a fine has been levied and paid." "Is there anyway Sir, that I can pay you a fee now and you let us continue on our way? " Kevin pleaded. "This shipment is urgently needed to continue our very important work." Kevin asked. "You mean a bribe?" "No Sir, just a fee to address the problem." "Do you know I can have you imprisoned for very long time for offering bribe?" "I'm not offering a bribe Sir."

The police Commander reached for his pistol, but before he could remove it from the holster Kevin grabbed the man by the wrist and crushed his trachea with a single rapid blow. Ted pushed the other two policemen against the wall preventing them from being able to reach for their weapons. Kevin shot both of them in the head. The two customs inspectors made a desperate dive back onto their patrol boat. A lone gunner was loading his machine gun with a belt of ammunition as Kevin emptied the dead police Commander's 9 mm pistol into the Machine Gunner's chest.

The inspectors were rifling desperately through their duffle bags in search of the pistols they should have been wearing. Ted drew a quick breath and took them both out with head shots with the 9 mm he had taken from the dead policemen. He then threw the three policemen's bodies back onto their patrol boat. Kevin quickly poured the patrol boat's spare gas containers on the bodies and the engine area. Kevin then yelled to Ted to shoot a flare into the patrol boat as he gave his own engine full power toward the South China Sea. The patrol boat exploded in flames in all directions. The boat sank so quickly that the return of darkness caused red and white spots to fill the vision of both Kevin and Ted.

Kevin squinted as he piloted the freighter toward the high seas. He ran under a complete black out and both men prayed they wouldn't be intercepted before they were free of the Vietnamese coast line. Team Bravo had drawn first blood on the mission. Ted thought to himself. That should be worth some beers and women when they returned to Phnom Penh, he thought. Ted was about to mention this to Kevin but thought better of it. They both knew these had been bad kills. Necessary, but bad. Not the kind you drink to celebrate but instead the kind you drink to forget. Ted walked down the stair to the galley and loaded his arms with cold Tiger beer. Kevin didn't offer a single word of protest as Ted opened two bottles on the rough ledge of a window.

"I bloody hate collateral damage Ted, but they bloody didn't give me a choice." Kevin lamented. "They bloody never do Kevin. Whether they are bloody innocent, or bloody eaten up with authority, they get in the fokkin way every time. It's like an ethnic death wish mate!" Ted observed. "Here Here!" Kevin said as they clinked their beer bottles and continued to devour the northward current with the ill fated vessel.

As dawn exploded out of the East the freighter drifted on calm seas, ever closer to their target. Kevin had timed his speed perfectly. They would reach the Kwai Chung Container port almost exactly at fourteen hundred Zulu today. The beer had all been finished on Friday afternoon and both men were drinking bottled water to rehydrate. Kevin kept thinking of the Vietnamese police. "They must have all had families and didn't need to die. The ones ahead were killers, who had already taken lives from our side. I won't bat an eyelash when they die." He thought. At thirteen hundred Zulu, they saw the first glimpse of the mountains that formed the natural harbor of Hong Kong. As they drew closer they could see the majestic high rise buildings and towers that made up one of the most beautiful coastlines in the world.

Kevin kept Lantau Island to his Northwest aiming his ship on a course that would allow him to just skirt the Eastern coast of Cheung Chau Island, then maneuver across some of the busiest sea lanes in the world to Kowloon and their destination. Ted saw them first. A small yacht had begun to trail behind them. Kevin used his binoculars to confirm it. "It can't be our hostiles." He thought.

They were setting up a tripod with what appeared to be a rather sophisticated video camera. He counted eight men and two women. Then, through the haze and trailing the lead boat, by no more than one hundred meters, he saw them. A large speed boat with twelve heavily armed men all dressed in black. "What did these two boats have to do with each other?" He wondered, as he continued onward to the Container Port.

Clive and Sean spent an uncomfortable Friday night in the shack on the roof. Clive spent most of the evening watching the hotel, then just after midnight he saw the SUV with dark tinted windows pull around the corner and circle the block once parking on the street fifty meters away from the hotel. Two men dressed in black unloaded two large canvas bags and made their way inside. After ten minutes a light came on in the sixth room from the front on the top floor of the hotel.

Clive ducked down below the perimeter wall and crawled further toward the Southwest corner of the restaurant roof. "No sense getting caught staring at each other through our sniper scopes this early." Clive thought. Clive pulled out a small, but powerful set of binoculars and watched the two men set up a table by the window. "This will be your firing position eh? My good fellow?" Another table was set beside the first. "Now your spotter has a table too?" The fact that he was using a spotter spoke volumes to Clive. "Wait a minute! Wat's this? He has an L-96!" "Fokkin 'ell! Maybe he has the same supplier we do!" Clive thought.

He was about to wake Sean but decided it would be better to let him sleep. He needed Sean at his best tomorrow. "What was it the Americans played on the telly?" Don't under estimate the value of a good night's sleep? No wat was the other commercial I saw on the telly when I took the missus to Las Vegas, the year before she left me for good and took the kids with her? I stayed at a Holiday Inn Express! That was it." "Always had some bloke who just did something impossible who always gave credit to the fokkin hotel. The Americans were funny bastards once you understood them. Understanding them was the hard part." Clive reflected.

"Wat in the fok do you think yer gonna do with that one Laddy?" Clive pondered in silence. "L-96. Killin' fokkin elephants are we?" Suddenly the drapes were closed. Five minutes later, the room went dark. "That's it me lovelies. Get a good nights sleep. Maybe the bastards had seen the same American telly commercial too. Better take the same advice me sel'," Clive decided. Clive crawled into the shack and placed his loaded XM-8 beside his leg and unsheathed his K-Bar laying it carefully within reach should he suddenly need it. He left the door to the shack open to be sure to catch the first light. Clive was an early riser, but it wouldn't do to sleep through this one.

He closed his eyes and drifted off into a fitful sleep. He was back in the strange feather like grass of the Falklands. Crawling between the clumps of grass looking for a place to set up and bring down some more Argentina army officers with his "love Angel" his pet name for his sniper rifle. David was impressed with Raptor five's ability to fly the Caribou. He gave David some thrills when he showed how easily the aircraft turned completely on its side to slide between trees and then level off again. Raptor Five was the only American mercenary in the entire group. John Mason had flown many missions for the CIA in Colombia, Panama, Nicaragua, The Dominican Republic and Costa Rica.

He looked up Bill when he first arrived in Phnom Penh and had been under close scrutiny as a potentially permanent pilot in Bill's organization. The only reason Bill hadn't accepted John with open arms was because John had flown only insertions and weapons deliveries. He had never been involved with drugs and Bill wasn't certain how it would settle when John found out he was dealing with an ex-CIA heroin drug King pin. If he performed well on this mission Bill had decided to lay it all in front of him and let him decide. Raptor six, was a brilliant tactician.

He served as a CIA advisor to the U.S. Special Forces during the take down of the Taliban in Afghanistan living and fighting, side by side, with the Northern war lords. Roy Schipper had applied his brilliance quite well in Afghanistan and it was he, who began to employ pro-Bhutto Pakistanis as Forward Observers and Spies that had accounted for so many Al Qaeda leaders being eliminated by Predator missiles in Waziristan. He laid out a plan to use two, two man Khmer teams disguised as fishermen to recon the Yunnan Rose to conduct an enemy head count and supply the best places of initial assault. Roy Schipper was an enigma. He spoke with a South African accent, but was unmistakably Dutch.

His involvement with U.S. Special Forces in Afghanistan was kept ultra secret, in an otherwise, traceable and logical past. Roy was quiet and never ventured any information that wasn't needed in a mission. Roy quite frankly gave Bill the creeps, but David saw value in him and so he was a team member based on that fact alone. Roy approached David after he returned from the test flight with John Mason. With one sweeping observation he saved the mission from certain disaster. "David, could you please take a look at your satellite map with me?" "Sure Roy, what's up?" They walked into the hangar which had now become an Ops Center. "You see these blurry areas just here and there? About one kilometer from the Yunnan Rose."

"Yes, what are they?" "Camouflage netting. Judging from the size and shape we have ourselves two attack helicopters . It doesn't make sense that a barge would be hidden so far away from town without alternate transport. It has been there for almost a week, yes?" "That's the info we have, yes." "What have they been eating and drinking? If the hold is full of weapons and munitions there should be some small boat, or other vehicle to run errands back to civilization. The serial photo just shows a tent and six people presumably guards, but no small boat. Also, look at this."

Roy pointed to a rectangular area. "What's that?" David asked."A thatched roof dwelling, makeshift barracks." "There could be thirty guards there, not including the six on duty." David observed. "Four shifts a day of seven guards. Leaders would bring the total close to thirty people." David remarked."David, we have two missions instead of just the one of capturing the barge and transferring the weapons to Burma."

"We must first take out the choppers. Do it simultaneously with the barge assault, or we will be destroyed by enemy air support." Roy said matter of factly. "Damn it Roy! You just saved our asses!" "That's what you are paying me for." Roy said with a smile. When David informed Bill of the attack choppers he took back everything he had ever thought about Roy. "I didn't think we needed it yet, but let's mount the 20 mm cannon on the ramp of the Caribou." Bill said. "We can take out the choppers with a pilot and a gunner while the river crew attacks the guard house and captures the barge. If they meet resistance at the guard house the Caribou can help take out the guard house too after it eats the choppers." David said. Bill and David worked with the mechanics several hours until the Caribou had been fitted with the new weapon.

The Khmer mechanics kept touching the six barrels and holding the one hundred gram rounds that looked like small flash lights with pointed tips. David explained why there were no firing pins. The weapon was sourced to the Caribou's electrical wiring. The barrels would be rotating so rapidly the rounds would be exploded by a precise electrical arc. "Six thousand, six hundred rounds per minute." David explained. "All six barrels rotate, Gattling style and the High Explosive rounds can tear a human torso in two, or penetrate light armor. It's called an M61-A1 Vulcan. It weighs about one hundred thirty kilos and it rains lead like an angry Monsoon." David said with a grin.

The Khmer looked dumbfounded and mumbled nasty names about the weapon in Khmer. "Yes, I agree with you it is the tail of the devil." David said. The Khmer were surprised that David had understood them. "But we have only eleven men to send against the barge and this weapon will make it seem that we have eleven hundred men." David assured them. The Vulcan was mounted on a cart with wheels that locked onto tracks that had been especially fitted for the cargo floor.

The cart had a large cylindrical drum attached to the frame to hold the coiled belts of ammunition. The cannon with six rotating barrels swiveled on a fulcrum that was blocked by bolts that prevented a wild gunner from shooting off the tail of the aircraft, or the sides of the fuselage bay. Raptors Five and Six briefed and readied the Khmer team. Anchaly had one man who had fired a twenty mm cannon before, but to be certain David had John fly a mock mission in a remote area and Boran, the Khmer gunner got to destroy an abandoned shed. With Raptor Five and Six in the lead the team boarded the Caribou and flew at tree top level all the way to their staging LZ ten clicks North of Houay Xay, Laos out of sight and sound of the Yunnan Rose.

In the Cargo hold were the weapons and munitions needed to carry out the mission as well as two small fishing boats the Khmer would need to get themselves close to the Yunnan Rose. The Caribou landed at the staging LZ at ten thirty Saturday morning Hong Kong time. As soon as they landed at the staging LZ the team set about the task of camouflaging the Caribou just in case the attack choppers may also be used for security-recon. The two Khmer teams unloaded their fishing boats and loaded their AK-47's, ammunition and RPG's into their holds.

With help from the other assault team members they carried the boats and the small gasoline engines that propelled them two hundred meters to the Mekong's edge and covered the weapons in the boats with canvas. By eleven fifteen Hong Kong time they had launched their boats and were maneuvering toward the estuary where the Yunnan Rose lay like a fat crocodile after a large meal. Using ear plugs and collar microphones the khmer recon teams began sending intel back to Anchaly who sat in the cockpit of the Caribou. "They say six guards lay underneath poncho tent to find shade. Wait!" Anchaly became animated.

"They count thirty one soldiers standing in line near thatched hut, waiting for soup and rice. All have weapons." John Mason spoke first. "Looks like you were right Roy. They definitely have us out numbered about three to one." "I thought you liked odds like that." Roy said with a grin. David and Bill had flown from Phnom Penh toward Hong Kong in their Caribou after Bravo team had departed for Laos. Bill's flight plan called for a round trip to Taipei Taiwan for the purpose of delivering hybrid rice for research at the Taipei Agricultural Institute. With only two ten kilo bags of rice in the cargo bay they had more than enough fuel to make it to Hong Kong where they would refuel.

About forty five minutes South of Lantau Island Bill radioed Hong Kong Tower and requested a deviation landing to "address a maintenance problem". He was given permission to land and was escorted to the private aircraft maintenance hangar. By eleven thirty Hong Kong Tower told Bill that he could expect about a two hour delay until an inspection could be completed. Bill and David agreed and presented their extra-flap bogus passports to Hong Kong Customs who issued them a twenty four hour visa based on maintenance concerns of their aircraft.

They took a helicopter to Hong Kong where a private car, a black English taxi had been waiting near the heliport driverless since they arranged for it twenty four hours earlier. They climbed in and Bill drove toward the Blue dragon restaurant at twelve thirty. David felt beneath the seat and found two .32 Calibre Beretta pistols with crotch holsters that could be worn directly over the pubis a place where macho guards seldom, if ever consider feeling during a body search. They waited until fifteen minutes before their fourteen hundred hours meeting then they strapped on their Berettas and began the short walk to the Blue Dragon.

They were frisked and sent to the second floor where they were met by two armed guards who frisked them again. For a stressful moment the guard looked at the slight bulge in David's trousers, but thought better of it and signaled to Ma Fai-Zhi that both men were clear. Then one of the two guards headed for the pull down stair that led to the roof. Luckily Clive heard him fidgeting with the pull down strap and quickly got Sean to crawl with him behind the shack just before the guard's head appeared through the hole in the roof. The guard walked to the edge of the roof and lifted his binoculars aiming them at the window where the sniper team was waiting. The sniper and the guard exchanged a wave and the guard squatted down against the shack.

With Sean holding Clive's legs Clive was lowered down the side of the wall of the shack. He grabbed the guard by the head poking his fingers into the guard's eye sockets and slit his throat so deeply with his K-Bar that Clive heard the neck bones crack beneath the force of the razor sharp blade. Clive recovered quickly to the shack's roof aiming his XM-8 at the hotel window across the way.

Had the Khmer recon boat simply passed by the estuary things may have gone according to plan, but inexplicably one of the Khmer boats actually negotiated itself inside the estuary about fifty meters away from the Yunnan Rose and all hell broke loose. The guards on the barge opened up with their AK-47's and the two Khmer barely made it to a fallen tree where they took up firing positions among the branches to return fire. The Khmer fired RPG's into the thatched barracks as two dozen men dropped their rice bowls and returned withering fire. Instantly, a leader of the group was on his radio. One kilometer away two attack helicopter pilots scrambled to get the camouflage netting away from their blades.

The second Khmer recon patrol came ashore and sprinted the distance from the Mekong to the fallen tree and began firing at the guards on the barge. Upon hearing the fire fight crackling as the Khmer reported by radio they were taking fire, John revved his engines and pointed to the twenty mm cannon where Boran was already taking his position. Team members were diving into the Caribou even as its ramp was lifting as it rumbled down the dried dirt trail. John Mason headed Southeast toward the attack chopper site. Within seconds the pilots and their ground crew had removed the camouflage netting and had begun to fire up their turbines. The choppers, two Cobras were loaded with missiles and cluster grenades. John lowered the ramp just before the Caribou flew directly over the warming up choppers to allow the twenty mm cannon a clear field of fire. Boran sat frozen, staring at the choppers below.

John, not hearing the cannon banked the Caribou to make a return pass. The attack Cobras were starting to lift when the Caribou passed overhead once more. Anchaly slapped Boran across the face and screamed, trying to be heard over the sound of the engines. This time Boran opened up and the cannon made one huge burst that sounded like a million elephants roaring. It deafened everyone who were cheering as they watched the Cobras both disintegrate into a billion pieces in a fiery explosion of combustive flame and chunks of metal. John banked once more and headed back toward the Mekong to the fire fight that had already claimed two of the Khmer recon team. Roy hesitated for a second and then placed the call that would break radio silence. Bill's satellite phone buzzed against his thigh.

He wondered whether it would be Bravo, or Charlie team, but whomever something had gone horribly wrong. He put the phone to his ear and said "I told you don't disturb me, I'm in a very important meeting." Bill could hear small arms fire crackling in the background. Roy, replied. "Leader One, Raptor Six. We are intractably engaged. We are taking casualties and will now complete the mission for better, or worse. I will give you a final report within the hour. If not, assume me dead and that our mission has failed. Out!"

Bill took a deep breath. I'm sorry Sir, you are?" Ma Fai- Zhi introduced himself as the new representative of Ma Sik- Yu. "From now on you will be dealing exclusively with me. Ma Sik-Yu has decided to retire. If you will please view the video feed on the screen, you will see that your heroin freighter is not concealed from us." Just then, the triad leader of the Yunnan Rose Contingent attempted to call Ma Fai-Zhi on his satellite phone. Ma Fai-Zhi tried to stop the ringing and wound up shutting off the phone.

Kevin looked at his watch. Thirteen fifty five Zulu. "Launch the speed boat Ted." "But we aren't at the port!" Ted complained. "Close enough old boy, besides look! We are about to be boarded." The two boats had now pulled along parallel and were screaming into a loudspeaker to lean to. Ted pulled the handle down and the speed boat slid sideways down onto the open ocean on the port side away from the two approaching boats. Ted snapped a link onto a lead cable and rappelled down into the speed boat and started its engines. Kevin locked the Captain's wheel throttled down and snapped his link onto the cable rappelling, as Ted had done to the speed boat below.

Ma Fai-Zhi became belligerent as White Powder Ma looked at the floor, shaking his head. "You can see on the screen that my people are boarding your f--cking freighter Mister Bill. No money transfers today. Instead I'm afraid it's the end of the road for both of you geriatric f--cks!"

Eighteen triad men armed to the teeth had scaled cargo netting and were now being videoed from their own boat as they commandeered the S.H.A.R.I. freighter. Kevin had managed to get clear of the freighter a few hundred yards when he dialed the cell. The screen in the Blue Dragon conference room suddenly recorded a huge blast just before going completely blank with snow. The freighter rose fifty feet in the air and rotated one quarter turn as it came down hard, sliding nose first into the sea. The two boats that had delivered twenty triad members to their place of final doom were also both blown apart. Kevin and Ted's speed boat surged, first toward the exploding freighter and then twice as fast away from it. Kevin regained his balance and headed full throttle to Discovery Bay. Within fifteen minutes they tied the speed boat to the dock and were walking in the direction of the public bus.

Realizing that he had been outwitted by the nefarious Mister Bill Ma Fai-Zhi pointed to Bill which was the signal for his execution. When Clive saw the sniper release his safety he slowly inhaled. As he exhaled he squeezed the trigger and the top of the snipers head blew off. The spotter tried to raise up from his chair to run for the door, but Clive put two shots at the base of his skull. The second guard hearing the shots from the roof raced up the stair. As he poked his head above the roof aperture Sean's XM-8 ripped his upper torso to shreds. In accordance with the Ops order Clive threw his Sharpshooter configured XM-8 down the side of the building into the dumpster and picked up his snub XM-8.

Clive joined Sean as they dropped down into the room below. Ma Fai-Zhi tried to pull a pistol, but both Bill and David put two rounds each into his forehead. They signaled for Clive and Sean to take the lead and assisted Ma Sik-Yu down the stairs. No fewer than twelve guards having heard the shots rushed the front door, but couldn't come in because about thirty restaurant customers who had been hiding beneath the tables were now making a desperate escape through the front entrance. Bill, David and White Powder Ma ran through the kitchen to the alley. Clive and Sean realizing that no forward progress could be made through the front door ran back up the stair until they were again on the roof top. They switched to full automatic and poured suppressing fire down on the street below killing seven of the twelve guards.

The remaining guards hunkered down behind parked cars until they heard the sing song siren of the approaching police sedans. Clive and Sean leaped from the roof of the Blue Dragon down onto the trash heap in the alley dumpster. They crawled out and then ran the block toward the black English taxi diving in as it sped by. No one said a word until Bill exclaimed; "Excellent job Clive and Sean! We would have never made it past those triad guards without the two of you clearing our path."

"Not to mention taking out Ma Fai-Zhi's sniper who had a bead on us the entire time." David added. "Thanks Bill, thanks David," Clive replied, "but I shan't breath easy until we are in the air. Have you heard anything from Kevin and Ted?" "Not yet. You should have seen the explosion of the freighter." Bill continued. "You saw it? How?" Clive asked. "Courtesy of Ma FaiZhi. He set up video so we could see him stealing from us during the meeting. Twisted bastard! When he saw it explode taking twenty of his triads with it he looked like he was going to shit himself." Bill said.

Clive and Sean slapped each others hands in a high five then Bill remembered that in spite of the fact that Ma Fai-Zhi would have killed White Powder Ma without a bit of hesitation it was still his brother's son they were talking about. Out of respect, Bill drew a line across his own throat to signal an end to the conversation. They were soon nearing the Hong Kong International Airport. "David, you fellows check in with maintenance. I left instructions and payment for refueling. " Bill said. "I will go with Ma to his plane and then meet you at the Caribou." Bill walked with Ma Sik-Yu to Ma's Lear Jet. When Ma was safely aboard Ma shook Bill's hand Vigorously. "I am so sorry this happened Mister Bill. I am without words to express my gratitude to you for saving my life." Ma's eyes teared.

"I will never again deal the White Powder, Mister Bill but I will remain in the middle for you until this gets sorted out. You have just destroyed about half of the Hong Kong distribution channel. It will take a short while, but my nephew will be replaced by someone who I am certain will pay you far greater respect. The triads own the distribution network for "China White" throughout the entire USA and Europe. You most obviously own what is left of the "Golden Triangle." "They cannot distribute without your production and you cannot sell your production without their distribution." Ma observed.

"It is a whore's contract, but it is what it is." Bill Murphy said. Bill had never bowed to an Oriental man in his entire life, but now he bowed deeply as he bade White Powder Ma a respectful goodbye. "Ma." "Yes, Mr. Bill." "Please call Li Jing Xan and thank her. Tell her that her sister is dead. She and her sister were the ones who saved your life." "Yes,I know this. Yes, I will tell her. Very kind of you to remember them. Thanks again Mister Bill."

John Mason swooped down on the fire fight with a vengeance as Anchaly strapped himself to a "D" ring near the edge of the ramp. Anchaly spotted his two remaining men running through the jungle, pursued by a dozen followers firing as they ran. He pushed Boran away from the cannon and took aim at the pursuers. Suddenly, came the horrific sound of six thousand rounds, per minute, of 20 mm cannon fire. The solid burst looked and sounded like fire from Hell as the projectiles became a stream of molten lead between the gliding Caribou and the tree tops below that fell to the side like wheat stalks as the men in pursuit were chewed into fodder.

John found a short strip of hard earth and landed the Caribou on a dime. Roy, Anchaly and the remaining four Khmer ran toward the river meeting the two recon Khmer half way. Anchaly translated from the two recon Khmer that about six enemy remained at the barge and were starting its engines in an attempt to escape. Roy rallied the group in the direction of the Yunnan Rose forming a moving oval formation with security to the flanks front and rear. When they neared the river they could see that the six remaining guards were frantically attempting to full throttle the engine to escape, but one of the tie downs was still fastened to tree roots along the bank. The barge made loud sputtering noises and swayed left and right. When the guards saw Roy's group they threw down their weapons and raised their hands in the air.

The men yelled out in Cantonese Chinese which seemed to excite the Khmer. "No! Anchaly, stop them!" Roy screamed, but it was too late. The Khmer mowed down the Taiwanese cutting them to pieces. Roy was a quiet man but suddenly, he lost it. "Why in the f--ck did you do that? They were unarmed! I could have gotten them to disarm the booby traps, or at least show me where they were, so now it's your fucking job you fucking idiots!" Anchaly was about to translate when he realized what would happen next if he did. They would turn their weapons on the crazy Barang if they knew what he had said. Anchaly thought. Roy slowly and carefully examined each area of ingress and egress and found booby traps in both places. He stretched a wire taut between the simple spring loaded detonator and the railing and cut the trip wires.

He then plugged the detonators and removed the charges. Soon the Yunnan Rose was untethered and on its way to the cross loading point. Roy placed his promised call to Bill. "Leader One, Raptor Six, over." "I've been waiting on pins and needles Roy, is everything OK? What happened?" "Enemy has been destroyed and the freighter is now at the cross load point. Booby traps have been dismantled. "That's excellent news Roy. Casualties?"

"Two of Anchaly's Khmer, KIA. They triggered the fire fight early so it's their own f--cking fault, but they did fight bravely. Did it damage your mission? over." Roy asked. "Our target's phone rang, but he decided it wasn't important and didn't answer. We never lost the element of surprise. Over" "That's good. I'm glad, over." Roy said. Post your security and await our arrival. We'll stop at Phnom Penh just long enough to refuel and we will fly on to your location as soon as possible. Please relay my gratitude for an accomplished mission. Over." "What of the dead? Over." "Put Anchaly's dead on the Rose. Over." "I'm talking of the enemy dead over." Bill at first thought the question strange.

Who gave a f--ck about a bunch of dead triads? Bill wondered. "What do you recommend? Over." "Well if we leave them where they fell you will be providing someone with an intel bonanza. I don't know whether that's a priority of this mission. Over." "Damn!" Bill thought. "This Roy was the kind of man he needed. Too bad he wasn't in on the planning from the get go." He thought. "Sorry, that one got by me." Bill said. " It's getting dark. We don't have time to round up enemy dead at this point. Just leave them where they fell and hope the worms are in a hurry. Over." Bill concluded. "Roger, leader One. Out." Roy shook his head. "Amateurs." he thought. "It's a bitch to be broke. You wind up taking jobs that could get you killed, or arrested."

Roy was still angry at the Khmer and did his level best to sit alone while they were cross loading the weapons cargo. Roy worked on re-positioning the 20 mm cannon after the cargo hold had been filled. He wondered if it would be used again tonight. " Not my f--cking problem." he thought. " At least it will be ready if they need it again." Khmer were stoic about death, but Anchaly's eyes misted over when he thought of the task of telling the dead men's mothers and wives that they fought with the utmost bravery.

It was already dark when the Yunnan Rose slipped Southward through the surly waters, toward Phnom Penh. Ted and Kevin rode the bus to the airport and walked to the private aircraft lounge. Their stomachs almost turned when they found it empty then Kevin looked out at the runway and saw their Caribou idling with the lights flashing, waiting for take off instructions. They pleaded with security that they were late for their flight, presenting the U.N. FAO photo documents Bill had given them with fake ID and passports and were quickly cleared by the security personnel. They ran across the tarmac and leaped up the ramp. The Hong Kong maintenance supervisor looked at them curiously, but had already signed off on the maintenance records.

Bill lifted the ramp after the supervisor bounded back onto the tarmac and into his jeep. The Caribou received its clearance just moments before the police shut down all departing aircraft as it climbed homeward to Kampuchea. Bill informed the others that Charlie's mission had been triggered prematurely, but that Charlie team kicked ass and successfully completed its mission. "Two Khmer soldiers died for us tonight. A moment of silence please." "Hear Hear!' groaned the Sergeant Major. They were all accustomed to death, but it always managed to find an untouched place on the surface of their hearts whenever a brother in arms was taken. "Asian heathen, or Foreign Devil we all bleed the same." The Sergeant Major thought to himself while looking down at a darkening South China Sea.

John and Roy took turns at watch until finally in the small hours of the morning Bill called and asked them to pour two streams of fuel one on each side of the landing strip to create a flare path. Bill suddenly saw the flare path about two kilometers ahead. He brought the Caribou down for a perfect landing. David checked the weapons cargo and when he was satisfied that the pay load wouldn't shift in flight he poured the extra cans of fuel into the loaded Caribou.

He checked the Vulcan which was wedged in tight at the ramp, but would be ready if needed as soon as the ramp was opened. After some solemn hand shakes and good byes John and Roy taxied their Caribou around taking off above the dark Mekong toward the hangar North of Phnom Penh. Bill left instructions with his hangar guards to set out some flare path lights as soon as John radioed that he was thirty minutes out. Bill slowly taxied further toward the wood line as David walked ahead to look for sumps in the path.

The fully loaded DHC-4 Caribou even though it was the best STOL, Short Take Off and Landing aircraft ever made would need some extra dirt to reach the sky this night with its belly so full of weapons. Bill calculated the distance to John Kern's Tachilek camp to be about two hundred twenty kilometers West. The manual said that with a max load the range was three hundred ninety kilometers on a full tank. "Hell!" We have three fourths of a tank. That should give us forty extra kilometers of impassable jungle and hostile terrain to play with." Bill mumbled.

David chose to ride near the Vulcan. If they had a sudden need for it he wouldn't be able to climb over the cargo quickly enough to get it. He put on his wireless head phones which played soft music, but was connected to Bill by intercom whenever they had something to say to each other. He felt the weight of the bird as it roared down the water buffalo trail. He strained with it as it lifted skyward barely brushing the tree tops screaming for air. Once it seemed to stall, but Bill played with the throttle and its two powerful Pratt & Whitney's digested the strain and sent the aircraft ever higher in the direction of Burma.

Bill knew that the Junta had spent a great deal of their drug profits on beefing up their air defenses. They called it the Myanmar Integrated Air Defense System, or MIADS. Headquartered in Rangoon the system divided the country into six sectors. Each sector having its own Sector Operations Command, or SOC. Each SOC reports directly to the National Air Defense Operations Command. What all this meant to Bill was that if he showed up on their early warning and tracking system radar he would be turned over to an Air Intercept Operations Center which would probably kill him with a mobile SAM surface to air missile. If dying could get even worse it would be at the hands of one of the Junta's Chinese Chengdu F7 Airguard interceptor jets.

Bill knew them to be an upgraded Mig-21 with state of the art avionics and armed with French R-550 Magic Air to Air missiles. The closest air base to Tachilek was at Keng Tung. He stayed at tree top level and hugged the Thai border until he reached Chiang Rai where he flew Northward toward Tachilek. When they passed Chiang Rai the sun was just barely sending high angled haze to the heavens above. Stars which had been clear and bright now twinkled in a dull half light as one by one, they disappeared. Bill was so pleased with the successes of the day that he wondered whether any if not all of the six mercenaries might consider a permanent contract with him.

David thought of Srey An and how she had drained the last amount of romance from his broken life. Without her life would never be the same. He knew instinctively that just as it is when you fall from a horse you have to get right back up in the saddle he should keep his heart open to falling in love just once more, but old cliches' didn't fit anymore. He simply didn't want to risk the pain of letting someone get that close again. If you keep people outside of your perimeter they can never hurt you in a place that never heals. Besides, he still had battles to wage with his devils of the past after Vietnam left him so hollow inside.

He had been so bereft of expressive feelings when he first returned from the war zone, that ordinary Americans seemed like Aliens from another planet to him, the reverse just as he thought he must have seemed to them. He knew he would probably never be able to communicate with them again, on a deeper level. He felt stripped of a culture and a people who were only too ready to wish he had never been born. "How can you build a bridge back to a place that no longer exists for you?" He thought. He could negotiate his way through a grocery store, or buy gas, speak in American slang and local dialects, but existence would never rise above low level banter and meaningless drivel, such as "How are you?" when no one really cared about the answer.

His years in Europe didn't break the isolation, it merely provided him with more comfortable camouflage for the reasons he kept to himself. Until and unless they had all seen and done what he had seen and done they were forever in their world and he in his and never the twain shall meet. He felt like a cell phone with two SIM cards. One he used to communicate with his alien countrymen and the other with that rare contact which occurred when he met a brother in arms, regardless of his nationality. "Hell, I'd be more comfortable in the presence of an ex-North Vietnamese soldier opposed me on the battle field than I would be with people I knew in high school and college." he lamented. He slept with a .357 Magnum under his pillow and it had been several years before he stopped checking his perimeter at night.

The campus police at Wharton had been informed of his Post Traumatic Stress Disorder, P.T.S.D. They considered him a harmless joke when they watched him check the perimeter of his dormitory each night before setting trip wires inside his apartment, but the muggers nearby knew he wasn't a joke. One had tried to put a choke hold on David one night and wound up in the emergency room with two broken arms and a fractured jaw. "Muthah F--ckah crazy!" they would say of him as they gave him a wide berth.

In Vietnam David lived in a world of constant death. His world was deep within territory where North Vietnamese Hunter teams searched constantly for the long range patrols responsible for calling in B-52 air strikes that wiped out entire battalions and regiments of NVA. If capture was imminent the leader of the LRRP's responsibility was to shoot each of his men in the head saving the last round for himself. It had nothing to do with avoiding intelligence losses by torture. "F--ck that!" David would say. "Tell them everything." It was only about ensuring a quick and merciful death for his team, which was the only thing the enemy could not control.

The NVA were beyond a doubt the most cruel torturers in the history of humankind. He remembered again as clearly as if it had been minutes ago the sound of their panting and squealing whenever they believed they were close to a capture of the hated Americans who brought death without warning. These were the things of David's dreams. He hated sleep because the dreams hardly ever changed. Occasionally in America his need for adrenalin had been so great that he would ride his motor cycle in excess of one hundred miles an hour between trucks.

At other times, he would chamber a round and spin it with the barrel at his temple. Sweat filled his eyes as the sharp metallic click told him that death wasn't yet ready for him just as it hadn't been when he was gravely wounded on the battlefield earlier. Death was like a razor that traced and glided along life's artery. At any time of its own weight it could bring life's game to an end. The blade could over take you and bleed you out and nothing could prevent it. If it didn't yet want you it would leave your heart beating in panic without laying a glove on you. The element of not knowing and the horror of opening its final door left a vast emptiness inside that had driven many less strong to insanity.

In America David's escape from the draw of insanity would have itself seemed insane to many. He would trek deep into the forest at night and squat beside a tall tree not moving even in torrents of rain. Staring blankly into the abyss. Once a deer had come so close to David its nose brushed against his chest before leaping in the air so high it appeared to be flying in order to escape. Sex offered a healing escape from David's suffering soul. He figured that as soon as Bill's opium was processed and delivered as China White he would take a long sex vacation to Rio then Venezuela and Colombia and work his way back to Jakarta and Surabaya, in East Java.

"Maybe I should do the jungle bars in Borneo." he thought. "F--ck that!" he spoke out loud to himself. They say that after a while, the women start resembling the Orangutans. Maybe I'll just start in Bangkok and f--ck my way through Isaan all the way over to Phnom Penh. David stared at the 20 mm casings on the floor and began to laugh, maniacally. Today death had been quite busy. He had either killed, or caused many others to be killed he thought. A day of death. No sex in violence, he thought. Sex was the opposite of violence. Whenever he caused death, it made him long more intensely for life.

To be closer to life kept him from staying outside beyond the limits of his mind. Sex was the very heart of life its Alpha and Omega. "Til death do us part." he thought as an image of Srey An changed brutally from her beautiful face, to the mask of death he had seen when he looked under his bed. "Kill, or be killed." he mumbled. "Live and let live." "F--ck, or get f--cked!" David was struggling to dominate his own mind which was slipping away as a result of the exhaustion he had felt since Srey An's death. "Kill and F--ck!" "No! F--ck and Die!" he shouted as he collapsed across a pile of web gear, into a fitful nightmare.

Bill was somewhere between a day dream and his own complete state of physical and mental exhaustion when the air to air missile swooshed past his windshield missing the Caribou by only a meter. "Jesus!" Bill yelled into the inter com. He immediately lowered the ramp to free up the 20 mm. Had David not secured himself earlier to a D-ring he would have been swept out of the aircraft. "Someone just missed us with an AA missile David! F--ck! I can't see shit! It's probably a f--cking F-7. Man are we f--cked!" Bill screamed. David's calm and even voice soothed Bill's momentary panic. "It isn't an F-7 it's a Bell Ranger chopper probably a Thai border patrol. He's about to get us on radar lock for a second shot. Bank hard right and then left again." He said with utter calm.

Chapter Nine: Bait And Switch

"That should give me a good angle for the 20 mm." David said calmly. Bill did the zig zag David asked for as David walked an arc of molten lead straight into the Thai chopper. The chopper became a mist of fire and exploding fuel that lit up the sky for fifty miles in all directions.

"Hot stuff! You nailed that bastard! Yeah! We're just minutes to Kern's place. Hope we get there before any F-7's come around." Bill shouted. "Get a grip Bill." David said calmly. Bill called General Kern on the radio. "Jon it's Bill sorry to wake you, but we are close by with your package." "You didn't wake me we had some probing attacks from Junta forces and I've been involved in sorting out some after action details. Was that you who just shot down an aircraft?" "Yeah. Bell Ranger. Thai Border Patrol. He almost tagged us with a missile." "Good shooting! They are always attacking my ground forces. Glad you gave them some payback." General Kern said.

"I have to go Jon. I'll be landing at your compound in Tachilek in just minutes from now." "See you soon then Mister Bill." Bill landed heavily and rolled almost to the main gate before coming to a halt in a cloud of red dust. He attended to his instruments before shutting down his engines and lowering the ramp to the ground. General Kern arrived driven in an open jeep. He jumped out to greet Bill and David near the ramp of the plane. He admired the Vulcan and was very pleased to see the weapons and ammunition in the cargo hold. "Nice 20 mm cannon is that what you used to bring down the chopper?" He asked. "Yes. Lucky shot." David quipped. "Listen, I know you fellows must be exhausted, but can I have a few more minutes to show you something while my men off load your Caribou?"

Bill and David jumped in the back seat of General Kern's jeep and were driven to a large hangar. Inside the enormous building were two C-130e extended range Special operations designed aircraft with dual mounted 30 mm cannon. Bill and David's jaws dropped. "Both of these aircraft are identical." General Kern explained. "Each can carry in excess of forty thousand pounds and have an extended range of two thousand miles fully loaded. What isn't clearly seen and understood, is that both aircraft are equipped with a state of the art IFF system. The Thai General who sold them to me included an identifier code that allows these aircraft to fly unchallenged and undisturbed over Thai airspace.

The code identifies the aircraft as a Thai Special Operations forces plane on a secret mission. Any Thai interceptor is prohibited from even raising these aircraft on the radio lest they be giving away its secret position to eavesdroppers by creating a radio signature that can be plotted." "Damn! This means you can fly product across Thai airspace at will and never be challenged by either the military, or the police." Bill remarked.

"Exactly. The short distance between Chiang Rai and Tachilek where Junta forces sometimes patrol with J-7's, would be the only vulnerable air space you need worry about. If you fly at canopy level you should be able to avoid MIADS but would of course have to keep an eye out for Border Patrol with SLAR, or Side Looking Airborne Radar as you just experienced." "What's the catch Jon? These aircraft are at least fifty million U.S. each." "I got a good deal on them Bill, I paid mostly with methamphetamines." Jon replied. "Anyway I am not selling them. What I propose is that you equip both of your Caribou with twenty mm cannon and let me use them. They are much more practical for my needs because they are better bush aircraft than the C-130e's.

"I won't be using them to transport opium, I already have a satisfactory system in place for that. I would use them to haul troops on short notice to places where airstrips are not available. In your case, these two C-130e's can deliver the entire season of opium in one trip reducing excess exposure to interception with a great deal less danger and risk to yourselves. This season's crop yielded eighty thousand pounds of opium which you will reduce in process by a factor of ten.

After heroin production, you will have a net product of four tons of 99% pure China White. That should be easier to deliver to your buyer as you will only need one C-130e for final delivery. After you make final delivery just bring back my C-130e's." Jon said. "I have been concerned about drawing too much attention with two Caribou in Phnom Penh. This will solve everything." Bill said. "We will only have a big plane profile once a year for a few weeks. Jon, I am going to give you the Caribou along with the eighty five hundred pounds of weapons and munitions free and clear." Bill said firmly. "That's very generous Bill!" Jon said. "Not really Jon. The weapons and munitions were a gift from the triad.

The Caribou may have eventually drawn the Police to us, so I would much prefer giving them to you in trade for a regular annual use of your C-130e's. I'm very pleased with this deal, if you are." "I am." Jon said sincerely. "David and I can fly both Hercules loaded with opium back to Cambodia this trip and then return with your other Caribou within a few weeks. Is your complete crop ready to be transported?" "It's waiting in the warehouses. Then I have your hand on it?" Jon asked. Bill vigorously shook Jon's hand. "The C-130e's won't be loaded until tomorrow morning. You can leave tomorrow, or whenever you please. By then the bank transfer I assume will have already been confirmed? Jon asked. "Yes, absolutely!" David said. "Good. Then my driver will take you now to your quarters."

Would you like companions during your stay?" "Yes. that would be nice." Bill answered. "Not for me thanks." David replied. Jon looked surprised. As David walked back to the jeep Bill explained David's circumstances. "The triad killed his woman in cold blood, as they were trying to kill him.

Very bad people. The same ones who told you I was dead." "I see," Jon answered. "Well, if he changes his mind I will send him a nice companion. When one loses a good woman, other women are the only antidote." "Quite true," Bill replied. "I think he will be looking for an antidote in large quantity after we return home." Bill said.

Jon spoke in Hanto to his driver, who in turn called someone on his radio. By the time Bill and David were driven to separate and exquisite bungalows three women were waiting in Bill's living room. Alone in his place David fell across his huge bed fully clothed and fell into a deep sleep. Bill fell asleep after the three beautiful Burmese women undressed both him and themselves and neither he or David awakened until Jon called to invite them to dinner. To say that Jon lived well, would be an understatement.

His expansive mansion, centered within a jungle fortress was truly enchanted. His olympic sized swimming pool was full of women, some just girls who couldn't have been older than fifteen, but the majority were eighteen, or a little older. It was plain to see that the women and girls were there to please the wide variety of guests who he did business with. That evening David and Bill were ushered to Jon's state room where expensive oil paintings of himself and his mentor the late Khung Sa decorated the expansive walls. Some had Khung Sa sitting atop an elephant, yet others were of Jon on horse back in a blue uniform strangely reminiscent of Napoleon Bonaparte. His wall decorations ranged from Han dynasty China, to medieval India and ancient Burma.

Jon was perhaps as wealthy as the leaders of the Junta, but he brushed off compliments by reminding anyone of his humble beginnings in Khung Sa's Kuo Ming Tang army. "Please join me in my study for a before dinner drink." Jon implored. His study could have been carved from the Royal Palace in London. Dark mahogany furniture bordered by emerald green tapestry, a copper sheen ceiling and paintings of Fox and wild boar hunts established an old English motif. One had only to part the drapes to be reminded they were still in the tropics, but short of that the atmosphere stirred the craving for a fist full of single malt and a Churchill Cuban cigar.

"I know Bill likes my single malt, but I am not aware of your preference, may I call you David, Mr. Anderson?" "Yes by all means." David cordially replied. "Do you like cognac? I have just opened a bottle of Louis The Fourteenth. Will you join me for a glass?" Jon asked politely. "Delighted." David marveled. Jon passed around a sleek, dark brown cherrywood humidor filled with a variety of Punch, Romeo and Julieta and Cohiba cigars. David wondered if Jon knew that his excellent taste in cognac single malt and cigars would have been more enjoyable after dinner, but he realized he was being plied by conspicuous consumption more than looked after appropriately, as a guest.

David instinctively avoided putting the cigar in his shirt pocket to savor the excellent tobacco later, after dinner. He was expected to drink and smoke so Jon could enjoy being King of Burma "so drink and smoke we shall." David mused. In a way he felt sorry for this uneducated Asian drug King pin. "He must hunger for people who understand his lavish life style just to have a sounding board for tastes that he must have worked hard to collect." David thought. David tried just as hard to fight his deep rooted opinions and feelings that were only now coming to the surface. He knew he had to ward off the sanctified infection Manny had attempted to inject him with.

Yet Manny hadn't started the war of conscience in David's mind. It was always there, but he did bring it out into stark transparency. He was beginning to hate Jon, Bill and most of all himself for being involved in a death enterprise. For the sake of his friendship with Bill he had tried desperately to fight the surging current, to remain upstream but he was tiring now and he felt the under current take him downstream to where the reality of the effect of his life, his karma, was claiming real people.

David closed his eyes and then gasped at what he saw. Millions of wretched souls were injecting themselves with the poisonous China White he and Bill had killed in order to deliver. "Are you alright?" Jon asked, with seemingly genuine concern. "Yes, I'm fine." David lied. "I'm not accustomed to liquid this rich. I'm afraid some went down the wrong pipe." he lied again. Both Jon and Bill feigned laughter at David's explanation. David had actually felt satisfaction to put two bullets in Ma Fai-Zhi's head earlier, in Hong Kong. He didn't feel a single pang of guilt when he watched the triad people die on the freighter. After all, they had killed Srey An, or had they really? Wasn't it David's life style that had killed her? Wasn't David really the one who had destroyed perhaps his very last chance to be happy in life?

"Stop it!" David screamed inside his mind. Mercifully, Jon announced that dinner was being served and the three walked out into Jon's enormous dining chamber where a table was filled with Asian and English delicacies. An entire wild boar was centered in the middle of the table surrounded by roasted Asian pheasant and lobster flown in from the Eastern United States. After dinner Jon excused himself for matters pertaining to the skirmish his troops had the night before with Junta forces. Matters which apparently required his urgent attention. In actuality the most senior Junta officer who had been taken prisoner had just had a heart attack while being tortured with cattle prods and Jon needed to revive him to extract further intelligence before letting his men finish the job.

Bill had awakened earlier in the afternoon to discover that his trousers had been tampered with. His wallet had been rearranged as well. He told the women he would no longer need their services and shooed them out the door. He double checked, but nothing had been removed just examined. Then, he used a small microphone detector he had kept from his CIA days and found a bug in every single room of his bungalow. Bill asked David if he would mind having a swim before retiring. At first David was about to decline, but when he saw the look in Bill's eyes he quickly accepted. They were given robes and swim suits by a servant in the men's locker and soon they were splashing out toward the center of the softly lighted pool. "David, our rooms are completely wired." Bill whispered. "I had suspicions." David whispered back. "Is that really unusual Bill?"

"I suppose not, but this whole thing about the C-130e's and fly free transponders has me vexed. I have never known Jon to have a generous bone in his entire body. I smell betrayal." "Well, would he destroy two expensive aircraft? Why not just kill us? We are pretty much at his mercy in this compound wouldn't you say?" David observed dryly. "I know it doesn't make sense. It just seems a little strange, that's all." Bill said. David fell silent for a moment. "Bill, let's suppose you are right. We buy from him for five hundred U.S. per kilo of raw opium. The dealer price in Afghanistan is U.S. seven hundred a kilo. What if someone has made him an Afghan offer? Suppose he wants the weapons and your two Caribous and of course our cash transfer, then he drops the axe, keeps the dope and our money and the weapons cache too. But he would have to wait a few days because we won't deliver the second Caribou until then." "Nah!" Bill said. "I think it's even more f--cked up than that. I'm thinking he made a deal with the triads that he can't back out of. He needs them more than he needs us. They have a network across the U.S.A. We are just a production processor, who takes a cut upstream. " Bill observed

"Dealing directly with the triads who have almost never gotten involved with processing heroin out of opium makes Jon the big man in the Triangle, just like his boss Khung Sa used to be. I think either the triads, or Jon Kern's opium army, or both, have cut some sort of deal. A deal that has us processing four tons of China White for them and then they kill us." Bill said.

"You're right Bill. That is f--cked up. So when do you figure they'll make their move?" David asked. "I figure they'll wait about a month. That's how long it's going to take Hamilton and his teams to process this much junk. White Powder Ma will set up a meet with the triad leader whom ever the f--ck that is and as soon as they fix the location of our huge production of China White they will disintegrate our asses." Bill whispered. "We took out some of their key people in that slew of f--cked up henchmen in Hong Kong, as well as Ma Fai-Zhi. Whatever payback they may want for the next delivery of China White it's going to be as tempting as an entire herd of African antelope at a stream to a starving pride of lions. Expect them to pull out all the stops to take over the Triangle, kill us and take our shit." Bill said.

"Jon knows that his share, which is two million dollars for the raw Opium is chicken shit compared to the street value of four tons of White, which is a cool quarter billion. He wants to bump us out of the middle and take what's ours. If he were holding four tons of China White I'm sure the triads would give him at least twenty percent which give, or take is what we are set to make on this deal." Bill said. David nodded in agreement. "So now what?" David asked. "Let's brainstorm this shit for a while. I think they won't make a move until after we bleach the Morphine and get it loaded on their C-130e's." Bill said. "Damn! I should have guessed." Bill groaned. "Jon has always spent his money on his own ass. Sixty to a hundred million dollars worth of C-130e's with two way IFF transponders? Yeah! Transponders alright." Bill growled.

"From the minute we take possession of those C-130e's until we bring them back they will know where we are at all times. That should have rung the bell for me straight away. I'm getting too old for this shit David!" "It's not your fault Bill. He plied you with single malt and pussy. That seems to work on you every time." 'F--ck you!" Bill laughed but he never the less silently weighed the truth in the statement. "Well David, I may be getting old but don't count me out. Did you notice that the nose cone of our Caribou is sealed? Smooth as a baby's ass, no rivets." "Sealed? Why?" "Because inside that nose cone is a state of the art telephone communications monitoring system designed by NSA. I didn't plan on it, but two can play the same f--cking game. After we leave that Caribou is going to be a Trojan horse. Every phone call Jon makes will be automatically recorded and transmitted to me in Phnom Penh. If he is in fact betraying our asses I will know with whom and in real time." Bill grinned. "Wow Bill. That's great!" David almost spoke out loud.

"Bill?" "Yeah." "What if we just walk? Leave it all where it f--cking sits and just walk away man." "Are you f--cking crazy?" "No. Think about it. I have the books, right? We have a billion and change right now in the f--cking bank Bill. I know I'm a junior partner. I''ll be happy with forty percent. You can have six hundred million man. Who gives a shit?" David said. "Manny got to you didn't he? Admit it you prick!" Bill said cynically. "Yeah, well sort of. Man there's some heavy karma collecting behind this shit Bill. Think about it! We're taking greed beyond the f—cking envelope." David whispered. Bill looked perplexed. "David you know you're like a real brother don't you?" "Yeah and you're mine Bill!" "Look at me. I swear on my mother's grave, if you stick with me for this one last job I will walk with you, or f--cking swim with you to Fiji, or Brazil and we will f--ck big tittied women until we can't get erections ever again, but stay with me for the last mile mother f--cker." Bill said with a scowl.

David sank beneath the water and his whole body trembled. When he surfaced he held Bill's shoulders as he stared directly in his eyes. "OK. This is the last one Bill! If you want to stay in this shit after that, you're alone man!" Bill hugged David. "I swear David, this is the last one God strike me dead if it isn't! You promised me another year, but if you stick it out until after this last deal we'll both retire I f--cking promise."

At breakfast Jon was overly apologetic that he had to leave early the night before. Using his wireless laptop he smiled broadly as he read his confirmation of funds transfer. David had wired two million dollars into Jon's bank account using his satellite phone before going to sleep. Jon in turn informed Bill that both C-130e's were fully loaded with opium and topped off with fuel, ready for take off. "I look forward to a long and prosperous association." Jon said as he shook first Bill and then David's hand at plane side. "Remember to fly the canopy until you reach Chiang Rai and then fly between ten and fifteen thousand feet all the way to your place in Cambodia. Also although these aircraft are short take off and landing and are stated to be able to land within six hundred feet because you are fully loaded you may wish to add a few hundred extra feet to your landing plan." "Thanks Jon, for every single thing." Bill said mysteriously.

Within minutes both aircraft were greeting a Thai sunrise as they climbed to twelve thousand feet and pressurized for the remainder of the trip. Just as they approached Kon Kaen two Thai F-16a interceptors appeared from nowhere and were in a tailing position of both C-130e's. Within seconds they received their IFF messages and closed to level positions beside the C130e cockpits. The Thai pilots made thumbs up gestures and peeled away back into the clouds they came from. Bill called David on a closed frequency. "Amazing, but this shit really works." "Yes, too bad about the rest of it." David replied.

"Roger that out!" Bill signed off. Within an hour and a half they were circling Bill's hangar in Phnom Penh. Bill's airstrip was fifteen hundred feet long, about twice what was needed. Bill landed first and taxied to the hangar as David landed close behind. Doc Hamilton had a ground crew waiting to off load the cargo holds to a convoy of two and a half ton trucks. After the opium was loaded on the trucks that each displayed S.H.A.R.I. logos bags of rice were used to cover the opium bags. While Bill and David were gone, per instructions Doc Hamilton had reopened four extra heroin labs about twenty minutes into the countryside from Bill's hangar. He would now distribute the opium evenly to each lab and some very long hours and hard work would take place on a 24/7 schedule until they processed and packaged four tons of China White.

As soon as the two C-130e's were airborne Jon placed a call to Hong Kong. A matronly voice answered. "Yes Jon I've been expecting your call. Did they like my airplanes?" "Very much Madame Shian." Jon replied. "That's good. Did they take the entire crop?" "Yes Madame Shian. Everything is going exactly in accordance with your plan." "Did they give any indication that they know of the Junta's destruction of all of your heroin labs in the Shan State?" "No, Madame Shian." Jon replied.

"They communicated nothing to that effect." "That is very good news. If your labs had not been destroyed you could have merely disposed of them both, but anyway let them process our product in their labs." She said with a chuckle. "I shall have a nice surprise for them when they turn it over to me. After this season is finished and you have taken their place, I shall send you some of Hong Kong's finest chemists and we will re-build all of your labs and as many more as you need to convert the opium into China White." "Yes, Madame Shian. I will serve your needs with the utmost of pleasure." "Yes. I know that to be true. Wait a minute General. What of the listening devices?"

"What was recorded?" "Nothing Madame." Only the Bill Murphy took whores. The one called David refused them." "What about the devices in the flotation material in the swimming pool?" "Nothing Madame they would have had to whisper to evade such technology." "You god damned fool! Then they whispered! They know!" Madame Shian' exclaimed. "I would bet my life they know nothing." the startled General retorted. "I accept your bet. Goodbye General." "Goodbye Madame Shian'." Madame Shian' Ming Xian was the highest ranking female among the Chinese triad societies, which were the 14K, the Sun Yee On and the Wo Shing Wo triads. She was in fact the most powerful member who sits above all three of those largest triad organizations in Hong Kong.

The triad was born of political necessity at the end of the Qing dynasty, in 1760. A need driven by the despised Manchu leadership of the Qing Dynasty. An organized movement to restore Han Chinese rule. No outsider to China could truly appreciate, or understand the power of this secret organization that changed with the exigencies and political realities of each successive generation in order to keep the heart of Chinese culture and ethnic history alive at all costs.

Madame Shian' Ming Xian understood it. That is how she rose in the shadows like a hungry serpent. Other male triad leaders were kept from exercising delusions of grandeur and power fantasies by the brilliance of Confucianism which kept the triads small in organization. Splintered, yet connected by Chinese patriotism . Madame Shian consoled the Mountain Masters and assured them their time would come and that she would help them gain the wealth and power they so richly deserved. Yet, it was Madame Shian' who had gotten rich. Celebrated figures in history had been members of triads. Sun Yat Sen who was considered the "Father Of China," was a triad. He drew the lion's share of his funding from triad business.

Sun Yat Sen's close friend and protege' Generalissimo Chiang Kai Shek was himself a triad member who often used triads to torture followers of Mao. The triads had grown in number through China's bitter history until today, perhaps more than five hundred thousand practice the Guan Gong rituals from mainland China to Taipei, Hong Kong, San Francisco, New York and Los Angeles.

The original symbol of the triad, is a triangle reflecting the connection of heaven, earth and man. The original organization "San he hui,"or the "Three Harmonies Society," which was the forerunner of the present day triad societies was formed since its inception to keep Chinese pride alive, even when its institutions failed. Bruce Lee would never have come to the United States had he not fallen out of favor with the triads in Hong Kong which have complete control of Chinese cinema. Chinese scientists who defect to China with precious secrets of aerospace and nuclear weapons even after a lifetime of living in America have been reached by the triads. Many Chinese are prepared to sacrifice everything to give it life. The triads are the patriotic Chinese heart transcending ideology and geopolitics.

Somewhere along the line Chinese patriotism got confused with materialism and the "Dragon Syndicates" evolved. Ferocious and unforgiving, traditional triad elimination of enemies was done by two degrees. The second degree was reserved for those who had simply been in the wrong place at the wrong time. These misfortunates were merely buried alive in a tradition called Tongchi. If even a fragment of revenge had been involved then the first degree of Tongchi was delivered with personal vehemence, whereby the enemy was cut by a hundred thousand tiny razor slices then buried alive so that the dual displeasure of slowly bleeding to death could be joined with the experience of complete darkness, in an atmosphere of depleting oxygen. Such were the people who ran the heroin network from Hong Kong to the U.S. and Europe.

These were the people who were sworn to hunt down and bring to triad justice the likes of Bill Murphy and David Anderson. Bill, as an enemy deserving of triad revenge David as a man in the wrong place, at the wrong time. Both dead, as surely as the morning would bring the light of another day followed by the inevitable darkness of another night.

Edward Thompson was a pedantic little man. He had served with the CIA for nearly thirty years as an intelligence analyst. His wife, now a chubby Hawaiian lady had once been a beautiful airline hostess. She relentlessly badgered Edward to transfer to any job as long as it was in Hawaii. When they first laid eyes on each other she noticed how kind, but chronically shy Edward was. They met during a flight from San Francisco to Washington D.C. and it was love at first sight for both of them. As a reward for loyal services the CIA transferred Edward to the JIATF-W, or Joint Interagency Task Force-West, Hawaii a year after the destruction of the Twin Towers in New York.

His personal motto printed on a placard on his desk at Camp H.M. Smith, Hawaii, which was a part of the Nimitz- MacArthur Pacific Command Center, was; "I'm Slow but I'm Goddamned Thorough." Never had a description of anyone been more accurate. Edward's job was to sift through HUMINT, Human Intelligence spot reports as well as perform detailed analysis of all aerial surveillance and satellite missions that had been ordered to identify (TNCO's) or Transnational Criminal Organizations.

He had AWACS support, as well as the fusion support of the National Security Agency, or NSA. Recently, a Bird had been tasked to provide satellite photos of a river barge suspected of drug transportation activity but the black source who had ordered the mission had failed, or merely forgotten to file a post mission report.

Edward hated loose ends and was as tenacious as a bulldog until all reports had been received and classified. As he perused the satellite images he noticed the blurry rectangular shape one hundred meters from the barge and determined it to be a thatched roof dwelling, possibly a guard house as it appeared six men lightly armed were guarding the barge. Then, he scanned sector by sector and found two camouflaged areas large enough to conceal a helicopter in each location about one kilometer from the barge.

This peaked his interest. Rather than follow the least difficult route which would have been to discard the file because the originator was part of a black operation Edward decided to order another Bird mission on the same location. When Edward began to analyze the second set of satellite photos he nearly spilled his coffee. "Jesus H. Christ!" he yelled. Other analysts nearby began to crowd around Edward's desk. "Whatcha got there Eddy?" Navy Captain Al Peterson asked.

Al Peterson was the Chief of Special TNCO analysis and happened to be walking past when Edward, who was known to be like a church mouse actually yelled and swore at the same time. "Sir this Bird task was conducted last week. See the barge and a possible guard house here? See the camouflaged positions that may have been concealing a couple of choppers? Now look at the same sector coordinates of a Bird task from yesterday." Peterson perused the photos. "Damn, look at all the bodies must be thirty, or so, strewn about. The camouflaged locations are now widely scorched earth. Someone had a shoot out at the Ok Corral. Look the barge is gone." Captain Peterson observed.

"Edward, prepare a report for Admiral Donaldson. Cross reference this with routine aircraft signatures. Not many planes flying in a remote area like that. Go back to the day the first bird was tasked. Have NSA provide any radio traffic or telephonic chatter they may have for that location on that specific date." "Sir, the requestor is from a Black Ops source." "I don't give a shit! If someone is releasing souls in my area of responsibility I want a f--cking explanation." "Yes Sir!" Edward replied.

By the very next day Edward received a thick report from NSA. Benjamin Alexander, the Chief JIATF-W Liaison officer from NSA followed up with a phone call. "Hello Edward, It's Ben Alexander, how are you old friend?" "I'm fine Ben. I just received your report." "That's why I'm calling." Ben said. "Americans and European Nationals were involved in your little fire fight, along with Khmer and quite a few Chinese suspected to be Taiwanese, from their specific accents. Because it took place inside the Golden Triangle, there's going to be a lot of interest all the way to HQ at Homeland Security. I gave my report a CRYPTO classification suggest you use the same security level."

"You will find in the first appendix, a reference to a Bird task over Myanmar, that indicates some sort of aerial combat took place that same day near Tachilek. Probably Shan Army and Junta forces. First glance, it also looks like a Thai border chopper was shot down. Cross check with your Thai Fusion Liaison to see if he confirms that." "Appendix two shows SAT imagery of two Thai Air force C-130e's with Black Ops IFF, leaving Tachilek and crossing Thailand without interception into Cambodia like they own both countries. We tasked a special bird where they went down near Phnom Penh. Twelve deuce and a half's are parked there on what appears to be a crude airstrip. Because of the Golden Triangle we are putting some Bird dedication on Phnom Penh, as well as the place in Tachilek." Keep me informed from your side, OK good buddy?" "Sure thing Ben."

Admiral Ralph L. Donaldson frowned as he read the JIATF-W TNCO Recent Activities report. Sitting across from Admiral Donaldson was Captain Al Peterson, Chief Of TNCO Analysis and Rear Admiral Michael Slater, Head Of The Asia-Pacific Drug- Related TNCO Database, as well as Chief Of Operations for the IFC, or Inter-Agency Fusion Center. "Mike, what do you make of this TNCO report out of the Golden Triangle database?" Admiral Donaldson asked.

"Nothing you're gonna like Ralph. There are three ex-CIA ex-special Ops people who have gone rogue, still in our database. One is in Bangkok running a few beer bars and a massage hotel that's a brothel. There's another who we believe to be dead, without confirmation and one other who is providing arms to Drug dealers, but as far as we know, on a very small scale." "Well Mike, I don't believe someone who is in the pussy business is who we're looking for. Who's the dead guy?" Admiral Donaldson asked. "A guy named Bill Murphy. He started out being mentored by the old OSS Kuomintang guys in Laos." Admiral Slater noted.

"They taught him everything from agriculture to processing. He helped set up the Air America distribution to fund the CIA secret war that used Hmong Tribesmen against Ho Chi Minh's forces. Then he drops off the radar until the mid-eighties, in Afghanistan where he ran the whole banana, from Poppy cultivation in Afghanistan in the Helmand province to a chain of heroin labs in Waziristan. He kept the Mujahideen supplied with weapons and then he disappears again. Haven't heard from him since what is that about twenty plus years?" Slater asked. "That's your Boy, I'll bet my f--cking retirement on it." Admiral Donaldson exclaimed.

"It lines up with the killing of those DEA and Interpol guys about a month ago on the Mekong. That investigation came to a dead end in Phnom Penh where a Thai agent got whacked and now fire fight along the coast of Laos on the Mekong?" Admiral Donaldson continued. "Turf war is what it sounds like to me. They had a shit load of triad people get waxed in Hong Kong last week. NSA tells us that the dead they found where a barge was being guarded on the Mekong in Laos were Taiwanese. If they have triad tattoos this shit will start getting connected, I have a feeling. Who owns this place in Tachilek?" Donaldson asked.

"That would be General Kern Sir. He took over after Khung Sa passed away last year." Captain Peterson enjoined. "Al, line up a SEAL team and put them in mission preparation mode for about a month." Admiral Donaldson ordered. "Get someone from HUMINT to see if we can get some local Khmer asset to infiltrate this guy Bill Murphy and find out what the f--ck he's up to. No local government types, I don't trust those F--cks! Get a CIA agent who is ethnically and linguistically Cambodian. It's bad enough we're up against Asian terrorists and you name it, but I will not f--cking tolerate Americans getting involved in heroin production and distribution especially when it's one of our own and an Operator to boot. What makes an American get involved in killing his own f--cking kind?" Admiral Donaldson asked, rhetorically.

"Money Sir!" Captain Peterson replied. "Well, let's see how well he spends it with a SEAL team on his ass!" "Yes Sir!" "Ralph, do you really believe it's just money?" Rear Admiral Slater asked. "If not money then what Michael?" Admiral Donaldson asked.

"Ralph, we get these guys when they're just kids and then we drop them in the Devil's asshole with a mission Dante couldn't have dreamed up and then, when the politicians say "Tilt," game over, we expect them to come back to who they were before we turned them into f--cking killers. It isn't just money Ralph, it's the f--cking adrenalin rush and crazy, take it to the limit power addiction. Survival of the fittest. Mistakes at the top create rogues."

"You're probably right Michael, but when our trained killers do something to rain shit down on their own country we have no choice but to hunt them down like any other wild dog of a clear and present danger." " I sadly agree with you Ralph." Admiral Slater concurred. "Admiral Donaldson, I have drawn a Player/Incident chronology chart to facilitate data fusion." Captain Peterson said. He pulled down a chart. "Beginning three months ago, the Myanmar Junta initiated a massive campaign to destroy General Kern's heroin labs forty seven in all. Our sources inform us that he was operating 50% of his drug business in methamphetamines which he easily exported into Thailand and the rest in heroin which he sent into China.

 His heroin capability was ended. The primary reason the Junta clings to its military dictatorship is because it knows that if a civilian government took power there it would lose its drug enterprise. The Shan represent a competition both in methamphetamines and heroin that the Junta cannot allow to continue. The Junta is also jealous of Kern's connections in Thailand that go all the way to the top General staff. These connections were originally made possible through triad and Kuomintang connections with two Thai Army Generals. Connections that go all the way back to General Chiang Kai Shek. This explains how he was able to acquire the Black Ops Thai Air Force C-130e's." Captain Peterson observed.

"Al, as money hungry as the Thai are it still defies the imagination that any Thai General would turn over those kind of aircraft to any military person in Burma, without some sort of guarantee they wouldn't be used on Thai forces." Admiral Donaldson observed. "Jesus those planes cost us about a hundred million each. He has that kind of money to throw around? Plus it must be costing Kern a shit load of tea money to keep the Thai Air Force contacts bribed. My educated guess is that the triads have guaranteed the Thai, as well as paid them somehow. Kern has an army to feed." Admiral Donaldson exclaimed.

"Yes, Sir. We know that Khung Sa, Kern's mentor was kept under house arrest in Rangoon since 1994, but he arranged a "Hands Off" policy with the Junta which he paid highly for, but it kept the Junta away from his labs. Without leaving his home in Rangoon and using Jon Kern as his surrogate he was shipping several tons of China White each year through Riuli on across the Yunnan province to the South China Sea. He paid off the Chinese using triad connections both in Yunnan and Guangdong that connected his distribution to the triad network in Hong Kong and eventually across Europe and the United States. Kern just lost all of his heroin labs. This must have rocked his world. It makes sense he turned to the triads in Hong Kong to get not only sophisticated aircraft from the triad's Thai contacts, but a free pass over Thailand to ship opium. " Captain Peterson said.

"Al, drugs and money, like a serpent create strange heads at the top when you follow the trail. When Khung Sa died his implicit understanding with the Junta died with him. Kern and pretty much everyone who does business in Myanmar and the rest of the Golden Triangle, are now directly vulnerable to the caprice of the Junta." Donaldson said.

"They all lost their special status. I believe the Junta saw heroin as a product that was making the triads rich, but cutting into their lucrative amphetamine business, so they ordered General Kern's labs to be destroyed. This provided an immense opportunity for processors to step in and fill Kern's vacuum and treat the Shan State, as a larger source of raw opium. I also believe this Bill Murphy, to be a key player in Kern's post heroin lab destruction phase." Admiral Donaldson concluded.

"If Murphy is processing heroin in Cambodia and delivering it to the triads, it would complete a circumvention that became necessary after the Myanmar labs were destroyed. It would also tie in with the drug interdiction episode on the Mekong two weeks ago. The processed heroin was shifted from the China corridor to the Mekong." Admiral Donaldson explained. "I see. Murphy was perhaps a player all along, but now has become a super player as a result of what went down in Myanmar. But why all the blood letting in Hong Kong and Laos? Admiral, that just doesn't seem to make sense if Murphy is working with the triads."

"I know. That doesn't appear to make sense. Maybe it's an intra-triad thing, where someone wanted to replace Murphy and got the worst end of the deal. Murphy is obviously a tricky son of a bitch." Admiral Donaldson remarked. "Had to be to stay alive this long. We'll just have to let this play out more to figure out the nuances. It's all just theory at this point." Admiral Donaldson concluded. "The two C-130e's with a free pass through Thailand might indicate that a big cargo is in the offing." Captain Peterson mused. "I agree. Ok. I want an immediate briefing on any new discoveries and keep me in the loop on the operations planning for the SEAL team. Keep the birds dedicated and let me know when and where those C-130e's are at all times." "Yes Sir!"

Edward was anxiously awaiting Captain Peterson's phone call to learn whether Admiral Donaldson had any further requests for his TNCO report when Captain Peterson walked into his office area. "Edward, bring a copy of the report and come to my office please." "Right away Sir!" As Edward settled in, Captain Peterson smiled and poured Edward a cup of coffee.

"Edward, I cannot express my gratitude enough to you personally for your alertness and dedication to professional analysis. Expect a monetary reward and some extra vacation time once we put this incident to rest. For now, however, I still need your assistance. The potential of your discovery is mind boggling. We may be able to bring a lot of bad guys down and effectively eliminate the Golden Triangle as a source of heroin if we play our cards right. Get in touch with the CIA JIATF-W Liaison today and tell him we need some toes stepped on at Langley until we find out whose access code was used to task the first Bird on that Mekong barge in Laos. Whomever tasked it is the key to bringing down the whole goddamned Triangle!" "Yes Sir!"

"Then and until this mission is complete I would like for you to personally task and analyze this hangar facility north of Phnom Penh and the two C-130e's that are parked there every single day. There will soon be a Navy SEAL team in pre-mission mode. They will need your vigilance all the way to mission execution. I will let you know when they will conduct the actual assault and I'd like some live infra red feed in Admiral Donaldson's conference room when they do the take down." Captain Peterson explained. "Yes Sir." Edward replied.

In spite of the fact that Edward hand carried his request to Elgin Phillips, the JIATF-W CIA Liaison, Elgin put Edward's request on a stack of other work. He eventually got around to calling his counterpart at Langley, Virginia. "Ted we have a Level Six Priority Request to run down a Bird task that was made on the twelfth of May. Access code number three, three, Alpha, twelve twenty two X-ray. Apparently this had a Black Ops requestor." There was a silent pause. "Elgin is this some sort of f--cking joke?" "Absolutely not!" Elgin replied. "Elgin, you just gave me the access code of the Director of the Central Intelligence Agency!" "Shit!" "Yes, Shit!" Ted answered. "OK Elgin, don't do anything until I get back with you." Ted said. "This is going to have to be handled at the top. I will at least put the communications forensics together, but what ever it is you are f--cking with, it just turned red hot!" "Roger that!"

As soon as Ted began to trace all computer and voice communications sourced to the Yunnan Rose Bird task on the Twelfth of May with the CIA Director's access code Bill's CIA contact went ballistic. When Bill's special Satellite phone with a very expensive scrambler rang, Bill was almost too shocked to answer. "Yeah!" "It's Fred, Bill."

"Yeah, I know. What's up Fred?" "This is your Burn Notice Bill. As soon as we hang up destroy your phone, I'll do the same on this end. You have a level six JIATF-W special mission on your ass old friend. SEAL team and all. They traced you somehow from the archives. They sourced your Bird task on that barge to the access code I used." "They traced it to you?" "F--ck no. I'm not that stupid. I used the CIA Director's access code because it had the least chance of being questioned." "Will they set a trap for you Fred?" "I am way beyond that Pal. As soon as I hang up I will become an altar boy until I retire besides I'm under a lot less threat than you are for the moment. "

"Their search for me will run off the track when they discover that the bird task was made from the Assistant director's lap top which he leaves signed on like a dumb ass from time to time." Fred mused. "You now have a dedicated Bird on some hangar complex you have near Phnom Penh. I have no idea how far away you are from the actual SEAL assault. Me? I'll just crawl back in my hole and I should be just fine, but thanks for your concern. Needless to say, I can't ever be in contact with you again in this life." "I know. Thanks Fred, I'll never forget you my friend."

"Don't get all sentimental on me Bill. We're even for the times you saved my bacon along the Ho Chi Minh Trail." "Thanks again Fred!" "Bye Bill!" Bill dropped the phone in a bucket of acid, then walked out and looked up at the sky outside his office. Bill opened the panel on a black device which had been recording Jon Kern's telephone calls from the Caribou since he and David had left it at Tachilek. He leaned against a railing and pushed "Play". Most of the calls were in Han dialect, so he fast reversed to the very beginning and listened to the call General Kern had made to Madame Shian' as soon as Bill and David were in the
air. He recorded the phone call into a miniature recorder he carried in his pocket. "Looks like this shit is getting more interesting." He thought to himself. Bill walked out onto the street and hailed a Moto Dop which he rode to within a block of David's villa near the river front.

David was exercising in his home gym when Bill rang. David's guards recognized Bill quickly and let him in through the heavy steel gate. "Where's your SUV?" David asked. " I just felt like a little fresh air and took a Moto." Bill replied. "That's not very smart considering recent developments." David scolded. "I know. Listen the shit just got a million times more complicated. Let's talk in your living room with the stereo cranked up." David turned the music up loud. Wagner's ride of the Valkyries was playing.

"David, we have the JIATF-W crawling up our asses." Bill whispered. "Sorry Bill. I haven't kept abreast of all of the military nomenclature, what in the f--ck is the JIATF-W?" "Joint Inter Agency Task Force West. They fuse all of the biggy's DEA,CIA,FBI and Interpol together into one big happy family. It's headquartered in Hawaii and they have operational responsibility for nearly every country and Island from China to Myanmar, Thailand, Cambodia, Laos Vietnam, you name it, anyway all over South East Asia."

"They are commanded by some admiral who has unlimited military resources, not the least of which is a shit load of Navy SEALS. We're toast man. They even have a dedicated Bird on our hangar which can of course trace our asses to the labs. We're perfectly f--cked. Time to split up the funds and run for the f--cking hills. Man were you ever right." Bill said with bitterness. "How much time do we have before the SEALS come to call?" "F--ck, I don't know. You know more about those kind of Ops than I do David." "Well if they just picked up our scent, my guess is they were surveilling Kern's place and attached themselves like fleas on a dog's ass as we left with the two C-130e's. Unless there's a hostage situation, or a ticking nuke, these guys don't allow themselves to be hurried.

They put the capital "P" in the word "Professional Operator" trust me on that. They will put HUMINT spies on the ground before they make their final move. Ask Anchaly if anyone has been trying to get on board lately. If the answer is yes, hire the sonofabitch so we can spoon feed him what we want the JIATF-W to know. In the meantime we can set up a "di di" plan to exit gracefully. Starting now let's always play music and whisper what we have important to say to each other. NSA is probably already getting a fix on the institute and our private residences as we speak." "David,why the change of heart? I nearly had to beg you to continue in Tachilek."

"No change of heart Bill. I meant it when I said this was the last job and I still mean it. We simply don't have that option anymore. It would have been enough to have been hunted for the rest of our natural lives by triads, but now if we just walk we will also be hunted by Special Operators. Unless you want to live in a f--cking cave in Waziristan, like Osama Bin Laden we have to end this shit one way, or the other, for all time."

"I see what you mean. OK. Let's put together a plan but put this plug in your ear and listen first to a phone conversation between General Kern and a Madame Shian' Ming Xian." Bill said. David listened as Bill played the taped conversation until the end and shook with anger. "I want this dirty bitch personally Bill! Who is this bitch he's talking with?" "Madame Shian' Ming Xiang. She is the supreme leader of all of the major triad societies in Hong Kong and Macau." Bill said. "I believe her networks have been receiving our product from Ma Sik Yu and then distributing our heroin to America and Europe for these past six years. She is apparently in control of General Kern, but needs us to process until she can rebuild Kern's labs. White Powder Ma will no doubt set up a meeting between her and myself soon. We need to plan a surprise for her and Kern after we get paid." "Roger that!" David said.

Captain Peterson was agitated as he picked up the telephone to call Admiral Donaldson. "Sir Peterson here." "Yeah what's up Al?" "Sir, I just learned that our TNCO inquiries have uncovered the operations of a mole in the CIA. The CIA Director's own access codes were used to task the original Bird in Laos. The Director is steaming. He is demanding that the CIA take over our entire investigation and assign a self investigative CIA team to smoke out the mole." "It's too late for that Al. He should have been more vigilant, then he wouldn't have the embarrassment."

"He wants all files and reports from us and an acknowledgement that we are no longer the principle investigative team." "F--ck him! Let him want in one hand and take a dump in his other hand and see which one fills up the fastest. This is precisely the reason JIATF-W was formed. Tell him the answer is no and that if he wants, he can send special agents to assist, but we will remain the lead on this one. Hell, this is our core competency and it was our analysis team who discovered everything.

If he wants to go to the President he can, but I doubt he will get very far once the Secretary of the Navy and the Director Of Homeland Security get involved. Send a "For Your Eyes Only" Intel summary to the Navy Secretary so he won't get broadsided." "Yes Sir!" "Have you assigned a Seal Team yet?" "Yes Sir.

Seal Team Six out of Coronado is sending two SEAL platoons of sixteen men each. One platoon will be broken into four fire teams and the other into two squads. The platoon in fire teams will do advance recon and set up mission support from the U.S. Embassy in Phnom Penh while the platoon in squads will comprise the main assault force and hunker down in a safe house not far from the target objective. Both Platoons will be involved in the assault Sir." "Sounds good. Make certain that the ones who set up at the Embassy have diplomatic ID's and cover stories.

I don't want the local drug police to be included in the information loop until the last bullet is fired. Then they can take credit for the entire take down, for all I care. Those f--ckers are as corrupt as they get and would sell out the mission for thirty pieces of silver. What about HUMINT? Did they come through with some local assets for us?" "Yes Sir. His code name is Mongoose. He has worked as a field agent on contract with the CIA since the coup de etat against Sihanouk."

"How in the f--ck did he survive the Pol Pot era?" "He slipped into Thailand and ran patrols until the Khmer Rouge fell." "Bring both platoons here first, for an initial briefing and then fly them to Cambodia immediately thereafter." "Yes Sir."

White Powder Ma had learned his lesson well. When you have a net worth as large as the GDP of the country you live in you really shouldn't skimp on security. His villa atop his sky scraper had been nearly re-built. He had a small army of top notch security experts set up checks and balances. His phone calls were carefully screened. He lay on a lounge chair most of the time watching the dozen, or so security monitors in his room behind triple layered titanium steel walls that could repel a direct C-4 charge.

Rarely did his personal phone ring as most calls were merely turned away outright. It was ringing now and it startled Ma so much that he almost didn't pick up. "Sir, a Madame Shian' has called three times today. She is now threatening me personally if I don't connect you." "Yes, I will take her call." "Ma SikYu?" "Yes Madame Shian' it is I." "Why don't you answer your phone? I have tried to reach you all day and your secretary has been most insolent and rude. If I am still your friend you will fire her to please me!" "Ha! Madame Shian' so sorry, I will lecture her about her rudeness and I beg of you to let me keep her. It has taken me so long to train her." "Well, as long as she crawls the next time I call."

"Ha! Madame Shian' still the Dragon lady I adore." "Who called me that? Did you get that started?" "No Madame Shian' I think I heard you call yourself that once." Madame Shian' cackled. "Ma you running dog! I suppose you know why I am calling." "I suspect you would like for me to introduce you to Mister Bill? You will both be needing to transact a very large shipment?" "Yes. How soon can you arrange it?"

"I suppose within a week, or less time. He will understandably be more than cautious after the damage Ma Fai Zhi caused. Anyone who is connected to the triad will be especially ominous to him at this juncture." "Yes. Well, it seems he is now the primary source of fully processed China White in the entire Triangle so if he promises to be civil and doesn't hold a grudge tell him he will actually enjoy his new business associates. Why are you leaving the business, if I may ask Ma Sik Yu?" "The White Powder has brought me only misery and besides my hexagrams all tell me to cease my discourse with the devil.

Madame Shian' you are a very elusive woman. You complain that you cannot reach me yet it is I who will have the utmost difficulty to inform you of the meeting with Mister Bill." "I have my reasons for never sleeping in the same place twice. Can you write down this number? You and one other trusted person are the only ones I have given it to." "Yes, I have it." Ma said. "Good night Madame Shian'." "Good night Ma Sik Yu."

Within the hour Ma called Madame Shian'. "Madame Shian'?" "Yes Ma." "I spoke with Mr. Murphy and he wishes to meet with you tomorrow. He understandably wants to meet with you in a neutral place." "Yes a neutral place is fine with me. Where does he consider a neutral place to be?" "This may sound strange but," "Well, spit it out! Where?" "He wants to meet you on an Air China charter flight from Hong Kong to Singapore. He has already bought all of the seats on the flight including the two first class seats for you and himself which means no body guards, or hired assassins from either side will be there. His conditions with the airline were that the flight would hence forth be closed except for you and him." "That isn't strange Ma it is something I would do. That is brilliant! Tell him I accept." Madame Shian' had to call in receipts from many years ago to be able to replace the China Airways charter flight Crew with her own loyal assassins, but it was worth it to her.

If Bill Murphy insulted her, or threatened her in any way, she would have him killed and dumped at the Singapore airport as common waste. How dare he think he could control Madame Shian' through trickery and pay offs? When Madame Shian' showed up at the China Airlines counter in Hong Kong, only to be informed that her flight had been changed to an immediate departure with Air Singapore with the same set of flight circumstances, she was both livid and somewhat in awe. Bill Murphy had bought all of the seats on a second major airline denying her the ability to control the staff.

"Goddamn him!" She thought. Madame Shian' boarded the aircraft. She was about to turn around and get off as the entire aircraft was empty including the assigned seat section of Bill Murphy and herself. Only the complete airline staff were present, adjusting seats and blankets in over head storage as though the aircraft were full. Suddenly, Bill Murphy appeared from nowhere and offered a full set of apologies for having changed the aircraft at the last moment. Madame Shian' was surprised. Bill Murphy should have been an old man with a large beer belly, like most of the Western men she had seen chasing the young prostitutes in Hong Kong. Bill, was not only absent the beer belly, he was in excellent condition and somewhat irresistibly handsome to boot. Sean Connery was her first mental comparison.

"Well, Mister Bill, it was somewhat disconcerting to learn of the change in aircraft, but hopefully you now realize that I am serious about our business at hand." "By all means Madame Shian'. Champagne?" "Why not?" For his part, Bill had expected a spider lady with extra layers of makeup. Not a thirty eight year old Chinese woman who looked ten years younger. By the time they were on their second glass of champagne, Bill had her cackling and wondering why she hadn't insisted on meeting him earlier.

An hour into the flight, Madame Shian' insisted on discussing the details of the exchange. Bill described his proposed plan. "Madame Shian', I have organized the opium into four processing Lots. Each lot will be processed in one of a total of four laboratories. Each lab has three trained chemists and a work team of eighty laborers." "Working around the clock seven days a week we predict with the utmost of certainty that we will be finished within three weeks from today with two C-130e' aircraft loaded with two tons each of 99% pure China White."

"How shall I take possession of the heroin if it is on your aircraft?" "Well, I have been assured by our mutual friend and colleague, Ma Sik Yu that you are interested in a long term relationship." "He was right. I am interested in a long term partnership." "Fine." Bill said. "So am I. Which means that if you trust me by transferring my commission which amounts to 20% of the street value of a quarter of a billion dollars worth of heroin, or fifty million dollars, then I can trust you to return two hundred million dollars worth of aircraft back to me after you have off loaded your product."

"I like the sound of that. Mutual trust and the fact that I am holding more collateral than I am being trusted to pay you." "Indeed Madame Shian'." Bill said with firmness. "Now then, Mister Bill, how shall the transfer take place?" "Since we will have already loaded both planes, I suggest you send two capable pilots, who can each fly a C-130e aircraft along with a chemist who can test the product at plane side while you view the arrangement via SAT phone. Once you transfer my commission using this account number and it is confirmed on my side your pilots can fly your four tons of heroin to any destination you please and merely bring back my empty planes." "I like it. Clean and well thought out with collateral in place at all times." She said. "We agree. I should have arranged a shorter flight for our meeting." Bill remarked.

"What in heavens name for?" Madame Shian' asked as she placed her soft hand on Bill's thigh. Within moments Bill was caressing her shoulder and then kissing her deeply. Bill gave the Chief attendant a crisp five hundred dollars to ensure other attendants would not enter the first class section for another hour as he slowly removed Madame Shian's dress and underwear. They had passionate sex until climaxing together, followed almost exactly by the pilot's announcement that they would soon be touching down at Singapore International airport in fifteen minutes.

As the plane opened its doors, Bill zipped up the back of Madame Shian's dress. "I will soon be in touch with a date and time for the exchange." Bill said. "You now have my number. I will be awaiting your call." She purred. "Enjoy your flight back to Hong Kong Madame Shian'." "Indeed I shall. But I can't leave Singapore without doing some shopping first." Bill smiled, nodded and disappeared in the direction of his return flight to Phnom Penh. Bill went straight to David's villa when he returned to Phnom Penh. Both Bill and David were acutely aware of the latest state of the art satellite imaging and listening devices, as well as the airborne pin point data and voice collection systems employed by NSA. This time, however, David waved Bill away from the stereo. David mouthed the words "I want them to hear this." Bill nodded yes.

"So how was your trip Bill?" "Excellent. The buyer has agreed to our terms and as soon as our last batch is processed, I will arrange for the exchange." "Sounds good. You can call her tomorrow because the last batch will be loaded in only fifteen more days." That means the exchange is set for the Saturday, week after next, at twenty hundred hours local time at our hangar in Phnom Penh." "Care to listen to some Vivaldi ?" David asked. "Sure why not." As the music played, David whispered. "Did she agree to twenty percent?" Bill nodded.

"Will she send two pilots and a chemist?" Again the nod to the affirmative. David yelled, "Did you f--ck her at thirty thousand feet?" This time a vigorous series of yes nods. "You f--cking dog!" David yelled and both men laughed uproariously. Captain Peterson delivered the flash message to Admiral Donaldson, which contained the most recent conversation between Bill and David. "Did NSA decipher any of the recording made after they started listening to music?" "Yes Sir. "

"Something about f--cking at thirty thousand feet and then David calls Bill a f--cking dog." "I'll be a son of a bitch!" The Admiral shouted. "Their client is a woman. F--cking at thirty thousand feet. They had their meeting in an airplane and apparently the deal was sealed with sex. If it weren't for the business he's in, I could actually get to like this Murphy guy." The admiral said. "OK. We have a transaction date and time. Get this to the SEAL team. Tell them to plan their assault accordingly. If the C-130e's attempt to leave at anytime before the transaction time, that will trigger the assault automatically. It is most probable they will test the product before money changes hands, so we will have all of the actors in the same place at the same time. That's when I want to hit their asses." "Yes Sir."

Bill knew his phone was tapped as he placed the call to Madame Shian'. "Madame Shian? I have good news. The last batch will be loaded by Saturday the 28th. We can conduct the exchange at twenty hundred hours Phnom Penh time at the hangar GPS location I gave you." "That is good news Mister Bill. Very well, expect my team of pilots and Chemist to arrive shortly before." "Good night Madame Shian'." "Bill?" "Yes Madame Shian'." "Thank you for the pleasurable experience on the way to Singapore. If we can keep our business on the right track, I look forward to traveling with you again sometime." She purred.

"So do I Madame Shian'." "You may call me Ming Xian after our business has been concluded. Good night Bill." "Good night Madame Shian'." Bill leaned near David's face and whispered. "Can you believe that cold hearted bitch is still playing me?" " She spoke as though we may f--ck again even though she plans to have me whacked and steal my junk all on the same evening." "She's a real Pro Bill. That's why she's the bigga bossa." "She's f--cking heartless David. I would love to f--ck her again with pain involved next time." "Bill, there ain't gonna be a next time." David whispered. Admiral Donaldson listened to the recording twice, but he couldn't hear the whispers. "Do we really know who this Madame Shian' is Al?" "Yes Sir."

"As we previously discussed, her name is Madame Shian' Ming Xian. A rather wispy, shadowy and elusive character, she is believed to be the real decision maker for the largest three Hong Kong triad societies. She has ordered hits in both Europe and the USA and is the unquestioned boss of heroin distribution from China and now, apparently Myanmar to the West." "Can we tap her phone in Hong Kong?" "Sir, she has a better security system than Al Qaeda. "We don't even know where she spends the night from one day to the next." "Well, we have her tapped whenever she speaks with Bill. That will have to suffice." "Yes Sir."

"Are the SEAL platoons in place yet?" "Yes Sir. Platoon Alpha is at the embassy and has begun direct surveillance of both residences, the S.H.A.R.I. Institute, the hangar and all four labs. HUMINT has been relaying reports from Mongoose. His reports confirm that White Powder in clear plastic bags gets transported from the four labs to the C-130e's almost constantly by two and a half ton trucks and also that chemical container trash gets taken down to the river and thrown in the hold of a barge. Mongoose can't leave his post as a security guard to check out the barge without drawing suspicion."

"No need. It's perfectly normal that they have a trash problem with all of the chemicals and Bleach they have to use to convert the Morphine into heroin." "Yes Sir."

General Kern was in the swimming pool, when a servant brought him the phone. He leaned along the pool decking to take the call. "Yes Madame Shian'. How did your meeting with Mister Bill go?" "Splendidly. I have him eating from the palm of my hand like a dog. He even wants me to send two pilots to fly my own C130e's back to me. Wasn't that nice of him?" She giggled. "Do we stick to the original plan?" The General asked. "But of course General. Nothing has changed. He has set the time and date for the exchange, for Saturday the 28th at twenty hundred hours Phnom Penh local time. I will send two pilots and a chemist by helicopter."

"I will send to you today a copy of the map Bill gave me that pin points his location. The chemist will test the heroin and then I will transfer his money." "What he doesn't know is that your assault team of thirty assassins will arrive by the Caribou he gave you and you will wipe out his small force. You may kill everyone except Mister Bill and his associate David. David will be tortured until he returns the money transfer I will have just made.

Then, after he divulges where all of the rest of their funds are located we will make him transfer all of it per our agreement. Half to your account and half to mine. After that, he will receive the lesser Tongchi and be merely buried alive." "What will you do with Mister Bill?" "He will taste the greater Tongchi and be cut by a razor one hundred thousand times, while being also buried alive. He has drawn triad blood and must soon pay with his own. That is our custom, that is our law and even I cannot change it even if I wanted to." She reflected.

"In fact, he has killed many of our triad soldiers and can never be pardoned. Remember General Kern. Under no circumstances will your men kill Bill or David and they will be sent, securely bound, with the heroin back to me."

"It will be as you have ordered Madame Shian." Bill and David removed the plugs from their ears and sat motionless for a few moments listening to the loud music. "I thought since you f--cked her she might let us off the hook Bill." David whispered. "Guess you should have sent me to meet her, then she would have pardoned both of us." David whispered again. Bill shook his head, partly in surprise and partly in hatred for Shian' Ming Xiang. He knew he would have to kill her himself to end her death sentence on his and David's lives.

Bill's hangar was both perfect and completely imperfect, as a location of defense. Traveling the road from the Mekong one could see its roof from three kilometers away. The open expanse that surrounded the place made surveillance for the defender simple, as there was nothing to hide from anyone who harbored malcontent from a long distance, in every direction. At the same time, however there was no possibility of escape without being watched as you departed, for an uncomfortably long time. The hop scotch of rectangular rice paddies were a maze with no continuity of ingress, or egress.

They were made so, by the fact that the patches of land that separated them were active mine fields. Only the rice farmers whose relatives had lost a limb here, or there, knew the unwritten map. Very narrow foot paths led one back out again. When the SEALS made their plan of assault it was clear that only a
parachute drop on the runway using HALO, high altitude low opening as a jump strategy would allow at least a semblance of an element of surprise. Aircraft could be heard if not seen from quite a distance, before they reached the hangar.

A tank might be of use, but theirs was to be a lightning strike, not an armored invasion with artillery to soften the target. The problem with HALO was that there would be too many SEALS coming in from the sky at the same time. Combat formations, post drop, would be ad hoc at best according to who landed close to whom and there would always be the possibility of a gust of wind taking at least some of the assault force into the mine fields. Rally points may already be occupied by enemy forces, which would deny the SEALS the ability to organize according to plan.

These SEALS had lived together, trained together and behaved both psychologically and physically like a precision Swiss watch, but if the platoons got mixed around both platoon leaders could very well wind up fighting in the same platoon. They had been trained to fight as individuals which would have no doubt still been enough to accomplish the mission but the SEAL casualties could double, even triple, before the assault could be concluded. The date and time of the assault was in the hands of the enemy and on the Saturday night in question the weather prediction was for a cloudless sky and a full moon. Navy Lieutenant Chris Billings, Platoon Leader Alpha Platoon came up with the perfect plan.

They would chopper to an LZ a few kilometers from the Labs, reach the labs on foot using the connecting road take out the lab guards and two and a half ton truck drivers who slept in their trucks, then drive the trucks to the hangar. Seeing their own trucks being driven to the hangar would cause just enough confusion and delay to allow the C-130e's to be taken and the resistance eliminated before the element of surprise had been lost. Lieutenant Billings wrote the operations order for both platoons and made ready for a helicopter insertion at the appointed LZ.

A mock LZ and a mock lab were constructed in a remote area on the other side of Phnom Penh and the SEALS rehearsed their insertion over and over. By the time their rehearsals were complete, they knew every move every mission imperative, even with their eyes closed. They were more than ready for the "Take Down". At exactly nineteen fifty hours on Saturday, Bill used electric landing torches to wave in Madame Shian's helicopter. According to plan the two C-130e's pilots and Chemist were ushered into the hangar while their helicopter pilot remained with his chopper. Suddenly Anchaly's men arrested the chopper pilot and Madame Shian's team binding them with cord and lining them up inside the hangar. Mongoose was tied up and placed with Madame Shian's team.

Bill gave Anchaly a nod and Anchaly signaled one of his men to bring in a mesh crate. Visible inside were two angry King Cobras that were hissing and spitting. "In a moment," Bill said to the Chemist, "I am going to untie you and you will use your SAT phone according to your plan to contact Madame Shian'. You will be on video testing a heroin sample at random from each C-130e's cargo hold. You will attest to the purity of the heroin to be 99% pure China White.
You will also confirm that the bulk load appears to be exactly two tons, per plane. If you falter, or fail to mention your prearranged code word to Madame Shian' she will refuse to transfer my funds. You will then be immediately bound again and the Cobra snakes will be turned loose upon you and your friends. Speak English at all times, no Mandarin, or Cantonese, understood?" The man's eyes grew large as he carefully watched the snakes launch strikes against the sides of the crate. He shook his head vigorously, yes. Bill took the Chemist to the C-130e's and reached the Chemist back his own SAT phone.

The Chemist dialed and Madame Shian's voice filled the hangar. "Reach the phone to someone who will video you making the test!" She said. "Yes Madame Shian'," he said as he reached the phone to Bill. Bill held the camera lens of the phone in the direction of the Chemist who carefully pretended to take a random sample from inside the massive heap of White Powder in clear plastic packaging. He combined the chemicals of the test and studied their color and consistency and lied about the result. "99% pure China White." he said. The test was repeated at the cargo hold of the second C-130e then Bill spoke to Madame Shian'. "The tests are now complete please transfer our commission." "I'm doing that now Bill please wait." Madame Shian' replied.

David stood by with his wireless laptop and within a couple of minutes that seemed like an eternity he suddenly announced that the funds had been received by their account in Hong Kong and had already been divided and sent on, per prearranged instructions to their bank accounts in the Caymans.

Madame Shian's team was bound securely together and their bindings were tied to the trap door of the snake cage. If they struggled to be set free they would inadvertently open the cage. Bill spoke in the phone to Madame Shian. "Your pilots are preparing to taxi to the runway. Your Chemist and Chopper pilot should reach Phnom Penh within minutes. You should be able to reach them by radio in a few minutes. It was a pleasure Madame Shian. I will be calling you soon." "Thank you Mister Bill. Likewise." She grinned.

A hand written note was pinned to the shirt of the Chemist which read:

Dear SEAL Commander:
You will find a ten kilo bag of 99% pure heroin in each of the aircraft. The rest of the cargo is enriched flour. The amount of heroin should allow you to seize these aircraft and arrest these men who are part of a transnational criminal organization.
Regards,
Bill Murphy
CIA Field Agent (retired)

Bill already sent the Yunnan Rose to an estuary along the Mekong with its cargo hold packed to the brim with four tons of 99% pure China White in used chemical boxes. His men would conceal the barge there until he gave them the order to abandon the barge and go home.

Bill started his Caribou. David joined Anchaly and his team as they marched up the ramp stopping one last time to take a last look at the hangar and Madame Shian's crew. Within minutes, Bill was soon landing the Caribou in an open field not far from the floating restaurants, along the Phnom Penh river front. Bill and David hopped out of the plane for an emotional goodbye with Anchaly's crew. The Khmer had been paid very well, but knew they would probably never see either David, or Bill, ever again. Bill lifted off, his fuel tank full, he set a course for Malaysia. At precisely nineteen fifty hours SEAL Platoon Alpha's point men reached the first lab.

The Place was unusually dark and two, two and a half ton trucks sat quietly in the shadows in front of the building. "Alpha Six, this is Spearhead One, over." "Come in One, over." "Six, I have reached the trucks. No guards in sight. I will now take out the drivers, over." "This is Six Roger that, out." The point man unleashed his K-Bar knife and moved quietly to the cab of the truck. He leaped inside and buried his knife into the seat of the truck. "Six! This is One. The Trucks are empty, not a soul in sight, over!" "Spearhead One, clear the two trucks for booby traps and IED's and wait. I will be at your location in one minute. Out."

Spearhead Two point man checked the Labs for personnel and booby traps, but found nothing. Spearhead One point man checked and cleared both trucks. Lieutenant Billings ordered both platoons to mount the trucks and they raced to reach the hangar.

Captain Peterson and Edward had just turned on the infra red screen at twenty hours in time to see two trucks apparently loaded with SEALS headed with speed toward the hangar. They could no longer see the presence of personnel at the labs and all of the other trucks, ten in all were lined up at the river front. The barge was missing! The Caribou was missing! But the two C130e's were still at the hangar. A chopper they hadn't seen before was sitting cold at the hangar, as well. Inside the hangar they detected heat sources of a group of personnel who were immobile. Admiral Donaldson walked in and was immediately briefed by Captain Peterson. Admiral Donaldson picked up the SAT phone to Lieutenant Billings. "Alpha Six, Eagle Six SITREP please!" "Eagle Six we are one minute from the hangar. No bodies alive, or dead, at objective One." "Only two deuce and a half's that we are now using to get to Objective Two. Over." Admiral Donaldson coughed and then exclaimed. "Sonofabitch!"

"Alpha Six, it looks like we've been taken. The Caribou is missing and the barge is missing. Your missing ten trucks are parked down by the river. You will find what appears to be five immobilized individuals in the hangar. One of them is no doubt Mongoose. Debrief him and send him to the Embassy alone. The rest will probably be bad guys. Arrest them and take them to the Embassy for interrogation. Put a Marine Embassy detail in charge of the. C-130e's. Finally,Give me a sign off when our SEALS are at the Embassy." Donaldson concluded.

"Al, Goddamn it how did the Caribou and barge get moved without you knowing about it?" The Admiral grumbled. "Sir, at precisely nineteen fifty hours we received notice from Langley that the CIA Director ordered his bird dark and removed from our mission. I quickly tasked a bird to substitute from NSA." "By the time our IR screen was back up the barge had been moved and the Caribou was gone." "Jesus!" Admiral Donaldson exclaimed. Admiral Donaldson's SAT phone buzzed. "Eagle Six, Alpha Six, over." "Come in Alpha Six." Admiral Donaldson replied. "Eagle Six, the Caribou is returning on a direct approach over." "Goddamn son. Hide your SEALS and conduct an assault as soon as it lands. Shoot to kill anyone who resists arrest over!" "Roger Sir!" Admiral Donaldson spun around to watch the infra red screen.

The Caribou landed and began to taxi toward the hangar when General Kern's pilot saw the SEALS running toward his plane. Kern's assassins were already running down the lowered ramp when the pilot throttled for immediate take off. The SEALS shot out his tires, slowing the Caribou to a crawl. Small arms fire erupted and six of Kern's men were killed instantly. One of Kern's men manned the 20 mm and was ready to open up on the SEALS, who had formed a skirmish line and were proceeding toward the Caribou.

An alert SEAL with a L.A.W. Light Anti-tank Weapon immediately fired at the 20 mm gunner. Suddenly, the Caribou exploded in a white hot ball of gaseous fire, killing all on board. SEAL Platoon Bravo secured the C-130e's as SEAL Platoon Alpha secured the hangar. Lieutenant Billings helmet video brought Bill's note into focus. "Good job Alpha Six. Secure the prisoners and the heroin Murphy left for us to use as evidence." "Have the trucks driven to the Embassy after you check them for drugs. I doubt you'll find much, it seems the big fish has eluded us. Fly the C-130e's to the Embassy air strip and a JIATF-W liaison will sign for them. I expect quite a shit storm will ensue tomorrow about who owns them between Bangkok and Washington. Destroy the chopper in place. Call in a SEAL chopper to recon the Mekong. I doubt you'll find the barge but it's worth a shot."

"Sorry we lost the treasure Sir!" "Not your fault SEAL. I was outsmarted by an old operator. It hurts less to think of it that way. Also, we have an internal inter-agency problem that could have cost us some SEALS. I'll get answers about why SAT support was removed during a SEAL assault and I'll fix it you can depend on that!" "Yes Sir!" "Navy SEALS Sir!" "Eagle Six, out!"

"Madame Shian' was screaming so loud into the phone that she was gasping for air. "What do you mean you have lost contact with your assassins Kern?" "My assault leader and pilot of the Caribou radioed me that he was landing at the objective hangar when I heard shots ring out. I could hear him commanding his men to dismount and counter- attack. That's when all communications went dead. He was obviously under attack on the runway ambushed by a huge force." "But I thought you said Bill Murphy typically never had a force larger than ten, or twelve people!" "Yes. Well typically that has been the case, but he must have had a sizeable force on call, in reserve."

"Well, when will you hear from your men? When will you bring my heroin and my aircraft? When will they bring Bill Murphy to me?" Madame Shian screamed. "My triads have already been assured by me personally that Murphy is already dead. Now they are waiting for their heroin!" "Madame Shian I have just lost thirty of my best fighters and an excellent aircraft." "Who cares what you have lost? I have just lost two hundred million dollars worth of aircraft and four thousand kilos of China White! Who can I turn to besides you to get it back? If I tell the triads, they will kill both of us." Madame Shian' whimpered.

"Madame Shian. I suggest you come immediately to Tachilek. Charter a small plane and come straight here. We are in this together. I have a ten thousand man army. No one can harm you here. Together we will devise a way to capture Murphy and torture him until he pays for taking your planes and heroin and for killing my best men." "What you say makes sense General. I shall come to Tachilek immediately." "Call me when you arrive. I shall have my driver pick you up at the airport." Kern said.

As soon as they neared Phuket, Thailand Bill began the number string to call Admiral Donaldson. " Well, David it's time to execute the final phase of your brilliant Ops order. Do you really believe he will go for it?" "He has to. He's an officer and a gentleman and his main incentive in life is to keep heroin away from the United States. Besides, it's our last hope in Hell to keep those SEALS off of our asses." "This is Donaldson." "Sir my name is Bill Murphy." "Murphy you're a low down..." "Wait Sir, hear me out! I have an offer I hope you can't refuse." "What? Turn yourself in?" Bill looked at David, who made rolling forward motions with his hands to get Bill to finish. "Sir, if that had been my only option I would have waited for the SEALS to arrest me."

Admiral Donaldson pointed at Captain Peterson and mouthed the word TRACE, but waved it off when Bill Murphy stated that his phone call was routed around the globe and would be untraceable. That the call was originating from a remote device in Pennsylvania. "I hope no SEALS were hurt during the assault." "You can thank your lucky stars that they weren't." The Admiral said with sincerity.

"Our SEALS took care of a force that I am assuming belonged to either Madame Shian, or General Kern." "Very good Admiral! Yes, some really bad people that the world will never miss." "OK. We did your laundry for you. I'm still waiting to hear what you have to offer Murphy!" "Yes Sir! Well, I want a free pass for life from your SEALS for myself and my partner David Anderson. He was the one who wrote my Ops order."

"Damn good Ops order. I could use a man like him. OK a free pass, for both of you. What do I get?" "As once loyal federal servants to the CIA we will swear an oath to leave the drug business for good." "Is this a joke Murphy? If my SEALS hunt your asses down and kill you I can get the same thing for free." "Wait Admiral. I was saving the best for last. How about if we give you the GPS coordinates to the barge that is holding four thousand kilos of China White? The Khmer guards on the barge must also be released without punishment." A silence followed.

"How do you know I'll keep my word?" "Because you are an officer and a gentleman and a man's word is who he is. It's his bond in life." "OK Murphy. If the heroin is there, you've got yourself a deal." Bill gave the Admiral the coordinates and within minutes a Navy SEAL helicopter was hovering over the Yunnan Rose. A loud speaker told the Khmer in their own language that Bill Murphy was a mutual friend and that he asked them to leave the barge and go home to their families.

The Khmer at first refused until a recording by Bill was played over the loudspeaker with the same appeal in Khmer and English. As soon as the Khmer departed the estuary in a small motor boat the SEALS brought the Yunnan Rose out of hiding.

A bright beam shone down on the barge as Lieutenant Billings led his team to the hold of the barge. Lieutenant Billings who had been trained in testing drugs for identity and purity scooped a sample from a bag he retrieved from near the bottom of the pile. He then took three other samples from every corner of the hold. His helmet mounted video camera sent back clear images of the cargo from a panoramic view as well as close ups of the clear plastic bags to Admiral Donaldson who watched him perform each test. "Holy Virgin Mary! Eagle Six this heroin is 99% pure China White and my estimate is that it is even more than four tons." "Roger Alpha Leader! How much C-4 do you have on you?" "Four fifty pound blocks in the chopper Sir!" "Use it and blow that monster to hell. That is too much heroin to risk transporting to any port just to please the press. They will have to be satisfied with your video feed Alpha Leader." "Roger that Sir!"

"Alpha Leader, do I hear a quavering in your voice?" "Just thinking of all the souls this shit will never touch Sir!" "Roger that SEAL!" Admiral Donaldson answered firmly. Both Lieutenant Billings, the Admiral and even Captain Peterson's eye's got misty with that exchange. Within minutes the video feed was recording from an ascending chopper as the C-4 blew the Yunnan Rose into a trillion tiny bits. Captain Peterson looked at Admiral Donaldson and said "Sir we have a fix on his location. He didn't have a global computer network call after all." "Where is he?" "His Caribou is just passing Phuket,Thailand. Looks like he's heading for Malaysia. Should I scramble some F-18's? We have an aircraft carrier in the South Indian Ocean."

"Captain Peterson, your word is your bond. It's who you are. Let him go." "Sir do you really believe he's out of the business?" "Yes, I do. He didn't have to turn over the four tons of pure heroin. He could have found a buyer somewhere. This triad bitch, what was her name Madame Shian? That's who I want to bring down. Her and that General Kern. Let's focus on Myanmar and Hong Kong to see what shakes out of those two places. Arrange a video conference between the Secretary Of The Navy and the Secretary Of State. Show them this video feed and inform them that this heroin came from the Shan State in Myanmar and ask them to see whether the Junta might be interested in some private, covert, military assistance in eliminating the private army of General Jon Kern." "Yes Sir!"

The international press gave incessant coverage to the world's largest heroin bust saying that it was only through the courageous cooperation between the JIATF-W and the local Phnom Penh drug police that such a monumental and historic success in the global war on drugs had been made possible. The President Of The United States announced that a large monetary reward would be delivered by check to the Cambodian Anti-Drug task force commander.

Not a single SEAL was referenced although both platoons had performed bravely and in accordance with the highest standards of courage that American men could ever hope to ascend to. Their only reward was knowing inside that another day had found them living up to their own standard of excellence.

Chapter Ten: The Lotus Dream

Hundreds of thousands of new drug customers would have to get their ruinous product from someone else. This heroin had been eliminated by SEALS! SEAL Platoons Alpha and Bravo shook Admiral Donaldson's hand as they filed to the all black 747 that would take them home to their loving families, in San Diego. Ready for another day on the hot cinder when their country needed them, once more.

Bill placed the call to Omar. "Omar, it's Bill. Sorry if I awakened you but could you light your air strip? We are about five minutes out." "Yes Mistah Bill. I have electronic lights now." Within minutes, Bill saw the narrow pathway that was lit up on both sides by what appeared to be blinking Christmas tree lights. He brought the Caribou down like a feather and taxied to a stop in front of a barn that Omar had converted into a hangar. Bill and David jumped down from the ramp that still had the 20 mm cannon attached. Omar marveled at the weapon and then warmly shook both men's hands.

"How long can you stay this time Mistah Bill?" "Would two weeks be too long Omar?" "No, you can stay forever!" Omar laughed and Bill and David grinned widely. "I will bring same girls? Yes?" "Absolutely!" Bill said. David looked at the star filled sky and mumbled, "Hell yes!" Both men were bathed by the women and properly put to bed where they all slept like a den of lion cubs once again. The men awoke in the early afternoon and walked to the beach where they sipped green coconuts and drank beer until sunset. At dinner, Omar loved the compliments about his new dwelling and when Bill told him that the Caribou and its new gun were a gift, he nearly broke down. "You really should be an Islam man Mistah Bill because I believe Allah send you to me."

This was the highest compliment a Muslim could have ever given to an Infidel and it truly humbled Bill. "Omar, next week, David and I must go to Singapore to buy a boat." "No need go Singapore Mistah Bill. I give you my boat!" "I am honored with such a gift, Omar, but I am afraid the boat we need is as large as a house." With this, the entire house, including Omar's wife and children and the women, broke out in uncontrollable laughter.

After dinner, Bill, David and the beautiful women returned to Omar's second house and made love until sunrise. When Bill looked out the window, he saw Omar patiently standing by the Caribou. Bill opened the window and yelled. "You are up early Omar." "I will wait until you teach me to fly plane and shoot gun." For the remainder of the month, Bill and David taught Omar to fly and how to operate the 20 mm. He proved a fast learner, although both Bill and David confessed later to heart palpitations, each time he brought the Caribou in for a landing. A month and a week went by and the day to go to Singapore to buy a boat finally came.

The women cried when Bill and David hugged them and then stepped into the taxi. All, from Omar and his wife to the women, who Bill and David had grown to love, in their own special way, as well as Omar's children, knew they would never see Bill and David again. Stoicism and acceptance of fate, was a trait they had known since birth so they all looked at the sky and hugged each other, as the taxi disappeared in a cloud of dust. Only Omar remained, transfixed on the image of the disappearing taxi, for a long long, while, until his wife finally nudged him and pulled him away from the still lingering cloud of dust, back up the hill to the Great house. "What makes it harder to leave this place every single time?" Bill wondered out loud. "They're the closest thing either one of us have had that resembles a family, that's why." David said.

"Yeah. Guess you're right David. It sure choked me up some this time. Did you see the kids faces get all twisted up?" "I couldn't see much, my eyes were sort of swimming in a haze, myself," David said softly. "Hey Bill, tell me about this boat. Fishing rig? Fighting Chair?" "Ha ha. wait until you see it." "I wanted it to be a surprise David, but since you will be transferring the money to pay for it, I may as well get you in the loop sooner. A little more than eighteen months ago I planned our retirement. Why do you think I went balls to the wall in Tachilek when it looked like you were going to bail on me?" "I don't understand, what's that have to do with a boat?" David asked. "Well, remember when you said you were willing to take four hundred mill and give me six hundred, give, or take?" "Yeah, so?" "Well my math is a little different than your's man."

"You saved my ass a few times since I've known you. You've become the only f--ckin' family I've got David. I want a fifty, fifty, split of all the assets. That comes out to five hundred fifty mill apiece man. The fifty mill we just pulled from Madame Shian' is going to be needed to pay for the boat." "Bill, I am overwhelmed man, but can I ask you a f--cking question?" "Sure." "What kind of f--cking boat costs fifty mill?" "Ha ha! Ours David. That's what kind. Eighteen months ago it was just a steel hull, waiting for the buyer to custom order the finished product. One hundred eighty feet or fifty five meters long. Displacement is six hundred tons. It's a luxury power yacht, driven by twin Cat diesel engines that have 2,200 horse power each. It's a f--ckin' mega yacht man. I had two professional interior design companies do the interior. Hand sculpted Italian marble floors, no expense in furniture, woods, leathers, or accessories, was spared. The Galley has walk in refrigerators and meat lockers. The toilet seats and basins are all 14 karat gold. She has a professional billiard room and even a sports bar. A swimming pool aft on the Main deck."

"It has ten private luxury cabins and Crew quarters on the lower deck. Besides it was only thirty mill. I spent the other twenty on a small attack chopper and armory full of special Ops weapons. I got us an AH-6 Little Bird Gun, configured for special Ops. It has two 7.62 mm six barrel Gattling guns front mounted, two Hydra rocket pods with twelve rockets each, two strut mounted fifty calibre pods, two 40 mm grenade launchers two TOW missile pods with two each pod, two Hellfire ATGM Air To Ground missiles and two Stinger AAM Air To Air missiles."

"Damn Bill! I thought we were going to retire!" "We are, but with a triad vampire and one hundred fifty thousand man triad organization behind her what's a baby chopper with an attitude, in the over all scheme of things? "You do have a point. So it has a helipad?" "Yep! Aft on the fly bridge." "Goddamn! I can't wait to see this boat, I mean yacht!" "Won't we need a crew Bill?" "That's been arranged. I thought we'd do a little maiden voyage to Surabaya, stroll around Dolly and then head up the Strait of Malacca to the Indian Ocean. Head for the Red Sea and up the Suez to the Mediterranean Sea. Do the Gold Coast of Spain, hit Marseilles, Nice and then cut across to Brazil, transit the Panama Canal then head back for Asia stopping of course in Fiji, Samoa, Tahiti and then back to Singapore to get any wrinkles taken care of before docking in Phnom Penh and turning the sucker into a houseboat."

"How long will this trip of yours take?" "Oh, about two years depending on how long we get hooked on the pussy we enjoy in any given port of call." "Bill, I'm beginning to feel retired. Are you feeling retired yet?" "Yeah, for about a month now." The two grinned and then laughed from deep within their weary souls. Although neither cared to admit it they both felt uneasy in large modern cities. Singapore, in particular, with its high rises, and glitzy discotheques.

Although they were rich, by anyone's standards, Bill and David preferred the rural, jungle atmosphere with simple sweet women. The prostitutes in Singapore weren't even Singaporean for the most part, but instead, were Filipinas Thai, Russian even American and a few Japanese. Men from Singapore used them frequently, and paid them exorbitantly. As they walked into the Yacht Brokerage facility along the water front of Singapore, they saw a handsome African American man, with a beautiful Thai hooker on each arm. The show room was filled with nervous sales representatives, distinguished looking customers and a small news crew that was milling about near the dock that led to the water front display.

The African American man, who had the physique of a young Muhammad Ali, joked with his Thai friends in English about the reception being readied for himself. David believed him, at first, guessing that the man was perhaps a famous athlete, even a boxer, but the closer he looked the more he realized that the man was too old to be an athlete. David judged him to be mid to late forties. "Looks like you're pretty popular here." David remarked. "American! Damn, I had you two pegged as Aussies."

"All Decked out in your jungle clothes and all." The man said jokingly. The man extended his hand as a fist and David just stood there looking at it. Bill crossed in front of David, extending his fist against the man's fist, as though he Bill, were thoroughly familiar with Black culture. David laughed out loud at his own clumsiness and at the simple manliness of the gesture itself, then he extended his fist toward the man. The man bumped David's fist in a salutary gesture and introduced himself. The name is L.J. Jones. Pleased to meet both of you. Bill looked down at the jungle khakis he and David were dressed in and compared them with L.J.'s sleek yachting jacket and white tropical slacks.

"I guess by the way we're dressed, you probably thought we were here looking for part time jobs?" Bill said with a smile. "I never judge a man by his clothes, what I said about you being Aussies was just a joke." L.J. responded. "You probably thought that I was a pimp, by the way I walked in this place with a woman on each arm." "No offense, but yes the thought crossed my mind." Bill said. David felt embarrassed. He wasn't sure which way this was headed and the last thing they needed was public attention from an incident. L.J. laughed a deep rich laugh. "I love the honesty. Rare amongst most White folks." Bill grinned broadly. "I have to agree with you on that one." " I have to admit, I also thought that you two looked out of place, but now I know it wasn't the clothes. You stood out because you are real folks." "Thank you." David said sincerely.

"What do you do for a living? Bill asked. L.J. reached each of them a business card. "I own a string of eye clinics from Guam to Tokyo and Singapore. I'm an eye surgeon." "I'll be damned!" Bill blurted out. "That's really something!" "Something to really be proud of man!" "Should we call you Doctor L.J.?" "Don't you dare. People might think I'm a Rap artist!" All three laughed hard at that one. "What do you guys do for a living Bill?" "We're drug king pins." Bill replied. L.J. laughed hard, but David just looked down at his feet as Bill grinned and beamed proudly. "What attracted you guys here today?" L.J. asked. "Just out for a stroll." David answered. "Well, I came here to look at a yacht I ordered, but with this crowd, I'm not sure I will be able to get through long enough to see it. It's still in progress in the factory just down the boardwalk. Cost me ten million. I doubt when I pick up my yacht that I will get this much attention. The crowd is here to witness the purchase of her." L.J. pointed at the huge show window, with the Lotus Dream moored straight beyond. From stem to stern, the enormous yacht filled the panoramic show room window, with elegance, design and sheer size.

"I heard that the Sultan of Brunei is buying this one." L.J. embellished. At that moment, the yacht broker who Bill had been dealing with, spotted Bill and rushed to him, to greet him. "Hello Mister Bill. I was beginning to worry that something happened to you." "Bill leaned over to the man.

"Who in the hell organized this cluster f--ck?" "Oh, I'm sorry Mister Bill. We make the delivery of all of our mega yachts with a bit of marketing fan fare." "I wasn't consulted." "So sorry Sir." "OK. here's what you do. Get rid of the news reporter. Let her take a few shots and tell her that the Sultan of Brunei is the owner who will be taking delivery in absentia." "But you are the owner." "Not if you don't do exactly as I say. Understand?" "Yes Sir."

"Now then, it's OK to take marketing photos, but neither myself, or my associate, had better be in them. Is this clearly understood?" "Yes Sir." "Good. We will remain outside of camera range until you finish your marketing and then I want to be taken on an engineering and architectural structural detailed tour of my yacht." "At that time, we can meet in one of your conference rooms and accept title as well as transfer funds." "Yes Sir!" L.J. felt embarrassed about his earlier assumption that Bill and David were curiosity seekers. "Goddamn it fellahs. That's really your yacht?" he asked. Bill smiled. "Yes, but we are not snobs."

"That's very cool. I like that. Low profile wealth. I'm working on that myself, but occasionally it's hard not to enjoy money, even though it makes others stare. To be honest, the conspicuous consumption aspect can be a real f--cking turn on at times." L.J. confessed. Impressed with L.J.'s honesty, David said "Don't get us wrong, my friend Bill and I were a couple of your conspicuous consumption admirers when we first checked out your Thai friends." L.J. laughed hard at that. "Oh, so now it's your turn to make a stereotypical mistake?" He said with joviality.

"At the risk of being completely and unabashedly nosy how much? L.J. asked. "Thirty mill." Bill answered. "I love capitalism. Y'all gonna make this Po niggah work his ass off to catch up wit dat!" L.J. mocked. Bill and David instantly liked this man, who could joke about race, while being keenly cognizant of who he was and obviously proud of his accomplishments without wearing them on his sleeve. They had to pry it from him that he was a medical doctor, an eye surgeon, no less and a successful businessman as well as an aficionado of Asian women. Confident, but not boastful. Solid traits to a fault.

"Care to have dinner with us on the Lotus dream tonight?" David asked. "Yeah and feel free to bring as many Thai friends as you please if they look like those two." Bill laughingly remarked. L.J. turned to David. "See? Man still believes I'm a pimp!" All laughed. "Bring a tooth brush. We are very spontaneous. We may just head for Jakarta, or Surabaya for a few days." David said. "I happen to be on a self-imposed two weeks vacation, so I may just take you up on that if you are sincere." L.J. replied. "Oh we are sincere about having an extended party right David?" "Absolutely!" David exclaimed. "Dinner will be served at eight. Party starts whenever the f--ck we all say it does!" Bill exclaimed. "I definitely like your style fellahs."L.J. said with sincerity.

The yacht marketing man rushed through the formalities and was soon introducing David and Bill to the engineering and architectural team who began a tour that lasted nearly three hours. From stem to stern, every detail and nuance of the mega yacht was discussed. At the end of the tour Bill and David were shown to their dual master chambers. Bill had insisted that each suite be appointed identically, with the other, to avoid any semblance of one being more lavish, or important than the other. Bill and David were brothers after all and would remain partners and friends for life.

They returned to the Brokerage office and in the presence of the Builder and Brokerage attorneys accepted ownership of the Lotus Dream. The title was transferred to a trust, that was set up to automatically provide survivorship to either Bill, or David, in the event of the death of either one of them. David brought his own laptop and transferred the paid in full funds, to the Builder's account and also transferred payment in full to the numbered account of the helicopter broker, arms dealer. No ordinance was listed and the weapons and ammunition already stored in the ships armory was completely clean of any sort of paper trail. The armory was not drawn into the ship's blueprints and was instead merely shown as dead space between Bill's master suite and the hull of the ship.

Access was gained by dialling a code number with a cell phone, at which time an electronically powered door slid open to the arms room. The Armory had six rifle racks, each holding six automatic assault rifles that were state of the art special Ops weapons, mostly XM-8's in various configurations. Two L-115-A3 sniper rifles in accessory cases. Two M-79 grenade launchers, several RPG's and several LAW rocket launchers, as well as two long cases full of a wide assortment of semi-automatic and automatic pistols, K-Bar knives and fragmentation HE hand grenades.

"Who are these crew members? How did you ever meet them?" David asked. We'll both meet them for the first time together, in the morning." Bill said. "What? You've never met people who may become as intimate as our ass holes for the next year?" "Yeah! I know. But what choice did I have? The Yacht Brokerage promised me the best available and that they would be bonded maritime tradesmen, certified and with references." Bill said defensively. "I'm sorry Bill, I know you did the only thing you could. How many of them will there be and when will they arrive?" David asked. "They are scheduled to arrive tomorrow morning." Bill replied.

Their passports and visas have all been taken care of by the yacht brokerage."A chef, two certified diesel engine mechanics, two laundry and cleaning women, who are conveniently married to the engine mechanics, a pair of boatswain's mates, who will share shifts steering the yacht and keeping her on course and a radio, electronics and computer, specialist repairman. "What about dinner tonight?" David asked. "I asked the brokerage company to have it catered. It should be here soon. I didn't know if we would have guests, so I played it safe and ordered food and drink for twelve people." "Man I'm really excited Bill! Thanks for the greatest surprise I've ever had man!" Bill smiled at this.

"We deserve it David, after all we've been through." The two men embraced. "Don't worry about the crew David, I'm sure they'll be just fine. Besides the brokerage agent said we can stay berthed here for a month with free rent and electricity and water, if we need that much time to get accustomed to the Lotus Dream. We can put the crew through Chinese drills as much as you'd like to make certain of their competence." "Nah Bill. It's as you say. I'm sure they'll be just fine." The two men went to their suites and got ready for an interesting evening, with a new yacht, a new friend and the beginning of a new life.

At exactly Eight O'clock, L.J. arrived with six women in tow. On a scale of one to ten, each was a ten. Two were Thai, the same two he was with earlier, two were Filipinas and two were Russian. He introduced each girl and then stated. "The women are my house gift. They are paid up for the week and are common to our brotherhood, meaning if you don't get the one you want tonight, she will be available tomorrow." "Bill and David were impressed by L.J's sincerity of wanting to contribute. The party started at dinner, but soon wound up at the pool and lasted all night long.

The crew reported for duty at six AM sharp sending nine nude people scurrying and laughing as they searched for their clothes. Bill wound up wearing a woman's dress wrapped around his privates like a sarong and absolutely no one was wearing the clothes they had on originally. The Filipinas were the funniest, as they modeled Bill and David's trousers which wrapped several times around their waists and the pants legs were rolled up above their knees. By twelve noon, the Lotus Dream was launched without fanfare. Its stores were full and its power systems checked and topped off. "First Jakarta and then if we decide, on to Surabaya," Bill ordered the Boatswain's mate. David couldn't believe how smooth the Lotus took the waves. Even when large vessels passed in other directions, she cut through their wake with barely a notice of surface change. David was astonished at how seldom he saw any crew members. They had been trained to remain invisible unless called for. One of the Boatswain's mates named Hakim had shifty eyes and always looked down at the floor when spoken to.

David mentioned this to Bill, who agreed he should be watched more closely than the rest, but "let's not let anyone stop the fun we're having." He replied. L.J. turned out to be quite a philosopher and well read man. His knowledge of obscure subjects was vast. If a book were written on any given subject, from existentialism to financial strategies, L.J. had already read it and any further editions from the author that were worth reading. He was a traveler at heart. He worked about six months out of the year and traveled every chance he got in between. He knew of pubs and places to have good romantic times with women, from Scandinavia, to Paris and Rio de Janeiro. If it was worth a good time L.J. had been there. He even surprised the Russian women with intimate knowledge of their cities of St. Petersburg and Moscow, repeating places he had been that few outsiders had ever seen.

He was truly a brother and was held in the highest regard by both David and Bill. "Why don't you do a world trip with us?" Bill once asked, after L.J. described a wintry night he had spent with a big bosomed German girl, in the back seat of an old Mercedes, in a place called Wildflecken Germany. "We both knew we were going to freeze to death in that blizzard, after the battery died." he recalled. "So to ensure that my Manhood was the last thing to perish , she selflessly swallowed it all night long, to protect it from freezing, only occasionally coming up for air." Even the women laughed at that story. L.J. stared off in the distance taking his time to answer Bill in just the right way.

"I honestly cannot think of anyone I have ever met in my entire life who I would rather see the world with than you two guys, but the timing isn't quite right for me." "I have a total of ten clinics, and about thirty doctors who I am responsible for. I'm about two years away from being where you two are right now. I will have my businesses ready for a maximum pay out in two years. If I am fortunate enough to be able to cross your paths again, I can only hope you are still on the move." L.J. said.

"Oh we will be," Bill answered firmly. "David and I are rolling stones. We'll only stop rolling when death takes us and even then I'm not so sure about David. He'll be raising hell from hell, I can guarantee you that. Everyone enjoyed Jakarta so much, that it was decided Surabaya would have to wait until the other end of Bill and David's voyage. No one would forget their short week together, they thought as they watched the waterfront harbor, of Tanjung Priok, Jakarta fade into the morning mist. "Would you guys mind, after we drop the girls off in Singapore, if I sail with you as far as Phuket?" "L.J., I wish you could do the world with us especially Brazil. Man, your experience there would be invaluable." Bill replied. "Me too Bill. Someday bro!"

Chapter Eleven: East Of Egypt

As the women waved goodbye at the Singapore pier, Bill said aloud "Now there goes the crew that I wish I had hired." "You'll find plenty more like them where your funky asses are headed!" L.J. laughed. L.J. excused himself to take a bath and sip on some more great champagne. He wasn't a real drinker. He just liked to sample luxury. Each suite had a large, flat screen HD TV. L.J. played with the remote, as he searched for the channel that had soft music and Hawaiian surfing. He felt warm from the champagne and drifted off to sleep.

Caveat Emptor! Buyer Beware! In this case, the warning wasn't about the Lotus Dream. She was, even at thirty million, an excellent buy. Buyer Beware, in this case, was about the thieves who coveted the Lotus Dream. The Brokerage agents had been trained never to mention Malacca Strait and "Lanun", or Pirate, in the same sentence. Bill's broker had only been informed that they planned to sail to Jakarta and then perhaps Surabaya. No one mentioned the Malacca Strait, so why should he? The crew were like sheep. Wherever the yacht owner wished to go, they followed. Their lives as peasant farmers and fishermen taught them obedience and silence in the presence of the rich. Why should they change now?

Once, the second Boatswain's mate, Muhammad, had mentioned that perhaps Mister Bill should be warned of the Strait, but Hakim grew angry and threatened him if he broke ranks, just to gain favor with the foreigners. They were, after all, just rich foreigner Infidels and would exploit their workers. Since the early eighteenth century, the Malacca Strait has offered the most direct route for merchant ships traveling from the Indian Ocean to China, by way of the separation of the land masses of Sumatra from Malaysia.

Known as the Northern gateway to China and South East Asia, via the South China Sea, the Malacca straight surrendered horrible stories of mutilations, forced drowning's and disembowelment by Parang knives, to force victims to divulge, where their precious possessions were hidden. It became legendary. Large ships had been attacked and diverted by the Malaccan Pirates in order to steal cargo. Between 2002 and 2005, some two hundred and fifty eight Pirate attacks forced Lloyd's Of london to declare the Malaccan Strait a war zone, suspending, in some cases insurance, until ships had passed well beyond the place.

Neither Bill, David, or L.J., had seen the fast boat escort they picked up in Singapore, as the Lotus moved Northward into the surly waters of the strait Of Malacca. The pirates of Malacca came in three flavors. Loose unconnected gangs desperate from poverty, who overwhelm a ship, or vessel, with what they refer to, themselves, as "Flying Squirrels", or men who climb ships. The second variety are guerilla groups, such as Abu Sayef or Jemah Islamiah, who kidnap foreigners for ransom to support their political cause.

The third variety, the ones who wanted the Lotus Dream are those who belong to a multinational syndicate, such as the Hong Kong triads, who capture an entire ship, for resale or to off load its cargo. Millions of gallons of oil, or refined fuel, that can be auctioned off, in places like Mogadishu, Somalia, to the highest bidder. This was the variety who had been watching the shipyard waiting for the Lotus dream to be delivered and hit the high seas. That its owners had elected to travel through their homeland, made it even better. Hakim stood aft, watching the fast boats closing the distance. It was dusk, not yet dark enough. His watch wouldn't begin for another thirty minutes. He sent them a text, telling them to add a little more distance, until he gave them the signal to mount the attack.

It would be then that he would cut the engines and lock himself in a storage room, with the ignition keys, until his comrades had taken control of the Lotus Dream. As Hakim approached the Control room, he noticed Bill standing next to Muhammad, asking questions about the radar screen. "Muhammad, I have arrived early for my shift. You can go get some dinner now." Hakim spoke over Bill. Bill became somewhat unsettled by this almost rude interruption. Muhammad ignored the interruption and continued to explain to Bill that the three red spots on the radar, were seaborne craft, that had been maintaining the same formation behind them, since they left Singapore.

With this, Hakim ran out and began to call his conspirators on his cell. David had watched this little episode, from outside the control room and lunged at Hakim just as he yelled into the phone "Do it now!" David knocked the cell phone over board. L. J., who was still in his bath robe, ran up to David as he was breaking both of Hakim's collar bones. Hakim was screaming in pain. L.J. grabbed David around the neck to try to pull him off of Hakim. Bill yelled at L.J. "L.J. let David go, GODDAMNIT! Hakim is a f--cking pirate who has brought his buddies here to kill us all." "Jesus! Sorry David, I didn't know!" L.J. let David go free.

"How many Goddamnit?" David shouted in Hakim's face. "Fifteen men, each boat, three boats forty five men." David glanced down at Hakim's shaking arms and immediately saw it. The unmistakable dragon tattoo of the K-14 triad. "Goddamnit! F--cking triad! Bill I've got it here. Get the chopper revved up. I figure we've got less than three minutes." David stood back and then twisted Hakim's neck quickly, breaking the spinal column at the base of the Medulla Oblongata. He threw the limp body over board. "Whoaa! What the f--ck? David why the f--ck did you just kill that man? He wasn't resisting." L.J. screamed.

"No, his resistance has already occurred. He brought forty five pirates down on our asses L.J. They'll be here faster than shit man. They want this boat and they won't leave witnesses." "Shit! I'm sorry man, I didn't understand." L.J. exclaimed. "I've just never seen anyone killed before." "That's OK. No time to get into it now, follow me." David led L.J. to Bill's suite. He entered and quickly dialed the cell. the door slid open to the Armory. David rapidly loaded L.J. up with six XM-8's and several pistols and grenades, and as many boxes of ammunition as he could carry.

David grabbed two "Dupers", or M-79 grenade launchers and several RPG's and a couple of LAW's. "Will we need all of these?" L.J. asked. "They're all locked and loaded. Quicker to change weapons than reload magazines." David explained. He ran back out on the Flying Bridge, just as Bill yelled down to change over to the choppers frequency. Within seconds, Bill lifted off with the "Little Bird Gun" and headed back South toward the Fast Boats which had nearly reached the wake of the Lotus Dream. All three Fast Boats opened up on the Little Bird Gun, with small arms fire.

Bill had on the directional helmet and he looked down at the nearest boat. His dual Gattling's rotated with Bill's line of sight. He opened up with the Gattling 7.62mm's and the boat disappeared into an explosion of splinters. The outside boat maneuvered to the starboard side of the Lotus Dream and several grappling hooks were thrown onto the yachts railing. The "Flying Squirrels" began to climb their ropes when David saw them. David had L.J. stack the weapons and quickly checked L.J.'s XM-8. "Safety is off, just pull back the sliding mechanism, that's it, you're ready to fire. When it's out, drop it and grab the next one.

If you get to the last one when the magazine is empty push this button to release it. Point the bullets in the same direction as the barrel, shove it until it clicks and then repeat the sliding mechanism and fire." "Got it." L.J. said firmly. "Good, we have bad guys climbing up ropes. I'll see to them. You take these weapons and magazines and watch the port side. Shoot them before they reach our decks." "Got it!" David looked over the side and opened up, unloading an entire magazine, killing seven of the Malaccan pirates. L.J. peered over the port rail. Twelve men were scaling ropes. He squinted as he opened up, chopping six of them to pieces. He quickly grabbed another XM8 and opened up on the remaining six, killing four. Two made it onto the lower deck.

The pirate boat on the starboard side withdrew to give the remaining men a chance to recoup for another attempt. That was what Bill had been waiting for. He opened up with his dual fifty calibre's disintegrating the boat and the men on board into shreds. L.J. pulled two of the fragmentation grenades from his pocket and pulled the pins, dropping them down into the pirate boat below. He heard the driver scream as he veered away from the lotus in a chaotic circle. The boat flipped over in mid air and L.J. saw the frightened looks on the faces of the men he had just doomed, just before the explosion tore them apart. He sat there staring at the frozen memory of those faces, as tears filled his eyes. L.J. heard a noise behind him.

Thinking it was David he began to speak. "I am so ashamed".... when the sharp blade of the Parang cut through his voice box, severing both carotid arteries, nearly beheading him. David had gone down to the lower deck. Finding one of the attackers he shot him between the eyes with his 9mm. By the time he ascended it was too late. The man who killed L.J. jumped down on David, wounding him with the same Parang he used to kill L.J. David saw L.J.'s face contorted in surprise and frozen in death.

David unleashed an evil fury on the assassin, virtually sending his rib cage into his heart, with a powerful double kick. He then emptied his 9 mm into the man's face. Bill landed the Little Bird Gun and ran down to the Flying Bridge. He saw L.J. lying in a pool of his own blood and saw David looking out at the black water, his entire body shaking. Aware, that approaching David now, could be dangerous he softly said "The good always die young David. Anyone who gets it and has a heart they get to them first David." "But why him? He even tried to protect Hakim that's how innocent he was Bill."

"I know David. I know. He sure as hell wasn't collateral damage. I saw from the air that he fought like an Operator. He helped save our asses." Bill bemoaned. "How will we get his body home?" David whispered. "Look at what the dirty bastards did to him Bill." "I saw David. Let me figure this one out. Go get the crew. We're going to pay them for the whole f--cking voyage and let them off in Georgetown. Just get them to clean up all the blood and throw the assassins in the water."

"Have them put L.J. in the meat locker, until we can get him in a proper body bag. Shit David! Your shirt's soaked in blood." "Just a scratch Bill. Bleeding has stopped. What we gonna do for crew?" "We'll crew this big bitch ourselves. It's so computerized, it almost runs itself. " Bill said. Bill dialed his SAT phone. "Omar, it's Bill. Listen buddy we're about two hours South of you. We got shot up pretty bad by Lanun. Yes, David's OK too. We lost a good friend. Can you please bring your boat out to us and get his body? I'll provide an address for you to fly the body to by tomorrow. I'll leave you money to take care of the body. " "Yes, good friend, all here very sad. Omar, I will need to get re-supplied with ammunition and fuel. The fuel I can get at Georgetown, but can you get me the ammo? I'll have a list for you. Intshallah Omar. Thanks."

Bill went through L.J.'s pockets and choked up when he saw the family portrait of his lovely parents and brothers and sisters. David was looking over Bill's shoulder at the photo. "We're f--cking cursed Bill. We're the lowest of the damned. We can't even make friends with anyone without getting them killed. I saw a K-14 Tat on that f--cker Hakim. I thought he was Muslim. How could he belong to a triad?" "He was ethnic Chinese. A minority in Singapore and Malaysia, but they never forget their roots." Bill said.

"Every time we relax and start to feel normal, we will constantly be looking at our sixes, because they will always be one step behind us and forever in our shit Bill. This is a really f--cked way to live man!" "Let the ass holes come David! They will always get twice as much as they give, I shit you not!" Bill shouted. "They got L.J. because he was innocent, man. We didn't jinx him. He could have gotten killed by f--cking Muggers in Jakarta with that much innocence. He fought like a f--cking lion before they got him though. I'll sure as hell give him that!" Bill concluded.

Bill took the bridge and told Muhammad to help the others prepare to leave the Lotus Dream in the Morning. "So sorry, Mistah Bill. We not know about pirates and Hakim. Many Lanun live here. Come from Batam. Very dangerous place. Many poor people. Bad to do things." "Don't worry Muhammad. We don't blame you. Just bad Joss my friend. Intshallah!" "Muhammad was surprised at the Islamic word and bowed his head, in sadness, as he left the bridge. Omar met Bill as the sun was rising, along side the Lotus Dream. He had a wreath of orchids that he placed on the water, beside the yacht as a sign of respect for the dead. Quietly and solemnly, David and Bill carried L.J.'s body to the side and wenched the litter down into Omar's boat. Bill's ammunition store was replaced and the Lotus Dream steered a course for Georgetown, to off load the crew.

They were paid handsomely and given money to fly back to Singapore. David's wound was sutured and soon the Lotus Dream was on a northwestern course toward the Indian ocean. Bill looked down from the bridge at David lying beside the pool with his XM-8 beside his deck chair and his 9 mm firmly gripped in his right hand. Bill wondered about steering the Lotus Dream past Somalia and into the Red Sea. Would there be more pirate attacks along the way? He studied the bridge maps and saw the Maldives. He decided they should probably put to port there until David kicked his current bout of P.T.S.D.

Bill stared at his SAT phone for a very long time before he reached down to pick it up and dial the number. A gentle smooth, matronly mother's voice answered. "Hello, may I help you?" "Is this Mrs. Jones? Mother of Doctor L.J. Jones?" "Yes, it is, why? Is L.J. alright?" Bill choked up. After a brief silence he forced himself to continue. "Ma'am in just a short while he became like a brother to us." Ma'am, I'm so very sorry to have to tell you that your son has passed away. He...." Bill was interrupted by a crying scream. Bill was over come with the pain, that was being delivered to him, directly from that poor woman's soul. Bill almost hung up the phone. He couldn't bear the weight of L.J.'s mothers grief. It was worse than he could have ever imagined it would be.

He hated being the one to deliver such a message, but he hated even more, the idea that she would have been contacted by a U.S. Customs officer. Some uncaring bureaucrat, or worse, a thoughtless policeman on a power trip. They would tell her that the child she had nurtured in her womb, the young boy she held in her arms, the young man who had made her so proud, that she thought her heart would burst, when he received his medical degree, could be picked up at the airport morgue. Abruptly, a deep, man's voice came on the phone. "Who is this?" The voice trembled with anger. "I'm so sorry sir."

" Are you L.J.'s father?" "Yes, I am." "Sir, I only knew your fine son for a short while, but in that brief amount of time, I grew to love him like a brother. He's passed on sir." "What happened?" The deep voice shook ready to break. "We were motoring up the Strait Of Malacca when we were attacked by a large group of pirates who wanted to kill us for our boat. L.J. fought courageously, killing many of the assassins, before they were finally able to kill him."

"Now wait a damned minute! You couldn't have known my son. He worshipped life. He could have never harmed anyone. He was a doctor who saved lives. For all I know you were the one who killed him." "Please Sir. This is hard enough for me as it is." "Where is L. J. now?" "I made arrangements to fly him to your city." "You will be contacted by the airlines when his remains arrive." "Give me your number. I can guarantee you there will be a police investigation." The bereaved father said.

Bill looked out at the great expanse of the ocean and then up at the even greater sky and suddenly felt smaller than he had ever felt in his life. He gently turned off the phone and tossed it out to sea. He looked down at the world atlas in its glass case. He saw immediately, that he was too far east of Egypt and had been, for a very long time. Bill looked down at David again. The last living relic of what seemed to have been Bill's entire miserable life. "Hey David. I hear the Maldives are a good place for snorkeling and f--cking Swedish chicks." "Shut up you horny old goat!" "Can't you see that I'm trying to catch up on a few years of sleep down here?" Bill smiled. He knew that David would wear the weapons all the way to the Maldives, even sleep with them but by then, his post traumatic stress disorder would be some how put back in its cage, until the next time. Until then, he and David would try to forget who they were in the arms of as many women as they could find.

Bill was startled, when, one moment he was looking at David, sleeping by the pool and the next moment discovering David standing behind him with his XM-8, cradled in his arms. "Damn it David! Don't sneak up on me like that, you'll give me a f--cking heart attack! You know how much I hate that shit! We're on a fifty five meter yacht and you can't give me a f--cking phone call or even yell to me that you're on your way?" Bill protested.

"We have to talk, Bill." "Talk is good." Bill joked, trying to recover from his over reaction to David. "I'm serious Bill. What we're doing now is just stupid. You really believe that staying out of Asia for a year will make it all go away? Triads never forget and never forgive. They will stay in our shit until the end of time. There will be no truce. Do you think that global port hopping, in places we have no contacts, friends or back up, while riding on a one hundred and eighty foot long target under our asses is a good plan? We don't need crew, we need soldiers! Violence is what the triads live by, violence is the only thing the f--ckers respect. We have to deliver it to them before they deliver it to us."

"Deliver it first and with a finality even they will have to accept. Maybe, just maybe, they will realize that f--cking with us is just too costly. We sure as hell can't set up a perimeter out in the Indian Ocean. Do you actually think that riding this Onassis class yacht into internationally famous resorts is keeping a low profile? It's f--cked up Bill and you're f--cked up if you believe such shit!" David said with anger. "Too bad I killed Hakim. I should have locked him in a closet. It just seemed like the right thing to do at the time." "Why do you regret killing that slimy bastard?" Bill asked. " Because I could have tortured his ass until he gave us who his immediate controllers are, then we could have started with them until we got to who they were working for all the way to the top. He was planted on this yacht with an agenda.

His back ground file was faked. Your yacht broker was bribed to add him to our manifest. He wanted the yacht as a secondary mission. His first was to capture us and bring us back to Madame Shian' in Hong Kong." "They have spies all over the globe. They probably had you watched since the first time you visited the yacht brokerage in Singapore."

"Your points are all well taken, David. I'm guilty of thinking with my dick and with my heart. I just wanted you and I to taste the good life a little before we die. We were both robbed of our youth by the CIA and a government that considered us expendable, in general. A government that taught us violence and then walked away from us. I'm every bit as tired of this shit as you are. I hate the killing too. But it's like a poker game with the Devil. Apparently, you can't just take your winnings and go when you want to leave. That Kenny Rogers shit about knowing when to fold up, doesn't apply to the game we've been into. Maybe the part about knowing when to run does and that's what I thought we could do, but I see what you're saying is the cold and bitter truth, we can run, but we can't hide. Especially in a forty million dollar luxury yacht."

"So you're the Operator, David. Tell me what to do and we'll do it brother." "For real Bill?" "Of course for real. I'm in this shit with you for life, man. So instead of hauling ass out of Asia on a mega yacht, what do you recommend we do?" "The first thing we need to do is get back to invisibility. Lower our profile to harder to see than we ever were. We need to turn this Albatross around and deliver it back to the Singapore brokerage for dry dock maintenance and storage. A few thousand bucks a month and our toy is controlled by us, instead of the other way around. We can always collect it again, with our own hand picked crew and take the world cruise when we know the war is really over for us." "OK. What then?" Bill asked.

"Then we get our mercenaries back and I'll write an Ops order to end all Ops orders. Our mission? Assassinate the entire leadership of the three main triad societies in Hong Kong. "They are the ones who are trying to assassinate us. We take their plan and burn them with it, before they can burn us. Then we can leave the poker table because we will have cashed in all of the players who don't want us to leave without stripping us bare."

"David, you have opened my eyes and now I see. It isn't enough to just want to live your life in peace. You first have to set in motion a defensive perimeter on your own terms. The war stops when we say it stops and here I thought you were just a P.T.S.D wing nut who likes guns. Your assessment is deep and clear my friend." "Wing nut. Is that what you think about me?" "Hey, you're the one who goes swimming with an automatic rifle and a pistol!" "OK my last recommendation for our new plan is that you strap on until the war is over!" David said with a smile. "Yes Sir! " Bill replied with a grin.

" Do you think our previous team will work for us if they find out we once were involved in a heroin operation?" Bill asked. "Who has to tell them? We aren't in that business anymore. This mission is a pre-emptive strike against people who are trying to kill us first, based on their own agenda and principles. We can probably get, not only the six we had before, but a dozen new mercenaries to boot. It's not like we are short on funds!" "Turn this beautiful tub around Bill and let's make ready to travel straight back through pirate alley. They will be totally unprepared and shocked that we have the balls to return there so soon." David said. "Remember the strategy for getting out of ambushes in Vietnam? Attack the main ambush element head on and get behind the ambush where you can inflict the highest damage. Ambush the ambushers." "David you're beautiful man."

"Going back to Phnom Penh is the only real option we have." Bill said. Bill tapped in new GPS data into his control panel and the yacht began its wide arc, reversing its direction back to the South East with a new, one hundred and eighty degree azimuth change. Bill turned the bridge over to David and ran a complete weapons system check on the Little Bird Gun. The Little Bird Gun had a cruising range of two hundred fifty miles. Half way back down the Strait Of Malacca, where the pirates seemed to be the thickest, Bill would fly recon to see what the hundreds of inlets and scores of tiny islands, that peppered the Malaysian and Sumatran coastlines had to offer. The Northern mouth of the Strait was about two hundred and fifty miles across, at its widest, but the further South one traveled the narrower the Strait became.

Its narrowest range at the lower end, was just ten miles wide. From the bridge, David watched the dark waters like a hawk. He waited for the sudden change, along the horizon, that would quickly become a hazy view of shapes, that got clearer, as the fast boats would be expected to approach with surprise and malice. If they came again, they would have the taste for revenge fresh in their bellies, for what had been done to their brothers. It would be a hard fight, but David and Bill were feeling like wild animals with their backs against the wall and were spoiling for whatever the sea would bring them.

David thought about his conversation with Bill and secretly weighed the risks. "What if Bill was right? Leaving and laying low would have been the best plan. But not on this mega yacht. Not enough flexibility and way too high a profile." David thought. Would lopping off the head of the triads work, or would it just stir their anger and resolve even more. David didn't know. He only knew they had to do something, even if it was wrong.
He blamed Ma Fai Zhi and Madame Shian' for how things had turned out. Definitely extremely bad karma.

Chapter Twelve: Tin Hau, Queen Of Heaven

"Stop thinking about things you cannot change!" David scolded himself. They were now committed on a course that demanded focus and the expenditure of all resources necessary to accomplish the mission. This time, more than any other time in his life, David understood they were playing for keeps. Winner take all, loser will die, were the stakes and there were no other rules. Bill hated going in a reverse direction. He was the kind of person who would drive one thousand miles forward, before he would consider going even one mile back.

Yet, his instincts told him David was right. They weren't giving up on the world tour, or the good life that Bill always dreamed of, they were merely delaying their schedule, long enough to wrap up some loose ends. What nagged at Bill was not being able to comprehend who the enemy really was. It could turn out to be like trying to kill a weed, only to discover that the weed was a sapling from a root of a one hundred ton tree. Would the act of beheading triad leaders really kill the beast? Bill knew it wouldn't but it may buy some valuable time to build a real defense. A defense in depth that would swallow anyone who opposed you.

If things went south, for David's protection, Bill would split with him and lead the assassins away. David was never involved in the actual production, or distribution of heroin. He didn't deserve to die for it as much as Bill knew that he did. Madame Shian' fit Winston Churchill's apt description. She was indeed a mystery wrapped up inside an enigma. She controlled millions of dollars, decided who lived and who died, meted out rewards for success and punishment for failure, stopped petty bickering and swayed the outcome of complicated plots, that would have been the envy of the Guelfs and the Ghibellines, all without an office and a secretary.

Her office was a hand bag. She had never been arrested and certainly no one had ever managed to directly threaten her life. She had brushed past an Interpol agent on the streets of Kowloon once. By the time he realized who he had just seen, he turned around and she was gone. Who could have ever dreamed that she would eventually be compromised by a brilliant chip designer in Santa Clara, in the heart of the Silicon Valley?

The chip was called a "Chip on board" design, because it had everything an entire computer would need to function. Power supply, memory, both random and operational and a sensor that would allow a deaf person to hear and a blind person to see. It's short coming had been size. Micro circuits rely on gates, to direct electronically powered signals and commands to be sent in appropriate and logical directions. The gates are traffic cops, so to speak. For decades shrinking the size of a micro chip was inhibited by the inability to shrink the size of the metal gates. The line width of the circuits, were already sub-micron, but there was just so much one could do with metal.

The brilliant discovery involved using liquid, instead of metallic gates and eureka! the brave new world of atomic micro-circuitry was born. What this meant for Madame Shian' was that global interface satellite systems could now process every voice recovery in the world, simultaneously and that her system of throw away cell phones to maintain obscurity had been rendered obsolete. Her voice was discovered in a routine scan and relayed to Admiral Donaldson. "Al, it's all in Mandarin, but the boys in NSA are 100% certain it's her.

We traced the cell to Kern's place in Tachilek. Listen to the translation."

"Yes! You imbecile, it's Madame Shian' but I'm growing tired of excuses. You were given more information on the man than would have been needed by even a semi-skilled person to capture him and his associate, yet I sit awaiting the success of your mission, looking at an empty chair where he should be." "So sorry supreme Madame Shian'. We placed a man on his yacht and even though we could have taken him as he left Singapore, we followed your own directions and waited until we received the signal to board his yacht, from our planted man, before we took action. We were not informed that there would be three gunmen and we were also not informed that they had air attack capability with heavy weapons and rockets. The men we recruited in Batam were eager and obedient but they were chopped to pieces by the air defense. All forty five." "It took us months to recruit them, now, thanks to this we are no longer welcome in the back streets of Batam." "I must hang up imbecile, your whining has used all of my telephone time. Know this:" "If your triad cannot handle the matter, I will consult the other two Dragon Heads and make plans that no longer include you." "As you wish supreme Madame Shian."

"Man, what a bitch." Captain Peterson observed. "Yeah. She would make one hell of a woman Marine First Sergeant." Admiral Donaldson quipped. "Sir, that isn't nice." Both men laughed. "Al who in hell do you think she's talking about?" "It could only be Bill Murphy and David Anderson. They're the ones who gave us her heroin. She must be burning like an ember about that, not to mention, from the NSA taped conversations that day, we believe she paid for it before it was given to us." "Hmm. Yes, that would have caused her at least an ulcer, I should think. So the man she spoke with was whom?"

"The boys at NSA tell us it was an exact voice fit for Chao Cheng Lei. He's the Dragon Head of the Wo Shing Wo Hong Kong triad. They have responsibility for alternate Asian safe houses for the China White network." "They seldom do business further South than Phuket, Thailand because it's an automatic death sentence in Singapore and Indonesia to be caught with as little as a few ounces of heroin. Mind you things aren't any friendlier in Thailand, but at least there, it's still possible to bribe your way out." "Any confirmation it was really him?" "Yes Sir, the CCC, or Chinese Commercial Code was Chao (6473) Cheng (8721) Lei (9490). Hong Kong police put him in Interpol's data bank years ago when he was still a "Red Pole", or enforcer for the Wo Shing Wo." "I see. Amazing. China has so many f--cking people the only way the police can keep track of them is to assign four digit numbers to each of their three names. Boggles the f--cking mind."

"Yes Sir. There's probably a few million Chao Cheng Lei's but only one with those three sets of numbers." "I told you Murphy would go straight. That's why she wants to kill his ass so badly, I guess." Admiral Donaldson reflected. "It did sound personal, Sir." "What of General Kern? What's he up to these days?" Admiral Donaldson asked. "He is working his Meth labs overtime, probably trying to compensate for the heroin loss." "Heroin? I thought because the Junta took out his heroin labs his involvement was now limited to raw opium and Meth." "Yes Sir, normally it is, but again, our NSA tapes reveal he had a deal cooked up with Madame Shian'." "Their deal called for Kern to take half of the middle man profit, for eliminating Bill Murphy and his people, which we of course, prevented, by taking out General Kern's people with our SEALS, when they invaded Murphy with the Caribou." Captain Peterson explained.

"Damn but that Murphy is slick. He gets us to eliminate an enemy for him, while he sells four tons of pure heroin that he gets paid for, but delivers to us instead. If you had any doubts about him returning to the business, that should dispel them. He burned his last bridge with that caper." "Does that mean our deal with him is off Admiral?" "Hell no Al, a deal is a deal. He reneged on drug dealing triads who were trying to kill him. I would have done the same in his shoes." "Yes Sir." "Looks like we will have to treat General Kern and the triads as two separate issues. I don't see the two of them getting back together soon, do you Al?"

"Not soon Sir, but the growers need the processors and distributors. Unless Kern breaks out of Myanmar and replaces the triad heroin network that took the triads decades to develop, they will have to kiss and make up sooner, or later." Captain Peterson considered. "I want to take both of those entities out Al. Can you imagine what that will do to the Golden Triangle? Yes Sir but it's not going to be easy." "Nothing is ever easy Al."

After signing a berthing and maintenance lease and insuring the Lotus Dream, Bill and David, using fresh fake passports then caught a plane for Bangkok. They stayed a few days in Pattaya, but only took women they already knew from beer bars near Soi two, to avoid running into anyone who may spread the word they were in town. Soi two was close to their hotel, which Bill thought made it safer. They dined in and turned in early with their women, strolling along the beach walk only after dark. One morning, after getting a massage at their favorite Thai massage parlor, they caught a hired limousine to Bangkok and flew Air Cambodia into Phnom Penh.

They appeared to be just two typical sex tourists and were ignored at the airport, except for being over charged for their visas. Normally Bill would have raised hell with the immigration agent, but this time, he merely paid the fifty U.S. dollars and walked outside to where a line of taxis were waiting. "Can you believe that son of a bitch? David?" "Glad you let it go Bill." David said. Within thirty minutes they were driving past their NGO S.H.A.R.I. Two Khmer policemen were standing guard at the gate which was locked with a heavy chain. They took rooms in a small, but clean hotel along the river front, that even boasted of two rooms on the top floor with a terrace view of the Mekong. Later on in the evening, they took an old reliable private driver and toured past David's villa. Sitting parked halfway down the block was a black SUV with dark tinted windows. "Triad goons!" David remarked.

Their private driver didn't slow down when they passed, as he had been instructed not to by Bill and the men inside the SUV didn't become suspicious. When they drove past Bill's villa, an exact SUV was waiting and watching a half a block away from Bill's front gate. "You'd think they'd be creative and have a different vehicle at each house." Bill said. "Perhaps they think we're stupid enough to come home separately," David responded.

"OK, let's get out to our safe house and see how good these guys really are." Bill said. They drove a few kilometers out of town in the direction of Sihanoukville and turned out the lights as they entered the old dirt road that led to their farm house. No vehicles were around, but Bill and David both chambered rounds in the AK-47's their driver had brought them and loaded their 9 mm pistols. David circled around the house and Bill walked onto the front porch.

Each had a key and both entered, clearing the house, room, by room. "All clear!" David yelled. "All clear in the front!" Bill replied. The house was immaculate and kept so by a rice farmers wife, Bill had hired six years earlier. "How soon can you bring in the team?" Bill asked. "I will call them all tonight and give them the time and place in a code I left with them." David said. "Great! Look the frig is full of Barang food and beer. Let's eat here tonight and get some sleep. Tomorrow we will see if we can recruit some people." Bill said. "Starting tonight let's get your driver to bring in some of his best security people and post them in shifts." David said. Just then another vehicle pulled into the driveway with three Khmer men. "Already taken care of David. Those are Bonarith's brothers." David checked out the new men and was satisfied they were professionals. Thanking them for their vigilance, he shook hands with each man and returned inside the house. "Bonarith, Bill's driver, showed the men to the downstairs bedroom where two would sleep, while the other two, including himself, were on shift.

Before sunrise, the mercenaries shuffled in from the covered farm truck, David used, to bring them to the safe house. Each eyed the surroundings warily. "Quite a change of digs mate." Clive said to David. "Don't let the surroundings throw you," David replied. "We're stronger than we ever were. We have a new situation and we had to go to the mattresses," Bill added. All six of the original team were there and one extra man, Mitch Ellis an American, who was vouched for by John Mason, Raptor Five, who flew the mission at Houay Xay Laos. "Mitch went through Special Ops training for pilots with me," John explained, which was good enough for everyone except Bill Murphy. He would wait until later and have a word with David. In the meantime, Bill had Bonarith assign a man to follow Mitch and to place an undetectable bug in his room, until he was certain the man was trustworthy. "David will you brief our friends?" Bill asked.

A lavish table of food and drink was set out and the meeting was informal. "We seem to have stirred the hornets nest with our Ops in Hong Kong and Laos." David began. "Three of the largest triads in Hong Kong, the K-14, The Wo Shing Wo and the Sun Yee On, all have us on their radar." "They have active sanction orders for Bill and myself and anyone who is working with us. Anyone who has studied the triads are aware of their tradition of Tongchi, or burial while still alive. They have sworn themselves to capture Bill and myself, alive, in order to give us a burial of one hundred thousand slices, or razor cuts, that will cause us suffering, as we are buried alive. Don't worry, if they capture any of you, they will merely bury you alive without the razor cuts." David said without smiling. The entire room burst into nervous laughter.

"Our principle targets include a Madame Shian' Ming Xian, who is the real decision maker for over one hundred fifty thousand triad members world-wide. The Dragon Masters, or top leaders of each of the three societies, start with Chao Cheng Lei, supreme leader of the Wo Shing Wo." "The Wo Shing Wo are primarily involved in gambling and casinos. They own a large portion of the action in Las Vegas and Reno, but wisely let the Italian American mafia draw all of the attention. They started out in Macau and even stretched their tentacles into Monte Carlo. Drugs account for less than ten percent of their total operation, but they are very much involved in providing security for the heroin network that stretches from Hong Kong to San Francisco Los Angeles and New York."

"The second triad is led by Feng Hong Hui, who is the Dragon Master of the Sun Yee On. This society, by far, is the largest and most powerful, of all triad societies in Hong Kong. It's membership exceeds twenty five thousand members in Hong Kong and about fifty six thousand members worldwide." "It has a hidden share of major movie companies in Hollywood and virtually controls all film making in Asia.

Bruce Lee was almost murdered by this triad and escaped Tongchi, only by taking flight to the West. Some believe that his strange death and that of his son, was triad revenge. This society goes all the way back to the Heung family of the Guomintang, or Kuomintang and has unlimited resources in Taiwan, as well as Hong Kong."

"Finally, in no small measure, the most threatening is the K-14 triad society. It has the most global members of any triad society, somewhere between one hundred and one hundred twenty five thousand members world-wide." "It has been the primary creator of international heroin delivery networks throughout the world. This triad has engaged us with assassins already and this triad, more than any other has vowed to destroy us. It's leader, Hung Jian Yu is a very dangerous man." By now, you have probably surmised that our only hope of surviving such a focused effort to eliminate us, hinges on our ability to preempt our enemy, to kill them in their kitchens, before they have a chance to cook us in their pots.

Your mission, if you decide to accept, is the complete annihilation of Madame Shian' Ming Xian, Chao Cheng Lei, Feng Hong Hui and Hung Jian Yu, four targets, four hits." "The sooner, the better, before they find us and take us out first. We believe that eliminating these four leaders, will so disrupt the international drug networks, they may never fully recover. "At the very least, it should give us the space we need, to live out the rest of our lives, without constantly looking over our shoulders." "Those who take the place of these four, will be too busy trying to hold on to their new inheritance of power and will, most likely, not even care about hunting down those who caused their sudden promotions. We have about a fort night to prepare for this mission. That is when the Tin Hau Festival will take place on the 23d day of the third lunar month. It is during this festival that new triad member initiation rituals are performed.

This tradition almost demands the presence of all four triad leaders.""According to my sources in Hong Kong, they are scheduled to be there. We will send an advance team within two days to photograph our targets and gather intel regarding their habits and repetitive movements."

"The secondary mission, is the elimination of a certain Shan General named Jon Kern, who supervises a large drug operation center in Tachilek Burma. We will issue detailed Ops orders by tomorrow, for any who wish to engage the contract." David concluded. "There is one small difference between this mission and the last one," Bill enjoined. "The last mission paid fifty thousand each, with a ten thousand bonus. This one pays one hundred thousand, with a twenty five thousand bonus."

"American dollars, paid into any account number you provide." A silence filled the room. "Questions?" David asked. "David, I know you to be a bloke who delivers on his promises and as a fellow operator I would follow you into Hell, but by Jesus, there's something bloody missing here what? We are professionals, do, or die and all that rot, but you Goddamned owe us all of the information we need to make a decision, whether to join you again, or not and you know I am right!" "Sergeant Major, you are right." Bill said. "The truth is almost always simple, but not always easy to describe. The simple truth Sergeant Major is that I have been involved in running heroin distribution for the CIA, since the Vietnam war." Bill confessed. "I offer no apology. I was a f--cking drug king pin and I did my job well. Too well, I suppose.""My karma finally caught up with me and I was forced to either quit the business, or be taken down by one hell of a mean Navy SEAL team." "They were sent to end my operations, by a man of high respect, an Admiral Donaldson of the Joint Inter Agency Task Force West, based in Hawaii." "They operate missions with SEALS and other Special Ops organizations against terrorism and drugs. I saw the light.

I read between the lines, I found Jesus. I gave Donaldson my word of honor, if he'd let me go, I would never get involved in drugs again and I f--cking meant it, I never will. I aim to keep my word." Bill said with deep conviction. "I could drown you now with morality and idealism, as my reasons for quitting. I'd be lying. Every man should know when he has gone too far. My guts simply told me it was no longer as it used to be and that my time to die for nothing, had come, or I could just walk away. I chose to walk away, while I still could." "The triads are my last obstacle to walking away and have made themselves a heavy burden for my having lived a rotten life. If they kill me it will be a strange sort of justice, because both God and the Devil know I deserve it." "If we kill them first, we will have the pleasure of knowing we stopped the evil that I became entrenched in, for so many years. I simply want to go away with my friend David and f--ck as many Asian whores as an oriental society will allow." Bill concluded.

"He left out one small detail, Gentlemen." David interjected. "He turned over four tons of 99% pure China White to Admiral Donaldson no favors asked, other than to just be allowed to leave and live a celibate life as far as future drug Ops are concerned." David said. "Don't make me out a hero, David. Remember that Madame Shian' had already paid me for it before I gave it to the good Admiral." The room erupted in applause and laughter. "Jesus, four tons, that was the bust we saw on the evening news. No wonder the triads want your bloody balls on a nail! David, Bill, I believe you." Clive said. "But do you believe the triads would really want to end you, before they get back their China White?" Clive asked. "We assume they know the China White has been destroyed, but wait, it gets better. He f--cked Madame Shian' at thirty thousand feet and he must not have hit the sweet spot." David chimed in. The house came down. Bill turned crimson. "Did you really shaft that bitch?" Clive asked.

Bill looked at the floor, genuinely embarrassed and shook his head vigorously yes. "Even after that and my perfect willingness to treat her with respect, she tried to have General Kern's henchmen kill me with my own airplane and rob me of my hard earned wealth."

"So I robbed her instead." Bill said sheepishly. "I told him that he should have sent me!" David said. "I would have had her give every man here a b j just because you're my friends." Again the house came down, until Bill clapped his hands and tried to return to a professional meeting. "Well Sergeant Major and the rest of you, are you with us?" "Wouldn't miss it for all the tea in bloody China" The Sergeant Major roared. He was followed by a unanimous raising of the glasses as Bill screamed out "Death Before Dishonor!" The Sergeant Major leaned toward David. "Why does he always say that?" "Beats the shit out of me, I think he saw it once in a movie." David replied.

"Here! Here!" the men all shouted. Suddenly, Mitch stood up and drew his 9 mm pistol, shooting it into the ceiling. The room became silent. All eyes were on Mitch as he put his pistol back in his waistband. "Gentlemen, the time has come for me to blow my own cover. My name is really Mitch, but I am not yet a mercenary. I am an active duty SEAL Commander. I was sent here by Admiral Donaldson to determine if Bill Murphy had indeed lived up to his word." "I am now convinced that he is sincere. The camera that is allowing Admiral Donaldson, to have been a silent participant of this meeting, was planted here, by me, a few minutes before you started your meeting. Admiral can you hear us?" "Loud and clear Mitch!" Came the Admiral's voice over Mitch's cell phone loudspeaker. "Jesus!" Bill cried out. "How in Hell did you breach our security?" "That's my fault Bill. I trusted the Son Of A Bitch!" John Mason said. "Hold on! Goddamn it!" Admiral Donaldson shouted.

"If I wanted you dead you would all have already been taken out." Admiral Donaldson growled. "Gentlemen. It seems that your mission, as discussed by David Anderson and Bill Murphy, is a mission that we want to support you with." "We share the same enemies. That means that I will now ask both Bill Murphy and David Anderson to work for me. If you agree, you will immediately have two MC-130e Combat Talon II aircraft at your command, as well as a complete SEAL Team at your disposal.

I need not remind you, I'm sure, that a complete SEAL Team consists of six platoons of sixteen men per platoon, or ninety six special operators, who have been trained to fight to the death." "Lastly, if any of your mercenaries need to come in from the cold, we will not only pay them for you, per your agreement with them, we will grant them a free pass." "That means we will eliminate anything they may desire to expunge from their past, no matter how gruesome." "Even the wrong side of Rwanda, but I sure hope that won't be the case."

"Sir, we cannot imagine a greater honor than working side by side with you to end the Golden Triangle but we don't need ninety six SEALS and just one of those MC-130e Talon II's would be sufficient for us in Tachilek. I will issue a detailed Ops order by tomorrow, but we will need a way to get four Sniper teams into Hong Kong, in about two weeks without drawing any attention. Not a suitable mission for a Talon II. A Navy submarine would allow us to infiltrate at night, bringing our weapons." "If we have to fly in commercially, we may draw attention from our last visit." David said. "Good! I have a submarine you can use and I have a CIA operative, in Hong Kong who will meet you near the sub and bring you to shore on his yacht." "He will bring all of the Sniper gear you request. What else do you need?" The Admiral asked. "Well, we already have one crack sniper and spotter. I am sniper experienced and can train one of our mercenaries to spot for me.

We could use two more snipers with spotters preferably ethnic Asians, so we don't stick out like a sore thumb. That will allow us to take out all four targets simultaneously. I have a contact in Kowloon who informed me just a while ago that our weapons supplier was murdered, after our last mission, so your CIA agent will come in handy with picking us up and delivering our weapons to us." "My source also informs me that our four targets are scheduled to officiate over some triad initiations at the Tin Hau Temple in two weeks."

"This will happen on the day of the Tin Hau festival which takes place in exactly two weeks. I'd like to take out all of the targets at the same time as they ride on their Guests Of Honor Float." David said. "You won't have to train anyone. I have both Sniper and Spotter experience." Mitch remarked. "Great." David said.

"I will lead the triad assassination mission. Bill, along with our other four mercenaries, can do an insertion at Tachilek, with your Talon II and paint the place up pretty well that same evening. Admiral could you start tasking a bird daily on General Kern's complex in Tachilek right up to the night we hit him?" David asked. "Done! I will ensure that Mitch gets detailed SAT photos with analysis on a daily basis." The Admiral assured David.

"Give me the names and whatever other information you have on the triad targets and I will have the CIA get you up to date photos and daily routines of each of them. Be sure to include the CCC's so we don't kill the wrong Chinese." The Admiral added. "Roger that!" David agreed. "Admiral, if you could assign four Predators of the T-8 Drone class, each with three Hell Fire missile pods, I guarantee we will be able to lop off the head of Kern's drug Ops at Tachilek." David said confidently. "That's what I've been waiting to hear!" Admiral Donaldson almost shouted.

"If any of your men do not wish to partake in our operation, please put them under house arrest with reasonable per diem, which I will pay, until our operation is concluded, for security reasons of course." David scanned the room. "All in favor of joining with the JIATF-W for the duration of both operations, please raise your hands." David took the head count. "It's unanimous, Admiral. We all will join your team for the two Ops." David said. "Good! Work up your Ops orders David. Make them like your last one, which caught us by complete surprise." Admiral Donaldson said. "Give Mitch my copy. He will get it to me in our diplomatic pouch marked Ultra Secret. Mitch will act as my boots on the ground until the operations conclude." "Thank you Admiral!" Bill shouted.

"To the contrary, I thank all of you for finally getting on the right side of things!" "Admiral Sir!" Bill called out suddenly. "Yes Mr. Murphy." "I accept this mission only if David and I are Commanders on the ground. Your man Mitch can advise us, but we make final decisions." A moment of silence ensued. "God damn but you are brazen Mister Murphy. Except for the two sniper teams and the crew of the C-130e you won't have any one from my side to give orders to. Mitch will observe and assist as a spotter in Hong Kong, but that will be the extent of his involvement. If Mitch tells me you have wandered off the reservation, I will pull all support even if I have to leave you walking.

If you f-- ck this mission up, I will deny that this meeting ever took place. Is that understood Mister Murphy?" "Perfectly clear Admiral Sir!" Bill said with a grin. "Mitch, how soon can we get the MC-130e ?" David asked. "How soon do you want it?" Mitch replied. "Yesterday?" "Roger. It will be at the Phnom Penh airport tomorrow Morning." "Good, I'd like Bill's team to do some practice missions with it before they go live." David said. "There's some remote farmland the Cambodian army used to use for parachute training jumps, that I know about.

No minefields and the farmers are used to seeing parachutes." David told Mitch. The MC-130e is a special operators dream aircraft. It flies, day, or night, in clear, or stormy weather, with equal efficiency. It's electronic systems are state of the art. Its DIRCM, or Directional Infra Red Countermeasures, incorporate sixty different systems, which interface with other on board systems, to enhance the aircraft's survivability, against all known infra red guided missile systems.

It even has a system that locates infra red guided missiles, before they are launched. It is equipped with hardware and software that virtually eliminates its own IR signature, making it nearly impossible to detect at low flying altitudes. It flies securely at canopy level at night, or in severe weather, using TFTAR, or Terrain Following, Terrain Avoidance, Radar. In addition to oversized doors and ramp for HALO, or High Altitude, Low Opening parachute insertions, as well as LALO, Low Altitude, Low Opening, it has a Fulton Air Recovery system. FARS makes it possible to extract Special Operators, without having to land the aircraft.

The Special Operator takes a sitting position facing the oncoming aircraft and releases a helium balloon that is securely connected to a very high tensile strength wire that is four hundred fifty feet in length. The aircraft is flown beneath the balloon and a snare collects the wire. The Special Operator is then reeled, hydraulically into the open ramp end of the aircraft. The MC-130e has a range of 3,110 miles on one tank of gas, fully loaded with twenty six fully armed, combat equipped paratroopers. It is powered by four Allison T-56-A-15 Turbo-Prop engines, with 4,910 shaft horse power per engine. David knew about each of its available technologies as he wrote his operations order for Bill's mission.

Bill knew the risk Admiral Donaldson was taking, by associating with members of a TNCO. He knew that if things went south, the Admiral would be reprimanded, a star would be taken from his three stars and he would be forced to retire. He also knew that Donaldson was an original SEAL who had helped convert the initial Navy frogmen, from mere demolitions experts, into Special Operators, who had grudgingly won the respect from Marine Force Recon, and U.S. Army Special Forces.

He knew how badly Donaldson wanted to end the Triangle and the personal risks he was obviously prepared to take to accomplish his objectives. In another time and place he would have enjoyed serving under such a man. He became a rogue agent after the CIA abandoned him twice but it didn't blind him to the patriotism and heroism of others who he secretly and deeply admired.

He was pleased that Donaldson would be at the Com or in charge of the ship, so to speak. He made his remark about authority earlier to get an exact read on just how much support he could expect in Tachilek. The answer was honest and clear. If things get f--cked up, you're on your own! Admiral Donaldson thought about Murphy after he hung up the phone. He would have loved to have had both Murphy and Anderson if they hadn't been ruined by the CIA years ago.

Yet they were powerful, dangerous men. Perfect for what he needed now. After Admiral Donaldson hung up the phone Captain Peterson weighed in. "Sir, did I just observe you make a pact with the Devil?" "Al, I guess that's one way to look at it." The Admiral said dryly. "But think about it Al. I can't send a SEAL team into Myanmar. My ass would be on fire all the way back to my court martial in Washington. Murphy, on the other hand can go in with his mercenaries and destroy the Shan army with Predators.

If it goes south we can claim our MC-130e had radar problems and veered off course. Once the fire works start the Drones will pull out and the Junta, glad to be rid of Kern won't complain about a violation of their airspace. SEALS are a different story. If they started taking casualties, we'd have one hell of an international incident on our hands. Mercenaries are in it for the money and who gives a shit about mercenaries other than me?" "What about Hong Kong Sir?" Peterson asked.

"Hong Kong is easy Al. The minute the CIA agreed to put their field agent in charge, when I approached them earlier it became their operation. I won't even task the Marines for the two Shooter teams. They will. They'll even lay on the submarine. We'll just pass on the requests." "If Bill, or David get captured in either place, it will look like a drug war gone bad. Our only risk is the MC-130e but I have our asses covered even on that one." "I have two Raptors on call at all times to protect my MC-130e. I feel sorry for anyone who approaches from the air. That leaves ground fire. If I'm that unlucky, I guess I'll just take the punishment." The Admirals eyes narrowed into two slits making him look like a wise Mandarin, as he sipped his tea and pondered the missions that lay ahead.

" Al, it's all about character. " "If it had just been Murphy, I would have probably passed on the whole show but there's something about that Anderson guy that makes me think we may just be able to pull this off. Character is what is left after everything else has been stripped away. Anderson is mucho Hombre Al and he has the cajones to succeed under impossible circumstances." "Al get that MC-130e to Phnom Penh as soon as possible and follow up on the arrival of the two shooter teams also in Phnom Penh, on the day of mission execution. Keep me copied on the details of the submarine rendezvous as well. Ride herd personally on the T-8 Predators and make sure they are on station when they're needed.

We'll get involved with the Special Delivery SEAL vehicle the day of the rendezvous and once the CIA agent picks them up, we go back to an observer role." "Make sure the two Hitter teams are ethnic Asians. Otherwise let the CIA worry about their own details." "Yes Sir!"

Neither Bill, David, or even Admiral Donaldson really knew and understood the triads. They made the popular mistake of believing the triads were a simple ethnic Chinese mafia, a criminal organization based on birth right. To be certain, the triads were all of these things, but much much, more. The triad societies were created in the late seventeen hundreds, when a secret society named Tian Di' Hui was formed for the specific purpose of overthrowing the Qing dynasty, that was saturated with hated Manchurian leaders.

Everywhere, in every province, the common people of China yearned for a return to the Han dynastic rule. By 1911 the Heung clan, which grew from the Tian Di Hui, succeeded in overthrowing the Qing dynasty however, the patriotic society, itself, had not participated directly in the uprising. As a consequence, the society, which, by then was referred to as the "triad" society, from the fact that it used a triangular symbol, to represent the harmony, between Heaven, Earth and Man, struggled for a consciousness and a cause to justify perpetual existence. It managed somehow, to become the national soul and allegiance of a China in trouble and became both an embodiment of Chinese history, as well as a collection of China's primary philosophical resources, from Taoism, to Confucianism and finally, Buddhism.

The main heroic character of the triad societies was a man named Lord Guan Gong, a heroic figure from the Han Dynasty and the period of the Three Kingdoms. Lord Guan Gong emblazoned the concept of humility into the Chinese psyche as being superior.

Understatement versus overstatement, remains the guideline of all Asians, who wish to be known as civilized. His legacy was the embodiment of the six qualities of a humble man; humanism, righteousness, ritual obedience wisdom, loyalty and trust.

To this very day, all triad societies worship the character and example of Lord Guan Gong, however, no one can explain just how the triads eroded, from a patriotic institution into a nearly fanatical criminal enterprise, over a period of two and a half centuries. To overcome this, the triads have observed historic rituals, in an attempt to establish legitimacy. The Tin Hau festival, that David chose for an assassination mission, was one of a dozen such ritual festivals observed by the triads, but he couldn't have known just how fervently patriotic this festival really was. His mission could be compared, in some ways, to deciding to assassinate the President of France on Bastille day. On such a day, if the Chinese learned that foreigners had assassinated important Chinese leaders, especially triad leaders, no foreigner in Hong Kong, not protected by the police, or in possession of an iron clad alibi would be safe. Tin Hau or "Queen Of Heaven" is revered by Asians especially along the coastal regions of the China Sea, from Vietnam, in the South, to Taiwan in the North, as a protector of fishermen and sailors. Known also as Matsu, she was once a real person named Lin, who drowned at the age of twenty eight.

Neither Taoist, or Buddhist, she is revered by both religions. Born during the Song Dynasty, in the Fujian province of China, she became a folk legend that lasted until the present, as a young Goddess who drowned trying to save her father and brothers from a typhoon. According to the folk legend, she flew, magically, down from the clouds to pluck her family from the sea. Now she watches over all sailors and holds back the mighty sea until they become safe again.

Tin Hau is, herself, protected by two spirits. The first, Qiyan Liyan, or spirit with a thousand eyes, who is believed able to see a seafarer, in trouble, from a thousand miles away. The second Shun Feng, or spirit with favorable ears is believed able to hear cries for help, as far as the wind can travel. Each spirit alerts Tin Hau of peril at sea. There are several temples dedicated to Tin Hau, but the grandest is the Tai Miu Wan, on a hill top above the fishing village of Sai Kung overlooking Joss House Bay. Each year, on her birthday a procession of boats make their way from Hong Kong Island to the fishing village of Sai Kung, in the New Territories, all decked out in an explosion of colorful flags and decorations. Seafarers go ashore, at Causeway Bay, to join a procession of floats, that wind their way to the temple along Tin Hau road to honor the Queen Of Heaven.

This Tai Miu Wan temple, was used often by the triad Wo Shing Wo to film Kung Fu movies. In just two more weeks, it would become a slaughter house for top triad leaders. A place of revenge and a place of ominous reactions. Who would Tin Hau protect, on this bloody day? It would be an evil day of killing, caused by the poisonous vendetta of the vicious serpent, known as China White.

Alex Fong, the resident field agent for the Central Intelligence Agency in Hong Kong and Macau, was born in Hong Kong, but educated in San Francisco. He had done a miraculous job of keeping the agency out of the many pit falls, that lay ahead, during the Chinese reclamation of Hong Kong. The mainland Chinese were convinced he was just another rich Hong Kong art dealer, who loved China and could be counted on to do occasional favors in exchange for access to the art of China's greatest artists, that included the likes of Wu Zuo Ren, Li Keran, Wu Guan Zhong and Huang Yong Yu. When he began, the CIA had Alex enroll at the Yang Ming Shan Cultural Institute in Taipei, where he studied traditional Chinese art, to support his cover in Hong Kong.

Alex' expertise in Chinese art and calligraphy was unquestioned. His training convinced the Hong Kong elite that he was the genuine article, yet they still considered him a harmless product of an American education and considered his fluent english an oddity. The triads quite strangely never attempted to recruit Alex treating him as a pariah, they went out of their way to avoid him. Alex never understood why, but he was grateful not to have been compelled to add that sort of complexity to an already challenging job. He was known to his brethren in the CIA only as Mako. He had been one of the highest regarded assassins ever to graduate from Langley. One hundred and thirty kills. Not a trace had Mako left behind.

From Ricin, to long range rifles, no modus vivendi, no preferred method of operation, was provided to supply the smallest clue, that all one hundred thirty targets had been killed by the same man. Alex had been quite busy these past two weeks, after reading the Ops order, sent by Admiral Donaldson. He would make the rendezvous today at 2100 hours Zulu, at the GPS coordinates in the Ops order. He had already reserved a suite at the luxurious Causeway Bay hotel where the hits would be made from. It's flat roof would offer an unparalleled vantage point of the Lion Dance parade that would wind its way toward the Tai Miu Wan temple below.

Alex told the hotel manager that a band of musicians from Singapore would be staying for one night only, in order to play at a private party following the day's Tin Hau festivities. The manager obligingly had his bell staff carry the musical instrument cases to the suite, which held the four L-115-A3 super sniper rifles for tomorrow's hits. The Ops plan had been quite clear. The procession would reach a curve in Tin Hau road just one kilometer from the hotel roof top, that would provide a full five seconds to verify and execute the kills. Alex had, himself looked through a sniper scope and determined this exact location to be superlative for a simultaneous hit.

He, Alex, would act as group leader, to give the synchronous command to fire at just the right moment, after he first confirmed the identity of each target. Following the hit, the group would be picked up from the hotel roof by a chopper, displaying Hong Kong police insignia and delivered to a warehouse near Alex' slip in the Hong Kong Harbor. Alex' yacht would then be waiting to deliver them to a departure GPS coordinate. As a consummate professional Alex had gone over every detail both in his mind and on the ground. The plan was flawless, but he knew from experience that the Devil was always in the execution.

Alex always worked alone, but the mission called for a simultaneous hit and four targets would have been a bit much, even for someone with his experience. Alex walked through a fisherman's market stopping to buy a kilo of cooked shrimp. He ate shrimp as he drew a long mouthful of Tiger beer and gazed out to sea, from the lower deck of his sixty four foot yacht. It was another hot day that made the cold beer and shrimp taste twice as good. In a while, Alex would take a shower and get ready for the evening.

Ironic he thought. Tomorrow is the celebration of seafarers. His seafarer's would be coming from beneath the ocean not its surface and their mission was to take life not defend, or celebrate it. Alex was intimately familiar with the meaning of this festival. He knew that once word got out about the hits the Chinese people would be insane with rage that someone would dare draw blood on such a sacred day. He would do his best to get the killers back to their escape submarine and then, himself go deep underground until the shyte blew over. He was, after all, an operator and couldn't let anything get in the way of his job, not even his own people and their long held traditions. As David walked across the tarmac, at the air strip in Phnom Penh, he felt dread rise from deep within his stomach. He suffered frequent nightmares of the day he was shot in North Vietnam.

The weight of his dead comrades on his own body and his inability to speak, or even blink to let anyone know he was alive. This thing now, was completely different. His mind freeze framed. He saw the grotesque faces of the dead, the enemy soldiers he had killed. The faces of his own men and their lifeless bodies, now filled him with the shame of not having been able to save them, from death. The helplessness, was unbearable. The freeze frames moved rapidly across the vast terrain of his tortured soul. Suddenly, he was back on the search patrol in North Vietnam. He saw the frightened faces of the work detail as his men fired on the NVA squad before them. He saw the horror in the eyes of the NVA soldier he stabbed to death. Then, the look of disbelief on the face of the NVA soldier David shot.

Suddenly, a long faceless line of the dead marched toward David. Their clothes were soaked in blood and a stench preceded them like a fog. The smell of death so pungent, so nauseating. They forced David down and all began to climb on top of him, pinning down his limbs and ignoring his mental screams to be set free. David tried but couldn't stop the columns of bodies from coming and weighing him down. He tried to close his eyes, but he couldn't force his eye lids to move.

His mind reeled with the horror and he felt his face move across the rough, hot tarmac. His knees buckled and the burning pain brought David back from the precipice of Hell. As he opened his eyes, he saw the contorted faces of Mitch, Clive and Sean glaring down at him, as though he were some sort of curious object that had fallen from the sky."Are you alright David?" Mitch asked. "Yes, I'm fine. Guess it's the heat and the fact that I haven't slept for a couple of Days. I'm fine now." David muttered, as he regained his balance. "Here's some bottled water Mate." Clive said. "Sorry I don't have some American whiskey to throw in. You should be well revived soon Mate. Cheers!" Mitch stared.

"Are you sure you're up for this David?" Mitch asked. "Yes! Absolutely." This had been far worse than any previous nightmare and David knew it. He had just experienced a panic attack. "Claustrophobia." David thought as he walked toward the chopper that would soon take him to the most dreaded and greatest psychological challenges he could have ever feared. He would soon be confined in a small space in a submarine several hundred feet beneath the sea. Can't think about it! It's just another f--cking way to catch a ride! He screamed to himself, in his thoughts. The chopper lifted with David Mitch, Sean and Clive peering out through the open doors. David looked down at the split tributary of the Mekong river as it rushed past the river front of Phnom Penh.

Sooner than he expected, they were flying over the delta near the mouth of the Mekong. David watched as the muddy water gradually became deep blue ocean. They dropped down and flew low out past the coastal islands of Vietnam and due North across the South China Sea. Finally, the chopper circled and hovered as the men made the last minute adjustments to their wet suits and UBA, Under Water Breathing Apparatus. Mitch signaled the pilot by tapping the top of his head that the men were ready to exit the aircraft. The pilot spoke into his microphone and suddenly, a white spray parted the ocean as the submarine came nose high out of the sea. It appeared at first to be a large Blue whale, breaching for air. The pilot gave Mitch a thumbs up and a salute and the men jumped down from the chopper.

They swam to the submarine, removed their fins and climbed the ladder up onto the small deck and down into the body of the sub. They were met by Captain Marvin Wilson who welcomed them aboard. They stowed their UBA gear and joined the Captain for refreshments. David was amazed at how much room there seemed to be in the hold of the submarine. "Almost like being inside a 747 Heavy, without the windows," he thought.

They were soon introduced to the other two Sniper teams and to the crew of the Mark 8 SDV, SEAL Delivery Vehicle. The two Snipers were both Marine Recon Gunnery Sergeants. Each was ethnically South Korean, one from Los Angeles, the other from Flint, Michigan.

Their spotters were both Lance Corporals, also Koreans and nearly as qualified as Snipers as their Gunny Sergeants were. All had seen action in Afghanistan, Iraq and Somalia. Per protocol, no one was introduced by name but instead by Team Leader One, which was David, Team Leader Two which was Clive, Team Leader Three, who volunteered his first name as Doug. Team Leader Four merely grunted and stared through everyone. Their assistants were simply referred to as Spotters, One, Two, Three and Four. The SEAL Commander of the Mark 8 introduced himself as Navy Lieutenant Brad Olson.

"Gentlemen, there are only two Mark 8 teams in the entire world. SDV Team One, which is my team, is based at the Naval Amphibious Base in Coronado, California." "The other SDV team is based at the Naval Amphibious base in Little Creek Virginia. Our team normally consists of a SEAL Platoon, which is sixteen men. Myself, ten other SEAL Operators, one dive medical technician and four fleet support maintenance technicians." "Because of the nature of your mission, our team for this mission will just be myself, as driver, my navigator and the dive medical technician. We are all SEAL qualified. It gets a little tight in a Mark 8 with sixteen personnel, in full UBA equipment and combat gear, so we left most of our team behind, to give you a little more room tonight." David tried not to show his relief with Lieutenant Olson's last statement. "The Mark 8 is essentially a mini-submarine. It is completely powered by re-chargeable Silver-Zinc batteries which we keep at 100% and it is flown through the ocean like an airplane." "My joy stick moves rudders elevators and bow planes, to control direction using ballast and a trim system."

It has a computerized navigation system that keeps us from getting lost in the blackest of waters." "The Mark 8 is 22 feet long and shaped like a fat torpedo. It is black as the night and runs perfectly silent, avoiding state of the art radar and sonic detection systems." "It has several roles, but tonight, it will be used in its primary mission status, which is clandestine insertion. We will get to your contact vessel which, I believe is a Sixty four foot yacht. You will exit the Mark 8 at thirty feet below the yacht and slightly to its starboard side, as that is where we are informed its ladder will await you. We still have a few hours until the rendezvous, so I would like to show you the Mark 8 and practice one load and exit."

David felt the cold sweat on his forehead and he could imagine that he was going pale, when he experienced the panic attack on its way. He bit his lip and began to imagine the ecstasy of finally climbing the ladder of the yacht. "Here we are Gentlemen, this is our little SEAL delivery vehicle." Olson said. "I would like to ask you to don your equipment even though we will not change atmosphere for this Mark 8 practice loading." The Mark 8 has an intercom system, so even though you will be breathing behind your masks, you can talk and be heard. We like to use FILO here, so Team One you will move in first and will be the last team out followed in numerical sequence by the other teams." David felt as though he had been hit in the chest with a hammer.

He was not only trapped inside all of this aquatic gear but he would be crammed all the way inside this metal coffin and wouldn't even have the comfort of knowing, that he still had even the smallest amount of control over his own little space. If he were at least allowed to sit closest to the door able to leave if he felt he'd reached his limit, he could survive, but now, at the mercy of others, who blocked his escape, men, who he would rather die, before letting them see his fear, how could he stand it?

His knees felt weak as he moved further inside this torpedo shaped craft. Once, he almost turned around to push his way out, but he began a mantra, Srey An had taught him. "Om Mani Padmi, Um." He closed his eyes and repeated the mantra, over and over and then he saw her. He saw a little bird flying into a white light. He chased her in his mind and she stopped flying away. She stood there in a sheer gown, her puffy red lips parted in a smile. "Srey An, my little bird. You've come to comfort me my love." David thought. Then like an echo, in a deep dark tunnel, he heard Lieutenant Olson's voice. "Sir, we have all exited, will you please join us? Some people love our Mark 8 so much they hate to leave her?" He said with a laugh.

David scurried out and knew he would never have to be afraid of small spaces, ever again. "Srey An would never leave him again" he thought and he drew incredible strength from his knowledge of this. The time passed by slowly, but at last Lieutenant Olson announced that it was time to get suited up for the delivery. David was anxious to breathe fresh air again and was suited before any of the others. He expected at least some light when the cold ocean water surrounded him, but it was as black as a cauldron of oil, when he emerged from the Mark 8. He fought the sensation of panic and disorientation. Suddenly Mitch broke a chemical stick and started ascending to the surface. The rest of the pack followed. David looked back into the nothingness, to see if the Mark 8 was still there but all he felt was a swirl of ocean current.

It was just as Olson described. They emerged on the starboard side of "Mako's" yacht. Soon, they were all aboard stowing their equipment and exploring the yacht which moved silently, without lights, ever Northward toward Sai Kung. Alex showed them to his master suite, where each took turns taking a shower and getting dressed in the clothes Alex had waiting for them.

The clothes and shoes fit each man perfectly and in each of the eight baskets, the men found their fake passports traveling documents and nine thousand U.S. dollars, per man to be used in case things went South and each man found himself escaping alone.

The four Korean American Marines had North Korean passports and David, Mitch, Clive and Sean had Chechnyan passports. Pictures of the four triad targets were posted on the wall of the flying bridge, for each team to study. Before arriving at the harbor in Sai Kung, the photos and all written intel would be shredded, including the operations order. David went over the Ops order again, carefully with all four teams. TV dinners were microwaved for their dinner.

There would be no risks taken either with restaurants, or room service, once they reached the hotel. Alex had already checked the men in at the hotel, when the documents had been finished. A windowless van brought the men to the underground service elevator and the men were led by Alex to the adjoining suites, where they would remain isolated until the mission started. Each suite had an L-115-A3 case lying beneath the bed.

The Snipers all used the cleaning kits in each case to completely disassemble, clean and then re-assemble the weapons. Even though the weapons were already spotless they were cleaned, because this was the protocol of a professional sniper. It allowed him to know the current status of his weapon, down to its smallest moving parts and to know that when the weapon was critical, it would work because he had been the last to put its pieces back together. Each Spotter was issued a Glock 17 and several clips of ammunition along with stun grenades and K-Bar knives. Each team had a suite and after some small talk security watch was assigned and the teams not on watch went to bed.

In the morning, each team went with Alex, separately to see the roof top and to be shown the curve, on Tin Hau Road, where the hit would take place, at 1500 Zulu. The quiet Korean stared at each of the other team members measuring each against himself. In spite of his cold blank almost evil expression, it was possible to see that he had already decided, that except for the transportation, he was on a solo mission. As far as he was concerned, he could have made all four hits and everyone else could have stayed home, even his Spotter.

At the harbor on Hong Kong Island the Seafarers were getting more excited. Small and Large Junks, side by side with fishing boats and luxury yachts were covered in an explosion of colors, bright red blue green, yellow and even purple flags, pennants and banners. Seen from a distance it gave the illusion that a large bed of flowers was floating on the sea. Sea Gulls dove between the boats looking for scraps and pieces of fish. The megaphones began a cacophony of sing song Cantonese and the boats circled to establish a convoy.

A cannon was fired and the Tin Hau procession was officially launched. At the Fisherman's Pier in Sai Kung, the floats had already begun to get in line in their pecking order. Each float told a historic tale of Tin Hau's courage and prowess in fighting back typhoons, or depicted her swooping down from white puffy clouds to pluck fishermen from drowning disasters. Float number three which represented Tin Hau's ascension from her own death, had a long white Chaise Lounge riding at the very top. This comfortable place was reserved for the triad leadership who would come to pay homage, to an honored character of Chinese history and culture. A canopy was erected, to shade the VIP guests, who would arrive later on their luxury yacht, in the Seafarer's parade of ships. Triad security was heavy at the Fishermen's Pier at Sai Kung. Serious looking men in dark sunglasses checked business frontage, while a black shiny helicopter without markings hovered above.

The helicopter then slowly flew the route of the Lion Dancers Parade. The procession started at King's Road, then on to Tin Hau Road and ultimately to the Causeway and the Tai Miu Wan Temple. Alex saw the chopper and paid the hotel maintenance manager handsomely, to erect four large blue and white umbrellas on the roof top with large tables beneath. He explained that his group wanted to watch the parade from a distance and that the umbrellas could be taken down by night fall.

As the chopper made its second sweep, the triad enforcer aboard noticed the change on the hotel roof, but figured it was related to a party at the hotel. Just the same, he used his radio to give instructions to his ground patrol to check it out. The ground patrol entered the hotel and were met by the Concierge, who called the maintenance manager. "Oh, just some guests who want to have some beers and watch the parade." The leader of the ground patrol was satisfied and the ground patrol left.

Alex ordered a case of Tsing Tao beer on ice and stated they no longer wished to be disturbed, locking the doors with a heavy chain. After the Seafarers disembarked from their boats and climbed onto their assigned floats, the procession moved along King's Road. Above, a News Helicopter circled and made low level passes to get better footage of the parade. The black helicopter swooped down occasionally but, otherwise, remained high above the procession below.

The parade moved faster than expected. Arriving a full fifteen minutes early. Float number three was moving nearer to the curve on Tin Hau Road. Alex used his field glasses to identify the targets. The sniper teams were still adjusting for windage, when Alex yelled out "Gentlemen acquire and prepare to engage your targets." David yelled out; "Where in the f--ck is my target? Where is she? Where is that bitch Madame Shian?" "Only targets Two, Three and Four are present!" Alex shouted. Engage on my mark!" Alex yelled.

"Fire on my mark! Ready! Aim....Fire!" Alex commanded. Through his scope, David could see that target Four was a miss. The cold, confident, Marine, had missed his target by a foot, because the sudden rush to fire had interrupted his methodical preparation. He was enraged that he missed and he abandoned his target to finish setting his windage. David saw the two headless bodies of targets Two and Three still sitting where they had sat all along, but target Four had stopped screaming and had begun to climb down from the Chaise lounge. David took aim and slowly squeezed his trigger as he exhaled. Suddenly the man's head was blown off.

In the distant background, Alex heard the whine of a chopper. Thinking it was his escape chopper, Alex yelled out for the teams to prepare to board the chopper. All across the news and cable networks that were providing coverage of the Tin Hau festival, the TV audiences suddenly saw live feed of four assassins and their assistants. They were dropping sniper rifles into large canvass bags.

A switch to Camera Two on the ground showed the carnage of the slain triad Leaders on Float Three. David turned his weapon on the News chopper, aiming at the pilot. The pilot seeing this, swung his chopper to the left and straight up, just as the black triad helicopter was coming in for a closer look. The choppers collided, creating an enormous explosion in the sky. Hotel guests and staff, who had been watching the event on television, recognized their hotel and went screaming up the stairs, with meat cleavers and beer bottles in their hands. The crowd forced its way onto the roof top and began throwing meat cleavers and bottles. The Korean American Spotters opened up with their Glocks, killing at least fifteen people in the first ten seconds.

Alex was on his SAT phone, screaming for his chopper but the pilot, seeing the explosion of the news and triad chopper, as well as the carnage on the roof top, waved off and bugged out. Suddenly, a police chopper swooped down and began firing mini-guns at the roof top. All four of the Marines were killed instantly. Clive and Sean fired at the police chopper pilot, wounding him gravely. His chopper began to spin out of control, skidding to a stop at the edge of the roof. The pilot slumped over and fell off the roof, impaling himself on a steel spear topped fence below. David yanked the Police Lieutenant out of the front passenger seat.

Alex pulled out a pistol and executed the policeman. He then stooped down to check the carotid pulse to confirm each Marine was dead. Clive and Sean dove into the rear of the Police chopper. David took the dead pilot's seat and Alex jumped in the front passenger seat, while Mitch strapped himself with a D-ring to the right doorway, resting his feet on the landing strut. David lifted the chopper skyward, just in the nick of time, as the triad security group came crashing out onto the roof with guns blazing. The Police chopper hurtled out across Joss House Bay. Clive and Sean watched the triads kicking the dead American's bodies while they beat their own chests in rage.

David pointed to the head phones and Alex put them on. "Why did you execute that man?" David demanded. "He saw my face. He was a cop. Any more questions?" "We have about a fourth of a tank of fuel." David said. "What is your fall back plan Mako?" David asked. "I don't have one. We were supposed to have been evacuated by my pilot, before the police or the news choppers arrived." "Man I knew this was going to be bad Joss today. Of all f--cking days to plan a hit, besides I always work alone." Alex complained. "So do I, but let's get back to the here and now shall we? What do you suggest we do now?" David asked.

"If that news chopper got a good shot of my face, there is no next for me. I'm well known in Hong Kong. With my cover blown and my connection with this fiasco revealed, the triads will execute me on sight." "Well the best thing you can do then Mako, is try to stay alive until you watch the evening news, to see for yourself if you were mugged." "OK. OK. You're right. I left my yacht at the harbor in Hong Kong. We were supposed to already be on her, headed out of the harbor. Fly there now." Alex gave David a heading.

"The yacht is all decked out in multi-colored flags and pennants. As soon as we get on board, we can blend in with hundreds of other sea craft." "Turn South East. OK, see that large warehouse? Land between those two buildings. We can hide this Police chopper in that warehouse, while I go pick up the yacht. I'll come back for you guys in about fifteen minutes. Once we get beyond the naval and police blockades, I'll call the sub and coordinate the GPS location for the rendezvous." "OK, Mako. See you had a fall back plan all along." David said. "Yeah, sure!" Alex replied. David maneuvered the Police chopper into the warehouse, landing in the center. He shut off the engines and electrical system.

"Mako, I understand that the live feed from the news chopper was being simultaneously recorded in the studio. If they didn't get your face before the choppers collided you're still not home free. This chopper has a live video cam. We need to find it and destroy it." David said. "Thanks, but I already thought about that. It would have been recorded back at the Police home station, just like the news chopper." Alex said. "Well there it is." David said, pointing to the small silver box. Alex wrapped a cushion around the barrel of his pistol and shot the video camera into shards and pieces. Mitch Clive and Sean took up positions near the large doors. Because it was a week end, few dock workers were present in the entire dock area.

Alex pushed a button and the large doors began to close. "Don't stay here with the chopper. Follow me." He said. Alex led them to a pile of fish netting beside a lean to shack where lunch was served to workers during the week. It was empty now. "Stay inside the shack. I'll return in fifteen minutes, or less with the yacht. I won't be able to tie up to the dock. You'll have to leap onto the deck as I go by really slow."

Fourteen minutes later Alex steered the yacht to within a few feet of the wooden pilings. Clive and Sean took up firing positions, while David and Mitch took a running jump onto the deck of the yacht. They in turn took up firing positions on the yacht, as Clive and Sean leaped onto the yacht as well. The men clambered below deck as Alex headed due south skirting Lamma Island, with a course for the high seas. Alex reasoned, that at least for now, the attention would be paid to blocking the sea lanes from Sai Kung in the North, to Po Toi island in the South. Within the hour, the net would close the Southern exit from Po Toi island, West to Lantau Island and back North to The New Territories. This would effectively seal the coastal regions of Hong Kong.

David joined Alex at the helm. Alex kept the yacht distant from other sea craft. When they were past Po Toi Island, he asked David to have the men remove all pennants and flags from the boat. The further they sailed from the havoc at the festival, the less valuable it was to resemble a festival adorned yacht. David went over the details of the mission in his mind. "That slippery little bitch!" He thought. Had she been tipped off? Or was she just lucky? A cat with nine lives. How many were still left? She was the primary target, but had eluded death, once more. At least they had erased the top leaders of the triads, who had become the greatest threat. David knew it would be too hot in Hong Kong for another attempt. He would just have to wait for a sighting elsewhere in Asia. David regretted the loss of the Marines.

There would be hell to pay if Donaldson, or the CIA who managed them, were unable to keep their files black. They were all ethnically Asian, stripped of anything including shaving articles, that had been purchased in the U.S.A. Korean toiletries from Pyong Yang as well as prescription medicines in false names and even a few letters from girlfriends in North Korea would be found on their person.

The same care was taken with those posing as Chechnyans. Items only available in Chechnya, or Russia would be found on their person. There hadn't been time to retrieve the only item connecting the Marines to possible U.S involvement, which was the U.S. currency, but that couldn't be helped. Alex turned on the small TV set in his pilot room that he watched for weather reports. He used the remote to find the local news channel. An attractive female news anchor was already reporting the story in english:

" From this video feed we recorded live before our chopper went down, we see that several assassins took part in today's brazen execution style murder of three prominent Hong Kong Businessmen. All three were active in charitable organizations and will be missed throughout greater Hong Kong. A special report will cover their tragic deaths and the effect on their families on the ten O'clock news. The assassins were able to obscure their identity as no usable photos were recorded before the fatal crash."

Alex switched off the TV. He knew the circumstances would be different with the Ten O'clock news report. By then the Hong Kong Police will have turned over clear photos from their recordings during the "f--cking" fiasco. Alone on the bridge, Alex pulled out his SAT phone. "Hello Sir. The mission was a miniature disaster. The primary target Madame Shian' was a no show. Targets Two through Four were secure kills."

"Both Marine teams were killed by a Hong Kong Police chopper, firing mini-guns. I had no choice but to sanction a face to face Police Lieutenant witness. The Local News is reporting they have no usable facial shots of any of our team. I'm sure the Police will have a different story when they go over their recordings. I was abandoned by my own pilot who bugged out." "Yes Sir. I'm minutes away from the GPS rendezvous location. It appears we slipped the blockades but I can't return. After the rendezvous, I will head for the Taiwan safe house and await your instructions. Sir, please give me only solo assignments in the future. I don't work very well with amateurs." " Alex, I will bring you up to date on several important matters during our next communication. Finish the mission out!"

"Team Leader One!" Alex called out to David. "Just call me David, Mako." "Then call me Alex, David." Alex replied. "I just received the GPS coordinates for the rendezvous with your SEAL Delivery Vehicle. We are about forty minutes away. Get your guys suited up about fifteen minutes before launch time. The Mark 8 will be shadowing us again on the starboard bow, but this time, at a depth of about seventy feet. Please bring me one of the extra UBA suits in case of emergency." "Sure thing Alex." David replied.

David went down below the main deck and delivered the information about the rendezvous. "Mitch will lead us to the Mark 8. Just in case, Mako gave me some chemical sticks to help us stay close together in the dark water." David said as he reached each man some chemical sticks. At fifteen minutes before rendezvous the men donned their wet suits and UBA equipment. They sat backwards on the railing to await the command to roll into the water when the first Chengdu-7 made its low level pass. The shock from its after burners nearly knocked Clive off his perch on the railing. Alex yelled into a mega phone from the bridge. "Prepare to abandon ship!"

"We are one minute from the rendezvous about a thousand yards to the starboard straight ahead. You'll have to swim for it. Follow Mitch! Stay close together!" "What about you?" David yelled. "Don't worry about me. I'll lead the Chengdu's away from you. Don't use the yacht as a reference point. I'm veering off course now. JUMP!" Alex yelled. The four men rolled off the railing backwards into the black water, just as the second Chengdu came in for a strafing run.

Alex began a zig zag pattern just as the first Chengdu-7 locked on with two air to ground missiles. The yacht was vaporized. The jets came in for an inspection pass. Satisfied that the target had been completely destroyed the two jets climbed to fifteen thousand feet and headed back to their mainland base near Guangzhou China.

Lieutenant Olson both saw and felt the fiery explosion on the surface. He was sure the men had been killed, but he refused to leave the rendezvous point. Then he saw the blinking strobe from Mitch's belt and the small string of chemical lights as the four men approached the Mark-8. As soon as the men were inside the Mark-8, Olson asked, "Where are the others?" "Four KIA at the mission site and our rendezvous leader KIA about two minutes ago." David replied. "He sacrificed himself so we could make it to you." David said solemnly.

Just then, a clinking sound came from the skin of the Mark-8. Olson stopped the Mark-8 and slid open its cargo door. In swam Alex. Everyone cheered, their spirits lifted by his survival. Soon the Mark-8 was back inside the mother sub and the men were checked by the Chief medical officer then led to the operations room. A large flat screen displayed Admiral Donaldson's image, which started the de-briefing.

Mitch recounted each detail of the after action report and then the Admiral began to speak. "Gentlemen, first, in behalf of the American people, I would like to thank you for a job well done. The targets you eliminated were responsible for 100% of the distribution network that brings pure China White heroin that is produced in the Golden Triangle into the United States and Europe."

Chapter Thirteen: Tong Chi

"Although it is true, that the lion's share of heroin now comes from the Golden Crescent, we must be prepared to dismantle drug operations with every single opportunity we receive." David intervened. "Thank you Admiral, but our primary target, Madame Shian' escaped her fate. As long as she is alive, we can only expect her to assign others to replace the leaders we killed, which will allow her operations to continue unabated."

"Split the screen." The Admiral ordered his audio-visual technician. "This SAT image was taken recently, above Kern's villa." "As you can clearly see, Madame Shian' is being escorted from a chopper to her quarters in General kern's villa, a place you may have stayed at yourself from time to time." "As we speak, your five man Tachilek mission team, led by your friend and colleague, Bill Murphy, is enroute to General Kern's complex in my MC-130e.

Per your Operations Order, a parachute insertion will be made about three kilometers from Kern's complex. Bill has assigned himself the responsibility of painting Target One, which is Kern's private quarters, as well as the guest quarters, where Madame Shian' is staying. They will all be enjoying dinner when two Predators unleash Hell Fire missiles on the complex. We realize Kern keeps prostitutes at his swimming pool recreation area." "If they do not wander away from the pool area, they should remain safe. Everyone else should be effectively eliminated. There are four other targets. Each of your four remaining men will paint Kern's Meth labs and opium processing sheds, which are in four concentrations that will be attacked with the remaining four Predators." "Show time is in three minutes. Let us all sit back now and watch the live feed from a surveillance drone that is over the target area."

Admiral Donaldson's image disappeared from the screen and an Infra Red area coverage showed an outline of the MC-130e flying toward the drop zone. The camera surveillance defined the shapes and images of General Kern's complex three kilometers North of the DZ. Suddenly two helicopters lifted off near Tachilek and began flying in a Bee line toward the MC-130e. Admiral Donaldson could be heard reacting to this new event. "Eagle Six, this is Eagle One, abort the mission! over. Eagle Six do you copy? over."

It was too late. Five Infra Red orange and red spots could be seen in a descending pattern behind the MC-130e. Bill's team had already begun the jump when Admiral Donaldson's order was given. "What just happened Admiral?" David yelled. "Two choppers lifted off from Tachilek and started heading for our Drop Zone, so I tried to abort the mission, but I was obviously too late. Bill's team is on the ground. They jumped from an altitude of five hundred feet. We knew that MIADS may pick us up at that altitude, but that reaction was far too fast, even for MIADS. More than likely, someone heard the MC-130e from the ground and launched a local interceptor team."

As the Admiral spoke, David could see the five orange and red spots which were Bill and his men, running toward a woodline. The two helicopters landed directly between the woodline and Bill's team and twelve men exited each helicopter. A brief fire fight took place and four of the five men lay motionless on the ground. A fifth ran into the woodline. It was Bill. "Eagle One, Eagle Six, over!" "Go Six!" "Mission failure, mission failure!" Bill shouted. "We flew over a part of the city and they sent a reaction force. Four team members dead. I'm being pursued. Can't speak now. Contact you later out!" Two of Bill's pursuers caught up with him and tackled him from behind.

David and the others watched helplessly, as they saw members of the reaction defense force, kicking Bill while dragging him off to the lead helicopter. A few of the defense reaction force members fired into the four dead bodies of Bill's team. Then all of the reaction forces boarded the helicopters and departed in the direction of General Kern's compound. "Goddamnit!" David yelled. "Sir, can we keep surveillance on that place? I need to know where they are keeping Bill. I have to get him out of there!" David said pleadingly.

"There's no more element of surprise David. Anyone who tries to enter that place now would be committing suicide." The Admiral said with firm conviction. "Where's the bloody SEAL team you promised?" Clive said angrily. "That was in support of the initial two missions in either Thailand or Cambodia. We can't go into Myanmar." The Admiral spat back. "Besides, David said you could do the job with Predators not SEALS!" The Admiral fired back angrily. "Let's not get into a pissing contest!" David said.

"Admiral, it looks like it was just some bad luck. I don't expect you to commit SEALS now anymore than I did from the beginning. You would dash your career if you sent American forces into Myanmar without Defense Department approval, even if we were successful. I do need a ride though Sir and if you're still interested in taking out Kern and his drug operations, I could sure as hell still use those Predators." "Are you thinking about going in there alone? If so you're a bigger fool than I thought you were. It's suicide man!" The Admiral was in awe of David and had to pretend the opposite. "He won't be goin' in alone Admiral!" Clive said. "Yeah, that's right Admiral." Sean said. "Our bloody contract isn't over yet." Clive said. "You're all three fools then but by God I'm not going to stand in your way."

"Get your asses back to your Safe House in Phnom Penh and I'll have an MC-130e waiting for you. Your Predators will be back on station too. If you hope to rescue Bill, we'd better get you there by tomorrow night." "The longer they have with him the less the chances are he'll still be alive. Mitch, you are hereby ordered to give all the support you can from the Safe House, but you will not enter Myanmar, is that clear?" "Yes Sir." "David, please get at least an impromptu Ops Order to me ASAP. We obviously cannot do another LALO, or fly anywhere near Tachilek." The Admiral observed.

"Roger that Sir! We'll do a HALO insertion. I'll plan it for tomorrow night at 0300 hours zulu.That will give us time to find Bill, use the Predators on the planned targets and just have enough light at dawn for your MC130e pilot to be able to see our helium balloons, to execute a four man extraction." "If Murphy isn't able to walk you can't extract him. The shock would break his back. I guess we'll cross that bridge when we come to it. We'll keep that place under a microscope for you until you get there." "Thank you Sir!" David said. The Admiral nodded and the screen went blank. "Mitch, will you please get the MC-130e filled with ordinance and HALO gear for our insertion? I will work up an Ops order ASAP!" David asked. "Done!" Mitch replied.

Bill gazed up at the bamboo mesh, just inches above his nose. For a few eternal seconds, his mind traced the symmetry of the folded straw patterns, as though they may hold a secret clue, that would allow an escape from this God forsaken hole in the ground he had been thrown into. His mind reeled in shock. He demanded to speak with General Kern, but was brutally mistreated. The Officer was smoking one of Kern's cigars, the same ones he and David had enjoyed when they had been here last. "Seems like centuries ago," he thought. The officer hadn't even tried to torture him for any information, he had simply held the hot cigar to his left eyelid without asking a single question. Bill knew it was a bad sign.

They had captured him only to kill him slowly. His eye was swollen shut from the burn he sustained. He saw stars when he touched his left eyelid. He supposed that was a good sign, probably meant he wouldn't go blind from the wound, if his optic nerve could still transmit visions of light or anything external. "I wish David had come on this mission." He thought. "He would have watched the f--cking pilot closer. He would have never let him fly over Tachilek, I mean how f--cking stupid was that?" "What a tragic and stupid mistake and I let it happen. Now John, Roy, Kevin and Ted are all dead. Damned good men wasted because we flew over a well lit city." Bill lamented.

Tears welled up in Bill's eyes which made his left eye burn as though the officer was still shoving in his cigar stub. "That cigar puffing mother f--cker is dead when I get out of here!" Bill mumbled out loud. He felt in the dark and discovered that he was in a two foot deep hole, just longer than his body, but not wide enough to rotate over and back again to keep his blood from pooling. He tried to touch his face, but the ceiling prevented him from squeezing his hand past his chin.

Then the panic set in. "What if he had been given his Tongchi?" Buried alive in this foul pit, without even a word of hatred spoken?" He felt lonelier than he had ever felt in his life. "Surely the Admiral would send in that ninety six man SEAL team to get these f--ckers and get me out of here." he thought. "Who are you f--cking kidding? You're on your own. Bull shit I am! David would never leave me to die like this." "He'll come for me soon and we'll both do some f--cking damage. You'll see!" Then he considered that David may have been killed in Hong Kong. "Maybe no one is coming." The panic attacks came and went so often that he was losing his ability to keep his nightmares separate from reality. Maybe he would wake up and this would all just be a horrible f--cking dream. "Yeah, sure, but you need to be asleep to be able to wake up." His eye hurt so much he was sure he wouldn't be sleeping anytime soon.

They stripped him and "even though it must be after midnight" he thought, the humidity was heart breaking. He lay in his own filthy sweat and he had relieved himself uncontrollably when his kidneys absorbed the shock of being dropped solidly on his back in this dark nasty hole. He felt his thighs and was relieved that there were no razor cuts. "This couldn't be Tongchi" he thought. "They would have surely already made the one hundred thousand cuts if it were. He wasn't even sure the triads were here. Perhaps it was just Kern looking to scare me into giving him a ton of money to buy my way out." he considered. "If that's what it is, I'll have him call David, who will do the swap on the Thai border. No, Kern would kill us both and take the money too.

I am hopelessly f--cked." Bill imagined that he and David were on their yacht in Rio de Janeiro. Big Hottentot assed, bronze beauties, were having sex with him. It helped with the pain and the misery, if just for a little while.
As he was making love with the beautiful women one was poking her finger in his eye, which prevented him from being able to achieve an orgasm. Then he imagined that he was walking in a field of barbed wire. His ankles were being shredded by razor wire. Abruptly, he realized that something was eating his flesh, the thin skin, along his shins and ankles. He kicked his feet rapidly against the sides of the hole. "That is when he felt them scurrying toward his face.

RATS! Goddamned rats. The rats stood on their hind legs and began chewing on the bloodied cord that held the bamboo ceiling tightly along the sides. He made a plan to capture the rats and choke them to death, so they wouldn't gradually eat him alive, but when he realized they were chewing on the cord, he allowed them to stand on his stomach and chest to continue their job. Suddenly, one of the rats was plucked from his chest. He nearly had a heart attack when he felt the Cobra slither across his stomach, to drag the rat out of the hole.

The second rat jumped up and down on his legs, until it found a way back out of the hole. He tried the cord several times and just when it seemed hopeless, the middle of the bamboo cover gave way. He pushed it high enough into the air to see that he was only yards away from a guard barracks. He carefully avoided the Cobra that was swallowing the rat. Crawling on the ground on all fours, he reached the dark shadows behind the guard shack.

He peered inside and saw six men playing a game of cards. One looked nervously at the open door. Bill guessed it was his turn to watch Bill's hole and he was on the verge of walking out to have a look. A shovel was leaning against the side of the guard house, "probably used to dig the hole I was in." Bill surmised. The guard threw in his hand and stood up to stretch. He adjusted the 9 mm in his web belt and walked toward the door. Bill picked up the shovel and faded further into the shadows. The guard walked over to Bill's hole and pulled his pistol when he saw the Cobra swallowing the rat. Bill crept up behind the guard and swung the shovel with all his might, severing the back of the man's head from the spine. Without a sound, the man slumped to the ground landing near the snake which had become extremely agitated, but unable to do anything other than swallow his rat.

Bill picked up the 9 mm and checked the man's belt for more clips but there were none. He tore off the man's clothes, which were too short and tight. He took the guard's K bar and cut the trousers into shorts. Luckily the boots fit. They would be the most important part of his escape. Bill began to run. He stayed in the shadows, heading for the long entrance road he had landed the Caribou on during the last visit. If he could just make the ten kilometers to Tachilek, perhaps he could promise a huge reward to someone who might have a way to get him to Chiang Rai along the Thai border. As Bill stumbled toward the gate, he saw two guards standing in the middle of the road.

"Damn!" Bill thought as he walked toward the cyclone fence. He would have to climb the fence and try his luck with the razor wire at the top. He suddenly felt a smooth wire tighten across his ankle, but it was too late. He thought at first he triggered an antipersonnel mine, but worse, it was a trip flare.

"What in the f--ck is a trip flare doing inside the wire?" He wondered. Then, he realized that Kern's place was just as often used as a prison, as it was a jungle fortress. The sky lit up as the parachute flare exploded. The guards ran toward him. Bill killed them both with his 9 mm. Then he scooped up an AK-47 from one of them, along with several clips of ammo. A jeep with a mounted fifty calibre raced toward him from inside the compound, while a truck load of troops sealed him off outside the gate.
Bill threw down the AK-47 and held his hands up in the air. The Officer ran up to Bill and kicked away the AK-47 and was about to butt stroke Bill, when Bill recognized him as the Officer who had shoved the cigar in his eye.

Bill pulled the 9 mm from his waist and shoved the barrel in the Officer's eye. "How does it feel ass hole?" Bill said as he pulled the trigger blowing the man's head apart. The soldiers wrestled the 9mm away from Bill and kicked in his ribs. They took Bill to the airport hangar where they tied him by his hands and feet to a leather and steel harness, that stretched him out like Jesus of Nazareth. There he hung drifting in and out of consciousness, until the blazing rays of the morning sun filled his skull with white hot orbs of explosive, burning pain.

She stood in the shadows, watching for a very long time. Enjoying the image of this broken man. Savoring each imagined blow, that cracked his ribs and cut his face. She felt not an ounce of pity. Instead she felt giddy when she considered how he must have shrieked for mercy, as each powerful blow had been delivered to exact maximum damage.

She imagined that he called out for anyone to save him, pleading for mercy from his tormentor. His helplessness and continued ability to feel pain, excited her. That she had once given him pleasure only heightened her sense of power and control over the man. She found a wooden pole nearby and poked at Bill's hanging hulk of bruised and broken flesh. "Wake up!" She shrieked. Bill opened the eye that hadn't been burned. "So you thought you could trick Madame Shian'? Yes Mister Bill?" He stared beyond her for a moment until his eye focused and he recognized her. "You have very bad karma, Mister Bill. You were never really a part of my plan. I would have killed you anyway, no matter how good the sex. But your childish pranks, insulting me before my triads has hastened your death.

Now, you will curse your mother for birthing your miserable existence. Death will come very slowly, Mister Bill." "I will give you a swift death only if you release to me your banking account numbers and passwords. The money you stole from me will do you no good now, but you can use it to buy a pass away from the Tongchi of one hundred thousand cuts, but only if you give me the data immediately." Bill stared at her through his right eye. He would have gladly used all of his money to buy an ounce of spit right now, he considered. It caused him immense pain, but he somehow found the strength to nod his head yes.

Madame Shian' couldn't believe her luck. She nervously scrambled in her purse for a pen and note pad to write down the numbers. Bill chewed the inside of his mouth, filling it full of blood. When Madame Shian' drew within a foot of him, he sprayed her face with blood and spit. She screamed with rage. Her torturer came running. "Begin The Cuts!" She commanded, blood dripping down her cheeks. She swirled around and stomped out of the hangar. Bill managed a smile just before he slumped back into his state of unconsciousness, as he hung like a side of beef in a meat factory.

Back at the Safe House, David studied the satellite photos of the Kern Compound intensely. Clive and Sean had a huge breakfast followed by a hot bath and then they went to bed, both falling into a deep sleep. They awakened twelve hours later and were immediately briefed by David on the mission and the layout of the compound. General Kern's army was estimated to number just under eight thousand men, spread from his main compound at Tachilek to the jungles along the Thai border where they escorted and guarded his network all the way to the border with China, at Riuli, in the Yunnan province.

David assumed that Madame Shian' had come to Tachilek to hammer out a deal with Kern, to devise a new drug distribution system, to replace Bill's operation, but this time to include Methamphetamine's, as well as processed heroin. Probably a land route through China, from Riuli to Guangdong. David assigned the barracks at Kern's compound, where nearly three thousand soldiers were staying, nearby, to Clive. Clive would divide his target centers between the sleeping quarters and the ammo dump complex, where armaments and explosives were kept.

Sean was assigned the Methamphetamine labs located two kilometers from Kern's main compound. David himself would be responsible for Kern's main compound, to include his aircraft hangar and the Opium sheds, located deep inside the main compound. Each of the three missions were assigned two predators each, with three Hell Fire missile pods per drone. David reckoned that both the Opium and Methamphetamine labs should have some secondary chemical explosions. He also calculated that the proximity of the ammo dump to the sleeping quarters of the troops, should augment the killing range of the attack. Each man would use a portable laser device to pin point the epicenter of the missile assault. Immediately after the Predators were launched, the men would rally at specific locations to be extracted by the MC-130e.

With its 40 mm Gattling cannons mounted on the fuselage, the MC-130e would be responsible for air defense and close air support it needed. David would be given thirty minutes to locate and rescue Bill. After which, he would initiate the Predator attack with a strike on the main compound and the Opium sheds. David's call sign was Eagle Claw, Clive was Eagle Claw One and Sean, Eagle Claw Two. Each wore an ear plug radio. David had Mitch call Admiral Donaldson to get the latest satellite intelligence. "Things are looking good on this end David. Madame Shian' was taken to General Kern's quarters for what appears to be a meeting and dinner. Several of Kern's officers joined them." The Admiral observed. "Any sign of where Bill is? "David asked. "Yes. Not too pleasant I'm afraid. They appear to have tortured him for some hours in their aircraft hangar, at least, he was carried by stretcher from the place about an hour ago."

"His Infra Red signature shows him lying, perhaps in a shallow hole, beside the guard house, about three hundred meters away from Kern's quarters. His heat pattern is very weak. He may be near death. It's hard to say." "Admiral, I want to move the assault to Midnight instead of 0300 hours. We should still be able to benefit from the element of surprise. I just can't risk Bill's life for another three hours." David said solemnly.

"Are your team mates on board with that?" "Yes we bloody well are Sir!" Clive bellowed. "Fine. Mitch alert the MC-130e's crew to be ready to fly at 2100 hours." "Yes Sir. Admiral, I request to be able to help crew the MC-130e." " I am trained on both their weapons system, navigation system and their Fulton extraction system. I can act as Jump Master for the HALO as well." Mitch's request was followed by silence. "Very well Mitch, but don't accidentally fall out of the f--cking plane while you're over Myanmar!" "Roger that Sir!" Mitch said with a grin. David adjusted his parachute and secured the night vision goggles that would allow him to see his target.

The exact jump locations had been coordinated with the MC-130e's pilot. David would jump first, followed by Clive and then Sean. Mitch would ensure that each man exited precisely. The pilot followed the Mekong until reaching the Myanmar Thailand border, then he turned on his terrain radar, which allowed the aircraft to ride the canopy. When Tachilek appeared on the horizon and while still in Thai airspace, he climbed to twenty five thousand feet. He then turned right and flew a direct course to the targets.

The red light came on and the men as well as Mitch and the crew, put on their oxygen masks. Mitch lowered the ramp and David made last minute adjustments to his weapon and equipment as he steadied himself in the powerful wind blast edging ever closer to the end of the ramp. Mitch received the command from the pilot just as the green light lit up the inside of the aircraft. David dove straight out and away from the ramp, assuming a half Delta position until he was able to visually acquire his target. The Mc-130e banked slightly right and Clive dove out followed by Sean.

David now assumed a full Delta position, his legs slightly apart and his hands cupped and held tight against his hips. He was able to track like a glider across the sky toward General Kern's main compound. He had a choice of either employing his chute manually, or waiting until he had fallen to an altitude of five hundred feet. At 500 feet, the pneumatic device would open his chute automatically. David was satisfied that he could toggle his way to a dark area near the Guard House so he pulled at 700 feet. Clive tracked to his target, as did Sean and each of them also manually opened their chutes just above 1,000 feet. David crabbed against a slight wind and landed as light as a feather, about 100 meters from the Guard House. David whispered into his microphone. "Eagle Claw One, Eagle Claw Two, please acknowledge when you are in position over." "This is Eagle Claw One, I have the bloody barracks and ammo dump in sight and am waiting for you to make some noise over."

"Eagle Claw, this is Eagle Claw Two. I have the labs directly sighted and am ready to paint them when I get the signal, over." "Roger Eagle Claws One and Two, I'll let you know soon. Out." "Eagle Claw this is Eagle Command. Have you sighted the hole yet? Over." "Not yet. Which side of the Guard House is it? Over." "I have you on the Infra Red screen. Move to the left side of the Guard House and proceed approximately 25 meters over." "Roger." David crept silently in the shadows, wearing his night vision goggles and then he saw it.

A makeshift bamboo latticed door, that was hinged to a bamboo frame with cord. He looked around and saw no one, but he heard laughing and talking from within the Guard House. He slowly opened the bamboo door and nearly collapsed at what he saw. Bill's swollen, nude body had razor cuts on virtually every two inches of space , covering his entire body. Even his genitals had been sliced open.

David frantically tried to find a pulse, but realized he was too late. His best friend and mentor in life was dead. Tears welled up in his eyes as the anger filled his mind and heart. "I'm so sorry Bill! I should have kept sailing the world with you, just as you asked me to." "These dirty sons of bitches are going to pay for this big time! I promise you my brother." "Eagle Command, this is Eagle Claw, over." David could hardly speak. "Eagle Command, they tortured him to death. Over." Silence. "I'm so very sorry Eagle Claw. Collect yourself, my friend, it's time for some payback!" "Roger that Eagle Command. Out." David tenderly touched the swollen face of his friend and said, "Goodbye Bill. It's time for some payback my friend. These rotten bastards are going to pay from the depth of their being for this. I swear this to you." From nowhere, a rifle stock was pushed against David's wind pipe from behind. A guard had walked outside to relieve himself and jumped David before he could see him.

David turned his head sideways, which rotated his wind pipe away from the crunching rifle stock and allowed him to continue to breathe while he drew his K-Bar from its sheath along his right lower leg. David slashed the knife in an arc directly behind his own head and felt the blade slide into the throat of the man behind him. His attacker released the rifle and David spun around stabbing and thrusting at the falling body. He sprinted toward General Kern's private quarters. Staying in the shadows, he saw the lone guard in front of the main entrance. Using a silencer mounted on his 9 mm pistol, he took out the guard with a head shot. David slowly entered the ante chamber. Strangely, no one else was to be found. "Damn it!" David thought. Had Madame Shian' eluded him again?"

"She's a f--cking ghost!" He thought. Then he heard the laughter of a woman and some follow on chatter with a man. He crept silently toward the back of the house and slowly opened the door. There, in soft candle light he saw General Kern lying between Madame Shian' legs, in the act of sex. He was nearing climax when Madame Shian' saw David and screamed. General Kern had just enough time to roll off and lunge for a pistol, at his bedside, before David put two holes neatly in the center of his forehead.

"We can work this out!" Madame Shian' said softly and pulled the sheets away from her body. She was still wet from the General's perspiration. David gave her a disgusted look. "You killed my best friend you evil bitch. There's nothing left you can say that will save you now." He grabbed her wrists and bound them with plastic hand restraints tying her securely to the bed. Then he pulled his knife and slid it lightly across her abdomen. Madame Shian' pleaded for her life. "You tortured my best friend to death, shut up, or I'll cut out your tongue! Your kidneys are here and here, but your liver is just here." He shoved the blade into her stomach and watched as the almost black blood emerged from her liver.

"You have about twenty minutes before you bleed to death, but only ten minutes until I blow you apart, so it looks like you are going to be more lucky than Bill was." Madame Shian's screams brought a squad of soldiers to the house. As soon as they saw the dead guard, they ran straight inside the front entrance. David killed the first four men with his automatic XM-8 and leaped out through a large window overlooking a garden.

"Eagle Claws One and Two engage your targets over!" David yelled into his microphone. "Eagle One engaging now." "Eagle Two engaging now also. Over." "Eagle Claw, Out. Each Predator had its own controller sitting in a booth not completely unlike what one would expect to see in a game parlor. The Predators each had a surveillance camera that allowed the man with the joy stick to see the terrain below on an Infra Red screen at JIATF-W in Hawaii. The two men assigned to each Special Operator received their laser signal beam and each began the launch sequence for the first round of three targets. David ran nearly three hundred meters before the first sequence of Hell Fire Missiles. The shock wave threw him on the ground and the heat from the war heads made the leaves on the foliage nearby wilt and catch on fire.

Whoosh, General Kern's private quarters and the Guard House disintegrated along with the aircraft hangar and Kern's precious helicopters, creating secondary explosions. David had reached a vantage point for his second laser, which he aimed directly at the center of Kern's opium shed complex. "Fire for effect! He commanded his Predator Controller. Within seconds, the Hell Fire Missiles created a crimson inferno, while secondary chemical explosions, kept erupting with chaotic frenzy, in a feast of white-hot flames, that lit up the entire sky. Clive had already made his first strike on the barracks complex, with a hellacious inferno that erupted killing all inside. The Ammo Dump took a direct hit and artillery, mortar and Rocket Propelled Grenades, were exploding, as if it were a fourth of July fireworks display.

Sean engaged his Methamphetamine labs with deadly accuracy and unleashed both of his Predators destroying all eighteen labs with six dispersed missiles that kept exploding with secondary detonations. "Eagle Claw this is Eagle Command, over!" "Come in Eagle Command over." "Eagle Claw, you sure as hell know how to ruin a man's night vision! Over."

"Roger that! Over." Abruptly, the Admiral changed to a serious tone. "Eagle Claw! Heads up! There's a convoy headed straight for your extraction site. Do you copy? Over." "How many vehicles? Over." "I count twelve two and a half ton trucks. That's about a battalion of infantry. Over." "I guess we're fresh out of Predators?" David asked. "Roger you blew the shit out of the place with all of your Predators. Over." "Where is Eagle Claw Three? Over." "He's circling your extraction point. Over." "Can you have him unload on the convoy with his forty millimeters? Over." "I'll put him on it right away. Wait. Out."

Admiral Donaldson gave the pilot of the MC-130e the coordinates and he flew a strafing mission chewing up the convoy. Fifty of the troops escaped the strafing and reassembled along a wood line. "Eagle Claw do you wish to extract at the alternate Bravo location? There is still a size- able force near Extraction Site Alpha. Over" The alternate extraction site was near Clive and Sean but about two kilometers from David's own location. "Affirmative Eagle Command. Shift to extraction site Bravo." "Eagle Claw Eagle Claw One. Over." "Eagle Claw One, come in, over." "You'll never bloody make it to Bravo. I have a large force in view, who are sitting right in the middle, between where you are and the Bravo extraction site, over." Clive warned. "Make your extraction. I'll be right behind you over!" Silence. Clive made contact with Sean and the two men headed for the alternate extraction site. Clive took a sitting position facing South and Sean moved 200 meters away taking a sitting position facing North.

"Eagle Three, Eagle One, over." "This is Eagle Three over." "Make your first pass. I'm facing South and Eagle Two is facing North, for your return pattern. Launching helium now over." Clive pulled the handle on his harness and a whooshing noise confirmed the release of his helium balloon four hundred and fifty feet directly above him. The light from the burning fortress lit up the sky and made the two balloons visible to the MC-130e's pilot. The plane flew level at four hundred feet. Clive grasped his knees and suddenly he was whipped upward into the night sky. The plane flew about three kilometers by the time Clive was hoisted inside the aircraft. The MC-130e made a U-turn and repeated the snare operation for Sean. Admiral Donaldson watched David's Infra Red image running from the fifty soldiers who had escaped the strafing of the convoy. David entered the wood line and cut across toward the main gate and the long road he had once landed on as a run way.

"Eagle Command, Eagle One over." "Eagle Command, come in Eagle One. Over." "Sir where the bloody Hell is Eagle Claw? Over." "He's nearing the main gate but his pursuers have nearly over taken him. There's no way we can extract him now. It would endanger you and your crew. Over." Clive grew fierce. He staggered to the cock pit and pulled his 9 mm pistol. "Sorry mate but I need you to land this bloody plane on the road by the main gate." "What? Are you out of your mind?" The pilot yelled. "No. But if you don't do as I say, I will bloody shoot you!" Clive placed the barrel of his 9 mm against the pilot's forehead. Mitch ran forward pulling his pistol along the way. Sean pointed his XM-8 at Mitch's chest and yelled. "Holster your pistol mate, or I'll fill ya full of bloomin' holes!" Mitch stopped in his tracks and put his pistol back into its holster. "You'll get us all killed Goddamnit!" Mitch yelled. "Then so fokkin' be it! We don't leave no fokkin" body behind!" Clive replied. The MC-130e's pilot brought the plane down hard on the entrance road.

"What in the f--ck are they doing?" Captain Peterson yelled to Admiral Donaldson. "Something I wish I had ordered. Goddamn those are good men." "Sir they're going to get the plane captured, or destroyed!" "Leave no one behind Peterson. Remember that old motto of the American Rangers?" David was running and shooting as he saw the ramp being lowered for him. Mitch jumped out and knelt down on one knee firing a LAW missile from the shoulder at the men who were running toward the plane. Clive and Sean also jumped down from the ramp firing their XM-8's at the approaching infantrymen. David leaped onto the ramp followed closely by Mitch, Sean and Clive. The snapping sound of small arms fire rattled along the sides of the plane, as bullets penetrated the skin of the MC-130e. The powerful aircraft fought mightily for altitude rising high into the skies above a hellish scene below. Everyone held their breath as the pilot made a beeline toward the Thai border.

The Air Defense officer suddenly yelled out. "Bandits on our Six!" "They have us on radar lock. They're engaging us now! Releasing counter measures now! Within seconds the sky was filled with flares behind the escaping MC-130e. Two Junta air force Chengdu H-7 Chinese made Jetfighters were preparing to strafe the MC-130e, as their missiles had all been stopped by the flares." "Eagle Command, we are about to be attacked by two Junta Chengdu H-7's over." The Air Defense Officer shouted. "Like Hell we are!" The pilot replied. "Eagle Command, please release the hounds of Hell over!" "Wait out." Admiral Donaldson had assigned two Raptor F-22 fighter jets as an escort, once the MC130e was enroute back to the safety of Thai airspace. The two Chengdu H-7's headed down toward the MC-130e for the kill when suddenly they were blown apart by missiles fired by the Raptors. The Air Defense Officer announced the destruction of both bandits. Clive looked down at his feet and shook his head yes. "Couldn't let em leave the Yank. Now the bloody job is done." He thought to himself.

David looked out at the shiny reflection of the Mekong below and thought how sad it was, they had come this far together, only for Bill to lose his life. He hadn't even thought very much about how close he had just come to losing his own life. He silently made a vow that he would donate ninety percent of the money in their bank account to orphanages all across Asia, starting in Phnom Penh. Genuine orphanages. Not the phony ones with moralistic crusades and politics on their agendas, such as the ones where the children had to reject Buddha and sing songs about Jesus to earn a meal instead, the ones run by local Asians.

He would also start a fund for any family his dead mercenaries had listed on their secret files. "Clive and Sean I can't thank you enough. I will double what I promised you." "I knew you were worth savin' ya bloody Yank!" Clive said with a grin. "Where will ya be headin' to next David?" Sean asked. David looked almost panic stricken. "I really haven't given any thought to that." He said, quite sadly. "Bill bought a huge yacht not long ago. He wanted so much to travel around the world with me on that boat but now that he's gone, I guess I'll just sell it and start from square one."

Abruptly, the radio crackled. "Eagle Claw, this is Eagle Command, over." "Come in Eagle Command. Over." "Job well done. Please thank your men for me. Sorry we were too late to rescue Bill, I am honestly without words about your loss of Bill." "Thank you Sir. I am really feeling his loss right now. I just wish I could have brought his body out." David said. "I know. We would have, however, lost you all if we had lingered another minute. Who did order the MC-130e to land?" The Admiral asked. "Oh, that wasn't your order Sir?' David said with a small hint of sarcasm. The pilot interrupted the transmission. "No, it was that bad assed Brit who scared the shit out of me by threatening to kill me if I didn't land."

"Good friends are hard to find, Eagle Three!" David said with a sad shadow across his face. "If any of you ever want a job, get in touch, Admiral Donaldson said. "Thanks Sir, but I'm retired. Perhaps my two men here may be interested. I'll give them your contact information." David said. "Good Luck then David. It was an honor working with you. Sorry about your losses." The Admiral said. "The honor was mine Admiral." "Until we meet again." David turned to Clive and Sean.

"How can I.... "Oh fok off ya bloody Yank!" Clive said with a grin. "I was just makin' sure you was around ta pay me, like." Clive said jokingly. "Actually Clive, your money with bonus is already in your accounts. I took care of that in case I didn't make it back. For the ones who didn't make it, I transferred their money in such a way, that if they didn't make it back, their listed next of kin would receive their pay." David said. David looked out the window at his beloved Phnom Penh. The first light of dawn was playing with the rose colored clouds, along the horizon, off in the direction of China. "Red sky at night, sailor's delight. Red sky at morning, sailor take warning." Another mindless couplet about the weather." David thought. David looked down at the Monastery where Srey An had visited as a child.

After the MC-130e made its landing and taxied toward the hangar, for an after action maintenance check David said Good Bye to Clive, Sean, Mitch and the crew and headed for the taxi cue. He had intended to return to the safe house to work on the charities list. Instead, he asked the driver to take him to the river front. Almost as if the driver knew his thoughts, he pulled into the drive of the monastery and stopped. David paid the taxi driver then climbed the high steps to the main entrance. It was early Morning and the large statue of Buddha had an aura of golden light reflecting from the open windows.

David couldn't remember the last time he had ever been in a holy place. He knelt down on the cold stone floor and looked up at the knowing eyes of Buddha, that seemed to follow David as he moved to another spot on the floor. Buddha had such a blissful expression. David smelled the burning incense and watched as a swirling cloud of grey and white smoke rose up toward the intricately designed ceiling around Buddha's head. David marveled that in spite of an oath of poverty, taken by each monk, a beautiful arrangement of orchids, sat at Buddha's feet, along with small bowls of sweet rice and tropical fruit. Some small birds flew inside the monastery and began to feed from the bowls of rice.

David attempted to rise up to shoo away the small birds when suddenly a strong, but gentle hand, was laid on his shoulder. David felt instantly at peace. He turned to see an old monk in his saffron robe standing behind him. "You carry much weight on your soul", the old monk said. "I'm very tired. I suppose it shows." David said. "It's in your eyes. The sadness is deep. You have suffered much." "You were about to chase away the birds?" "Yes, I thought the gifts for Buddha should be protected." "Not at all." The old monk replied.

"The tiniest and the greatest of creatures, all have a place on the Great Mandala." He said. "The birds take their place on the Wheel Of Life. It is good that they succor from the rice at Buddha's feet. It is as it should be. Each tiny bird has a spirit that has traveled far and will journey until they leave suffering forever." "You sound like a woman I know who came here as a child." David said. "You speak of the little Srey An. Did she find her Buddha?" David was amazed that this man, obviously remembered every person he ever met. "Yes, she found her Buddha. She loved the little birds and spoke of them fondly." David said sadly.

"She stopped coming when the Christian missionaries asked her not to return here." David explained. "Would you ask her to please come by once in a while, just to please an old man's heart?" The monk replied. David looked up at Buddha and then down at his feet. "She is dead." He said softly. The old monk touched David's shoulder. "She is not dead. She lives forever. In your heart and in your mind. Forever." Suddenly a small bird flew up from the rice bowls at Buddha's feet and landed on David's shoulder. He froze so as not to frighten the little bird. It nibbled at his collar and then flew straight up and out the high windows followed by the swirl of other birds.

David felt a joy and a connection with this monk, who had known his Srey An and this monastery, where she had been as a child and a young girl. No matter where he traveled, he would always return here, he thought. David stopped at a nearby internet cafe to access his account. David was surprised at how easy it was to transfer the funds to the orphanages. Each had a web site with banking instructions and account numbers. He made the transfers anonymously using untraceable mechanisms to prevent the money from ever being challenged, based on its questionable source. David then made arrangements to travel to Singapore to put the Lotus Dream up for sale. He booked an early afternoon flight for the next day.

He felt safer than ever before, knowing that the triads had been decapitated and he had himself, dispatched Madame Shian' and General Kern, but just to be safe, he called Bonarith and asked him to tell the rice farmers that he would mail the title to the safe house to them, to keep without any re-payment. He would never return there again. David stayed the night, in a modest hotel, near the River front and enjoyed a brisk walk along the rivers edge all the way from the International Press Club, to the Japanese bridge and back.

Alex Fong clutched the sealed metal case that hung securely around his neck. After leaving Mitch and David near the hangar, he walked toward the Diplomatic entry at the Phnom Penh airport. He unsealed the small case. Inside was a Taiwanese diplomatic passport, an ATM card with a balance of one hundred thousand dollars U.S. and the keys to a new, black Mercedes S-Class sedan. Alex knew that the last half of the passport numbers would match the number plate on the sedan.

After walking, without challenge, through the diplomatic corridor, he walked out the front door and found the sedan waiting. He opened the boot and saw a state of the art sniper rifle in its case. He breathed a sigh of relief. The rifle meant he had a fresh assignment. This could only mean that Langley wasn't going to hold his feet to the fire for the cluster f--ck in Hong Kong. He knew his Hong Kong cover would be blown as soon as the Police turned over their chopper video to the press. What possible use would he be to the CIA now, with a blown cover? He had already decided that if Langley offered him an early retirement, he would sure as f--ck take it.

Alex opened the glove compartment. He locked and loaded the 9 mm pistol inside and took out the satellite phone that was encrypted. He held his breath as he dialed his Field Agent Controller. "Hello Alex, I trust you enjoyed the submarine ride?" Listen Sir, I..... His Controller interrupted him. "Alex, I know you have a hundred questions and believe me, you have earned your need to know. We all felt that for your own safety and protection, you should be kept out of the loop until the operation concluded. The triads you killed were substitutes for the real Dragon Heads.""Imposters, with no clue that they were being sacrificed for the good of the Dragon Syndicates." "But I saw their faces and they matched the photos you sent." "Yes, photos we sent."

" We were given the photos by the Dragon Heads who were spared, because of our joint interests." "Alex, we will discuss this in further detail at your place in Hong Kong." "Sir, my cover was blown by a video feed from a Hong Kong Harbor Police chopper. It must be on today's evening news." Alex reflected. "Alex, the video feed you speak of, as well as an even better likeness, from the news chopper's live feed, were destroyed soon after they were recorded." "Your cover in Hong Kong is as rock solid as it ever was." There is an organization that I have sponsored you to become a new member of, that combines the triad societies the world over including in Mainland, China, with ex-CIA Directors, World Leaders and Operatives such as ourselves."

"We are dedicated to the elimination of Communism in China and the reunion of Taiwan with Mother China under a free Democracy and Capitalistic society. This organization is multinational and dates back to the Chinese revolution in 1949 when Mao Tse Tung stole China from mankind. We had to go deep underground when Nixon and Kissinger sold Taiwan out, as well as when Taiwan, only one of a handful of countries that kept their U.N. fees current, were kicked out of the United Nations. When the timing is right, with support from the CIA,Taiwan will re-take China."

"Most of our funds have come from the Golden Triangle so you can imagine how we reacted to the plan from JIATF-W that threatened to assassinate the leadership of our strongest allies in the organization. Thanks to you, the JIATF-W believe they have dealt a mortal blow to the triad societies, when in fact, they accomplished the exact opposite. By warning the triad leaders about what was afoot, we have gained their absolute trust. Madame Shian' as well as General Kern were greedy pains in the ass, who got what they deserved." "Without lifting a finger, we got rid of them and shall have much better relations, with the triads, than ever before. Murphy should have been sanctioned long ago.

This leads us to your next assignment. I believe you must have an idea of who needs to be sanctioned now?" "David Anderson." Alex mumbled. "Yes! We don't need any other loose cannons mucking things up for us in the Triangle, now do we?" "No Sir!" "Alex, between the JIATF-W and the Murphy-Anderson duo, we nearly lost sixty years of American foreign policy strategy, in one massively connected little episode. After you tie up loose ends you will find a new and larger yacht waiting for you at your slip in Hong Kong's yacht club." "Thank you Sir!"

David knew that Phnom Penh would remain too hot for a while, but he believed the momentary chaos of the triads would give him an opportunity to leave the city in peace. After the affairs with the Lotus Dream were settled in Singapore, he would island hop in Micronesia and Tahiti. Make his way to Brazil for Carnival and perhaps spend some time in Scandinavia and Russia, before finally returning to Asia, once more. Even after the charities, David still had over one hundred million in the Grand Cayman accounts. The proceeds from the Lotus Dream would be put in reserve.

David had never been flashy and now was certainly not a good time to start. He intended to just relax and enjoy life and try to recover from the blighted years he had experienced in the military. David hailed a taxi for his trip to the airport. He decided to pass by the monastery and then travel on to the airport. He left the taxi waiting in a small alley that connected the Monastery dormitory to the river front. He strolled to the monastery and gazed at the statue of Buddha for several minutes, through an open doorway. He returned to the alley but the taxi was nowhere in sight.

David began to feel something larger than anything he had ever felt before. It lifted his thoughts away from the taxi or his flight to Singapore. Life slowed down for David. He watched as a covey of birds circled the dome of the monastery. The noise of the traffic, fell silent.

He could see the blur of a hummingbird's wings slow down, as its long thin beak drank nectar from an orchid nearby. He saw the smiles on the children's faces as they passed by, then a brief glint from a window, a few blocks down the street. A voice inside his head, that was pure instinct screamed DIVE! But it was a split second too late. The bullet ripped through David's chest, nicking the Aorta along the way. David fell back onto the cobble stoned alley. He felt no pain at first, as the neural message system between his chest and his brain, was in utter chaos. Then sharply the unbearable burning began. He looked up at the dark red clouds moving in from the direction of the China sea. "Red Sky at Morning, Sailor take Warning!" crossed his mind.

As suddenly as it had begun, the pain went away. Just as he had experienced, long ago in Vietnam, it felt as if a heavy mill stone was lifted from his neck. David smiled as he saw Srey An's beautiful face in the clouds above. Before he could even think of how lonely he was, he died. The taxi crawled slowly back into the alley beside David's corpse. Across the street, a mother pushed her children inside and closed the door. "Just another foreigner, who was foolish enough to have gone against someone's power circle." She assumed.

The driver took out his camera. He would give the photos to Alex later, as confirmation of the kill. As Alex' spotter, it had been a part of his assignment. As the driver laid the camera on the seat and drove away, the Dragon Tattoo of the K-14 triad, on his arm, smiled at the scene of death in the rear view mirror. David's body grew smaller and smaller, in the distance. Fading steadily away, in the dust of another sweltering day in Phnom Penh.

The End

This 5 star review is from: East Of Egypt: The Secret War: Cia Drug Operations In South East Asia (Paperback)

Knowledge, Culture, Action & Emotion...its all in there, from start to end. Scott Grant has put together a fantastic piece of work here, that pulls no punches and delivers a fast-paced journey through SE Asia with two fascinating lead characters in Bill and David.

I too had trouble separating fact from fiction, which just adds to the overall appeal of the book. I gained insights into SE Asian cultures that I was not aware of before, as well as expanded my knowledge of CIA operations, military affairs and equipment and the underworld operations in Asia. Non-stop action and twists and turns in the storyline kept me glued to the book at every opportunity.

For those of you familiar with SE Asia, the book offers recognisable settings and events, that will draw you further and further into the storyline. For those of you less familiar with SE Asia, hold on to your seats, as you are brought in at the deep end, serving up a fantastic and emotional read.

95453897R00183

Made in the USA
Columbia, SC
12 May 2018